D0375714

For my husband, Greg.
I'm so blessed to have you in my life.

Praise for
STEF ANN HOLM

"A sweet, family-oriented romance."
—*Romantic Times BOOKreviews* on *All the Right Angles*

"Holm returns to her home state of Idaho with fresh, likable characters who will have readers rooting for the happy ending and relishing every step along the way."
—*Booklist* on *Lucy Gets Her Life Back*

"Holm's latest explores the flaws and foibles of her characters with a clear but affectionate eye. The novel also manages to often be hysterically funny, despite dealing with some very real issues...and readers won't soon forget mega-hottie Drew."
—*Romantic Times BOOKreviews* on
Lucy Gets Her Life Back

"Holm's delightful romance...shows that you are never too young or too old for romance."
—*Booklist* on *Leaving Normal*

"Holm's comedic flair is much in evidence in this fast-paced story."
—*Romantic Times BOOKreviews* on *Leaving Normal*

"Stef Ann Holm at her sexy and irresistible best."
—*New York Times* bestselling author Carly Phillips

"Nobody writes families like Stef Ann Holm."
—*New York Times* bestselling author Jennifer Crusie

"*Undressed* is a feel-good tale about people who find love and happiness in the most unexpected places."
—*Romance Reviews Today*

"Stef Ann Holm will make you laugh and cry and fall in love again."
—*New York Times* bestselling author Jill Barnett

"*Pink Moon* is tender and funny."
—*Romantic Times BOOKreviews*

Also available from

STEF ANN HOLM

STEF ANN HOLM

All That Matters

HQN™

If you purchased this book without a cover you should be aware that this book is stolen property. It was reported as "unsold and destroyed" to the publisher, and neither the author nor the publisher has received any payment for this "stripped book."

ISBN-13: 978-0-373-77313-8
ISBN-10:   0-373-77313-7

ALL THAT MATTERS

Copyright © 2008 by Stef Ann Holm

All rights reserved. Except for use in any review, the reproduction or utilization of this work in whole or in part in any form by any electronic, mechanical or other means, now known or hereafter invented, including xerography, photocopying and recording, or in any information storage or retrieval system, is forbidden without the written permission of the publisher, Harlequin Enterprises Limited, 225 Duncan Mill Road, Don Mills, Ontario M3B 3K9, Canada.

This is a work of fiction. Names, characters, places and incidents are either the product of the author's imagination or are used fictitiously, and any resemblance to actual persons, living or dead, business establishments, events or locales is entirely coincidental.

This edition published by arrangement with Harlequin Books S.A.

® and TM are trademarks of the publisher. Trademarks indicated with ® are registered in the United States Patent and Trademark Office, the Canadian Trade Marks Office and in other countries.

www.HQNBooks.com

Printed in U.S.A.

CHAPTER ONE

A SMILE OF APPROVAL lifted the corners of Chloe Lawson's mouth as she sampled her latest dessert creation. Rich chocolate from a bittersweet royale torte melted sinfully on her tongue. She'd gotten the cream glaze perfect. Not too thick and with just the right hint of cognac.

She loved being in the kitchen, working hands-on with the pastries and cakes she sold.

The sumptuous aromas of confectionaries floated in the oven-warmed air of her trendy bakery, Not Just Cakes. Having only opened five months ago, business had taken off in ways she'd only dreamed of. She sold a variety of desserts to local restaurants, and had been building a wedding-cake clientele with a steady stream of referrals. She'd had to hire extra help to keep up. Her instructions to Jenny and Candace were uttered succinctly and with time-tested methods that worked flawlessly.

"Chloe, do you want me to start frosting the cupcakes with the génoise?" Candace asked, standing at the worktable. Sandy-colored freckles dusted the bridge of her nose, her red hair pulled back into a loose ponytail.

Responding, Chloe said, "Thanks. That would be great."

Jenny filled piping bags with fresh white icing. "We have an order for six dozen of those cupcakes going to the Borah building later this afternoon. It's some official's birthday."

"Make sure we have the exact name, and I want you to put in a party praline as a special treat for them. In fact, when the stores open downtown, run up the street to the card shop and pick out a birthday card we can all sign."

"Sure, Chloe." Jenny set the piping bag down and jotted notes on a pad of paper.

That settled, Chloe refocused her attention on the torte and sampled another bite. Satisfied she'd done a perfect job, she smiled.

Cake-making was an exact process. Everything had to be calculated and balanced. For example, baking was only done in aluminum cookware. The shiny surface of stainless steel became too heat-reflective, causing the sides of the pan to cook the batter faster than the middle, creating a dry finished product.

Not only did Chloe like the intricacies of baking, but she also loved the variety of textures she created: the silkiness of butter creams and rich, thick mousses. Chocolate and vanilla sauces beneath fresh berries. The tart or sweet fruit fillings of a seasonal offering.

Baking drew out a blissful happiness from within her, linking her to the happy times of her adolescence, an otherwise blur in her young adult life. Decorating cakes had been the silver lining in her dark cloud when she turned fifteen, and the crazy-normal world as she knew it turned topsy-turvy.

Her aimless mother, Wanda, chose her boyfriend over Chloe, and left Chloe behind with Ethel Lumm—her mother's mother.

Chloe wouldn't have the confidence she had today without her grandmother's encouragement. Funny how being suspended from school in the ninth grade had been the catalyst for a new direction in her life. With a suggestion so simple, Ethel had been the driving force behind Chloe's change. Developing her skills in the kitchen had been the start of a fresh perspective during her teenage years.

Chloe had taken to being in the kitchen, rolling out her first fondant in junior high and landing first place in the Western Idaho Fair's junior division with a three-tiered rose cake.

Ethel, nothing like Wanda, had a giving heart, plus a savvy mind. She'd offered the encouragement needed to help Chloe figure out her talent. Today, Chloe was a long way away from that confused fifteen-year-old girl. Her baking skills were second to none and Not Just Cakes was proof of her talent. Chloe's future looked very rosy.

Due in large part to Ethel's suggestion, Not Just Cakes had located in the Grove Marketplace where Ethel had her own business. Ethel's Boutique, a clothing store, racked up sales from the full-figured woman who wanted to be stylish. Ethel wanted her customers to feel good about themselves and not to be identified as a plus-sized shopper. So Ethel was fond of saying that even when Oprah was at her largest, she always looked fabulous because she dressed with class. Given that, Ethel's Boutique marketed the clothing for the "voluptuous and sexy" woman.

Behind Chloe, the heat of the oven radiated next to her back. Sunrise hadn't shown its gingered hues yet, and already the kitchen was uncomfortably hot. She kept cooling fans running, but certain glazes and icings dried out as she applied them, so she took care to make sure the room stayed the proper temperature.

Chloe wore her blond hair in a ponytail. Beneath her kitchen whites, she had on a pair of capris and a thin tank top. Neither fit really well. She'd lost weight. Eleven pounds to be exact. It had taken her months to shed the results of too much sampling and not enough exercising. Now, with little time for shopping, she hadn't fully updated her wardrobe to the next size smaller.

Besides, she wasn't one to be overly concerned about fashion, something Ethel could not understand. If she could have, she would have worn rubber flip-flops from the discount store, but practicality, the desire not to smash her toes if she dropped a heavy pan on them, won out. Instead, she'd laced on a pair of white tennis shoes that already had fallen victim to pink coloring paste.

It was just another day as she began to decorate a cake.

The phone rang and Chloe's hand faltered just a little as she squeezed the piping bag to finish the reverse shell border. Her pulse skipped and she swallowed. The other bakers wouldn't have seen much of a change in her, if anything. But she felt her face flush from a momentary rush of heat.

Just as suddenly as it started, the phone stopped ringing.

Chloe glanced at the clock. 4:48 a.m.

The phone rang once more, startling her.

Setting the piping bag next to her cake turntable, Chloe ran her hands down the sides of her white smock, instead of using the damp cloth for this very purpose.

She grabbed the phone and, in almost an accusatory voice, she answered, "Hello!"

As had been the case from previous calls, nobody spoke into the receiver.

Chloe had had about enough of this. She had caller ID on her bakery phone, but the calls came in as "unknown." Originally, she'd assumed it was only a wrong number, or possibly a high-school prank at this odd hour. She no longer thought that.

An aching curl pooled in her belly, low and tight. She felt sick, as if she'd sampled too much frosting.

"Hello?" she said once more.

Nothing.

Finally, she dared to breathe into the receiver, "Bobby-Tom? I swear, if it's you—"

The line clicked dead and Chloe hung up with a twist of anger knitting her brows.

Attempting to compose herself, she didn't acknowledge either helper. But in her peripheral vision, she saw the women exchanging raised eyebrows. Chloe wouldn't make a big deal about this in case the girls thought there could be something sinister about the call. But she knew the truth. This was the sixth time in five days that someone had called her and hung up without saying a word.

And not just at the bakery. Last night, she'd answered her home phone and had had the same experience. This couldn't be a random incident. Someone knew who she was, but even more frightening, where she lived.

Looking through her reflection in the kitchen's row of narrow windows, all Chloe could see in the alleyway was the predawn gray, and the mellow light of a lamp illuminating the cook's entrance at the back of the Mexican restaurant.

There's nobody out there.

She blinked and her reflection came back into her view. Her appearance seemed unpolished this morning. Usually her ponytail didn't have a single strand out of place. Today, pale wisps framed her face, bracketing its oval shape. Her eyes looked a darker blue, almost a violet shade. The shape of her mouth didn't seem as wide, rather more narrow as she caught herself biting her lower lip again in thoughtful contemplation. She stopped the bad habit, reminding herself that she shouldn't worry.

The only person who'd pull a crappy stunt like this was Bobby-Tom Drake and she wanted to forget her ex-husband existed.

Bobby-Tom had called a handful of times since their divorce, all jacked up on liquor and blithering on about, *"Baby, I made a big mistake letting you go."* He didn't get drunk on a regular basis but, when he did, he spilled his guts like a roadkill rattlesnake.

He'd been making babies with his new wife since the day he married her, and the whole thought of his fertile procreation caused Chloe to wince as if she'd sliced her finger with a serrated blade.

Chloe had always been attracted to the bad-boy types, thanks to her mother's guiding light. When Wanda Lawson left, the seed had been planted in Chloe that a broken man is better than a good one, because a woman can fix a broken man and make him good if she loves him enough.

Yeah, right. Only if she can have six kids in just about as many years.

Squeezing her eyes shut for a moment to keep the unexpected sting at bay, Chloe remembered the day she'd first met Bobby-Tom out at the Firebird Raceway in Emmett. The racetrack was known for hard-partying boys who drove fast and liked their women thin and pretty. Bobby-Tom had been in between girlfriends and Chloe slid right in to take up the empty spot. Good old Bobby-Tom oozed more charm than a box of magically delicious cereal.

He had a swagger to his gait that showed off the leanness of his butt in his 501 Levi's. Just about perfect in every way, except he smoked a pack of Marlboros a day. She disliked the tobacco scent that clung to his shirts and skin, but forgot all about that the second he flashed her a straight white grin. He called her "baby" from the start because she looked younger than twenty-one, and it stuck for the nine years they'd been married.

"Baby, bring me another cold one."

"Baby, you sure look pretty today."

"Baby, let's go out and shoot some pool tonight."
"Baby, Bobby-Tom needs some loving."

Nine years was a long time for baby-calling. Long enough for her to try every fertility treatment known to man to try and have a real baby to take care of.

When they divorced, Bobby-Tom remained as broken as the day she'd met him. No amount of her loving could make him hold on to a steady job outside of racing, or not give in to his roaming eye—which he swore he never acted on. But those brown-eyed peeps had roamed just the same. He'd hooked up with another woman before their court date had declared them officially over, and he and Delilah had gotten married within three months.

Bobby-Tom hadn't called her in over a year, so the phone calls made her pause and wonder. The caller's silent approach wasn't her ex-husband's usual method.

Knowing that fact caused the hairs on the back of Chloe's nape to tingle.

Then again, maybe paradise with six kids wasn't such a paradise after all. Rather than blubbering in his beer, he was probably crying in it and was too ashamed to utter sincere words of remorse.

Chloe avoided the inclination to snort. Well, she sure wasn't going to be his life jacket. He could sink for all she cared.

"Jerk," she uttered beneath her breath, but loud enough for Jenny to respond.

"Yes, Chloe?"

"Sorry…it's nothing." Chloe shook the cobwebs from her mind, then looked at her surroundings.

The kitchen gleamed with cleanliness, her tools—

from angled spatulas and cooling racks to brioche pans and pastry bags—formed an orderly lineup against the wall. The stainless countertops gleamed, and the large utility mixing bowls churned dough for the day. Bright yellow walls and skylights gave the room a cheerful appeal.

Chloe should have nothing to dwell on. She had wonderful things planned for a successful future. And being scared by a stupid hang-up caller wasn't on her list.

With that, she began her workday anew, revelling in the idea that she had become her own woman.

With an optimistic smile, she didn't even care that she'd be turning the big four-oh this year, or that she was a divorcée of ten years, with no current boyfriend or prospective boyfriend, or prior kids….

Oh, please. Let's not be a martyr.

Chloe staved off a heavy sigh. She had a great little dog to keep her company and make her laugh while she spent her evenings alone, then going to bed early. Boo-Bear, her two-year-old bichon frise, sometimes chewed up the mail when it slipped through the slot in her front door. She missed a few bills every now and then, but figuring out which ones were which added some spark to her otherwise staid single life.

As Chloe tasted the last of her bittersweet cake, she couldn't help feeling a little bittersweet herself until she remembered something her grandmother always told her.

"Honey-bee, sometimes in life, things jump out at you that you least expect."

Putting a bright spin on Ethel's words, Chloe hoped

that the something jumping out at her today would be a good thing and not an ex-husband looking to patch a hole in his torn life.

Fixing broken just wasn't in Chloe's cards these days. She liked to think of herself as a woman who could be content with a man just as he was—if she ever met one who piqued her interest enough.

But she really had no time to think about romance when her fledgling business was busting at the seams. With the way the speciality cakes had taken off, her kitchen space felt as if it had shrunk. She needed to hire an extra hand just to mix the batter and icing, and do some of the baking.

Chloe had more bakery ideas she wanted to try, but she hadn't expected she'd be contemplating them this soon. There was a party line of cakes she could do, hosting events, in-home baking for those who wanted fresh bakery items right out of the oven.

And she could expand. The unfinished building butting next to her dining area wall spanned one hundred and twenty thousand square feet. Directly in front of that were two individual spaces at two thousand square feet apiece. A vacancy sign in the window called for tenant improvements. She could lease one of the spaces. Of course, her rent would double. But so would her business.

Biting her lip, Chloe pondered the possibilities.

"AT SIX-FORTY IN the morning, this is no way to start the day." John Moretti gave his nineteen-year-old son, Zach, a hard stare. "Where were you last night?"

"With friends."

John heard his blood pressure thumping in his ears, knowing where this conversation was headed. They'd had the same go-round a dozen times. "What friends?"

With hooded eyes, Zach replied smartly, "Freddy Krueger and Chucky."

John's lack of amusement was revealed in his un-flinching glare and lack of commentary.

Eventually, Zach grunted, "I was with VeeJay, Toad, Tom and Corey."

The usual four suspects, all from good homes, but none of the boys seemed to have their acts fully to-gether.

John ran his hand through his hair, walking the length of the galley kitchen. He paused, looking through the length of uncovered picture windows. The twinkling lights from the valley below were now gone as the city awakened for another day in early July.

The weather promised to be a scorcher. When John had stepped outside to get the newspaper around 4:00 a.m., the air that met his bare legs had still been thick and warm from the previous day. Wearing just a cotton bathrobe and boxer shorts, he hadn't readily gone back inside. He'd stood with his back to the double front doors of his sprawling Quail Ridge home, gazing at the view below, wondering how he could fix a problem that had been growing out of control since his wife's death.

Being up all night had put John in a foul mood. He should be used to this with Zach, but the hollow feeling of not knowing where his son was, and with whom, still left him shaken.

"I called you repeatedly," John said, glaring hard into his son's face. "Why didn't you pick up?"

Zach's shaggy hair fell across his dark brows, his mouth set in a grim line—as if he were the one who should be indignant instead of the other way around. "My cell died."

"Then why do I even pay for it if you can't remember to keep it charged?"

"I don't know."

Those three words happened to be Zach's stock answer these days.

John turned away, faced the coffeemaker and poured his fourth cup. He quietly sipped, wishing he had the right answers. Or at the very least, some wrong ones. Anything to be proactive would be better than the constant passive-aggressive battles he'd been waging with his son for the past three years.

Had it been that long since Connie had died? His sweet wife, his rock, his solid hold on life had been taken from him in a car accident. That day had shaken his world to the core and he'd never recovered. Not really. None of them had.

Prior to Connie's death, Zach had been a sophomore, and on the high-school football team. His grades had never been stellar, but he'd tried and passed all his subjects. John's daughter, Kara, had big dreams of trying out for the cheerleading squad at Boise High.

But none of that was to be. Connie had died, leaving John in charge of two teenagers he didn't really know. That knowledge had hit him hard. He'd always considered himself a good provider and an ethical man because he practiced law and knew the system.

He worked hard, late into the evenings, making sure he kept his wife and children in a lifestyle that suited them. The big house in Quail Ridge, comprised of three levels, spanned five thousand square feet, and sat on a hillside. It was a beautiful home with a main living area, a master bedroom upstairs, and the kids' rooms and media room downstairs. They had a swimming pool, a hot tub and a tennis court on the street level. He'd made sure Connie had a state-of-the-art kitchen with marble floors and heavy wool rugs imported from Italy, and a housekeeper once a week so she could stay active in the kids' lives.

While his wife put in uncountable hours at football clinics, Brownies and volunteering for the PTA, John had drifted away from the family nucleus, concentrating instead on keeping his law firm in order. He believed in gender roles. He made the money. His wife spent it and took care of the kids.

But the last three years of being a single parent had shown John that his 1950s thinking had been detrimental to the well-being of his kids. While he thought he'd been working to make life better for them, he'd really been shortchanging them and screwing them up in the process.

After Connie's death, it became crystal clear he didn't really know either of his children. And they reminded him of that fact whenever they had the chance.

They resented his absence in their lives. Now that he was making the effort to be here for dinner, they'd rebelled and all but isolated themselves, putting him between a rock and a hard place trying to repair a decade of damage.

There were moments, like now, when he felt like giving up.

"How are you going to make it to work on time?" John asked.

"I might not."

"You're going to get fired."

"Uncle Mark won't fire me."

Since he'd opted not to attend college, Zach worked for the family business, Moretti Construction. Under John's brother's guidance, Zach strapped on a tool belt. But, apparently, he thought himself above reproach.

"Make sure you show up on the job, Zach," John cautioned, but felt as if his words fell on deaf ears.

"Are we done?" Zach asked, slouching and stuffing his hands into his jeans pockets.

His son had classic good looks for a young man, and was old enough to get a girl in trouble. Who knew what Zach and his four cohorts had been up to last night. Probably drinking and pranks or something else stupid. The infinite possibilities had crossed John's mind many times last night while wondering where Zach was.

John had a briefing at nine this morning and the backs of his eyelids felt like sandpaper. The day would be long and arduous, but he couldn't miss work.

Ignoring the ache that enveloped his bones, John replied, "We're done."

Zach marched down the stairs, closed the door to his bedroom and amped his music up to a level that could pop nails from the Sheetrock.

The coffee in John's cup looked murky and black, much like his life. He knew he was messing up on a daily basis. Unable to see his way out of this, he'd consulted a family counselor and had taken the kids in a last-ditch effort to bring back some control.

Zach and Kara had hated the group sessions, and it had been an effort to get them to go before they finally flat-out refused and made themselves scarce during the appointment times. John's own family had been against him pursuing a therapist one-on-one, but John had gone anyway. His father, Giovanni—before he'd died last year—had all but called John an idiot for not seeking help within the Catholic church. To John's way of thinking, talking to a priest would get him nowhere.

But visiting the therapist hadn't helped much, either, and eventually, even John talked himself out of going, excusing himself by saying his schedule was too busy, or he had other appointments he couldn't change.

So much for trying to repair damages. The outcome had been unsuccessful and things had declined ever since.

It pained John to think he'd royally messed this up. Connie would be beyond disappointed but then, maybe she'd always felt that way and had never said anything. He'd put her on a pedestal, probably regarding her in a higher esteem than she wanted. And probably not listening to her when she'd tried to get her feelings across, pretending instead to give credit for being a super-mom.

Their children hadn't been able to come to terms with their mother's death, so rather than let him take care of them, they'd detoured down trouble lane.

And John Moretti had only himself to blame.

Bright sunshine burst into the living area, bathing the white sofas in yellow light.

He needed to wake Kara up and get her moving for summer school. She'd failed two classes, and the choices he'd given her had been either summer school, or he'd take her car away. So far, so good. Checks with the counselor's office confirmed she'd been attending when she should. Kara actually liked school, so it wasn't that she didn't want to be there. She just hadn't applied herself academically. She loved the social times she shared with her posse of best friends, attending football and basketball games, dances and parties. But after getting F's in math and government, she wailed, "OMG, I have to waste my summer at Boise High!"

She had a part-time job at the mall working in a makeup kiosk, and the income gave her financial freedom from her dad—a freedom that had produced a belly-button piercing against his wishes. He hadn't even tackled a punishment for that one. Right now, her education took priority.

John moved through the house with purpose, knocking twice on his daughter's door before entering without her permission.

In the slats of light peeking through plantation shutters, John could see clothes strewn on the floor, a purse knocked over on the bureau and various cosmetics laying across the desk.

Kara, fast asleep, didn't hear him come in because her slender figure didn't move in her queen-size bed. Her clock radio played music from the local rock station—apparently the alarm had gone off but had been disregarded.

John took a step toward the bed, dodging the land mine of junk on the carpet. "Kara, you need to get up for school. You're late—"

The words stopped short, as if sliced by a sharp blade.

His daughter wasn't alone in the bed.

Another person lay beside her, turned away from John so the face was indiscernible. All he could make out was shortish, sandy blond hair with a slight wave that fell past an ear. His daughter's bedmate hugged the down pillow with an arm that sheets partially hid.

Anger seething through his veins, John grabbed the covers and threw them aside, ready to kill the boy invading his home, his daughter's bedroom.

"Get up," he hollered.

"What's the matter?" Kara muttered, her sleek hair falling over her face as she rose to a sitting position.

"Who's the boy?" John spit out, ready to hit the kid. Assaulting a youth was an illegal offense, but rationality wasn't on John's short list right now.

The "boy," dressed in an oversize Boise High T-shirt and boxer shorts, stirred to consciousness and rolled over.

"Huh?" he said.

Kara blurted, "That's Ashley, Dad!"

Ashley sat up, pushing the sandy hair off her brows. Gazing directly at him, she stifled a yawn. "Hey," she said sleepily.

John backed away, the situation hitting him in the stomach as if he'd been punched. "Ashley?"

"Yeah."

"But I thought…"

"She got her hair cut yesterday, Dad." Kara's body stiffened as she slid her legs over the bed. "I can't believe you thought I'd sneak in a boy. We came home at ten o'clock when you were in the study working. I told you I had a friend with me."

John vaguely remembered that. Eyeball-deep into his briefs, he'd hadn't given Kara a glance.

"I didn't know she was spending the night," he said stupidly in defense. For an attorney, he floundered miserably right now to come up with a forgivable reason he'd neglected his own daughter.

There was none.

Kara flicked her long, black hair over her shoulder. "Ashley got tired and I didn't want her driving home so her mom said she could stay here. I didn't ask you because you never care."

John stared blankly.

"Sorry," he muttered, then headed for the paneled door. In an effort to retain some semblance of authority, he added, "Time to get ready for school."

"You know what the problem is in this house?" Kara's irritated tone trailed after him. "Nobody trusts anybody."

Halfway up the stairs to the kitchen, John didn't want to be badgered with a lecture. Not from a seventeen-year-old girl who hadn't experienced the world the way he had.

John gathered his belongings, snagging the brief-case from the leather bar stool.

Pulling a few deep breaths into his lungs to reset his racing pulse, he went to the garage and sat behind the wheel of his BMW.

He turned the ignition, adjusted the mirror, then gazed ahead at nothing. He took a moment to just chill before heading out into the craziness of the day.

It seemed as if everything in this house always turned around to make him the bad guy. Even when he tried to be the good guy.

Man, he really needed some help.

CHAPTER TWO

ROBERT MORETTI was a dream customer. He didn't scrimp, selecting Chloe's best bakery products for his Italian restaurant, Pomodoro. His orders consisted of cheesecake topped with amarena cherries, Pear Charlotte, raspberry tiramisu and triple chocolate cake. The dessert menu at his restaurant had received top review billing in the newspaper, and was noted to be superior like the food he served.

Chloe had been done baking for the day when Robert stopped by. She had stayed behind to work the register because her counter clerk hadn't shown up— and no answer on the girl's cell phone when Chloe had called to ask her why she hadn't come in as scheduled.

As an entrepreneurial business owner, Chloe had quickly learned that keeping employees on a regular basis was a constant challenge. She'd even offered a base pay of two dollars more per hour than minium wage, just as an enticement to show her faith in the help. But this was the third floor-clerk in five months who'd bailed.

But Robert's order put Chloe's frustrated mood back on track. "Thanks, Robert. I appreciate the business."

"I'm just glad I snapped you up when I did. You're always so busy." Robert's olive-skinned good looks and the comment about "snapping her up" captured her attention, but she reminded herself that a gold wedding band shone from his left hand.

"Never too busy for a loyal customer," Chloe replied with a soft smile.

Robert's nice looks attracted her, but anything but professional thoughts about him had to be curbed.

In Boise, it seemed as if all the good men had been taken back when cowboys hitched their horses on Main Street.

"Did I tell you about my expansion plans?" she asked, putting the quantities of Robert's order into her computer. She'd had a brilliant idea to bring a more diverse crowd into Not Just Cakes and she couldn't wait to launch it.

Not only would she be helping her wedding-cake division, but she'd also cater to the needs of hundreds of businessmen just waiting to be tapped into.

"Nope." He stood tall and handsome in a pullover shirt and a pair of relaxed jeans. His wife probably knew how lucky she was.

"I'm going to lease the space next door and put in a coffee bar. I'll serve specialty coffees and have a wireless Internet connection, as well as an LCD wall TV to broadcast headline news in the morning."

She'd done extensive research over the past couple of weeks. The businessmen who frequented Grove Marketplace on a regular basis were middle-class and educated. They drank their coffee black, wouldn't eat a sugary pastry with their morning java if you gave it to them for free, but they would indulge in a berry muffin or a bagel. Muffins to a pastry chef were a no-brainer. Bagel-making would prove to be more of an art—the dough had to be boiled, a rather unique process. But if it meant luring in new customers, she'd put in the effort. The menu, along with connections to the information superhighway, were sure to have these guys returning again and again.

Chloe had unveiled the idea to her grandma over lunch and Ethel had loved it. Ethel's approval always won points with Chloe. She valued her grandma's input.

"Well, you're in a great location," Robert said, pulling Chloe from her thoughts.

"Don't I know it," she enthusiastically replied.

The Grove Marketplace had been taking off by leaps and bounds, and the commercial space continued to fill. Luckily for her, there were spaces still available. And even luckier—the frontage next door remained unoccupied. Now Chloe would have to come up with final tenant improvement costs to take out the wall joining the two spaces, as well as figuring in some kitchen additions. Another oven for sure. The costs were going to be significant. She'd have to take out a loan, but it would be worth it.

Just then, the mailman came into Not Just Cakes with a leather bag on his shoulder. Bernie Schmidt walked with a rolling gait and his width was almost the same as his shorter-than-average height.

"Howdy-ho, Chloe." He fanned through the letters

in his hand like a human computer, knowing just when to start and stop.

"Hi, Bernie." She took the mail he offered her, then made an offering of her own. "Care to try a sample of our sticky buns?"

"Don't mind if I do." He popped a bite-size piece into his mouth. "That's really good."

"Thanks."

"Hey, got a certified for you. Sign here."

The back of an envelope was presented to her and she signed the green form.

"You take care now," Bernie said as he left.

Chloe finished Robert's order and totaled it while he fielded a call on his cell phone. While he talked, she fought off a yawn. By midafternoon, having been at work nearly twelve hours, she was wiped out and she longed for a nap. Robert was the only one inside the shop, and the lull in business offered a moment to unwind.

Glancing at her mail, her pulse sped in a pleasant way when she saw the return address on the certified letter.

Using her forefinger, she tore an opening in the envelope and slipped the letter out. Her earlier excitement deflated like a punctured balloon. The words jabbed at her, each one more worrisome than the last.

Her jaw dropped open and she softly uttered, "No…" Then with more clarity and firmness, she repeated "No!"

Robert, having quit his call, lifted his brows. "Are you okay, Chloe?"

Her chin shot up. "They can't do this to me!"

"Who?"

"The property-management company for the Grove. I asked to lease the space next door and they turned me down." She sank into one of the bakery chairs, her shoulders slumping forward. "Not only that, but they've given me a lease-termination notice." Gazing up at Robert, she blinked her disbelief. "In seven short months, I have to vacate. They aren't renewing my bakery space."

Robert's expression grew sympathetic. "That doesn't seem fair or right."

"But that's what they're doing." On a smothered groan, Chloe took another look at the letter, dreading a second read of the very sentence that had sucked the breath right out of her.

Feeling every ache of the day, her voice wavering, she added, "And that's only the beginning. It gets worse."

JOHN HAD TAKEN a paralegal out to lunch. He'd known from the onset that it wouldn't be good for him, and the hour spent at P.F. Chang's had been uncomfortable. His attraction to her had been mostly physical and he'd maneuvered himself into some mindless flirtation. But it hadn't been fair to either of them.

He wasn't in the right frame of mind to be dating right now.

He'd paid the check and thanked her for her time. She'd left with a confused look on her lovely face.

Now, back in his office, John sat behind his massive

mahogany desk and wondered how to get his personal life back on track.

In a relatively short amount of time, he concluded he needed a woman to talk to.

He'd been able to talk to Connie about anything. She may not have always agreed, but they always confided in one another and built resolutions based on love and trust. Their marriage hadn't been without its rocky roads, but it had been a comfortable one.

Staring out the window, John recognized a sad honesty within his heart. He couldn't remember the pitch of his wife's voice, or the exact smell of her skin. Or the potent impact of love that squeezed his chest at night when he cradled her in his arms. They were all gone.

All he had were memories.

Looking at the Boise skyline from his office window, he quietly reflected, somberly acknowledging a fact that had grown to a tangible reality over the years.

He wasn't in love anymore.

That quiet knowledge both saddened and freed him at the same time. It gave him permission to move forward, to make a new start and to be a better man the second time around.

He wanted to marry again and have a whole family. But not in the immediate future. Not with all the turmoil in his life.

He thought about his mother, Mariangela, who had suffered a devastating blow last year with his father's death. She seemed to be coping on her own after Giovanni's heart attack. Her strength and character molded her into a great role model, a strong woman his kids should look up to. John needed to invite his mom over to the house, to bring her into his world more than he did. He only went to her house for Sunday suppers. If he was lucky, his kids would join him. It would be good to have him, Zach and Kara to turn the tables and do a barbecue for his mom.

Sunshine reflected off the glass windows of tall buildings. The hour grew late. Time to head home. He thought about calling his sister, Francesca, to see what she was up to, but her world consisted of a new husband and overseeing the Grove Marketplace for Moretti Construction. Funny how his sister had fallen into that.

Both his mom's and sister's influences would be good for his children, filling in the huge gap that Connie had left. In John's roundabout thinking, his date today had been more a way to find a mother figure for his kids. Seeing the paralegal's sparkling green eyes and expectant mouth, he realized as soon as he sat down that he'd made a mistake in judgment.

John's phone rang and he picked up the call his secretary put through.

"Moretti," he said into the receiver.

"Hey, John," Robert greeted. "Got a minute?"

His younger brother was a good guy. The kind of man John respected and admired. "I've got more than that. What's up?"

"I need some legal counsel for a friend of mine."

The muscles in John's body tightened with displeasure. He didn't particularly like these calls, no matter if they were from family or not. Free legal advice could come back to bite him in the backside if he wasn't careful. The words he said could be twisted and made to suit the needs of others, completely neglecting the true legal ramifications.

Even in light of that, John said, "Go ahead."

Robert's voice carried through the receiver in an even and determined tone. "You know that bakery downtown called Not Just Cakes?"

"No."

"It's in the Grove Marketplace. Anyway, this friend of mine who I get my pastries from, she tried to lease the vacant space next door, but the management company in charge of the Grove said no. They're terminating her lease."

"Sorry to tell you, but that's perfectly legal." John piled some paperwork together and tossed it into the center of his briefcase.

"But here's why they want her out. Garretson's is taking over a hundred and twenty thousand square feet next door, plus the two frontages for another four thou. And they're getting the bakcry unit, too, as soon as she vacates."

Garretson's grocery operated a slick and trendy mega-chain in Idaho and Oregon. Some of their food prices weren't all that great, but they offered fine quality items in their delis and bakeries. The concept was top-notch product without warehouse-style aisles, and with price modifications on brand-name bestsellers. It was actually quite inventive marketing.

The bottom line: Every time a Garretson's went in, the shops around the superstore lost business.

"Nothing she can do, Robert. If her lease isn't renewed, she's got to relocate," John offered without emotion. "Our firm is one of several who represents Garretson's on different levels and you can't fight corporate."

"That's not fair."

"But it's the way it is. A leasing company can lease to whomever they want."

"You need to meet this woman, John. See for yourself she's a nice person who needs a break. Her store is doing great and I hate to see her have to start over."

John's cell phone vibrated but he let the call roll over to voice mail. "You know what, Robert—life isn't fair."

The line grew silent. John immediately regretted his crass choice of words. It had been a long day, and who knew what waited for him at home. He'd called the kids' cells once today and had gotten their recordings. Nothing new there.

John loved his brother and they had a good relationship, but it was a bad time for him right now, and he couldn't be bothered over some cupcake lady's problems. The woman could just relocate. No biggie.

"You know what your problem is, John?" Robert's voice grew abrupt. "You forgot what it's like to be the little guy. When you first set up your practice, it was all about helping those who didn't have the big bucks. Now you just care about the money. I didn't want to say anything because I know things are bad for you right now, but you aren't the brother I know." Robert's tone wavered as he drew in an audible breath. "For crying out loud—stop feeling sorry for yourself. You used to be the guy everyone in this family could go to. You were our rock, but now you're nothing more than a grain of sand."

Then the line went dead.

RATHER THAN GO HOME, John made a late-afternoon call to the CEO of Garretson's. Over the years, they'd formed a nonsocial relationship, with meetings dominated by corporate legalese. Bob Garretson had graduated from Boise State, earned a business degree and had taken over the family grocery chain. His enthusiastic point of view served him well, and he'd made a success of himself for his family. Stock prices were at an all-time high, and two new stores had opened in Oregon this year. Apparently one more location anted into the pot: The Grove Marketplace.

The Grove had cemented itself as an up-and-coming consumer niche where most businesses wanted to be. It had been John's father's dream to renovate the downtown site with quality craftsmanship. His vision of a vital future for the city streets had started with the construction, and the Morettis would see the Grove Marketplace project to completion.

"So, my brother mentioned this cake place to me, Bob," John said, leaning back in his heavy leather chair.

Bob's baritone sounded as if he smoked cigars all day long. "Dammit, leaks in this town spread thicker than palm grease. What about it?"

"The lease thing with the Grove."

"Oh, that."

"I'm assuming you'll take over her space for your new store."

"That's a hot spot so you can bet dollars to doughnuts on that one. Pardon the pun!" The gregarious man chuckled. "She's just small fries. Garretson's is Boise's big potatoes, John."

"I'm aware of that." John didn't know why he decided to put his neck on the line here. He'd never even met the woman. But it was what Robert said to him that had cut deep.

Stop feeling sorry for yourself.

John hadn't realized he had been acting that way. The observation had been biting, sending John into a long reflection. A million thoughts had raced through his brain, and most of them he hadn't liked.

"Bob, what's the big deal on the Grove space? You can lease elsewhere. There's vacant space across from the courthouse with a ba-zillion square feet. Some one hundred and fifty. Not even Wal-Mart is that big."

"Then let Walley World take it."

"Come on, Bob. The owner of the building is a client of mine and I could get you—"

"No can do, Johnny-Boy. I'm already inked with the leasing outfit for the Grove. We start building improvements next week. Miss Sweetie-cakes' shop is going to be my butcher block and part of my meat locker. If I could get her out sooner, I would." The phone connection jumbled, as if the receiver had changed hands. "In fact, since I've got you on the line, here's something for you. How about you help me get her out? I'd be willing to offer her a nice chunk of candy to take a powder sooner versus later."

John pinched the bridge of his nose, enjoying the temporary numbness to his sinuses. This call had gone in a direction he hadn't foreseen. He'd only been trying to do a favor, in a roundabout way, for his brother. Now he had to contemplate being placed on quite a sizeable retainer for a corporate grocery giant to buy out a little guy.

Nothing new here. This was John's speciality.

"Bob, I'll have to get back to you. It's a possibility, but I have a meeting I'm late for."

"That's what I like about you, Moretti." Bob's guffaw sounded more like a snort. "It's six o'clock and you're still going strong."

John left the office, his briefcase in hand. He no more had a meeting to go to than he had a dinner with the president. The lie had just slipped out.

He put Garretson's at the back of his mind and called Zach.

His son didn't believe in a normal ring tone, and when his phone rang, it played heavy metal music in John's ear, then went straight to voice mail.

"Hey, this is Zach-Attack. I'm not here, bro, so funk me up and leave me a message. Later."

John left a curt message for his son to return his call. Next, he dialed Kara.

"Hello?"

Relief flooded John. "Hi, Kara. It's Dad."

"What's up?"

"I'm just leaving the office. I thought I'd bring home a pizza for us."

"I was just going out."

Disappointment crushed his chest. "Well, can't you wait a sec for me? I can be home in thirty minutes."

"Um, I guess. Get extra cheese, 'kay?"

John stopped into Pie Hole on 9th and ordered a whole pizza instead of slices. Waiting for his order to cook, he sat at one of the greasy tables in the cramped pizzeria, his briefcase on his lap.

The clientele drinking colas and eating folded slices of pizza consisted mostly of college-aged kids and high schoolers hanging out in the downtown on a Friday night. Wearing an Armani suit and tie, John stuck out.

Garlic scented the air, reminding him of Sunday suppers at the Moretti house. Wine, pasta and bread, conversations, laughs and—sometimes—heated discussions. The atmosphere around the table had dimmed since Dad died.

John's thoughts tumbled together, a collage of the past three years working through his grief. He wondered if he should feel guilt for wanting to love a woman again.

These days, anger took the place that had once filled a softness in his heart. Anger toward the car accident that had taken Connie too early. Placing blame on the slick intersection had been an easy thing to do, when, ultimately, the cause of her death didn't matter.

She was gone.

BACK IN THE 1960s, Ethel Lumm had been a real dish. A fashion model for the Mode clothing store on Idaho Street, she'd been invited to all the elite homes in Boise to do special events for designers. But over the years, age and weight caused her to retire her runway career. She steered her life course elsewhere and took in her granddaughter, Chloe, and made her a priority.

After Ethel's third divorce, she gave up men and decided to live out her single years by taking a chance on her long-time dream. She opened her dress shop, Ethel's Boutique, in 1996. The grand opening of her State Street store had been a real razzle-dazzler.

Ethel catered to the beautiful-size woman, selling fashions that gave the pleasingly plump choices besides caftans at Sears and Roebuck, or polyester garments out of the plus-size catalogs.

Business had been so dandy in recent years that Ethel had moved to the up-and-coming Grove Marketplace late last year.

At age seventy-three, Ethel didn't mind her pillowy breasts, thick waist and cushioned hips. She ate whatever she wanted, whenever she wanted it. Five mornings a week, she speed-walked the tiled perimeter of the Boise Towne Square mall. Its climate-controlled interior offered comfort, and allowed her to exercise regularly, even in the blustery Idaho winters.

Ethel reasoned that as long as she kept her heart healthy, she could scratch starvation diets. Life was too short to live like a bunny rabbit on leafy greens with fat-free dressing.

So, instead, she indulged in honcho fries at

Woodchuck's, or had a chocolate milk shake, telling herself the pounds wouldn't add up as quickly if she engaged in some moving and grooving. Walking seemed to be her ticket since she disliked aerobics. She'd bought the Richard Simmons sweatin' tapes because his pitch for a healthier-and-happier you had won her over. She'd sweated to disco a few times before forgetting about them in her VHS cabinet.

Ethel closed her boutique for the night and pondered her dinner choices, her taste buds watering for a delectably yummy extra-cheese-and-sausage pizza. Pie Hole happened to be a favorite of hers. Its downtown location was right on her way home at the Imperial Plaza condominiums.

She had a ninth-floor corner unit. The building catered to the residents, from the health-club facilities— which she rarely used—to Jan's Imperial Palace beauty salon. Ethel liked her living space, and had decorated it in chic prints and colors. She'd always had a good decorating flare.

Swinging open the door to Pie Hole, she walked around a young man at the soda fountain filling a paper cup. She made her way to the ordering line, gazing at the wallboard to see if, perhaps, another flavored pie would tickle her fancy instead. Thai. Alfredo veggie. Sun-dried tomato and pepper jack.

The sausage still beckoned.

As bad luck would have it, they were all out of slices and she'd have to wait about ten minutes for the one in the oven to finish.

Ethel sat down and thought about her hectic day, but

only briefly. A very nice-looking man caught her eye. Not for herself, of course, but for Chloe.

He had to be in his midforties, modest strands of silver at his temple threading through his inky-black hair. She couldn't tell the color of his eyes, but guessed them to be dark. Tortoise brown. He had a nice mouth and an interesting nose. Not too big and not too small. Strong, but straight. His jaw commanded her attention; square and classically handsome.

An overstuffed, soft-leather briefcase sat on his lap, his hands resting loosely on the top of the opening. She honed in on his ring finger. Zip. No anchor around his ankle.

His face bore a strained expression, as if he carried the world on his shoulders. Ethel had seen this look on her dear Chloe's face today when she'd stopped into Not Just Cakes to say hello.

Ethel's nostrils flared as remembrance flashed through her in a hot wave of emotion. She'd always shopped for groceries at the food giant—Garretson's. Its location was convenient to her condo, and they offered a very nice line of cheese and spinach dips. But now that Garretson's intended to suck up the space where Chloe wanted to expand, Ethel would now patronize the Boise co-op.

There had to be a legal way out of this situation, so Ethel had suggested Chloe call a lawyer. Chloe had said she disliked lawyers ever since one had ratcheted through her divorce to Bobby-Tom. Be that as it may, a good shyster was what Chloe needed.

She also needed a decent man.

Ethel's gaze leveled on the suited gentleman and just as she was about to say hello, his order came up and he rose to his feet to take the pizza box.

On a sigh, Ethel watched him walk out the door.

Why was it the good ones always escaped?

CHAPTER THREE

THE FOLLOWING MONDAY, Chloe had to complete an order for a pistachio-and-rose wedding cake. Jenny would assemble the three tiers on a serving board at the reception this Saturday. Chloe could prebake the white cake rounds and freeze them today, but the gold lamé ribbon and dragées—little gold balls consisting mainly of sugar—would have to be done the day before.

With meticulous measuring and mixing, Chloe made the white cake batter and filled the metal forms. She'd just transferred them into the oven when her grandmother came through the bakery into the kitchen with purpose in her eyes.

"Chloe, I have an idea," Ethel called out. "You can sue the leasing company *and* Garretson's."

Unaffected by Ethel's outburst, Chloe finished what she had to do, then wiped her hands on a damp towel. Her employees weren't aware of what was going on, so Chloe steered her grandmother into her office and closed the door.

"Ethel, take a load off and chill." Chloe directed her to one of the mismatched, metal-legged chairs.

When Chloe went to live with Ethel, she quit using

the name *Grandmother* for her. It seemed too formal
for a woman who died her hair Lucille Ball-red and
wore it styled in a Doris Day bob. And if Chloe didn't
call her Ethel, she fondly called her "Mom," because,
in her heart, Ethel had been more of a mother to her
than her own mother had ever been.

Ethel's colorful hair matched her makeup—copper
eye shadow accenting her light blue eyes, a dusting of
rose blush across her flat cheeks, and a flat, red-pink
lipstick outlining her mouth. Her fashion sense had a
certain savoir...*flair.*

Ethel could pull off animal prints and faux suede,
but could also be quite stylish in knits, wool and
rayon. Today she had on a smart suit in summer
white with a black-and-white, zebra-patterned silk
blouse beneath. Her shoes sported a slight wedge.
She didn't go for super high heels because they aggravated her bunions. That said, she would suffer a
little because a heeled shoe made one's calves look
more shapely.

"Why are you shushing me?" Ethel queried, plopping down on a chair.

"Because my staff doesn't know about the deal next
door. I have a hard enough time keeping counter help
now. I don't need them to think I'm in any kind of trouble and I might pack up shop." Chloe sat and took a
sip of coffee, grimacing due to its cold temperature,
then pushed the ceramic cup away. "I have a new girl
working the front counter in the mornings. She rides
her bike here and raves about how close it is to the
BSU dorm. I can't afford to lose her."

"Sorry," Ethel muttered, "but I laid awake last night indignant for you."

"I can be indignant for myself. And trust me, I am."

Chloe had gone to the leasing office and, in person, pleaded for her lease to be renewed in seven months. Even if it meant no expansion. The agent, a barrel-chested man, called for his boss, a wiry man in a three-piece suit, who refused to budge.

Unwilling to believe this could be legal, she put in a few calls to lawyers. So far, none would give her any information unless she came into their office and paid the hourly retainer. What happened to a "simple question" on the phone? She had left messages with two others and was waiting to hear from them.

In the meantime, she'd temporarily put the matter out of her mind. She had too many orders to fill to let this heat her blood any further. If anything, Chloe put on a brave front in the face of adversity, but underneath, she was falling apart at the seams. The growing income from Not Just Cakes was her livelihood, and she'd done splendidly up until this point.

"Don't worry, Ethel. I'm not giving up."

"That's my girl!"

Chloe scratched her shin, her calf bare in a pair of tan capris. She would have worn shorts to combat the stifling kitchen heat, but didn't feel they were appropriate attire on the job.

"What are you going to do?"

Chloe folded her arms beneath her breasts and leaned back in her chair. "I'm going to talk to a lawyer."

"Great! Like I always say, the squeaky wheel gets the grease."

"And messy spokes."

Ethel grinned. "Honey-bee, you've got to work on your killer attitude."

"My mother had a killer attitude and look where it got her." The barbed words slipped out and she saw the streak of pain fan over Ethel's face. "I'm sorry."

"Oh, but it's true. Wanda had a wild streak to her." Ethel's eyes dimmed. "Sometimes I wonder where she is, if she's okay. I go along okay, then she calls me up and we talk a few minutes, but it's strained."

Chloe knew about these infrequent calls. Wanda never called her. She didn't have the guts. And that was fine with Chloe. If she never talked to her mother again, it would be too soon. While she tried to be sympathetic to a person's misfortune in life, Chloe didn't think she had it in her to forgive her mom for running out on her.

Nothing had been so bad for them that Wanda had to toss it all away and ride off with that long-haired, black-leather-jacket-wearing biker Zee. Who'd name their son Zee anyway? But Wanda fell under his spell and called it Splitsville.

Ethel rose to her feet and put her hands on her ample waist. "I wish there was something I could do."

Chloe stood and wrapped her arms around her grandmother. "You've been doing something for me for the past twenty-five years." Dropping a kiss on the older woman's soft cheek, she said, "You've been my mom."

"Thanks, Chloe. You're a sweet angel."

"No, I'm not."

"I think you are, Honey-bee." She tucked a strand of Chloe's hair behind her ear. "And one day," she continued in an endearing tone, "some man is going to see just what I see in you and you'll find a happily ever after on your horizon."

"Yeah, okay." Chloe's skepticism drifted into her voice. "But for now I'll settle for an extended lease on the horizon."

JOHN MORETTI wasn't big on eating sweets. The year he turned eleven, his great-aunt Romilda came for a visit from Italy. She made enough rich, chocolate-filled, chocolate-chip-crusted and powdered-sugar cannoli to choke a horse. Being a boy who thought dessert should be the main course, he'd eaten a battalion's worth. The color of his face had turned the green color of pistachio nuts, and he recalled waking in the middle of the night with a gut ache so bad, it had been like someone tied his belly into sailor's knots. He'd puked his guts out on his blue-and-red Superman bedspread. His mother had given him holy hell for not having the control to make a trip to the bathroom. Ever since, John hadn't been keen on eating chocolate, or anything with powdered sugar on it. Not even a doughnut.

The gooey smells in Not Just Cakes almost turned his coffee-logged stomach upside down. He'd had four cups this morning. Hopped up on caffeine, the acids were getting to him. He needed to eat something to settle things down, and since he'd been at the Grove Marketplace at a meeting at a client's office, John figured he'd check out the cupcake place and see what all the fuss was about.

Bright yellow walls splashed cheery color through the room. A long counter with glass cases below brimmed with frosted pastries, colorful tiered cakes and decorated cookies. The sugary aromas in the air floated in a thick cloud. Two clerks kept busy filling orders for the people in line. Customers occupied stainless steel and red leatherette chairs with old-fashioned Formica tables. Friendliness lent a good feel to the shop.

In spite of his preconceived opinions that he wouldn't like the sugar palace, John did. The atmosphere reminded him of the kitchen he grew up in. Welcoming and comfortable.

Taking a spot in line, John tried to view the case through those ahead of him to check out what he could buy that wasn't so stuffed with carbs that his caffeine buzz would have a sugar buzz on top of it.

When his turn came, he ordered a giant blueberry muffin and a carton of skim milk. John took a seat by the window facing Grove Street, turned his cell phone on mute, then took a bite.

His expectations that the muffin would be just ordinary were completely blown out of the water. Flavor exploded in his mouth, a delicate blend of flour and butter, and blueberries bursting with juicy sugars that had naturally been kissed into the fruit by sunshine.

Surprised not only by the quality, but also by the

light texture and the taste, he conceded "impressed" wasn't a high enough compliment for the baker. Curiosity about her had him considering asking to speak with her. But he didn't let the idea go further than that.

He hadn't called Bob Garretson back to talk more about his offer. John had been too busy to consider it. His desk had a pile of briefs laying on it and his court calendar had been booked for months. The firm already had Garretson's as a client, but this deal Bob wanted John to do would be good business for him to follow through on. Bob's position as CEO carried a lot of power and influence in town. He swam in a corporate sea of sharks that didn't bother to stop and think about the minnows. But this resolution to outing the bakery from the present location was actually generous. Ultimately, the cake lady would have to vacate anyway. So why not pack up early with some extra cash in her purse?

But John was still troubled by what his brother had said to him about his ethics. John had been thinking a lot about that. The truth couldn't be ignored—he *did* take on heavy-hitting cases for the large checks, but why should he apologize for it? John didn't think he had become arrogant because of the choices he made in business. Then again, it had become increasingly hard to muster sympathy for the guys in suits who really weren't all that interested in doing the right thing, but only in gaining the best thing for themselves.

Garretson's takeover was a perfect example of that.

John finished the muffin, catching himself licking

the tip of his forefinger to catch a crumb on the plate and put the last morsel into his mouth.

He left the table and stood in line again. He decided to buy a dozen blueberry muffins for the kids to snack on at home. And he'd eat a few or a half dozen himself.

Just as his turn came up, a striking blond appeared from the back to talk to the cashier then, rather than have the clerk help him, she helped him herself.

"Hi, what can I get for you?"

His silent response was *You*. But he kept that to himself.

After years in the courtroom, John didn't allow himself to be moved by a woman's presence, but this one's face held him captive. Her blond hair and blue eyes were a soft contrast to her tan skin. The hue of her eyes reminded him of a violet plant a client had given him once as a thank-you. Her hair had to be highlighted with all those golden streaks, or maybe it was naturally gorgeous. Her mouth was wide, an expectant smile on her lips. She wore a white apron that tied behind her neck and around her middle.

"Are you the owner?" he asked, disregarding her question and offering one of his own.

"I am."

"What's your name?"

Her brows lifted, definitely questioning why he wanted to know.

"I was just wondering," he added quickly, "who to talk to about the blueberry muffins. They're great."

"I'm the baker. I'm Chloe."

"Chloe, these are incredible. I'll take a dozen of them."

She nodded, then efficiently went to work on filling his order, arranging the muffins in a pink box and taping it closed. She gave him his total and he paid, unable to linger as there was a line of customers behind him, all anxious to be served.

John milled around by the cake counter, glancing at the many fancy cakes and decorated confections. They looked so good he could possibly be enticed to try some.

Chloe totaled something on the register, then a phone rang in her apron pocket, but she disregarded the ring. A few seconds later, the call came in again. She still didn't answer the cell phone, but this time she reached in her pocket and silenced the rings.

After helping another customer, John heard it ring again.

Now Chloe stepped aside by the big stainless refrigerator, and he couldn't help hearing her say, "Bobby-Tom, I've had it with you. I'm going to come after you like a pit bull on steroids if you don't cut it out." Then she ended the call.

Looking up, her eyes met John's where he'd locked in on her and had been staring. Without a word, she flashed him a polite smile, a smile that insinuated a whole lot more than a curve of her mouth. A flare of anger simmered beneath her expression—not directed at him, but John read her like a book. This Bobby-Tom better watch his step.

Chloe was not only a beautiful woman, but she'd

go down kicking and screaming rather than have somebody knock her out of the ring.

She was a fighter. Bob Garretson might be stepping in a wad of chewing gum if he didn't mind where he was walking.

"BOBBY-TOM IS CALLING me again," Chloe stated while helping Ethel set up a new window display.

The shop wasn't open on Sundays and Chloe usually came by Ethel's Boutique to visit with her grandmother and catch up on the week's events. The two women maneuvered around one another in the tight space. A half-dressed, pleasingly proportioned mannequin wearing a lacy bra and panties awaited the latest trend—a summer skirt and cami-sweater. Ethel felt that even a mannequin needed dignity and she put undies on hers.

"What did he say?" Ethel asked, evidently trying to make up her mind on which sweater—the soft pink or baby blue—to use on the mannequin. She settled for the pink.

"He doesn't say anything. He hangs up."

"Then how do you know it's him?"

"Because he's the only coward I know."

Ethel shrugged her ample shoulders, brows arching. "You've got a point there. Bobby-Tom Drake might have come across like a cigarette ad, but when it was time to saddle a horse and ride, he'd rather have sat in the corral all day and do nothing."

Chloe gathered a pair of plain pumps for the model, the patent white shiny in her grasp. "I know. I found that out too late."

"Knowing later is better than never knowing at all. There are some customers who tell me their life's sorrows, and being addicted to bad men is *numero uno* for most of them. Women need to have better self-esteem and value themselves a lot more than they do so they don't fall for these loser types. It's usually the voluptuous ones who lack confidence, and that's why I sell sexy clothes for them. They need to know that they're unique, no matter if they are in a size sixteen." Ethel worked the delicate sweater over the mannequin's head, then put her rigid arms through the holes. "Oh, nuts, Birdie's right arm is lose again. I'll have to fix that or she'll drop her purse."

"How'd you come up with the name Birdie? It sounds funny to call a dummy that." Chloe rested on the window's edge and took a sip of her diet pop.

"That's how the catalog listed her. She's a size eighteen-to-twenty and she retailed for a thousand smackers."

Chloe smiled, shoving thoughts of Bobby-Tom away. Ethel's word choices often tickled her.

Something cold and wet nudged Chloe's hand and she petted her dog's soft head. Boo-Bear got to come to Ethel's shop when it was closed, and the bichon loved to sniff around and sun herself on the carpet where the light streamed in through the window.

"Chloe, I hope you aren't smarting over that sap-headed Bobby-Tom for even a half of a second. He's yesterday's news and you're good to be rid of him."

Ethel and Bobby-Tom had had difficulties seeing eye to eye and, for years, Chloe's bond with her grandmother had been somewhat strained because of it. She'd had to side with her husband at the time, but now she realized that Ethel's instincts had been right on target.

"I ought to know," Ethel went on, ratcheting the mannequin's arm firmly in place. "I was married three times and it took me that many tries to figure out I have lousy taste in men. Now I can spot a rotten one a mile away, so I guess it wasn't a total waste of my time to bite into three bad apples. I've got the goods on defects now."

Chloe sat and quietly reflected on the female generations in her family. Ethel and Wanda had both had their daughters young. Yet Chloe had tried through her late twenties to have a baby, to no avail. Getting pregnant had been a cinch for the two generations before her.

Ethel had been eighteen and married when she delivered Wanda; then Wanda, an unwed teen, had had Chloe when she was just sixteen.

Then there were the marriages...

First Grandma had been married three times to men who were no good for her, then Wanda chimed in with her own two failures, and with innumerable shack ups. Chloe's one and only divorce rounded things out by placing this family of women high on the list of bombed marital statistics.

Ethel stood back and admired her handiwork on Birdie. "You know who would look fabulous in this outfit? Queen Latifah. I'd die and go to heaven if she ever came into the store."

"Maybe she'll shoot a movie in town."

"Oh, heck," Ethel said, her mouth souring as if she'd sucked on a tart candy. "The only movie that made Idaho famous was that dynamite picture."

"*Napoleon Dynamite*," Chloe gently corrected. "And hey, Matt Damon comes to the premiere at the Egyptian Theater whenever a new Jason Bourne movie opens. So you just never know, Queen Latifah might turn up."

"I guess." Ethel smoothed Birdie's skirt, then gathered the extra items she hadn't used in the display. With her arms full, she began to turn, but her limbs froze as she looked out the window. She recovered quickly and hid behind Birdie's full-figured frame, peeking around her to see, but not be seen.

"What's the matter?" Chloe rose on tiptoe to see what had spooked Ethel.

"It's that Buzz Lightyear," she blurted in a suffocated whisper.

"Buzz Lightyear? That's a cartoon character."

Chloe looked out, but didn't see anyone with a bubble helmet on his head and a gray plastic body. She did spy the man across the street cranking up the green awning for The Humidor—a tobacco shop that had recently opened in the district.

"There he is—right there."

"The cigar guy?"

"Buzz…" Ethel's posture softened and she gazed intently at the man wearing jeans that, by the cut, seemed to be Wranglers. A Stetson rested on his silver hair. He had a slight paunch to his waist that strained his button-down shirt. Overall, he didn't seem like a man to hide from.

"Why are you holding on to the mannequin as if you're going to take up ballroom dancing with her?" Chloe asked.

"I am not." Ethel's demeanor took on a proud air and she let go of Birdie and hopped down from the window. "I only mentioned Buzz because I don't care for him."

"Why not?"

Ethel set her things on the register counter. "I can smell the vile cigar fumes rolling out of his place when I keep my front door open on a sunny day. He's ruined the neighborhood with that nasty shop of his."

Chloe couldn't argue that point. After living with Bobby-Tom's smoking habit, she despised the smell of cigarettes to this day.

"How come you call him Buzz Lightyear?" Chloe asked, giving Boo-Bear a scruff behind her ear. Her tail wagged to show she was happy.

"Because I heard he's a retired astronaut."

"Really? That's cool. He's famous then."

"Famous is only an adjective. It all depends on the person, and not the infamy of his deeds."

"Flying to the moon is famous to me."

Chloe opened a box of silk scarves, admiring the pretty patterns. They made her think about a cake grid, a design she could do in a two-tiered cake. One scarf in particular stood out as exceptionally beautiful. Delicate pink pearls and seashells intertwined on a pale seafoam-green background.

"I'm buying this," Chloe said, setting it on the counter.

"Honey-bee, you can have it if it strikes your fancy." Ethel put a box away, then restocked her gift bags. "I didn't know you liked things like that."

"I don't. I'm going to create a cake pattern out of it."

Ethel folded her arms over her full breasts. "Chloe, I swear, if they squeeze you out of your shop..." Her soft voice quivered with emotion. "You're the most clever woman I know."

"If I'm so clever, how come I can't figure out how to get them to renew my lease and grant me permission for the expansion?" Chloe tucked the pretty scarf into her purse, her mind thinking about the ways in which she could create the same effect out of buttercream icing. Absently, she mentioned, "I have a meeting with a lawyer tomorrow. His hourly rate is obnoxious, but he came recommended so I'll hear what he has to say."

"That's wonderful. I'll bet—" Ethel's words were cut short as a *ping* tapped on the front window where the two of them had been not moments ago.

"What in the world?" Ethel went to inspect the glass, then let out a horrified gasp. "There's a bullet hole!"

"Get down!" Chloe yelled.

Ethel didn't move. "Well, maybe not a bullet hole. More like a BB, but still—somebody shot at my window."

Chloe jumped up beside her, heartbeat racing as if she'd just run a marathon, and examined the pocked depression. She gazed down the street, noting the absence of pedestrians.

The only person in view was the astronaut who stood on the sidewalk at his storefront. Holding on to a garden hose, he wheeled left, then right, as if to see if anyone else happened to be around. As if in relief, his shoulders relaxed, then he shot a concentrated burst of water on the murky pigeon poop marring his green awnings.

"I think we should call the police," Chloe said, stepping away.

"They can't do anything. The culprit is long gone."

Ethel gave a final inspection of the street, lingering over Buzz's figure long enough for Chloe to notice that the pulse at the hollow of her grandmother's neck grew prominent.

Blinking, as if caught in the midst of a stupor, Ethel left the window display.

Neither said anything for the longest time, and Chloe didn't like the feeling she had, the prickling of hair at her nape.

Bobby-Tom wouldn't be following her and taking a potshot at her grandmother's shop window just to get her attention…? That wasn't his style.

Then again, he might just have fallen off the bronco and gone a little loco.

CHAPTER FOUR

JOHN OCCUPIED a spot at the large conference table of Gray, Springer, Moretti and Hayes. Sunlight streamed through the smoky-tinted windows of the high-rise office space. No expense had been spared to make the large room luxurious and comfortable.

The dark brown leather armchairs had been imported from Italy, and the long table was constructed of solid Brazilian teak. Silk throw pillows decorated conversational sofas in a less formal alcove. An assortment of meticulously tended plants had been arranged throughout the area. Their leaves were given a weekly dusting and once-over by a guy who owned and operated his own plant service.

A marble-topped sideboard held gourmet coffee, real cream, as well as the artificial stuff, Earl Gray tea and candied sugar sweeteners. As an extra bonus today, a large box of bakery muffins, fruit pastries and croissants was front and center on the table.

John had made a quick pit stop into Not Just Cakes. Normally, he wouldn't have brought "treats" into the office, but it was the only way he could explain his impromptu visit to the baker's shop at the Grove. He'd hoped to see the owner, but only two young clerks helped the long line of customers. The place had been packed with morning commuters, many walking to their offices from the cluster of parking garages.

Double-parking to save time, John had received a lousy ticket for his plan to get in and out quickly, hoping to flash his smile at the pretty blonde.

So much for satisfying his curiosity about the woman Garretson wanted to run out of the Grove.

Shoving his disappointment aside and taking a bite out of his blueberry muffin, John settled into the meeting as best he could.

The usual Monday morning briefing on this week's cases was short one of the partners. Douglas Gray had called Louis Hayes to say he'd been up all night with the flu and felt as if he had one foot in the grave. Needless to say, he wasn't coming in.

John listened to the briefings recited by Macaulay Springer. His mind was not one hundred percent focused on the cases being discussed.

Last night he'd gotten into it with Zach for lying about being at work. The job didn't require much aside from physical labor and showing up. The fact that he hadn't, and that he had taken advantage of his brother's time had jerked John around one too many times.

In complete frustration, John had taken his son's Chevy truck keys away from him—even though it had been a gift. John probably should have yanked the keys long ago. While the vehicle was titled to Zach, John paid for the outrageously expensive insurance because of Zach's numerous tickets and previous wreck.

Zach had told him he couldn't do it; the truck legally belonged to him. True, but Zach lived at John's house, expense-free. All that was required of him was to show he was trying to better himself with a job. A job John had gotten him.

This morning, John had roused his son out of bed and driven him to the Grove Marketplace job site. Zach hadn't exchanged more than a few words—if grunts counted as conversation.

Stopping at the curb where Giovanni's beat-up trailer remained like a sentinel, John had stated he'd pick Zach up around four.

With an attitude, Zach had shoved the car door open with his elbow and had told him not to bother—he'd find his own ride. Then he'd slammed the door, thrusting himself away from the BMW with his construction belt held loosely in his grasp.

Hearing his partners' voices in the conference room, John only half-listened. Bad, he knew. But this morning's episode distracted him.

John leaned his back into the cushion of the chair, the supple leather enveloping him as he steepled his fingers together. He hated getting into his son's face, but he felt convinced that he'd done the right thing.

"And lastly, Doug had a ten o'clock with Chloe Lawson. Some kind of lease-termination beef." Louis closed the manila folder he'd been looking at. "It's probably a no win, so we'll reschedule her to next week."

Sitting taller, John said, "Excuse me? Who?"

"Chloe Lawson."

The first name was unusual, but John wondered. "A lease for what?"

Louis slid his glance to the barely open folder, his eyes hooded behind a pair of bifocals that perched on his thin nose. "Ahh, let's see. Bakery shop wants to go up against the Grove Marketplace leasing office. It's a waste of our time, folks."

Full awareness hit John all at once, but his face revealed none of his feelings. He extended his hand across the table. "I'll take the file and the meeting."

Louis's brows rose and he commented blandly, "Okay, Moretti. It's your time."

The meeting disbanded and the lawyers toted their files and coffees to their respective offices. John had a corner space with windows on both sides. The walls had been papered in a textured print-on-print in gold tones. He'd had nothing to do with it, but liked the outcome. An interior designer had concocted the exotic color scheme—reds, golds and black—as well as a scheme to get him to go out with her by flirting and wearing revealing blouses when she'd set things up.

Suzy Blaire. Good at her job, but a piece of work.

When ten o'clock drew closer, John caught himself tidying his office and arranging files on his desk in an orderly manner. He looked over the lacquered, ebony elephants on his end table, then fanned the copies of *Golf Digest* in a perfect line on the coffee table. He flicked dust off the red lamp shade in the corner, then took a satisfied look at his environment.

Very rich-looking. Almost standoffish.

"Well, hell," he muttered, but he couldn't do anything about it as his intercom buzzed and his secretary announced his ten o'clock had arrived.

John usually remained behind his big desk when a new client approached him. Often he was working on another case seconds before a new client entered his space. Time was money.

Money bought things for his family.

On that flat note, John pinned a smile to his lips and waited for Chloe to enter. He didn't sit down; rather, he faced his bookcase as if looking for a certain case history book.

He felt her before he saw her, almost as if she had touched him. Unable to explain it, he closed his eyes for scant seconds and gave his lungs a soft pull of oxygen. The room smelled like vanilla and a hint of sugar mixed in with an undefinable floral perfume.

"I was told Mr. Gray wasn't in today," she began, her voice a little uncertain. "And that I was supposed to talk to you. I believe I know your…"

John turned around, straightening his posture in an almost intimidating stance.

"…brother," she finished, a flush straining her cheeks. "I know you, as well. You came by the shop."

Nodding, John offered her a seat.

He took a spot in his executive chair behind the desk and she slipped into the petite chair before him, legs crossed, then together, then in a crossed position once again.

He made a mental note to himself: *Guarded*.

John purposefully kept two client chairs three feet

away from the desk. He did this to keep his eye on his client's body language as he listened to them.

Nonverbal messages were a good way to assess sincerity or lack thereof. He could read a lot about a person's thoughts by the way they conducted themselves.

He noted she wasn't wearing nylons, and her bare ankle revealed an easy-to-spot small tattoo. This surprised him as she didn't look the type to be inked. He couldn't make out what it was, possibly a butterfly.

A summer dress with some kind of abstract pattern in shades of pinks and greens hugged her body as if it had been custom-made for her. She had a woman's figure—not too skinny, but with breasts that were full and round, and a waist that didn't nip into a size zero. She'd tied a pale pink sweater over her bare shoulders and the soft knit set off the golden hue of her skin.

She'd left her hair lose about her neck and he hadn't realized how long it was. Its length fell to her midback in a straight curtain of sunny blond.

Chloe definitely captured his attention in ways that he had forgotten existed. Senses that had been dormant in his body seemed to come to life, heating his muscles and making the air in the room seem warmer than it was.

"Mr. Gray is out of the office today," John offered, resting his wide hands on her folder. "I'm John Moretti, Robert's brother."

"Yes, I assumed that. The name isn't all that common. When I made the appointment, I didn't know that Mr. Gray was part of a partnership."

"We work together, so if you hire one of us, you're getting all of us."

"But I haven't hired you yet." Her tone remained level as she pressed her hands together in her lap. "I only came for the advice."

In spite of himself, John smiled. "Miss Lawson, we don't offer advice here. We uphold the laws that govern the state of Idaho."

"Whatever you'd like to call it, I need some help." The edge of her teeth caught her upper lip, then she quit as if it were a nervous habit she'd like to be rid of. "I didn't know Robert had a brother."

"He has two. I'm the oldest." John couldn't fathom why he felt compelled to offer the clarification.

"Oh, well...I haven't known him very long. Just five months. He buys pastries from me for his restaurant—Pomodoro."

"I know."

"Yes, I figured you'd know the name of his restaurant."

"No, I knew he bought pastries from you. He told me."

"He did?"

John didn't respond. He opened her folder and glanced at it, but there wasn't anything written down aside from her name and today's date and meeting time, and one sentence outling her complaint.

"So what can I help you with, Miss Lawson?" he asked, picking up a Montblanc pen.

She opened her purse, then handed him a letter. She quietly waited while John glanced at the leasing company's statement regarding the termination of her lease and the effective date.

"Can I sue them?" she asked when he looked up.

The beautifully expressive concern on her face was enough to make him want to say *Hell, yes! We can crucify the bastards.*

But he couldn't lie to her.

"I'm sorry, Miss Lawson, but the leasing company is within its legal right to exercise their option of renewal—or in this case, not renewing."

Her chin lowered slightly and she sucked in a soft breath. Its sound pricked his heart. Then, she gave him a long gaze, her violet eyes pleading. "Are you sure?"

Biting back a smile, John remained silent a moment. He couldn't ever recall having his expertise challenged. "Yes, I'm sure."

"Shit on a stick," she muttered.

John couldn't refrain from laughing. "I'm sorry?"

"Nothing." She waved him off, adjusted her purse and took out a checkbook. "Who do I make this out to? The secretary said your office charges a hundred dollars an hour."

"This one's on me."

"That's a first. Thank you." She returned her checkbook and closed her purse. "Lawyers charge for everything, right down to a paperclip if I need one on my file."

"I take it you don't like lawyers."

"Nothing personal," she replied. "I just happened to deal with a couple during my divorce who would have done me better if they'd mud-wrestled each other instead of trying to sort out the best way to end things between my ex and I."

John couldn't help wondering how long she'd been divorced, but he didn't ask.

Holding her hand out for the letter, he returned the envelope to her. She tucked the bad news into her purse with a heave of her breasts and a sigh. "Thank you for your time, Mr. Moretti. I'm sorry to have bothered you."

Chloe made a move to rise to her feet, but he didn't want her leaving so soon, so he swiftly inquired, "What made you go into the baking business?"

She paused. "I learned a love of it from my grandmother. She taught me how to make a cake."

"My dad taught me how to hammer a nail, but I didn't have a talent for it."

"Sometimes desire outweighs talent." Her face softened as if dredging up memories. "I ruined a halfdozen cakes when I started learning, but I kept trying. I suppose I wanted to make Ethel proud. Or maybe I just needed something to keep me out of trouble."

There was a lot more going on in her words than she let on and John grew more intrigued by Chloe.

"What kind of trouble?" he asked.

She shrugged. "Just stupid stuff. I won't bore you."

John didn't think he could ever be bored by the way the golden shades of blond caught in her hair, or the way her fresh pink lipstick looked quite kissable on her mouth. She fascinated him in ways he hadn't thought possible.

"You really like it? The bakery business?"

"I dearly love it." Her heart-spoken response held passion, reminding him of the ambition he'd once had years ago when he first began his career. It had been a long journey from young lawyer to an older, seasoned man who no longer searched for the core values of a case, but the accumulation of billable hours.

"My business is doing so great," she went on, her eyes shining. "The very thought of moving to a new location—it's going to stink. My customers expect me to be a part of the Grove. I hate to give it up…but if I want to expand and—" She cut herself short, as if just realizing he was in the room with her. "I should be leaving."

She stood and he followed her to the door. He all but trapped her under the frame, his body towering over her form. She was tall, but his height dominated her by a good foot.

In that split second, where they stood suspended in time, she grew visibly flustered. And not by her lease termination. His presence did things to her.

He could sense it, feel it. See the flicker of confusion, and a mix of attraction in her eyes.

Reeling back slightly, she almost lost her balance. He reached out to steady her and she said something too softly for him to make out. He could only guess what she might be thinking.

"Robert never mentioned you," she mumbled.

John said nothing further as he watched Chloe walk down the narrow hallway to the reception area. When she was gone from his view, he returned to his desk, picked up the phone and made a call.

The receptionist patched him through.

"Hello?" the man's voice replied on the other end.

"Bob, John Moretti."

Bob Garretson's gravelly voice quipped, "Johnny-boy, I was wondering if I'd hear from you. I almost called another—"

"I'll plead your cause." John reclined into his large chair, feet on the edge of his desk. "But it's going to cost you. Big-time."

THE SPRAWLING HOMES in Quail Ridge fanned across the Boise foothills, creating a quiet neighborhood with earthy surroundings. Rim lots had heart-stopping views of the downtown city lights. The subdivision offered executive-style living at its finest, with amenities such as tennis courts, a playground and nature-jogging path. At the entrance, water cascaded from the tallest manmade waterfall in the Pacific Northwest.

Luxury Jaguars, BMWs, Lexuses and Mercedes parked in the long driveways. *Au pairs* pushed infants in prams passing beautifully landscaped yards with playing children. Cats sunned themselves on porches. The occasional loose dog walked down the road wearing a collar with tags on it. Teens drove new cars, gifts from graduations, down the winding streets, headed to the downtown nightlife.

The scent of meats roasting on barbeques filled the summer air in Quail Ridge. Soft music played from backyard sound systems. The community pool was nearly empty as most homes had their own.

A beat-up Mazda with a pizza logo on the door,

headed slowly up the road, pausing every now and then to look for a house number. Finding the correct address, the driver exited his car and carried four pies to the door.

Rock and roll music blasted from inside the residence. The double-front doors, framed by panels of glass, allowed an unobstructed view into the home's rich interior. The driver remained motionless on the stoop, as if unsure the doorbell could be heard.

Several rings later, the door swung open and a boy in his late teens filled the entrance. An exchange of pizza for cash was made, then the door slammed closed.

Zach Moretti walked through the dining room, the smell of sausage and pepperoni curling into his nose. Except for an Italian Sunday dinner once in a while at his grandmother's house, he lived on fast food. He would have rather had ziti tonight, but nobody was around to make it.

Several of his friends sat at the glass table on the patio while Toad and Corey ripped chords on vintage Fenders, power cables plugged into the amps they'd brought over.

Zach exited the open French doors, setting the boxes onto the table. "Chow time."

"Hells yeah," VeeJay said as he lifted one of the lids and steam wafted from the box.

Toad and Corey set their guitars down and joined them. The premier sound system, wired through every room, blared "Voodoo" by Godsmack out the patio's speakers.

The five of them dug in and ate, talking crap about people they knew, then VeeJay smacked sauce from his lips while asking, "Dude, when's your dad giving you back your truck keys? Kegger this Friday night in Garden City and I need a ride."

"Lemme see," Zach replied with a snort of irritation. "Since he only copped them from me last night, I'm thinking I won't have them back by Friday."

"Dude, he can't take your truck away if he gave it to you," Tom said, rolling a golf ball back and forth from hand to hand, across the table's surface. "I think that's against the law."

"Yeah." Corey laughed, tilting back on his chair. "Zach's dad ought to know. He's a lawyer."

Toad scarfed down his fourth slice of pizza and talked while he chewed. "Hey, man, when's your dad coming home?"

"I dunno. I never know."

"Crank up the bass, dude. I freakin' love this Godsmack tune. They kick ass." Corey wolfed down the last of his crust in two bites and washed it down with cold beer taken from the stainless steel fridge. "Tony Rombola plays a Takamine and rocks it with a Diezel amp."

The wrought iron side gate to the backyard opened and Kara showed up with her friend Ashley. She carried a half-full plastic bag from Garretson's market, and Ashley held on to a soft drink cup from the minimart at the bottom of the hill.

"Think you have the music loud enough?" Kara hollered.

"Nope," Zach replied, belching from the light beer he'd swiped.

"If Dad finds out you were drinking his beer, he's going to be pissed," Kara cautioned, making a face at her brother.

"Don't care. What's he going to do?"

Saying nothing, Kara dropped a hand on her slender waist and gave him a sassy smirk. A Tiffany charm bracelet encircled her wrist and glinted in the sunlight. She wore clothes from Abercrombie—a pair of pink plaid shorty-shorts, white layered tank tops and rubber flip-flops. Her hip handbag had been purchased online. The white, multicolored Louis Vuitton monogram cradled her shoulder.

"Well, I'm turning the music down. We're dying my hair and I can't hear myself."

"Later," Zach called after her.

"Your sister's hot." VeeJay caught Tom's golf ball and pitched it into the swimming pool.

"Jerk," Tom growled. "I was playing with that."

"Don't get any ideas about dating my sister," Zach warned. "I know what a loser you are."

The music took a drop in volume, but after two minutes, Zach got up and cranked the sound again.

Tom jumped into the sparkling pool, then climbed onto a raft and stretched out, eyes closed.

VeeJay fielded a cell-phone call. "Whad up?" He talked for a minute, then flipped his phone closed. "My girlfriend wants me to come over."

"Later, dude," Toad commented while strapping his guitar around his neck.

The iTunes music faded from Godsmack to a familiar guitar intro and Toad was all over it.

Tilting his skinny hip with a faux drug-induced attitude, Toad repeatedly played the tri-tone intro from Hendrix's "Purple Haze."

The double-pane windows on the back of the house vibrated from the deep bass as the song played on, Toad keeping up on his electric guitar.

A voice called from the wrought iron gate and Zach indolently glanced over his shoulder at the two Boise cops, one of whom said, "Boise Police."

Curses were muttered, and beer bottles swiftly pitched into the hot tub, disappearing into the jet of bubbles.

From the gate's vantage point, none of the evidence could be seen. Now that it was gone, Zach went toward the cops to address the situation.

"What's up?" Zach questioned.

"Can we come into the yard, son?"

"Uh, yeah…sure."

He let them in, glancing at his bros looking innocent-like, as if they'd all gathered to memorize their catechisms.

"Which one of you lives here?" the cop asked loudly, his hand poised at his belt. The music screamed at a high decibel level.

Zach silently pointed to himself, but made no appearance of being unnerved. He'd had a couple of run-ins with cops before. No biggie.

"We got a complaint about loud music."

"I'll turn it down." Zach feigned an easygoing attitude, then went to cut the tunes.

At that second, his dad walked out the French doors and onto the patio.

Glancing from Zach to the policemen, John Moretti stood for a long moment, sizing up the situation.

Then on a hot exhale, he said, "Great. Just great."

CHAPTER FIVE

AT SEVENTY YEARS of age Walden Griffiths had experienced three great loves of his life. His dear wife, Fanny, who had passed away a year ago. The NASA program—more to the point, the space shuttle *Columbia,* which had orbited him into space. And, lastly, the taste of a fine cigar as its smoke swirled around his tongue.

Basking in the sun outside of Humidor, his cigar shop, and rolling a Toraño torpedo cigar next to his right ear to test its pitch and crackle, he had to be honest about things and admit he actually had four loves.

The truth be told, he carried a big soft spot in his heart for his patchwork cat, Apollo.

Apollo laid on the concrete next to Walden's easel-back chair, his black tail softly curling and dancing as if conducting a symphony to the coo of rooftop pigeons.

Damn varmint cockroach birds.

The day was a drowsy Wednesday afternoon. Having lived much of his life in Florida, he enjoyed the scorching heat as it radiated off the sidewalk in hot waves. The cat would soak in the sun for about fifteen minutes, then wander off down the alley for a shady respite and to hunt down Dumpster mice.

Walden's shop in the Grove Marketplace was relatively new, a small clientele beginning to build. He wasn't in this for the money. His retirement checks from the government got him by just fine. He simply needed something to do after Fanny had passed away.

To this day, he missed her so.

The agony of loss made a sad bedfellow during long sleepless nights. There were times when his throat felt raw from grief and a hot tear would trickle down his cheek.

But today seemed to be okay for him. He was getting better at reconciling his broken heart, mending the tears with pieces of fond memories. That seemed to help.

While the walk-in humidor had to maintain perfect climate control, Walden could leave the shop door open to let the frigid air-conditioned air out, and allow in a little of the summer day. He was odd that way— he loved the heat like a lizard and could sun himself for hours.

Oftentimes, he took a canvas folding chair outside to enjoy the sunbeams dancing over his cheeks and nose—those rare occasions when he didn't go outside without his Stetson.

Walden had never ridden a horse—or even saddled one—in his life but, when in Idaho, do as the Idahoans did and Governor Butch Otter looked might-tee fine in his slick cowboy hat. Giving up his beloved Bermuda shorts for tight-in-the-caboose Wranglers had been quite the stretch for an old coot like him, but now he'd gotten used to the gear and actually liked it.

Given Fanny had died from skin cancer, Walden

didn't mess around with the sun. Each day he slathered that nasty-smelling sunscreen on himself. He hated its greasy coating on his hairy arms. He mostly wore long sleeves, even in the summer. But he held a love for the wind and surf in his soul, recalling days at the beach in Florida.

Fanny would be proud of him for going the extra mile and taking the precaution.

Walden wondered what she'd think of his shop. He did love a good stogie, always had. He'd wanted to start over in life and get away from the reminder of his former one in Florida. Idaho was a good place to begin again. AARP always wrote nice things about it.

Finding the retail vacancy at the Grove Market-place, Walden toured the building and felt it a good fit right from the get-go. He liked the neighborly area even though he was right downtown.

So far, business tottered forward on fledgling foot-steps but, much like the first spacecraft launched into space, time, determination and patience would make it a better journey. Walden was in no hurry, and he had the money to invest in the shop, so he didn't mind if the place stayed quiet for an hour or two during the day. Things would blast off if they were meant to be.

Covering all his bases, Walden had joined the RTDA—Retail Tobacco Dealers Association—to stay on top of things. He'd done all he could to present a top-notch shop, a place where a fella could enjoy the same passions as himself.

The Humidor sold premium cigars, pipes, tobacco, humidors and lighters. He'd set up a relaxing lounge toward the back, a place for customers to light up a Macanudo or Ashton, on Walden's recommendation.

Along one wall of the coffee area, he had a small museum dedicated to his NASA years. He'd set up informational displays and memorabilia he'd collected throughout his career as a mission specialist: official emblem patches, medals, a U.S. of A. flag carried on a mission, log books, security badges, some Orbiter pins, flight food menus and, of course, a detailed model of the space shuttle *Columbia*.

Walden felt his shop would fill a niche in Boise. A place where a man could be a man and enjoy a beautiful cigar, drink a strong cup of joe and retell stories about life.

Puffing on his cigar, Walden caught a glimpse of the woman in the shop across the street. She gazed through her window display at him, then quickly disappeared. It hadn't escaped his notice that she spied on him when she thought he wasn't looking.

He figured her name had to be Ethel given the shop's signage: Ethel's Boutique.

Ethel had been poking her nose in his direction, using those plastic broads in the window as decoys to keep her cover. He wasn't a nitwit. A guy with half a brain couldn't miss the real broad versus the dummy she kept primping over, changing its shoes and handbag every other day just so she had an excuse to gawk at him.

Her snootiness irritated Walden as he hadn't done a dad-gum thing against her. He considered himself to be polite and a true gentleman. And just to cement the

theory, his mind ran through a few of his best quali-
ties. He washed his hands after he used the restroom,
and he made his bed in shipshape order every morning
after his shower. On the day of expiration, he chucked
lunch meats from his refrigerator.

As a delivery truck rambled down the street sepa-
rating them, Ethel opened her shop door for an afternoon breeze. Not once did she look his way, an effort
that had to be forced because he noticed her head tilt
toward him, then her body posture grew rigid.

The old sourpuss.

His Fanny rarely had a grumpy day in her life, even
during the chemotherapy. Same thing even when she
went through the reverse curse, the big "change" to
nothing going on each month. She still kept a smile on
her face as she'd ironed his handkerchiefs.

Fanny had been a saint, even when he'd been a
mean and rotten sum'bitch devil because of…well,
just because of what he had once been like. But
Walden wouldn't dwell on that.

Instead, he stubbed the ash on his cigar and set it
in the sand can he kept on the shop's stoop. He rose to
his cowboy-booted feet and moseyed across the street
for a little welcome call.

Ethel almost ran into him in the doorway, evidently
having turned off her radar after opening her door.

"For heaven's sake," she sputtered. "I was just
going to close this door."

"But you only opened it a minute ago." His gaze
held hers and he noticed she had very blue eyes. So
blue, the color reminded him of the earth's oceans at

one hundred and sixty-six nautical miles in outer space.

With an offending wave of her hand in the air, she said, "The smell of your stale cigar blows across the street and into my store. I don't want my dresses smelling like an ashtray."

Walden stood there a little mollified, uncertain as to what to say first; that she wasn't being very neighborly, or that she had the nicest set of peepers he'd stared into in a long time. She wore some mascara, a hint of blush and some pretty lipstick. Her hair brushed at her jawline, it's color like a red ball of yarn.

They faced off, toe-to-toe, and there was something about her that addled him, got under his skin and boiled his blood pressure like a rocket thruster. He couldn't say outright he wanted to write her off, but he wished he could stop staring at her.

Rather than use the politeness that Fanny would have been proud of, he went into his NASA mode, where quips were traded in flight faster than the speed of sound.

"Roger that," he finally offered, touching the felt brim of his Stetson. "I hadn't realized the smoke could travel so far. I guess the exhaust from the cars passing by is like an atomizer of French perfume. Especially that diesel garbage truck. Makes a cigar seem stale, I guess, in comparison."

Her red-outlined mouth dropped open. "Well, aren't you full of applesauce?"

"I had a *Mac*Donald's for lunch." He didn't connect the dots in her comment and hated that he felt lame.

She laughed at him, and he felt the tops of his ears

burn red and hot like a launch pad seconds before lift-off. "I only came over to introduce myself."

Her laughter died, but her smile didn't crack so he pulled out the big guns and added, "Seeing as you keep looking at me as if I'm a prime cut of beef, I thought I'd give you a closer look."

The blue in her eyes darkened like a storm.

"I'm Walden Griffiths, owner of that fine see-gar store across the street—The Humidor. Feel free to come on over when it suits your fancy. We serve coffee daily."

She said nothing, just kept her eyes wide and then blinked.

Walden spoke for her. "And I'm thinking you'd be Ethel. Am I right?"

"Yes," she said, her throat scratchy.

"Ethel what?" he pursued.

"Lumm. Ethel Lumm."

He extended his hand, and she automatically slipped hers into his. "Nice to meet you," he said.

"Uh…okay," was all she said.

Her skin felt soft and peachlike. She must use a lot of cream on it. She came across as feminine and she looked pretty to him now that they got over that awkward beginning.

An ache circled in his heart, taking root right at the ventricle that pumped blood in a raging course down below where it had no business going. He missed having a woman. Missed the companionship that not even his cat could fully provide. Apollo couldn't shout out answers to *Jeopardy* with him.

"Well, I guess that's all then," he stated, letting her

hand go as he glanced around her place. Filled with enough froufrou to give a man a nightmare, this definitely wasn't his kind of digs. His throat tightened up and he felt the cold sweats coming on when he noticed a display of lacy panties.

Holy smokes.

"See you," he sputtered, then left the building, taking lunging strides to The Humidor. Once inside, he drank a cup of coffee in a long pull, not noticing he'd burned the tip of his tongue until after the last drop.

Screwing up his face, he gave Ethel's Boutique a second look from the sanctuary of The Humidor. He wondered what she'd do if she found out he'd accidentally popped a hole in her display window with his BB gun.

CHLOE LIVED a settled lifestyle—a far cry from the one she'd had in her early years. From infancy to fifteen she had moved all over the west with her mom in a beater Volkswagen van with everything they owned stored inside.

Wanda had been born in Boise, had attended Capital High but never graduated. She'd been a good-time girl. The one who livened parties and drank the most. She also had been in trouble at fifteen, gotten pregnant with Chloe and didn't know which boy had been the father. This was something Chloe never dwelled on as soon as she'd been old enough to comprehend that her mother had been a... Well, Chloe wouldn't even think the word. She preferred to think of herself as being born to be handed over to Ethel in later years. Chloe didn't know a whole lot about what her mother had done in her past, other than Wanda wouldn't have graced the cover of the *Ladies' Home Journal.*

There were those moments when Chloe gazed about her home off Emerald and Latah, and wished her mom could see how well she'd done with her life. But, truthfully, there was no point. Wanda wouldn't have cared a fig about a sofa and rugs bought from Pottery Barn, or her tiny porch with the wicker furniture.

Chloe's house had been built in the 1930s and didn't offer a lot of square footage. There were only six rooms and a dining nook. The house had a certain charm and sweetness, a Tudor-style that had been fun to decorate. Rustic brickwork had been used on the exterior, with broad timbers and alabaster plaster on the second story. The windows, comprised from a network of diamond-shaped panes in tall, rectangular housings, finished things off. Most of them opened with a crank rather than up and down on a sash.

Chloe's bedroom overlooked the front of the house, a vantage point that was useful in the wee hours of morning when she wanted to see if the newspaper lay on the driveway. The garage was in back, detached with only enough room for one vehicle, her lawnmower and basic yard tools.

The three bedrooms upstairs had windows on both sides. The dining room and large living room offered just enough space for her furniture and cookbook collection. Her kitchen definitely could be called cramped, but it was sufficient for her needs.

The rear of the home had a terrace where she'd situated a small table and four cushioned chairs. The leafy boughs of mature elms and sycamores moved in soft whispers when the wind blew. Chloe had planted a garden this year, but it needed weeding badly. The pink, tea-rose bushes on the front and side of the house could use a pruning as soon as time permitted.

These days, it seemed as if she got up, went to work in the dark and came home in the dark. She spent more time at Not Just Cakes than any place else. And on Sundays, after she slept in and took Boo-Bear for a walk, Chloe didn't feel like working in her yards. She wanted to go visit Ethel for girl talk, or go to Lucky Peak Lake and soak in the sun.

This week seemed to speed by. Already it was Wednesday evening, so Chloe decided to catch up on laundry and watch some cooking shows on the Food Network she'd recorded with TiVo.

She'd taken a cool shower when she came home, threw on a pair of her thin sweats and a cami top with a built-in bra. Walking through the house on her fuzzy flip-flop slippers, she'd grudgingly grabbed one of her starter herb plants and tossed it in the garbage beneath the kitchen sink. She had forgotten to water the four minipots on her windowsill and the basil had died. She gave a good soaking to the thyme, sage and oregano.

Dinner tonight had been compliments of the microwave—a lean meal on a plastic tray. She'd just poured a glass of wine to accompany it, turned on the television and pressed Play for her favorite show, when her phone rang.

"Naturally," she grumbled, snagging the receiver but talking away from it. "Boo-Boo, no!" Her bichon licked its chops over the unsavory meal of cubed chicken in an orange sauce. It may have been a lousy diet dinner, but it was her lousy meal and she wasn't going to share. "Boo—no!"

The dog backed off a few inches, but didn't leave its begging spot by the coffee table where the meal beckoned.

"Hello?" Chloe said, then under her breath, "Boo… *no*."

"Miss Lawson?"

"Yes."

"Did I catch you at a bad time?" The male voice seemed kind enough, but she didn't recognize it.

"Yes, actually. If you're selling something, I'm not interested. Good luck to you   "

"It's John Moretti."

Halfway to quitting the call, Chloe clasped the receiver closer to her ear. "Oh, hello."

Unbidden, she felt a wave of warmth heat her cheeks. There was no denying he could be called an attractive man, and attractive men weren't burning up her phone line.

The first time she'd talked to him in the pastry line, she'd been preoccupied, but his sexy brown eyes with thick, black lashes hadn't gone unnoticed. Her second encounter with him, she'd been more aware and sized up his finer attributes.

No doubt, John was cut from fine stock. Handsome couldn't begin to describe him. His tall, dark good looks beckoned women to take a closer look, but Chloe had been at his office on business, not on a date.

It had been her bad luck he'd been the one to talk to her about the lease expiring. After that day, part of her had wanted to go back to Gray, Springer, Moretti and Hayes and talk to Douglas Gray for his take on things. But, sadly, she suspected he'd give her the same dead-end answer.

John's phone call captured her attention. And piqued her female curiosity. For one bent moment, she thought he might ask her out or something insane. Stupid and ludicrous thoughts.

"Sorry to be calling you at home," he began, his voice deep and assured, "but I didn't have a cell number for you. I looked you up in the book."

With today's easy-access Internet, anyone could get her address, phone number and even her cell number. All they had to do was punch in a credit card, and presto. Instant information.

"It's not a bad time," she managed, watching her dog slowly stalk her chicken dinner.

His tone was filled with all business when he continued, saying, "I'd like to talk to you, in person. Sooner versus later, if you can."

"Really?" She relived those scant seconds in his office where he'd stood in front of her in the doorway, his body tall and muscular over hers. She ignored the tingles that prickled her skin. "About what?"

After confirming her lease could be legally canceled,

it didn't seem possible he would have anything else to say.

"It's better if we meet so I can go over a few things."

"What things?"

The line went quiet for a few heartbeats.

"Look…Chloe—" he said her name in a way that brought heat to her cheeks "—I called to talk to you about Garretson's."

This captured her attention, and hope welled inside of her like a spring. "Have they changed their mind about renting next door to me?"

"No."

The one word crushed her spirits.

"Then what do we have to talk about?" Chloe eyed her dinner and her dog's black nose, which was now within three inches of the plate. Boo's chin rested on the coffee table, her tail wagging ever so slightly as her body wiggled to grow closer…closer.

"I'd rather meet in person, but I can tell you this much—I'm not representing Garretson's against you—"

"Against me?" she exclaimed, aghast. "I haven't done anything wrong."

"Nobody is saying you have."

"Then what's this all about?"

He paused, as if trying to decide what to tell and what not to tell her on the phone.

Finally he uttered two words. "A remuneration."

She hated that she didn't know what that meant.

"Can you meet me and we'll talk about this?" His monotone statement felt as if he'd uttered it a hundred times to small fry in a big sea. She knew she was nothing to him, just a tiny bakery shop in the way of a giant store.

Undefinably disappointed, Chloe shook off the feeling. It had been too long since she'd talked to a man on the phone and she felt slighted. That she'd even, for a second, thought he might be calling to ask her—

Boo-Bear dove on her dinner plate, and in four gulps devoured the chicken chunks, scattering rice to the floor with sideways laps of her pink tongue.

"Have you had dinner yet?" John's casual question drew her attention away from her dog. "Meet me at my brother's restaurant. Pomodoro—you know it."

The last flecks of white rice disappeared as Boo-Bear covered her bases and sniffed for, then gobbled, stray pieces of food that had fallen under the sofa.

Chloe's empty stomach rumbled. "I'll be there in an hour."

CHAPTER SIX

JOHN'S RELATIONSHIP with his brother had been strained for the month since their phone conversation about Chloe. While they'd been sociable at family affairs, there definitely had been some hard feelings. So John headed for the restaurant's kitchen to seek him out and make things right before Chloe arrived.

Located at the corner of 9th and Bannock, Pomodoro had a classic Italian feel with its red checked tablecloths and full Chianti bottles on every table for the guests to serve themselves. Robert used an honor system for his patrons, allowing them to tally how many times they filled their wineglasses.

Savory flavors scented the air, garlic and cheeses, sausage and basil. The restaurant operated until ten, and since the hour was on the later side, many of the early-bird diners had come and gone.

John pushed the revolving door to the kitchen, spying his brother's back as he headed inside.

"Robert," John called as a pan on the commercial range seared and caught flame while Robert tossed ingredients.

Glancing over his shoulder Robert nodded, then set the sauté pan on the side of the burner. "Hey, John."

Robert Moretti never held a grudge, not even in their youth. He didn't seem to have a bad bone in his body. John admired him as a father and a husband, an all-around good guy.

"I'm having dinner in a minute." John approached the stove and leaned into the wall, watching as Robert sprinkled sliced basil into the dish.

"Special tonight is veal scaloppine marsala."

"Great. I'll let my guest know." John folded his arms over his chest. "I invited Chloe Lawson to dinner."

That got his brother's undivided attention. "Why?"

"I want to help her out."

"Amen for that." Robert clapped his shoulder. "I told you she was nice."

"Nice has nothing to do with it. I'll tell you more later."

"Sounds good."

Wearing soiled kitchen whites, Robert embraced him and gave him a hard hug.

John patted his brother's back, glad the air had been cleared.

He went into the dining room and sat at a table for two by the window, waiting for Chloe to appear. He ran through the deal she could get if she leveled with him about her income. Getting Bob Garretson to agree to *his* terms had been more of a challenge, but in the end, Bob had agreed.

Now all John had to do was get Chloe to accept the offer and everyone would be happy.

Chloe ran late, fifteen minutes beyond the time she

said she'd be here, but he didn't comment. She looked too beautiful for him to concern himself over a triviality like time.

Her blond hair cascaded over her shoulders, the top part by her bangs partially tucked into a hair clip. She wore minimal makeup. He mostly noticed the lipstick on her mouth. Soft and pink. She'd chosen a summer dress and heeled flip-flops, exposing her tattoo.

"Sorry I'm late," she offered in a breathless tone, the scent of her floral perfume clouding the air in a sweet smell. "I couldn't find a place to park and I won't do the parking garage at night. I had to circle the block like ten times."

As she hastily sat down, he dragged his attention off her ankle, still unable to make out what exactly the tattoo was.

"You're fine."

And she was fine. More fine than he recalled from their brief meetings. He wondered how long he could linger over dinner just to get to know her a little better.

Robert came to the table with a friendly greeting and a bottle of wine. "Chloe, great to have you come visit."

"Thanks, Robert."

Extending a bottle of wine toward Chloe, Robert's tone took a proud air. "It's on me. A 1999 Brunello di Montalcino from Banfi. You'll love it. I wanted to say thank you for all the wonderful treats you send me— so it's my turn to treat you tonight."

"Robert, how sweet," she cooed. "You didn't have to do this." Chloe situated her purse on the windowsill.

"But I wanted to." Cradling the wine bottle in his arm, Robert pulled the cork and poured two glasses. "Enjoy." Then to John he offered a heartfelt, "I'm glad you're here. *Buon appetito.*"

"*Grazie.*"

Robert left them with opened menus after reciting the specials and notable dishes.

Although he knew most of the entrees by heart, John leisurely explored the menu. Chloe made a peripheral study of her choices, but she seemed distracted. She fidgeted with her napkin, then drank a sip of red wine as if needing something to do.

She slowly raised the paper-thin wineglass to her lips, and he watched her take a tiny sip, then another.

The sexy arch of her brows raised. "Mmm. This is good. Really good." Her feminine purr of pleasure caused his heart to beat faster.

Retaining a calm exterior, John said lightly, "Robert knows his wines."

"I only recently developed a taste for wine." She took another taste, licking her lips. The gesture had him dragging his gaze to her full mouth. "Well, within the last ten years."

"And ten years prior—what did you drink?"

"I hate to say it, but mostly beer or those hard lemonades with a screw-top cap." The expression on her face grew distant, as if she were dredging up an old memory that bothered her.

"But you refined your tastes."

"Quite literally, yes. I got divorced." She quickly took another taste of the Brunello, smothering the words she'd spoken. Personal information she'd provided for a second time. So he decided it was legitimate for him to question her.

"Tough divorce ten years ago?"

"Yes, I'm a divorce statistic." As if to lighten the weight of her marital history, she countered, "Haven't we all, by our age?"

"True." John eased into his seat, allowing himself to relax and take things slow. He had the rest of the night to discuss business. "I gather you don't care for your ex-husband."

"That's putting it mildly." Her fingertip traced the rim of her wineglass; an innocent enough gesture but watching her do it put a coil of heat in his belly. "Living with Bobby-Tom was like living with a man a lug nut shy of a full wheel. He used to race over at Firebird and he never really grew up. I grew out of him."

Bobby-Tom. The name sparked an immediate connection for John. That's who she'd threatened on her cell phone the day he'd bought the blueberry muffin.

Chloe ran her hands down her arms, as if chilled. "I'm sorry. I almost never talk about my ex-husband. I was young and stupid and if I'd had half a brain, I would have seen the writing on the wall. But I just wanted a home and family to call my own, so I fell for the whole 'I love you so much, baby' crap and married the jerk."

John let her talk, watching the play of emotions run the gamut over her delicate features.

"We were all young and dumb once." She grew

visibly nervous and tagged on, "And I'm sure you have a story to tell about your ex-wife, too. Was it her fault things ended?"

In a thoughtfully low tone, John replied, "She died. She was killed in a car accident."

The color on Chloe's cheeks blanched. "Ohmygosh, I'm so sorry. I had no idea. Robert never told me. He and I have never talked about you so I wouldn't have known. I'm so, so sorry," she repeated. "Sorry…"

"If you say you're sorry one more time—" he lowered his voice "—I'm going to have to sit on your side of the table and put my hand over your mouth."

Eyes widening and her mouth clamping shut, she grew stone quiet.

John swirled the wine in his glass, gazing at its red depths then taking a drink. Gazing over the rim, he said, "I didn't mean for you to go into lockdown. I like a woman who speaks her mind."

"I can certainly do that," she almost whispered. "But I truly am…*regretful*…for my comment."

"It's understandable you'd make the assumption. I'm a rarity. A man my age—widowed." He held up his hands, as if in surrender. "I've never met a woman in her thirties, or forties for that matter, who's lost her husband. They've all been divorced, many two and three times."

The color returned to her face, a glimmer of her spunk coming back. "If you're keeping count, you can add me to the statistics, but only put me down for one divorce."

"I'm not tallying anything about you, Chloe. I wasn't

referring to women I've dated." He clarified in a deep tone. "I've done very little of that. I was talking about clients."

"Oh." The single sound was uttered between parted lips. The shape of her mouth kept beckoning his gaze, and he found he could hardly keep his eyes off her. He couldn't pinpoint why.

In looks, she wasn't anything like the type of women he was usually attracted to. He preferred dark hair. Black, like Connie's had been. Chloe's hair and skin made her coloring seem pastel in comparison. He didn't want to make comparisons between the two. His past needed to remain in his past, and his future shouldn't be marred with pieces of Connie—good or bad. His wife was gone and anyone he pursued would be uniquely different in mannerisms and looks. That pretty much made him think very cautiously before committing to any involvements. Which is why he'd remained single these past few years. He simply hadn't been ready to move on.

Staring at Chloe, he wondered why she had such an effect on him. He grew preoccupied by her appearance, the way she moved her hand in a fluid motion, or the way she tossed her hair over her shoulder. He hadn't sought the heated feelings; they'd just sprung into life by their own accordance.

A waiter came and took their orders. John went to pour more wine into Chloe's glass, but she fanned her fingers over its top. "No. I want to keep a clear head about me."

They'd been making small talk for the last several

minutes and now Chloe gave him a curious gaze. "Okay, so what's going on?"

"I don't follow you."

"Did you ask me to dinner to talk about the lease? Why not just tell me on the phone?" She absently aligned her silverware in a neat row. "And by the way, I had to look up *remuneration* in the dictionary."

Her resourcefulness put a smile on John's mouth. He liked that she had enough confidence in herself to admit ignorance, but also possessed the desire to learn and improve.

"I didn't want to discuss terms with you on the phone."

She gave him a hard stare. "I think I get it now." She all but smacked her hand on her forehead. "You didn't take my side of the case, but you took Garretson's. You're his lawyer, aren't you?"

"Not exactly," he replied. "My firm is one of many he has legal dealings with, but I'm not officially representing him. Or you. I'm a messenger, of sorts."

Chloe took a moment to process this information, her brows furrowing as she gave him a thorough gaze—as if to size up every line and curve on his face. "Will I want to kill the messenger?"

In spite of the serious nature of their discussion, a smile broke out on John's mouth and he laughed. "I hope not."

"Well, then, spill it to me. What's going on?"

"I called Bob Garretson. I wanted to see where he stood and just how firm he was on the Grove Marketplace. I suggested going elsewhere with his store. I even tossed out an alternate location."

Surprise marked her facial features, her shoulders squaring as if encouraged. "And?"

"He said no."

Defeat softened her posture, and she poured more wine as if needing the fortitude. "Of course."

"In the midst of the conversation," John said, "he mentioned that time is money and they would like to get going on their newest store sooner versus later."

"I won't do it." Fire sparked in her violet eyes, darkening their color to a deeper hue. "I have a viable contract in good standing and nobody can get me out of my space. It's legally mine until my lease agreement expires." Blond hair fell over her shoulder and she smoothed its golden curtain away from her face. "I can't believe he thinks I'm that stupid as to move out now."

"He doesn't expect you to leave early without compensation." John broke off a piece of warm bread, slathered butter over the soft brown inside crust, then slid the bread toward Chloe on a small white plate.

She murmured her thanks as he said, "I want to make myself clear—I'm not against you."

"But you're for Garretson's."

"Not true. I actually have your best interests over his."

"And why is that?"

John thoughtfully mulled over her question, but couldn't come up with a viable answer he wanted to share. It was too complicated to get into his entire legal history as a lawyer, his lapse in conscience and the false direction he'd caught himself moving in. "Just because."

"Just because?"

"Chloe, leave it at that." John went into business mode and, in an interviewing manner, began to interrogate her as if she were a potential client about whom he needed to know every detail. "Tell me how much your lease is per month."

"That's personal."

"I can easily find out. Save me the time," he stated bluntly.

She gave a huff. "Thirty-eight hundred."

"And your profits per month?"

"That's personal," she responded once more.

"I really don't care what you're making or not—I'm only doing this for a workable figure."

"I don't know," she said, but the fib could have been tattooed to her forehead her denial was so obvious.

John drew in a breath. "Any forecast on what you'll be looking at next year on profits versus rent?"

"I'm pleading the Fifth." She dug her heels in and folded her arms under her breasts, accentuating her cleavage in a way that was completely distracting.

John had to keep from smiling, or worse, leaning over the table and kissing her senseless. Where that thought came from, he didn't want to consider. It amazed him to think that questions as simple as these felt as if he were asking her about her sex life, or something equally as base.

"Look, Chloe, you have to work with me on this or I can't help you."

She squeaked, "I did ask you to help me and you said I didn't have a leg to stand on. I was willing to pay you and you said no."

"I'm still saying no about paying me," he said, trying to keep the irritation from his tone. Her demeanor stripped away his calm, level head. He'd never felt under attack by his own client—not that she fell into that category. Normally he held his own, and was very certain of himself and what he projected.

Chloe Lawson unraveled him a bit and he had to refocus to remember where his proposition had been going.

"Let me tell you about how Garretson's works," he said after a long drink of wine, finishing the glass and pouring another. "Each store they open is an instant moneymaker. They have a distinctive marketing strategy with quality foods, but discounted prices in some avenues. Some of their prices are double the warehouse grocery on Fairview Avenue—but still, more people shop for one day at a time at Garretson's rather than stocking up at the discount place. I don't know why it works that way, but it does."

Chloe gave him her rapt attention, but John felt she was being more polite than anything else. She tore bread crust and popped it into her mouth, slowly chewing as if needing something else to occupy herself while he mentally gathered his thoughts.

Damn. He felt as if this was his first courtroom case and, by hell and fury, he had to win or he'd throw away his career.

He rattled off Garretson's facts—anyone who read *The Idaho Statesman* would know the information.

After a few minutes, he pulled in a breath, watching as Chloe gazed about the restaurant as if looking for someone else to join.

"Are you listening to me?" he asked, annoyance in his voice sounding like a buzz saw incessantly spinning its blade. Not so much annoyed at her, but with himself. Neither in business, nor his personal life, had he had trouble keeping a woman interested in what he had to say, even if they found his topic out of their realm of expertise.

She leveled her eyes on him, then gave a perfect impression of him while reciting, "'It potentially costs Garretson's seven hundred to eight hundred thousand dollars a week in profit when they don't open a megastore on time.'" At the end of her mimicked oration, she gave him a cheesy smile.

John moved forward, leaning toward her with broad shoulders, doing the best impression of intimidation that he could muster. The effect over Chloe was as he desired—she blushed, then went stock-still as he traced the seam of her mouth with his fingertip. "I should have put my hand over your mouth when I had the chance."

Chloe swallowed thickly, evidenced by the lump in the slender column of her neck. "Well…you were getting on my nerves with all that blathering you were doing."

"Blathering? I didn't think anyone used that word."

"My grandmother does," Chloe replied slowly, as if cautiously testing the waters around them.

The air had gone from businesslike to something undefinable. They were talking, but he grew keenly aware of her and the amount of body heat radiating between them.

"Can you just tell me," she said, then licked her lips. "Just tell me what it is you want?"

At that moment, he wanted a lot of things and none of them had anything to do with Garretson's or deals or lease agreements. His every sense was focused on the woman before him. The way she breathed, and the vague pulse at the hollow of her throat. The way her hair fell over her brow. The scent of her perfume. Her beautiful face filled with strength and a resilience that caught his full attention, tugging at his insides and drawing him toward her.

Beyond the physical, there came an irrational emotional need.

For the first time since his Connie's death, John felt the bone-deep and primal urge to make love to another woman other than his wife.

He abruptly jerked back, as if singed by the thick heat around them. Every nerve ending in his body felt raw, on fire. Rubbing his jaw, he fought to gain composure.

Chloe seemed unaffected, and that bothered John more than he cared to admit. What was it about her that caught his attention to a distracting degree?

He maintained a business curtness as he proceeded. "Let's dispense with the history lesson of Garreton's grocery store." John clenched his jaw to kill the tic that suddenly pulled at his muscle. He shot her a pointed gaze. "Bob Garretson gave me the go-ahead to meet with you and offer you a one-time payment to buy out your lease early."

When she didn't profess her undying thanks, but rather gave him a blind stare, he wanted to... He wasn't sure.

Get up?

Walk out?

Forget he tasted one of her stupid blueberry muffins?

"Color me obtuse, but I thought that news might make you just a little bit—" he displayed his thumb and forefinger in a measuring gesture "—happy."

In a polished voice, as smooth as marble, she said, "It's not the money, it's the principle, Mr. Moretti."

"*John,*" he ground out between his teeth, finding himself once more rubbing his jaw with his fingers. "I don't know how to tell you this, but you're cooked. Finished. In six months you're out of a lease without squat. Why prolong the inevitable? At least this way you can leave early and get something out of it."

"You don't know me at all. I don't try and 'get anything' out of anyone."

"I'm not saying you are!" Each word rose in volume, and by the end of the sentence John grimaced at his harsh tone. Every muscle in his body felt stretched so taut it would snap. "I'm the one who put in the call to Garretson. I was doing you a favor."

"I didn't ask you to."

Taking a different course, he kept his tone softer and in check. "Think about your future earnings as a fledgling business. A remuneration could compensate you through next year. Give me a figure—whatever the hassle of leaving early is worth to you. I can run the number by Bob. If it's a reasonable figure, I can almost for certain tell you it's yours. He wants to give you the opportunity to get started at another location."

Chloe planted a dumbfounded expression on her face, as if in disbelief over the lengths he'd gone to secure her a financially beneficial way out of her trouble. The quiet undertones of her delicate features, the soft closure of her lips, the slow blink of her eyes, told him far more than he cared.

He'd insulted her beyond measure. And for reasons he didn't understand. This was proving to be the most tiresome argument he had presented in months. Possibly all year. The reasons she dug in her heels were beyond him, as she'd made no sense or given him a single complaint as to why she shouldn't take a deal.

Folding her hands, she lowered them onto her lap. Her pink mouth curved with rueful tenderness that shot straight to his rapidly pumping heartbeat.

Almost apologetically, she offered, "I appreciate your efforts on my behalf, even if they weren't initiated with my permission. After your impassioned plea to me, I believe you were truly thinking of my best interest and not your own or that of your law firm."

It was John's turn to remain silent while she spoke her peace.

"You may not know this, but I got my start right out of school decorating cakes at Garretson's first store on 18th and State. Back then, we baked everything from scratch. It's not like that anymore. Now their bakery department is what I call a 'fakery.' They get the breads and rolls partially baked from corporate and pop them into the oven to finish them off. Cakes come prepackaged in boxes, and already iced and decorated. All an employee needs to know at Garretson's is how to scribble 'happy birthday, so-and-so' with a piping bag. Anybody can figure that one out. Needless to say, I'm not a fan of their stores. But I did get my start at Garretson's way back when, not that anyone in their corporate office would remember me.

"During the year I worked there, I accumulated several hundred shares of their stock, and I still own it. I get their annual report and know for a fact that Bob Garretson made over five and a half million dollars last year, not counting his bonus of three million more." She met his gaze with a frown on her face. "Do you think he even cares about me or my store on any level whatsoever? I'm just a crumb on his pie plate of business affairs. He'd rather brush me off than deal with me."

"That's not quite accurate. He's willing to work with you."

"Only because you pleaded my case and he's aggravated enough to buy me off." She sighed. "When I first found out about my lease not being renewed, it wasn't about Garretson's. The Grove can rent to whomever they want—even if I disagree with that policy. But when I thought about the whole thing, the injustice of being shoved out by a corporation because they have more clout really got me worked up. How many times does this happen to people like me?"

In an undiluted voice, John said, "All too often."

"Then maybe you can understand why I'm not going to jump at taking money from Garretson's. You go back to Bob Garretson and tell him Chloe Lawson isn't quitting her lease early. He can put that in his oven and bake it."

CHAPTER SEVEN

IT WASN'T VERY OFTEN that Chloe mulled over the deathblow of being single and turning forty in a handful of months. On those occasions where she faced facts and acknowledged the big four-oh, and the lackluster progress in her personal life, she handled it with deftness and bravado.

She buried a clean spoon into a bowl of white chocolate cream cheese frosting and sampled her way into a sugar coma.

Today had dawned as one of those particularly annoying days in her life where she needed an infusion of chocolate to lift her spirits. The situation hadn't been helped by starting her period. Her time of the month came as reliably as a full moon. Go figure. You'd think with fertility problems she'd be all over the map when it came to her period. But no. Every twenty-eight to thirty days without fail.

Not one of the specialists she'd seen had pinpointed exactly why she couldn't get pregnant. She'd never even had a miscarriage, not that a false start would have made her feel better. There was something about her body chemistry that wouldn't allow conception, and it was no fault of Bobby-Tom's. She'd wanted to blame him and his sperm, but he'd been tested, and the results had made him say the one and only truly, truly hurtful comment he'd ever said to her that stuck all these years later:

"I told ya so."

Chloe measured scoops of soft flour into the commercial mixer and tried to put her marital past behind her.

She had no set plans for her birthday in October. The people she'd celebrated her thirtieth with at Humpin' Hannah's had been friends of both hers and Bobby-Tom, and seeing many of them now proved difficult. Probably because most of them were couples. And most still thought Bobby-Tom walked on water.

Thankfully Bobby-Tom had quit calling her and hanging up as soon as she answered. He'd gotten annoying, and she'd told herself that if he called one more time, she was calling him back to confront him and tell him to cut it out.

Now her cell phone hardly rang after work unless Ethel had something to tell her. That one time when John Moretti had called had been quite a surprise. Sometimes she wondered if he'd phone her again. Part of her wanted him to, just to hear his voice. That night at the restaurant, she hated to admit it but she'd liked the way he'd sounded when he spoke. Not that she much cared for what he had to say. That part of it she chose to ignore.

She was half-tempted to ask John what Bob Garretson had said about her declining his offer. But that remained a moot point since Chloe wouldn't change her mind and whatever Bob had to say didn't matter anyway.

With her milestone birthday zeroing in, Chloe tried to muster some enthusiasm about celebrating it, but nothing exciting jumped out at her. The prospect of drinking beers at Humpin' Hannah's just didn't hold the same appeal it once had. After ten years of being her own woman, Chloe had outgrown an evening out like that.

The number of Chloe's close friends had waned over the years—not because she didn't care for them, but working as hard as she did, she didn't have the free time to keep her friendships going. She'd pretended she would call the girls, but she never seemed to get around to it. The way she'd laid out her career path over the last decade, she hardly had breathing time.

Before opening Not Just Cakes, Chloe had been a pastry chef at Mortimer's downtown restaurant. John Mortimer ran a beautiful kitchen, and he'd been a delight to work with, but it had come time for Chloe to spread her wings and do her own thing.

Prior to Mortimer's, she had taught a class every now and then at Kandor, but it had gone out of business. Occupying herself didn't come as a hardship. Finding a moment to just relax was a premium. Taking time for herself didn't come easy for Chloe. It seemed as if she always forged ahead with ideas to help her business grow.

The Fourth of July had come and gone over a month ago. Lots of red, white and blue cupcakes had been purchased, as well as iced cookies with flag sprinkles.

Wedding-cake orders comprised most of Chloe's list of cakes to bake and assemble. She was working overtime, dog-tired and without much relief on the horizon.

After sliding in her pans of mocha chocolate-chip cake to bake, Chloe went to the front of the store to check on the bakery inventory. It wasn't her job to do this; Jenny usually took stock of things, but she had to leave early and go to the dentist.

At the noon hour, the seating area wasn't nearly as busy as it was in the morning, but the number of customers was respectable. About a dozen people sat and enjoyed pastries.

As Chloe made a brief tally of patrons, she thought once more about how much better business would be if she could expand Not Just Cakes.

Looking about the small rental space she currently had, she mapped out the layout in her mind to see if she could make it work for now—even with the clock ticking on her lease.

Where the couple were cozying up could be the sofa area, but it could only hold one modest-sized sofa, not two cushiony ones like she'd envisioned. The coffee creamer and sugar station would have to be in the middle of the shop and that just wouldn't work.

Changing directions, Chloe continued to ponder and rearrange in her mind. The location toward the back of the shop, where a hatted gentleman huddled over his plate, might work for the TV area.

As Chloe glanced the man's way, their eyes locked for a short moment, and his look gave her pause. An uncanny feeling prickled her skin, as if she might know him. She couldn't recall ever helping him, but there was something about him that was familiar.

She got sidetracked, ringing up an order while her clerk restocked pastry boxes. When she glanced at the man again, his gaze remained fixated on her. She slanted him a questioning look, a lift of her shoulders. But his expression remained unreadable, almost hollow.

Chloe opted to head straight for his table. "Hi," she said in a light greeting. "Have we met?"

"What's in this?" he asked, pointing to his plate of crumbs.

"It's hard to say since you've already eaten whatever it was."

From what she could tell beneath the fedora on his head, he had gray hair. Blue eyes, the color of a winter sky, seemed larger behind the lenses of drugstore glasses. The set of his mouth fell in a grim line, his nose bulbous at the tip. Facial features, swarthy and hard, seemed craggy, like the underside of a rough rock.

Given that, he wore a sharply cut suit that she knew had to cost big bucks. Very odd.

He clarified in a gravelly voice, "Swirly thing with pecans so light and flaky your momma would tell you an angel baked it from heaven's clouds."

"Why, thank you." Warm pleasure fanned across her cheeks. "We don't give out our recipes, but I can tell you it's the cinnamon and butter that make our pastries stand out above the rest."

"This—" he motioned to the empty plate and its

remnants of pecan pieces and white-icing smears "—could put Garretson's in-store bakeries down the toilet."

With that strange commentary, he rose on his freshly polished shoes and left.

Puzzled, Chloe watched him retreat.

The sweet scent of mocha cake filled the shop and Chloe went to the kitchen. Candace had taken the cake pans out for her. They cooled on wire racks.

"Thanks, Candace." She smiled at her young assistant, whose brunette ponytail seemed crooked on the top of her head, and her apron bore the battle scars of blue coloring paste. "Candace?"

"Yes?" The girl looked up from her Bavarian cream puffs she filled with a piping bag.

"I just wanted to tell you I appreciate how hard you work for me."

Candace beamed, a smudge of flour dusting her cheek. "Thanks, Chloe."

"You're welcome."

As Chloe began to get the ingredients she'd need to make an icing, her cell phone rang. She kept the slim phone in her apron pocket or, if she had been working on the register line, she tried to keep the cell on the alleyway windowsill so its ring wouldn't bother customers. That's where it lay now and she snagged the call.

"Hello?" she greeted, reaching for the canister of espresso to use in her cream filling.

"Chloe, hi."

Halting her movements, she recognized the voice immediately and uttered, "John Moretti."

He spoke in a friendly and easygoing tone. "How's it going?"

"Good," she responded automatically. Why did people always say "good" when things were lousy? Having cramps and a chocolate high made for a horrible combination. She felt a bad headache coming on.

"I know it's been a couple of weeks, but I wanted to get back to you with Garretson's latest offer."

Incredulous, she replied, "I never nibbled on the first offer."

"I understand. But I want to talk to you. In person." The line felt charged with sparks and Chloe's mind went in a dozen different directions.

Although she'd made herself perfectly clear about the payoff money Garretson's had presented, Chloe had thought about John a couple of times. Nothing to do with business—rather, on a personal level. She wasn't sure why she disliked lawyers. But she wasn't so prejudiced as to lump them all together.

Even so, she'd never met a lawyer she liked. Not that she had a lot of experience with them. Broadly speaking, they were all out to make oodles of money at anyone's expense.

While John claimed not to be representing the grocery chain, no doubt he would turn over a pretty penny if he got her to accept a payoff check from Garretson's.

"No thanks." Her decline might have been slow to come, but she held on to the conviction she'd made clear the last time she was with John.

"I know how you feel, but I think you're going to

want to hear this." John's tone came across steady and resolved, as if he weren't used to no for an answer. "Bob Garretson gave me a figure today that surprised even me."

Curiosity tugged at Chloe, but not hard enough for her to cry uncle. "No thanks."

"Let's meet for a drink at Pair on Main. Do you know it?"

"I do, but I won't be there." Using a damp towel, Chloe wiped powdered sugar off the stainless counter.

"I wish you'd reconsider."

"I won't."

"Is it me?" That question caught her off guard. "I could have one of my associates meet with you instead, but I'd rather it be me."

That he'd compromise knocked her off her high horse a bit. It didn't seem customary for a lawyer to believe in something so much that he'd go out on a limb for a client to hear the appeal.

Chloe almost changed her mind.

Almost.

The bottom line remained the same. She'd have to leave her location and start over elsewhere. The momentum that she'd been building would come to a grinding halt. She'd have to shop for another retail space, negotiate rent, cancel and set up a slew of utilities. The move would be a nightmare with her heavy kitchen equipment.

She understood that eventually all this would take place, but she didn't want the pressure of making these decisions overnight.

"I'm not moving until I legally have to." She responded with regret, almost wishing she had an excuse to hear him out and meet with him.

Chloe might have been resolute in her plans to forge ahead with things on her terms, but she wasn't blind. John had a nice face. And a muscularly formed body that hadn't gone without her notice.

"Please, Chloe. Reconsider. We're talking a lot of money here."

Sighing and leaning into the counter, she answered, "And I'm talking about principle, Mr. Moretti." In that flash of an instant, she wondered if she were doing the right thing. She rarely doubted her business choices, but a sizeable chunk of cash could pay for grander things at a new location that she couldn't readily afford right now.

She gave it several measures of her heartbeat to consider. *No.*

She still wouldn't bite on the bait.

Perhaps what set her off was the notion that powerful people like Bob Garretson always got what they wanted. "Garretson can't buy whatever he wants simply because he can." Before she could retract the words, she said, "You tell him that I'm not for sale."

Chloe clicked the call to an end and stood in the hot kitchen, trying to make sense of what she'd just done. Had pride caused her to spite herself?

Sticking by what she'd said might have just cost her a bundle of money. But she couldn't put a price on her business. The Grove had been good to her, better than she'd ever anticipated. It felt like home here. She couldn't throw it away for a check. That just didn't feel right.

Gazing out to the alleyway, she tried to put together some kind of a plan, anything that could keep her afloat here.

About an hour later, a glimmer of an idea began to take form, and by the time she closed her shop, she couldn't wait to call Ethel and fill her in.

JOHN HAD INSISTED that Zach and Kara join him for the family's traditional Sunday supper at his parents' house—rather his mom's now. About a year had passed and John still had difficulty thinking of his mom being without his dad.

Everyone in the Moretti family missed Giovanni. His presence at the table had been the heartbeat and soul of Italy's old country. It wasn't the same without him.

John's mother, Mariangela, had been coping, but she didn't laugh the way she used to. Coaxing by Francesca, John's only sister, had finally gotten Mom to consider going to the Amalfi Coast to see her aunt Romilda.

Before he died, Giovanni had purchased tickets for a surprise trip to Italy with his wife—a way to celebrate their forty-fifth wedding anniversary—but he hadn't lived long enough to present her with the surprise. He passed away unexpectedly from a heart attack.

In the months that followed, Mariangela hadn't had the energy or desire to make the trip without him.

Lately she'd begun to talk a little more about getting away and going "home."

As John fetched a cold beer from his mom's fridge, he thought it interesting that his parents had been in America since their early twenties, but they still called Italy home.

"John, there you are," Franci said as she made her way to him with her arms stretched open. She gave him a fond hug. "I haven't seen you in forever."

"I've only missed a couple of Sundays," he replied.

"Yes, and then I don't see you because you're so busy and I'm buried at work."

His sister had taken over the Grove Marketplace project to pull things together after Giovanni died. Moretti Construction had been the general contractor on the huge project, and they'd bring the job to completion thanks to Franci stepping into his dad's boots with her skill and organization. Although she had her own architectural firm, she also knew what it took to get things done. Mark, John's younger brother, was involved in the physical construction end of things and Franci's husband, Kyle Jagger, partnered in and oversaw the details.

Overall, the family had made things work during a time of sorrow and the job site had rarely missed a deadline.

"We should get together for lunch or dinner," John suggested, unscrewing the top of his beer. "And you can bring that guy you're married to."

"Gee, thanks." She smiled, then socked him playfully in the arm.

Seeing his sister so happy gave John joy. It also reminded him that he'd once had the same happiness. Marriage suited him. He'd liked it. The comfort, the love. The feeling of being a couple and raising a family.

Maybe he could find that peace and satisfaction again one day.

The front door burst open and four little girls under the age of ten poured into the living room.

"Oh, Robert's here," Franci commented brightly. "I've got to ask him something. He's catering a party I'm throwing."

John wandered through the house, stopping at the glass doors that led into the backyard. His teenagers had taken off as soon as they'd arrived, and he now found them both on the patio. Both with wireless implements next to their ears.

Cell phones.

So much for social interaction. John shrugged to himself. At least they'd come. He'd threatened to take their car keys from them for twenty-four hours if they didn't. He found that the consequence of no ride had been working. Too bad Zach went without a car almost three days out of seven.

For a nineteen-year-old boy, he certainly didn't have the same drive and ambition John had had at that age. John had finished his first year of college by then, had known his major and was going full force in the right direction. He'd been an overachiever, a straight A student and the golden boy on whom his father had lavished praise. Even though John hadn't gone into construction with the family, Dad had made him feel as if he'd done the right thing. For that, John would be forever grateful.

When dinnertime came and things settled down at the table, Mariangela served Sunday supper. The aromas were that of garlic and tomatoes, olive oil and the crusty warmth of breads. Everyone ate and laughed, told stories about their week, and the adults shared a bottle of wine.

John's mother seemed happier than she'd been in a long time, and for that, John grew encouraged. Nobody in the family had liked seeing her so distressed.

And nobody more than John.

His mother's grief had been a mirror of his own pain, and he'd been fairly certain that witnessing the sadness in his mom had been the catalyst to get him back on track in the land of the living.

Robert and his wife, Marie, sat on John's left with their kids as they passed slices of toasted bread down the table. Kyle and Franci were seated to his right. At the head of the table, John's kid brother, Mark, reclined easily in his chair talking about the latest drama on the project—a crane swinging too close to the parking structure and taking a corner out of the concrete.

Zach and Kara had been placed on either side of four-year-old Cora. She'd taken both their arms and, in her tiny voice, declared they had to sit by her.

"So, John," Robert asked in an easygoing tone, "how're things going with Miss Lawson?"

"John's dating?" Mariangela gasped, a pasta bowl in her hand. "Who? Where did you meet her? When are you bringing her over for supper?"

"Are you, Dad?" Kara asked, eyes wide.

"Hold on, Mom. Kara." John's hand raised to cease her string of questions. "I'm not dating."

Mariangela passed the bowl, tsking her regrets. "I got hopeful. You know I loved Connie, God rest her soul." She wistfully glanced at her grandchildren, then crossed herself with sadness. "But, John, *mio figlio*, you've been alone for a long time and you're due."

"She's just a…" The sentence trailed off. John couldn't exactly say client, or even friend, because neither were the case. "She's just a person I'm giving legal counsel to." To Robert, he added, "And I'm not at liberty to discuss the details."

"Okay. Just checking. As long as you're treating her right, it's all good."

John wasn't sure how "right" he was treating Chloe. He had done his best to offer a fair and reasonable solution for her bakery, but her stubbornness outlived a cat's nine lives.

Dishes were passed, and a week's worth of news digested over pastas and sauces, breads, wine and meats. Conversations flowed in different directions, laughter abounded, sometimes even a family lecture if the offender had done something un-Morettilike. That was the way of John's family. Love it or leave it. He kept coming back. He couldn't imagine a life without his siblings or his mom—even if they did get a little opinionated at times.

As John ate a bite of his salad, a thought crossed his mind: Would Chloe Lawson fit in here?

He remembered the first time his sister brought Kyle Jagger to a family dinner. He'd been eyed up and down so many times, the fact he could get up and leave the table with his clothes still intact and not shredded from harsh gazes had been a miracle.

John dredged up the conversation he'd had with Chloe, still in disbelief she'd turned him down flat, not wanting to hear a word he had to say.

He could think of a number of women who'd have a drink with him—just to go out and flirt for an evening. That said, his arrogance wasn't such that he thought himself this great guy. He just knew he was decent enough to date—if he were dating.

Why then, had he come up with dinner and a drink as a pretext to engage Chloe to meet with him? She'd bought into the dinner at Pomodoro and, considering their strained exchange, he'd had a nice time getting to know her somewhat.

He could have easily conferred with her on the telephone, but he'd pursued her in other ways. That she declined his recent offer still bruised. He took it personally. Rarely did he lose a case.

On that, John smiled to himself.

Chloe wasn't a case. She was a woman who intrigued him in ways he had yet to completely understand. He wouldn't give up on her.

More determined than ever, he'd make her see that she would be forgoing a large sum of money. She had to at least hear what Bob Garretson was willing to pay.

Crunching on a bread stick, Zach asked Mark, "When do you think they're going to pass inspection on the sixth floor of the new phase. I'm getting bored on two."

Mark Moretti had the best looks in the entire family. Dark, handsome and rugged, he wore masculinity as if it were a shirt and jeans. "Next week. And don't give me that bored crap. I know you like finish work. You have a good eye for it." Then to John. "Your son's got some carpentry talent."

John nodded his agreement.

There had been a time when John had encouraged Zach to be a professional and go to college to earn his degree. Connie had that hope when she'd been living, but John realized right after her death that simply wouldn't be the case. His son was uniquely himself and he had his own likes and dislikes.

Mariangela brought a thermal carafe of hot coffee to the table. "Zachary, your grandfather would be proud of you for following in the family's footsteps."

Slouching in his chair, shaggy hair hanging over his brow, he mumbled, "Yeah, I guess."

"No guessing about it." Mariangela stood at the head of the heavy wood table. "Who wants coffee?"

Responses were uttered.

As coffee was poured, Mariangela commented, "I'm fairly sure I'm going to Italy this fall. I spoke to Romilda."

"That's great, Mom." Franci's enthusiasm caught in her voice. "I think it's just what you need."

"I need your father, but I can't have him." A wistful sadness caught in Mariangela's eyes. "In any event, this will be good for me. It's what Giovanni wanted. I have to go."

"Amen," Robert remarked, passing a coffee to his wife.

The coffee for Marie passed in front of Cora. "I'll help!" She settled her hands around the cup's circumference. Taking hold too eagerly, coffee sloshed over the side and she yelped.

As she began to cry, both Zach and Kara comforted her. Zach slid her over to sit on his lap, and Kara examined her hand, top and bottom.

"It's okay, Cora. You'll be fine." Then she gave her cousin's hand a series of smacking kisses.

Cora's tears dried, but with a rubber lip, she said, "You come push me on the swing outside. Zach and Kara and Cora. 'Kay?"

"Okay, Co-Co." Kara rose from the table, her tank top riding up her tan midriff and exposing that ridiculous belly-button ring. But she had a comforting smile, with straight teeth from braces that had recently come off. She was supposed to wear a retainer, but he wouldn't even argue that one.

As Zach stood and scooped Cora into his arms, his jeans fell too low on his hips—that stupid gansta look that teens wore these days.

While his kids' appearances didn't please John, watching Zach and Kara comfort, hold and love a four-year-old filled his heart with warmth.

Underneath the rebellion and angst, his two kids were still the children he'd taught to ride bikes and dunk basketballs in hoops. He loved them dearly no matter what.

Even if they meant to torture him to the ends of the earth with their choices…he'd always have love inside for them. They were a part of Connie he cherished and took great pride in.

CHAPTER EIGHT

ON MONDAY, a courier delivered a bottle of red wine to Chloe at Not Just Cakes. The enclosed card read:

Since you won't have a drink with me, pour one for yourself and think about what an obscene six-figure offer could do for your business capital.

—John Moretti

The gall of the man sent Chloe into a foul mood the rest of the day. That Moretti had some nerve and, unfortunately, the taunt had tossed him into the cesspool of sleazy lawyers. Prior to his change in underhanded tactics, she actually thought he might not be that bad. Now she felt convinced otherwise.

When Wednesday came, the bakery's phone rang at 8:30 a.m., and Jenny fielded a call for a pickup order. Chloe thought nothing of the six-dozen pastries she boxed with tissues, arranging crullers, sticky buns, muffins and assorted sweets in a neat fashion. Orders as large as these weren't common, but they happened.

At 9:30 a.m. when a young man came in to collect the order, he told Jenny he had to speak with Chloe.

She rinsed the dough off her hands at the kitchen sink and went to the front of the store.

"Can I help you?" she asked, straightening her apron.

The young man wore a snappy dress shirt and tie, black slacks and polished shoes. His Adam's apple grew pronounced as he said, "I work for John Moretti and these pastries are for a meeting at his law office. I just wanted you to know he's an okay guy."

Chloe gave the man a skeptical glare. "How much did he pay you to say that?"

"Well, I get a weekly paycheck if that's what you mean."

"I figured."

"But that's not why I said what I said. He really is a nice guy."

"Hmm," she replied, sliding the tower of pink boxes toward the young man. "Tell your boss he's wasting his time. And mine."

For the remainder of her morning, Chloe tried to put John out of her mind, but he kept creeping back into her thoughts as she made a batch of sweet cakes. His persistence annoyed her, yet in a weird way, made her take notice.

Bobby-Tom had been a "love me or leave me" type of guy. He could have cared less if she went with him to a hot-rod show or not. If she told him she'd rather not go, he'd go without her.

Chloe sensed that John wouldn't do things without a woman at his side. He'd woo her and break her down until he got her to see it his way. She wasn't sure it was a good thing or not.

Being single for as long as she had, Chloe was set in her ways and liked things on her own terms. Having a man doggedly chasing her—even if it were for business—felt a tad bit thrilling.

Maybe it wouldn't hurt to meet him for that drink and at least find out what Garretson was willing to pay. Not that she'd take it. She had another card up her sleeve and had already set her plan in motion. So far, so good.

She wondered what John would say to her ingenuity?

Chloe took care of things in the kitchen, then went to check the register, and, if need be, remove the large bills and put them in her safe.

She noticed that man in the bakery again. He had a plate of doughnut holes, and was examining each one and dissecting it right down to the last granule of sugar. She would have gone over to speak to him if one of her regular customers hadn't stepped into the line.

Chloe helped him herself.

"Hey," she greeted. "You're here later today than usual."

"I overslept." The young man was fairly tall, had black hair and dark eyes. His tan had deepened to a toffee color as summer had progressed. He'd tucked his sticker-covered hard hat underneath his arm. The dark color of his T-shirt seemed faded, as if someone had used the wrong bleach on it.

As he reached for his wallet, she noticed he'd gotten a tattoo on the inside of his forearm. Clear plastic wrap and tape were still applied over the fresh ink. While she couldn't be sure, the drawing looked like an ornate cross with angels floating on either side.

The young man worked construction on the Grove Marketplace and usually came in each morning for a black coffee and a walnut muffin. She didn't know his name as their relationship hadn't gone beyond a simple hi and 'bye.

"Fresh Columbian coffee just finished brewing," Chloe offered while pouring him a large cup.

"Thanks. You read my mind."

"You look a little tired."

"Long night." He gave her a lopsided grin that spoke volumes.

Unbidden, she smiled. She knew those nights too well. She'd done her fair share of being up to no good—drinking underage and giving poor Ethel heart palpitations.

"I get it."

"My dad sure doesn't. He forgot what it's like to be nineteen."

Chloe didn't comment. She hated that she'd tortured her dear grandmother, and there had been no excuse for her behavior other than youth and stupidity…and being so pissed off at Wanda, she'd wanted to take it out on everyone else.

But the one Chloe had hurt the most was herself.

Chloe handed the bagged muffin to him. "Do yourself a favor. Get some sleep tonight. And maybe tell your dad you're sorry."

"Yeah, okay. Sure. I'll think about it."

She watched him leave and knew he wouldn't

utter a word of remorse. She'd been the same stubborn way.

Chloe thought if she'd been given the opportunity to have kids, she would gave raised them with a deep understanding of what it's like to have a dysfunctional family and why it's so important to support one another. Not that she'd wish the chaos on anyone, but she had taken away many lessons learned the hard way.

The rest of the day went by fast and, before she knew it, she'd let everyone go home and she closed shop herself.

Weary from being up since four o'clock, she didn't even have the energy to stop into the Pita Pit for a turkey wrap. For simplicity's sake and convenience, she'd have to settle for one of her diet meals. But the thought of rubbery chicken didn't remotely appeal to her.

No wonder they called them lean meals. The smell of nuked plastic in the microwave turned her stomach and she lost her appetite.

Chloe got into her car as the sun still simmered in the sky. Summer's twilight lingered on the horizon. She enjoyed the warm days, but her bakery ovens threw off so much heat, she went home from work feeling wrung out.

Turning down the narrow street, she made her way toward the shortcut onto Main Street. It seemed as if it was taking forever for her AC to kick in. Since Not Just Cakes was in the middle of the newer phase of the Grove Marketplace, she had to drive past the construction trailer.

She recognized the young man standing out front, looking up and down the street as if waiting for a ride.

His black coffee must have woken him up because he looked alert and agitated.

The chip on his shoulder was so apparent, she could have hit it with a chopstick and not missed. She sighed. Yet another thing she recognized as a commonality between them.

In her teens, whenever her life had been in the crapper, it had never been her fault—always someone else's.

Her customer wore his black hair on the longer side, a little shaggy but he looked okay with that style. The edgier appearance gave him an attitude. She recognized the streak of rebellion in his hazel eyes.

As she approached, she acknowledged him with a lift of her hand.

He stared at her, then did something unexpected. He waved her over.

Chloe maneuvered her car toward the curb, then punched the electric window opener and rolled the glass down.

"Hey," he said by way of greeting. He carried a tool belt in his hand. "You're the cake-shop lady."

She arched her brows, wishing she'd introduced herself on a prior occasion so he would have known her name. "Yes, I own the bakery."

"Yeah, hey, cool. You aren't heading anywhere near Hill Road, are you?"

His question somewhat flabbergasted her. "Uh, not really."

"Oh. Okay."

While she all but knew the answer, she asked, "Why?"

"I need a ride home. Mine didn't show up."

Hot air rolled into the car's interior, fighting with her car's air conditioner. It was a losing battle. The heat won.

While this was Boise, and the city could still claim a very low crime rate, there were those incidents few and far between that kept just enough fear in a single woman to carry a can of pepper spray in her purse. Chloe didn't know this guy, but she'd seen him almost daily, and had had many short exchanges with him.

In talking with him, he hadn't seemed psychopathic or anything. He came across like a normal—if there were such a thing—teenage boy.

Chloe bit her lower lip, then made a snap decision. "Get in. I can take you." She hit the unlock button on her passenger door and he climbed onto the seat.

The interior of her economy car seemed even more cramped as his tall figure filled out the seat. "Hey, thanks."

"Sure." Chloe accelerated from the curb and turned around to go in the opposite direction. "Did you call your ride? Maybe something happened to them."

"I'm not calling him." The boy scoffed, making a face. "Even if I did, he wouldn't pick up. He's always on his freakin' phone and I get his stupid voice mail."

"He sounds like he's not that good a friend."

"He's not my friend, he's my dad." The latter was spoken in an almost embarrassed tone.

Chloe gave an anxious cough, uncomfortable to touch on that subject.

She turned and headed toward the foothills. "I'm Chloe, by the way."

"Zach," he responded. "And thanks. You're a lifesaver."

"Is your car in the shop?"

"Uh, yeah," Zach replied, then gazed out the window. "Bad transmission."

"I hate when that happens." Then for added measure, and with just a little superstition, she gave her dash a friendly rap of her knuckles. "Knock on plastic, I haven't had any troubles with my car lately."

"Lucky," he uttered. His jeans were covered with splatters of something gray. Maybe cement. The backs of his hands had scrapes and nicks from working hard all day.

"How are things coming along on the Grove?" she asked.

"Pretty good. My uncle's easy to work for. He's the bomb."

"You like him?"

"Yeah. He's teaching me a lot."

"So, is construction a field you want to pursue?"

"I don't know. It's something to do. Mark's on top of his game, and he knows how things have to be just by looking at a set of plans. He's teaching me how to read them."

Chloe skirted the downtown and made her way to 36th Street. "So how long have you been at it?"

"Long enough. I was working at Old Chicago but I got fired for taking beers to a table." He turned his head in her direction. "I'm nineteen now so whatever, but at the time, it really pissed me off to get canned for something so lame."

Zach's long legs seemed to consume half the passenger space as he sat in easy comfort. "How about you? Do you like your job?"

"I do," she commented.

"Turn here."

She clicked on her blinker.

"Actually, I love what I do. It's a good fit for me."

The homes on either side of the street grew larger, situated on acreages that had spectacular views.

She glanced at his forearm. "So what did you get?"

Zach gave his arm a quick gaze. "Trinity cross and angels." A corner of his mouth crooked. "My dad's going to kill me."

Unable to stop herself, she asked, "Then why did you do it?"

Disregarding her question, he pointed. "This one. That's my house."

Chloe pulled into the massive driveway, her car motor idling and pinging in the heat. A shiny black pickup was parked in the driveway.

"Thanks. I really appreciate the ride," Zach said as he opened the door. "I'll probably see you tomorrow."

"Okay. 'Bye."

Chloe took off for home, a heaviness in her chest and a melancholy washing over her that caused her to reflect. Maybe she should volunteer at a youth center. Talk to kids about the errors of their ways and the mistakes they made. She knew too well how easy it was to walk down the wrong path. She'd been in their shoes.

As Chloe ate her dinner that night, the table had

never felt so lonely. After she did the dishes, her resolve broke down and she opened Moretti's wine bottle and vegged in front of the television.

Several times, she glanced at the card he'd sent, her fingertips tracing an outline over the phone number he'd penned underneath his name.

But the temptation to quell her loneliness and pick up her cell phone didn't tug hard enough for her to make the call.

JUST AS JOHN DUG into the court papers spread out on his desk, several flimsy boxes smacked down in front of him. Gazing over the rims of his reading glasses, he caught sight of Chloe spitting fire from her violet eyes.

"Okay, hotshot," she snapped. "You got my attention."

Sitting taller, he slipped the glasses from his head and gave the Garretson boxes a quick once-over. Even without the sugary greasy smell cloying his office, he knew what they contained.

Earlier this morning, he'd had several dozen glazed, chocolate and maple bars sent over to Not Just Cakes.

"Did you like the note?" he asked indolently, knowing full well his message had to have sent her blood pressure rising.

"Lovely." Her sarcasm grated, but her lyrical tone caused him to smile. "Next time just send over a coffin, okay?"

She drew herself taller and he admired her curves. A summer sweater in lavender hugged her breasts while a short denim skirt fit nicely over her hips and butt. She wore very little jewelry—just hoop earrings and a gold wristwatch. Her hair fell over her shoulders in a soft wave of golden tones. While she inched closer to his side of the desk, he saw the white sneakers on her feet and his smile deepened as he noted she was without nylons.

"I could do that if that would make you take Garretson's offer. But is it your coffin or mine you're after?"

She rolled her eyes and groaned.

John sat into his high-backed chair. "How did you get past my secretary?"

Lifting her hand for his examination, Chloe mimed her index and middle fingers into a scissored walking pattern.

"I see." His chin notched upward.

"She wasn't at her desk," Chloe confessed. "You need better security to keep the loony clients out."

"Are you signing on as one of my loony clients?"

"Not hardly." She plunked down in one of his chairs, crossing her legs at the knees. "Today's note really ticked me off. Monday's wine bribe was bad enough. Your Wednesday-morning errand boy proved equally as irritating, but now you've crossed the line."

Twirling his Montblanc pen between his fingers, John said, "I don't think so. I only wrote two words today."

Her brow quirked. "And I found them slanderous."

John recited the two words with feigned innocence. "'Indulge yourself.'"

"As if. I wouldn't take a bite out of a Garretson's stale bakery good if it were my last meal as a condemned woman."

"Ouch," John quipped. "That's harsh."

"But true." Chloe tossed her purse onto the chair next to her. She gave herself a minute to look around, then said, "I thought you lawyers golfed on Fridays."

"I don't golf."

"Then how come you have all those golf magazines?"

"They look good on the coffee table."

She gave him a quizzical stare, as if to say, *Is that how you live your life—setting things up around you that look good?*

The thought didn't sit well with him.

Putting on a business air, he addressed the issue at hand now that he finally had her full attention. "Chloe, I hope you'll consider taking the money Garretson is willing to pay. It's a sizeable sum of change and you could start over."

She made no response.

"I went to the mat for you on this one. Bob doesn't like having the screws put to him, but I told him you should be given decent compensation for your inconvenience."

"I didn't ask you to do that for me."

"I understand."

"I haven't asked anything from you, but you seem to be making me your business." Shifting, she angled her leg differently and inadvertently gave him a view of her thigh. Just a small peek before she tugged on the hem of her skirt. "Why is that?"

Rubbing his jaw, John thought about that. To tell her the true reason would be awkward. The core of his motives had nothing to do with her personally—he'd simply wanted to get back to his roots of doing good for the underdog.

He'd started his pursuit of this because she'd been a little guy, but once he'd met her he liked her. Too much for his own good. It came with problems and entanglements. Scared emotions that he'd thought long dead had resurfaced. But he'd felt a stirring of hope within his heart, and an energy about him that he didn't know how to grasp.

Connie had been his high-school sweetheart. He'd dated a few women prior to her. Of course he'd been all male, but he'd been a good Catholic boy, too. The fear of having to confess something in the confessional kept him pure. He'd probably been the only boy in their parish to listen to the priest.

In short, his Connie had been the only woman with whom he'd ever been.

Now John found himself faced with feelings for Chloe that he couldn't define. Although some had been blatantly sexual, he'd done a good job up to this point of keeping them at the back of his mind. It would serve no purpose to go forward with them. Even so, he was a man and he did have feelings... and needs.

Only it had been so long, he'd thought himself immune. And if anything, emotionally guarded.

But feasting his eyes on Chloe with her pouting pink lips and that short skirt, her fiery temper and the feminine voice that would sometimes purr—he found it hard to stay focused.

The question Chloe had asked loomed large. He might not have answered if she hadn't repeated herself.

At length, he replied in a tight voice, "Maybe because people like Bob Garretson get what they want too much of the time."

"That makes no sense. He wants my space and your plan is to give it to him early."

"But the privilege will cost him."

"Trust me, he won't care. He can afford it. I've seen the stock reports and—"

"Chloe, don't be stupid."

Her mouth snapped shut.

John tossed his pen, feeling a reckless frustration. They stared at each other through a ringing silence before he finally counseled, "Just tell yourself that winning is all that matters. Take Garretson's check and you win."

Chloe gazed down, her breathing soft and steady. Several long measures of time passed. "I've started a petition to keep my bakery just where it is. I wrote up an appeal to the leasing company and I already have a full page of signatures. Customers who come to the Grove count on Not Just Cakes to serve them quality pastries. I don't know how many ways I can tell you that you can relay to Garretson's corporate offices that I'm not quitting without a fight. People are telling me that if a Garretson's mega-store goes in, they'll boycott it."

"Chloe," he said softly, his heart aching for her

naiveté. "You can't fight a corporation. People will tell you they're behind you, but they really aren't. It's all about the bottom line."

She went to the door, her hand on the knob. Her eyes locked onto his and held for an eternity before she murmured, "I feel sorry for you. You're so screwed up you honestly believe that line of crap you're trying to feed me."

Then she left and he felt as if the breath had been sucked out of him.

CHAPTER NINE

REGENERATE SALON attracted the younger generation, but Ethel couldn't find another colorist in Boise who could dye her hair just the shade she wanted. A twenty-eight-year-old cosmetology genius, Fernando definitely had a flamboyant temperament. But when it came to mixing a batch of level-five-red, nobody could beat his formula.

Ethel had been going to him for about a year—ever since he'd moved his ultramodern salon from Bannock to the Grove Marketplace, making a trip to his chair very convenient. She booked appointments with him on either Wednesday or Thursday afternoons when Uma, her clerk assistant, helped out in the boutique.

Hammered, stainless steel countertops and black-washed walls greeted Ethel as she entered the hair salon. Irritating techno music throbbed from tiny speakers mounted on the wall. Ethel's left eye twitched with the onset of a headache. But Fernando, God bless him, catered to her distaste of the funky music.

Scissors held high in one hand, and with a few snaps of his fingers on the other, Fernando alerted the receptionist to switch music tracks. Within seconds, Frank Sinatra crooned "Come Fly With Me."

"I love you, Fernando," Ethel remarked gratefully. They had a relationship in which she could be flirty and her comments meant nothing. Fernando was as gay as Rock Hudson.

With a limp wrist, he pointed at her and smiled. "I love you more, Bubbles."

Arching her brows, and grabbing a magazine, Ethel couldn't remember when Fernando had started calling her Bubbles. It had just stuck and that's what he always called her.

The salon belched hot gusts of air from the hair dryers as Ethel took a seat to wait for Fernando. Popular with the MTV generation, he did a lot of unique color jobs—eggplant, inky black or bleached-platinum blond a la Marilyn Monroe. His skills as a trained colorist were in high demand.

While Regenerate's ambience was not exactly what Ethel would have preferred, she didn't like the old lady hair salons where they tried to talk a woman her age into a blue tint.

Already Thursday afternoon, the week had seemed to fly by. Uma Petersen came in at noon and worked on inventory. She'd been an employee of Ethel's for a year now. Reliable and sweet-tempered, she'd never missed a day. She helped business by the mere fact she was gorgeous, in her midfifties and wore a size eighteen. Being a real woman with perfect proportions, the merchandise looked fabulous on her.

As Ethel thumbed through *People* magazine, she reflected on how fortune had smiled on her. She truly lived a wonderful life and she had few complaints.

While she had her grumpy moments, she tried to live each day to its fullest. She lived in a great condo, drove a reliable car and her granddaughter was a true blessing. Her daughter, Wanda... Well, that was another story.

Ethel frowned. She lived a good life, but she also recognized the blemishes. Those early years when she'd been raising Wanda with her first husband had been a struggle. When they divorced, Wanda never really adjusted. She'd turned flighty in her teens, never stayed with the same boyfriend. And then Wanda got pregnant with Chloe.

Chloe's paternity had never been an issue. Wanda had simply said she didn't know. That choice had affected Chloe to this day. It was a topic that they never broached. Ethel knew that early on the unknown had bothered Chloe—mostly on her birthday. But as the years unfurled, Chloe spoke less and less about it, questions about a ghost father waning to nothing.

Now Chloe accepted the facts that she had no father and never would, and an absentee mother who didn't care enough to stick around or stay in touch. When Ethel thought about how great Chloe was, and how she didn't have either parent, it broke her heart.

Ethel hadn't heard from Wanda in months. If she thought about where Wanda could be or with whom, Ethel would go a little dingy fearing that something had happened to her daughter. She had to let Wanda go and not worry. Wanda had been running for close to twenty-six years. She still lived day-to-day.

Rarely did Ethel think a sin was unforgivable. But abandoning Chloe was one of them.

Shaking off the thought, Ethel brought herself out of the past. She didn't want to dwell on unpleasantries. Especially on a day as fine as this one.

The sun shone bright, weather was warm and customers had been steady all morning.

Ethel gazed out the window. The *People* magazine didn't hold her attention, even though she loved the movie-star rag.

She settled in and looked around the salon, observing Fernando's agile hands as he ran them through a girl's hair; fluffing, snipping, shaking and cutting.

Two rows of vinyl chairs on either side of the shop had clients at all the stations. The long mirrors reflected them as they watched their new dos taking shape. Cabinets held bottles of aerosol hair spray, gels and foams, and the pungent odor of chemicals could turn a nose inside out with the stink.

Combs, brushes, clips and frosting caps were in full use. The strong smell of bleach permeated the air.

"Almost finished, Bubbles," Fernando called to her. "Your color looks fab. You used the no-fade shampoo I gave you?"

She dutifully nodded.

Some would think it odd she came to a hair salon like this, but Ethel actually liked the diversity of the fresh looks and young trends. She'd lived them once herself as a model for the Mode. Those days seem an eternity ago.

At seventy-three, Ethel did have *some* predictable older person's habits. Insomnia. Waking up too early. Printing photos from real film rather than digital disks.

She saved rubber bands so she didn't have to buy them. And mall walking.

Ethel had had to skip her Wednesday-morning walk for a powwow with Chloe, who updated her on the bakery petition. The idea had enthralled Ethel and she hoped it would do the trick.

To make up for Ethel's missed day of walking, she'd been at the Towne Square early today for several rounds of the lower level, before changing course and heading up the escalator for some new scenery.

The regulars had been there. Couples older than Ethel. And the younger set, but not by much. That would be those in their sixties. That slaphappy retired National Guardsman, yet again, tried to put the move on her. Ethel didn't like his big smile. His partials were way too white. He reminded her of Micky Rooney with Regis Philbin teeth. He always tried to keep up with her brisk pace and wrangle a coffee date at the Starbucks on the upper level, but she declined. She didn't think he'd ever get the hint.

Sometimes Ethel wished she had a gentleman friend. Being thrice divorced put her off from ever marrying again, but she did miss the warmth a masculine laugh could offer. Or the fit of a large hand squeezing her own as they shared a private joke. Cooking a gourmet meal wasn't Ethel's strong point, but she wouldn't mind preparing a roasted chicken for a distinguished fella. Too bad she didn't know of any who appealed to her as much as she appealed to them.

Forty-five minutes later, Ethel's roots had oxidized into a deep bronze. A clear, plastic cap covered her head as she cooled down after being cooked under the dryer.

Ethel had colored her hair orange-red for so long, she wasn't sure of her natural color anymore. Her roots came in on the dark brunette side with threads of silver, but at least she hadn't gone all gray.

She drank a glass of mineral water, gazing out the window and marveling at the activity on the Grove's construction site. Steel girders had gone up and different tradesmen scurried to get things done. There had been rumors of another hotel to be added. That would be great for Ethel's business and—

That thought stopped as cold as the water in the glass in her hands. She blinked her eyes again, yet the image remained. The astronaut was staring through the window into the salon. Right at her.

Ethel froze, unable to move. What a sight she must be with a black cape over her shoulders and her head wrapped in cellophane. Her heartbeat pumped double-time and her breathing seemed to be coming out in choppy gusts.

To her complete and utter horror, the astronaut didn't keep on walking down the street. He opened the salon door and let himself inside.

Sitting in one of Fernando's vinyl chairs, Ethel pretended she hadn't noticed Walden Griffiths. Fat chance. He torpedoed himself directly at her.

"I thought that was you," he stated matter-of-factly, an unlit stump of a cigar clamped between his lips.

He cut a handsome figure. More than she cared to

admit. Dressed in those bun-tight Wranglers of his, he was a real hot tamale.

Ethel struggled for a reply and, in the end, said nothing.

"Are you changing your hair color?" he asked, brass as tacks. A real gentleman wouldn't inquire after such a thing as a woman's personal relationship with a bottle of hair dye.

He added, "I thought the red was interesting."

"Interesting bad, or interesting good?"

"Just interesting."

"I'm still red," she remarked flatly. "The color goes on different than what you'd expect."

"Tricky stuff," Walden commented, his cowboy hat riding low at his temple and giving him a John Wayne air. "I can only do the gray-away from the box. You know, the home treatment stuff you can rinse off in the shower."

That he'd admit such a thing flustered Ethel. She had a quick vision of Walden in a towel heading for the shower. With a peek at the base of his throat where his shirt buttoned up, she glimpsed the gray curls in the hollow, knowing he sported a carpet of chest hair.

Mercy! Ethel shook off the thought.

What was he doing in here, talking to her, as if they were old Sunday-school friends?

She didn't think they'd left things on very good terms the last time they'd spoken. In fact, she'd been slightly snippy to him. Then again, he'd volleyed a couple of prime shots at her.

Perhaps he wanted to let bygones be bygones....

"How's your cigar store doing?" Ethel asked the only question she could think of that oozed politeness.

"Dandy." He adjusted the tilt of his felt Stetson. He smelled like tobacco—an odor that displeased her, but she could tolerate it a moment longer the way he looked into her eyes.

She might look like a nightmare, and yet he gazed at her as if she were a real dish.

"And your frock store?" He tossed a question her way.

"Fine."

"Good. Good." His gaze drifted out the window, watching the pedestrians walking back and forth. "Well, I've got to be going. I'm meeting someone. I saw you in the window and I couldn't resist."

On that notable comment, he walked to the street and left her wits more scattered than a thousand-piece jigsaw puzzle spread out across a card table.

Ethel stared blankly at the spot where he'd just stood, then followed his figure as he stepped across the street. A woman waited for him, and Ethel could see her big smile all the way from here.

Moving closer to the window to get a better look, Ethel peered outside into the bright sunshine. Shock gripped her insides, suffocating the breath right out of her.

The astronaut was meeting Lois Pearl Ships.

Lois Pearl, a former glamour puss and one of Ethel's neighbors on the sixth floor at the Imperial Plaza, had more snootiness to her than a New York society matron.

Way back when, Lois Pearl used to be the top model for the Cover Girl Agency in Boise, and while Ethel's body had seasoned and gotten fuller, Lois Pearl remained as skinny as ever.

The fastidious rabbit diet Lois Pearl prided herself on following annoyed Ethel. *Lois Pearl* annoyed Ethel. She always seemed to be posting a notice for something on the community bulletin board at the complex. And she got herself involved in every event posted. Knitting committee. Charity mixer for the Veterans' League. Prayer group for Angels' Wings. Widow and widowers potluck. Docents needed at the local museum. Literacy groups forming for those who can't read.

Granted, they were all worthy causes—but something about a woman who had so many feelers out there rubbed Ethel the wrong way. There was always some group activity going on. She kept herself so busy, Ethel wondered how she could find time to meet with the astronaut.

But there she was, dressed in a St. John outfit. Ethel could recognize it a mile away. The knit skirt fit loosely over Lois Pearl's bony hips. A sweater with dramatic buttons emphasized the only flaw on Lois Pearl's string-bean frame—her shoulders were like a wide receiver's. Well, maybe not that broad, but they did stand out.

"Come, Bubbles." Fernando's airy voice broke through Ethel's thoughts as the astronaut and twiggy Lois Pearl disappeared around the corner. "Time for your rinse out."

Ethel obliged and followed him to the sink, unable

to shake the emotional feelings from her head. She simply refused to believe that, even for a second— even for a fraction of a second—she harbored a jealousy toward Lois Pearl.

This just wouldn't do.

CHLOE BASKED in the hot sun, loving the heat as it poured over her skin like cake batter. She'd been reading a suspense novel but had gotten drowsy and set the book aside to close her eyes. She laid on a beach towel, children's laughter coming from the lake, the sandy shore not twenty feet away. She heard joyous splashing and boat motors at the marina.

As she drifted half in and out of a doze, her mind wandered to the challenge that lay ahead with her bakery. Legally, there wasn't a thing she could do to fight Garretson. But get the people behind her to support her fledgling business, and she might have a chance. That optimism remained her only hope.

On summer Sundays, if she could manage the trip, Chloe enjoyed an afternoon at Spring Shores Marina on Lucky Peak Reservoir. She'd bring a blanket for Boo-Bear and a small umbrella to shade her. The dog loved it and would quietly gnaw on a rawhide and people-watch. Or simply snooze in the heat, and wake every now and then to lap up a drink of water.

This was probably one of the few hot September Sundays left. Hot enough to melt Chloe's troubles into a sleepy zone and she found herself nodding off while suntanning. At the same time, all the noises around her seemed to be heightened.

Inboard and outboard motors. The cry of gulls. Discussions taking place around her. The cash register's tally at the snack bar. Giggles. Dogs barking.

Lucky Peak was the pulse of Boise in the summer months. It drew people in on the weekends for some much needed recreation and relaxation.

The revved-up engine of a jet ski taking off out of the no-wake zone pulled Chloe from the dream she'd been having. She couldn't really remember what it was. Something about fondant and having a difficult time rolling it out. The edges kept tearing. Weird.

She laid on her back, wrist resting over her eyes and legs bent at the knee. She should probably get up and check the time. She'd planned on helping Ethel early this morning, but her grandmother had said she wasn't going in today. So Chloe had cleaned her house and decided to head to the lake early.

The emptiness in her stomach made her yearn for a cheeseburger, fries and a cola. But she'd packed a turkey sandwich and a bottled water. She was determined to keep off the pounds she'd recently lost.

Softly sighing, she felt the heat leave her body and opened her eyes just enough to see if an errant cloud had traveled overhead.

No cloud. Just a silhouette. And a tall one.

Chloe propped herself onto her elbows. She reached for her sunglasses so she wouldn't be blinded by the fiery ball of sun behind the shadow.

Focusing in on the man standing over her, she frowned.

He smiled.

Chloe inched her way to a sitting position, and Boo-Bear stretched her staked flex-leash to check out the newcomer.

Slowly wagging her feathery white tail, the bichon accepted the man without question. Traitor.

Frowning, Chloe eased her sunglasses higher up her nose. It didn't surprise her that the guy before her would be here. Boise, as largely populated as it was, was the smallest big town in the West.

A person couldn't go anywhere without running into someone they knew. Even when that someone was someone they wished they *didn't* know.

"I thought that was you," John said, his voice deep and easygoing—unlike his normal lawyer's tone that clipped tighter than a springform pan. "How are you?"

Considering John had had the enemy's dry doughnuts delivered to her bakery as a lure, Chloe didn't trust the pleasantries and kept her reply strained. "What do you want?"

"Ah…nothing."

She narrowed her gaze, skeptically giving him the once-over, and almost regretted that she did.

He appeared too sexy for words in a pair of micro-fiber swim trunks that fit his hips nicely. The turquoise color set off his tan in an eye-catching way. Why hadn't she noticed that before—that his skin had a rich toffee color to it? Perhaps because she'd only seen him in slacks and dress shirts.

To her dismay, he wore a shirt now. Short-sleeved. A Tommy Bahama—she knew the pattern and flow of the tropical silk. She'd once dated a man who favored them and that's all he wore.

Her interest in the Tommy Bahama shirt was marginal compared to the exposed slice of his chest revealed by the unbuttoned shirt. Her eyes widened.

John's chest had very little hair. Just a slight patch between his flat nipples. For a lawyer who had to sit around a lot, he was buff. No doubt. The peks on him were firm and his abs… A blind woman would love to run her hands across them and read the hidden messages in the taut skin and pull of muscles over his ribs.

Dang…why did he have to look so hot today? She'd already made up her mind to hate him, and here he was looking refreshing and cool enough to put on a Popsicle stick and…well, never mind.

John knelt down on one leg and stroked Boo-Bear's head and scruffed her ears, giving her enough attention that you'd think she'd just won the Westminister dog show.

The dog lapped up the attention, wiggling her barrel-like body as her wagging tail motored into high gear.

"She likes you," Chloe remarked. "Actually, she likes guys."

"I think most women do," he replied. He slipped a pair of sunglasses into his shirt pocket and viewed her through those handsome brown eyes of his, looking at her and then the dog.

Chloe had a hard time keeping her gaze off John's hand as he rubbed and stroked the dog. Boo-Bear rolled onto her back and, in quivering delight, received a belly scratch.

John's eyes met hers and she felt a bead of sweat roll down her brow. "You must know a lot of guys."

"Not really," she blurted.

"You said the dog likes guys."

"Yes—the UPS driver, the mailman, the electric meter reader. They all give her a biscuit and a scratch. She has a doggy door into the yard and works the system."

"Ah."

John remained hunkered down on a pair of Tevas, the black straps luring her stare. He had nice feet. Even nicer toenails. She never cared for men who had icky feet.

She'd only rub Bobby-Tom's for him if he wore socks.

Chloe banished that thought and lifted her eyes to John's. In that moment, she forgot to hate him. Studying his handsome face and disregarding what he did for a living, she thought he was about the finest-looking male specimen she'd run into in eons.

Her cheeks hot, she pulled her loose hair into a scrunchy.

Several children ran past, melting ice creams on sticks in their chubby hands. Chloe got a splash of chocolate on her knee.

A stretch of time ticked by before she said, "It sure is hot."

"I love summer," John remarked, swiping the chocolate from her knee with his finger, then letting Boo-Bear lick it.

Chloe fixated on her dog's tongue, then shook the clouds from her head.

"So what are you doing here?" she asked, almost too abruptly. "You don't strike me as the Spring Shores type. Don't you have a big pool or something to cool off in?"

"I do, but I also have a boat." He glanced over his shoulder to the dock. "It's tied at the marina. That blue-and-white one."

She followed his gaze, noting the sporty boat with a chrome boom.

"My son took it out with some friends last weekend and they damaged my outdrive and propeller. I had it fixed and wanted to take the boat for a test run to see how it handled."

"How's it working now?" she asked, suddenly self-conscious about her figure. If she'd been able to, without making a noticeable move, she would have put her sundress on.

Even though she'd lost weight, she didn't feel comfortable in a bikini. She wore a full coverage bathing suit. One of those tankini's with the high-waist bottoms and low-cut halter top. She'd got it at the Swim and Run shop after trying on a hundred options. The black spandex had been flattering—but as far as bathing suits went, nothing really flattered dimpled thighs.

"Don't know. I haven't taken it out yet." He stood and slipped his sunglasses on. Several women on the beach, some with families and husbands sporting rotund stomachs, ogled John and his muscular physique. "I just launched her and went to park my truck. When I was walking back to the marina, I saw you lying here."

Boo-Bear curled back onto her blanket and took her rawhide again.

Chloe gave a sigh and actually spoke the truth when she said, "Well, nice seeing you. Even though we don't like each other." A half laugh accompanied that latter part.

"I never said I didn't like you, Chloe. I do. Too much. That's why I want to help you."

"You can't help. We've already established I won't take your offer from Garretson."

"Maybe not, but I'd still like to be your friend. I wouldn't mind getting to know you better. There's something about you."

Chloe's breath hitched, and she had trouble keeping her head on straight.

Think, Chloe. Don't lose it.

It had been a long time since she felt the desire to flirt with a man, hear what he had to say about life, to want to be together and hang around on a lazy Sunday afternoon and do nothing with him.

"Sure. Maybe we can have coffee sometime." She couldn't believe she actually suggested a date. If she calculated how long it had been since she'd gone out with a guy, she'd be going back a lot of calendar pages.

"Or maybe a beer," he countered.

"Okay. Whatever."

"Great. Gather your stuff."

Brows lifting, she questioned, "Excuse me?"

John was already folding Boo-Bear's blanket and getting the dog's leash. "Boat ride and a beer."

"But wait—"

He ignored her protest as he grabbed her beach bag and stuffed her book, sunscreen and bottled water inside. An exaggerated pulse beat in Chloe's throat, causing her difficulty with simple intake and exhale of air.

Then John extended a hand for her to take. She stared at the width of his hand, his fingers, but didn't move. Finally he reached down and pulled her to her feet.

"Come on." His gentle command brooked no argument and she wondered how many times he'd gotten his way in court simply by being personable.

Boo-Bear sniffed her way along the beach, then to the marina dock. They stopped at John's boat. It looked larger up close.

Glossy paint and shining chrome accented the exterior, while the interior was clean and looked new. White vinyl seats had been cleaned to perfection, and appeared soft and comfortable to sit on. An ice chest was tucked under the rear seat.

The front panel had a lot of buttons and round dials with red needles. A single key with a flotation fob attached had been left in the ignition.

Chloe, liking the appeal of the jet boat and noting the speed it was capable of, asked, "You actually drive this?"

John jumped onboard and took Boo-Bear from the dock. "Why would you ask such a thing?"

"The golf magazines in your office and you don't golf."

Smiling, John shot her a flash of dazzling teeth that just about sent her heartbeat soaring to the moon. "You didn't see any boat magazines on the coffee table did you?"

"No."

"Then I really do drive this myself."

He helped her onboard, and she made sure Boo-Bear wouldn't freak out. The dog had never been for a boat ride before. She didn't seem bothered by the rocking motion of the water, sniffing from bow to stern and checking things out.

Before Chloe could situate herself on the passenger seat, John turned the engine on to idle and said, "I'll need your help taking the bumpers in."

"Is that like an anchor?"

His warm laughter evoked shivers across her bare arms. "No, sweetheart. Those are the rubber bumpers on the bow and stern of the boat that keep the hull from rubbing against the dock."

Chloe had not known that. She hadn't been around that many boats—just racing cars. Bobby-Tom had let her drive his once, but he'd had such a stinking hissy fit about her accidentally grinding the gears, he'd told her to get out after the first lap. She'd never been allowed another test run again.

Leaning over the boat's side, Chloe untied the bow bumper's nautical knot. John hopped onto the dock and undid the other. He told her to take the wheel and keep it straight as he used his leg to shove them off.

She worried he wouldn't make the jump into the boat as it started motoring toward the no-wake buoys, but with a single stretch of his long legs he stood on the driver's seat.

Rather than sitting on the seat, he rested on top of the chair's back and kept one foot on the seat, and one on the floor. His hand seemed to steer the wheel first left, then straight toward the open water, as if he'd done this a hundred times.

He turned the stereo on, tuning into a local radio station. She was surprised he got reception up here.

"Do you like going fast?" he asked, the wind kissing her cheeks as they kept a slow and steady pace.

She nodded.

He grinned. "Okay. Hold on to the dog."

Following his instructions, she cradled Boo on her lap as John pushed forward on the throttle and they gained speed.

As Peter Frampton sang about "feeling like I do" on the radio, the boat glided across the lake's surface as if it were a knife cutting through the finest and smoothest icing.

Chloe had to admit, the moment was beyond thrilling.

CHAPTER TEN

JOHN MOORED his boat in one of the lake's north coves where a bleached wooden dock bobbed in the water. Tucked into the brush and waxy scrub trees, a picnic table remained shaded from the sun's body-warming rays.

By all accounts, John thought the summer day couldn't get any better. Clear skies and calm wind, classic rock and roll playing from the boat as waves gently lapped at its hull, and a beautiful woman to share the moment with.

Chloe sat at the picnic table, her dog sniffing around the dead campfire. The bichon nosed and pawed at the cold ash pit, much to her chagrin. White leg fur turned a charcoal color.

"Boo," Chloe called. "I'm going to have to dunk you in the lake."

Completely uncaring, the dog continued her investigation.

"Somebody must have pitched some chicken bones in there," John said from his seat across from Chloe. He'd put his sunglasses on top of his head, settling in and relaxing.

The actions she'd taken before sitting down had intrigued him. She'd brushed off the bench, then draped her towel over it, then spread a paper napkin on the table to use as a substitute plate. Her sandwich laid in front of her, orderly and ready to eat.

He thought to himself: *She must be a neat freak.*

A person's demeanor and character traits had always fascinated him. He'd taken classes on it, felt he had a fairly good handle on how to read someone. Chloe seemed fairly straightforward, until she glanced at him with an expression that came across as unreadable.

Her eyes were stunning. And when that sexy gaze of hers lingered on him, John felt himself coming alive. Blood rushed through him, scorching and filling his muscles, his breath coming from deeper within his lungs.

No argument here—his attraction to her had a deep physical pull.

"Thanks for inviting me," she uttered politely. "I liked the boat ride. I sort of have a thing for speed. I drive fast, too."

"Any tickets?"

"Not yet. But I think I could talk my way out of one if I got pulled over." She gave him the sweetest smile that melted him to the bone, and he didn't doubt her claim.

Without asking, he twisted the cap on a beer to go with her lunch. Beads of cold moisture rolled down the bottle's neck. "I know you said you're not much of a beer drinker anymore, but it's what I packed."

"Thanks," she said with a note of gratitude. "I still like it, I just meant that I branched out to wine, too."

She held on to her turkey sandwich, nibbling on it, guilty she had herself a real meal when he hadn't brought one.

"Want half?" she offered, the sandwich halfway to her mouth.

John had to drag his gaze away. He simply shook his head, not trusting his voice.

The only food John had tossed into a grocery sack came by way of cellophane packages—snacks that were easy to pack. He kept things low-key when he came up here. He saved his culinary talent for the backyard barbeque. He could grill a salmon fillet or a thick New York steak to perfection.

"Are you sure you don't want half of this?" Chloe repeated the offering, her arm extended and her shoulders lifted with expectancy. "It's got deli cheese and fresh tomatoes."

"I'm good." He settled comfortably into the bench, casually straddling it with a leg on either side.

He enjoyed watching her, much to her evident fluster. She'd look at him, then look away as if highly engrossed at the lake beyond.

She absently swatted at a yellow jacket that buzzed in front of her. Back at the beach, she'd slipped on her sundress. The fabric had enough transparency to it that he could make out the outline of her bathing suit.

She had great legs—longer than he imagined the day she'd come into his office wearing a dress. Her tan had deepened since then. While her figure wasn't stick-thin, he wouldn't categorize her as heavy. She seemed normal to him; curvy and full-breasted. She had the kind of body that felt good next to a man. Connie had put on weight after being pregnant with Zach, then Kara. And over the years, she had stopped telling him her dress size, no matter how many times he'd insisted the number didn't matter to him. He'd loved her as she was.

The yellow jacket persisted to hover and Chloe waved it off.

"You're going to aggravate it," John commented, watching the bichon wander to the dock to stare into the water.

Her brow arched. "If it's dead, it can't bug me."

"You're not fast enough to whack the thing."

"Bet me. I can move pretty fast when I'm hot and bothered over something."

John smiled, allowing the implication of her words to settle over them. When she connected the dots, she blushed.

She shot him an animated roll of her eyes. "Come on, you know what I mean."

"I do." John drank his beer, the day sluicing over him in peace and contentment. Chloe's presence gave him joy, and caused dormant feelings to resurface in him that he welcomed. "So where'd you grow up? Here in Boise?"

"Not really. All over until I hit junior high. My mom settled here for a bit, but then we moved again when I was in elementary school. We came back and she got the road dust on her again and left me with my grandmother."

Her childhood sounded precarious to him. "And your dad?"

"My dad wasn't in the picture. And you?"

He wondered about some things she had said, but replied, "I'm a native. I have a big family, everyone's here in Boise."

"What high school did you go to?"

John countered, "Bishop Kelly."

"A good ol' Catholic school." The corners of her mouth turned up. "I ended up going to Borah. What year did you graduate?"

"Too many ago."

She somewhat snorted. "Tell me about it. I'm going to be forty next month."

"I've got you by four."

Pondering him a moment, she said, "You look good for your age." Then she cut the thought and drank a swallow of beer.

Her assessment pleased him.

John wanted to learn more about her, and since he finally had her captive, he intended on gleaning as much as possible.

Courtroom experience taught him that sometimes getting to point B required tracing information back to point A to refresh things a little. "So you're divorced."

Her expression soured as she aimed high at the yellow jacket who'd come back with a buddy. The pair flew over the half of her sandwich sitting on the napkin. "Yes—why remind me?"

"Sorry, I didn't mean that negatively."

"I guess since you aren't divorced, it's different. I'm not used to being with a guy who actually loved his wife until death do you part." Her face softened to a sympathetic smile. "And I don't mean that negatively."

"I know." John took a drink of beer, savoring the way her eye color could go from light to dark depending on what she talked about. The emotions in them kept him guessing as to what she might really be thinking. "So do you have any kids?"

An instant frown formed on the face. And not just any frown. But a deep crevice of distress on her forehead. And the sharp bolt of light in her eyes might as well have been a thunder-and-lightning storm.

Then John made a huge mistake.

He did what was commonly known as leading the witness's recollection of an event. John concluded and said aloud, "That Bobby-Tom guy didn't want any kids?"

Chloe grew as quiet as a church during prayer. The moment he said what he did, he knew he'd really screwed up.

"Actually," Chloe said, slowly licking her lips with a soft inhale of breath, "that Bobby-Tom wanted a passel of them and I couldn't get pregnant."

What seemed to be a long span of time passed. The incessant buzz of winged insects droned so loud, the noise bordered on deafening.

John's tone conveyed remorse. "I'm sorry."

"What for?" Chloe remarked, taking a bite of sandwich and thoughtfully chewing. "It's not your fault I never had a baby."

"Ouch," he replied quietly. "A sore subject. I'm clearly at fault for bringing it up when I don't know you."

"No." Chin down, she gazed at him through the fringe of her long lashes. "You don't know me."

John leaned forward, his forearms resting on the table's edge. "I want to."

She seemed visibly puzzled, her forehead creasing. "Why?"

"Try this one on—because I like you."

She vented an exasperated sigh, then opened her mouth to comment, but snapped her lips together. In the end, she offered nothing further.

Chloe now had a half-dozen yellow jackets flying around the table. Distressed, she dropped the sandwich and began swatting.

John quite calmly picked up the lunch meat and bread, then tossed it into the fire pit.

"Hey!" she squeaked. "What'd you do that for?"

He didn't reply. Within half a minute, the wasps followed the scent of meat and had gone after it. "That's why. This time of year, yellow jackets can be real pests. Make a note to yourself—always put a decoy food tray away from your camp. Then they won't bother you so bad." Grinning, he added, "Were you really hungry?"

"Well, kind of."

"Good." He popped the lid on his cooler and brought out the grocery bag. "Chips, candy bars and mixed nuts."

"I think my sandwich was healthier."

"But this will make you happier."

Her unexpected laughter warmed him, sending a pool of heat throughout him in a pleasant way.

She studied the offering, then said, "I'll have the Snickers."

John opened the can of mixed nuts and dropped a few into his mouth, then washed them down with beer. "It's great out today. Do you water-ski?"

"No. I'm not real athletic. I have a hard enough time getting on the treadmill."

"You work out at a gym?"

"Just at home."

"Where do you live?"

"Hey, you're grilling me like a cheese sandwich. Is this twenty questions?" she asked, venting a half-hearted smile of protest.

"Can it be?" he teased.

In spite of the reserve she sometimes tried to hold on to, she giggled. "Off of Orchard. My house is old, but I really like it." Her train of thought switched tracks as she yelled, "Boo!"

The dog had found its way back to the campfire and helped herself to the discarded sandwich.

"So now what?" she asked. "The wasps will come back and want my Snickers. I'm not letting you pitch this. I have a major weakness for chocolate." She coveted the candy bar in her hand, her eyes amused and bright.

"Let's put a towel down on the dock and sit in the sun."

John packed and relocated their things by the water.

Licking her chops from her snack, the dog sniffed her way toward the end of the dock to stare at her reflection. She gave a short bark, her feathery tail wagging.

The glassy water afforded a near-clear view to a five-foot depth and the trout schools swimming back and forth.

In the distance, the roar of boat motors and jet skis rocketed through the air. Two geese flew overhead, then swooped down onto the bank opposite them. Water rippled next to the dock when the waves created by boats rolled into the cove.

John sat with his long legs stretched out in front of him. He tossed his shirt onto the cooler and slid off his Tevas. He kept his sunglasses on, allowing himself to gaze at Chloe without her being aware of him.

She acted as if she didn't know where to look—at him or the lake. She'd gaze away to study the horizon, then slide her glance back toward him. The way her eyes drank in his bare chest, he could tell she appreciated the view. He didn't have a rock-hard, ultra-toned body, but he tried to work out a couple days a week in his home gym.

"Nice," she murmured, and he notched his chin up. "The, uh, boats," she stammered. "It's a nice day to be on the lake."

He loved the summers. He and Connie had come to the lake on the weekends when the kids had been little. That seemed eons ago. He found holding on to a cherished memory grew more difficult as the years had passed. He'd learned to store the good things in a safe place in his head, no longer needing to go over them and relive what would never be again.

Chloe sat on her towel, scratching her dog's ear as she gazed out at the large expanse of lake and the sloping walls of semi-orange rock. Then the dog took off for the water's edge.

The sun hit her legs and he found himself staring at them as she watched her dog playing in the sand. The vaguest hint of pale blond hair on her thighs glistened in the light. He started to imagine running his hands over them, wondering about the smooth touch. It had been a long time since he'd explored a woman's body.

Her figure reminded him of someone much younger and her skin had a healthy glow to it. Probably from the suntan lotion. She had the kind of body that would keep a guy up long into the night, thinking about all the "what-ifs" in life.

As John continued to study her, he knew Chloe was locked in memories of her own. Her eyelids lowered slightly, lashes thick, as she cast her gaze down. She seemed to be glancing at her hand. More precisely, her wedding finger.

"Do you still miss your wife?" she asked, meeting his gaze.

He answered in complete honesty. "Sometimes, but not as bad as I used to."

She smoothed her dog's dense fur. "You had children with her?"

"Two. Both teens."

"I'm sure they miss their mom."

"We don't talk about it much."

Clearly puzzled, she queried, "Why not?"

"We just don't. My kids are going through a tough time and are trying to figure out who they are. It's been really hard. My son is giving me grief. My daughter had to go to summer classes in order to advance to her senior year. She passed, but the fall school term started a few weeks ago and she's cut classes already—that I know of."

"Maybe you need family counseling."

"Tried that."

"Maybe you didn't see the right person."

"Maybe."

An upbeat arch curved her brow. "At least you have family in town. They can get involved. Robert is great."

"I also have a sister and another brother. You'd like Franci."

Smiling, she replied, "That sounds like a bad pickup line."

"True, but you really would like my sister." John ate another handful of nuts. "My mom lives up on the bench. My dad died last year."

"I'm sorry."

"It was a shock to the family. He died of a heart attack." John was enjoying the easy way they'd fallen into conversation about their lives. Outside of his family, and even then there were limits, he didn't talk to people about his personal life. He had no real close friends. If anyone, his younger brother Mark was closer to him than Robert. He should call Mark and see how he was doing, but with all the crap going on with Zach and Kara, he'd been zoning out most everything else.

"At least you had a dad," Chloe said quietly, her words breaking into John's reflections. "I never knew mine."

"He died when you were little?" The general question seemed reasonable to John, but he hadn't anticipated the answer.

"My mom didn't know who my dad was. She had several boyfriends at the time of my conception." The bland admission wasn't uttered with humility, but was simply an inarguable truth.

The sadness of the way she'd come to accept she had no one to call Dad wrapped around John's gut and squeezed. He thought of all the disagreements he'd had with Giovanni, and didn't regret a single one. Because with them had come memories over the years of a father who'd been there for him. Who'd taught him how to ride a two-wheeler, to build a fort, to throw a football.

"And I don't know where my mom is," Chloe added, as if needing to conclude the subject. "She and I don't talk."

John's sympathies rested hard on his shoulders. Just when he thought his life was hell at times he needed to remind himself how lucky he was. At least he had his kids around.

"But my grandmother is in Boise." Chloe's somber mood changed to a lighter one. "She's my best friend and I see her often. I love her dearly."

"Does she help you at the bakery?"

"No. She used to be a fashion model. She owns Ethel's Boutique at the Grove."

"I've driven past it."

The day fanned out in a breeze of warmth and easygoing dialogue that had them discussing favorite restaurants and foods, musical groups, recollections of high-school days, and even dating before they'd married their respective spouses.

John's admiration for Chloe grew and he found himself more and more attracted to her. She wasn't like any woman he'd been around in the past. She had a confidence to her, yet a slight bit of insecurity underneath her surface.

Clearly her marriage had scarred her in a way that he couldn't relate to. She was right—he was different for having loved his wife. He didn't know what it was like to be discontent with his partner and want to divorce himself from her. He'd known only love in his heart during his marriage.

He definitely missed the intimacies of being married, of having a wife to come home to. But he hadn't realized just how much until listening to Chloe's feminine voice, and smelling the sunshine in her hair as the breeze lifted it away from her cheek.

He opened another beer for each of them and he handed one to Chloe. A drop of water left the bottle and splashed her ankle. John couldn't help tracing his finger across her bare skin.

She visibly shivered, her eyes glistening as they locked onto his.

"I've been wondering about this," he commented, giving her tattoo his full attention. The colors were vibrant and the artwork on the delicate side for a smaller tattoo. "I thought this was a butterfly. But now I can tell it's a hummingbird."

"Yep." The single utterance didn't offer anything more, and John found himself still curious.

"Why a hummingbird?"

Chloe's hair spilled about her shoulders and she gathered the strands and pulled them away from her face. "They're beautifully colored and fearless." Her gaze fell onto his hand still resting over her foot. She had on pink toenail polish. "I was fifteen when I got inked. I lied about my age. Actually, I had a fake ID. I wasn't the person I am today. I mean, I was getting better by fifteen, but there were still some rebellious ideas I held on to. Poor Ethel had to deal with me, but she did and I'm grateful she kept the faith."

John thought about Zach's tattoo at nineteen and how it had ticked him off that his son would do such a thing to his arm. If he was trying to make a "statement," he definitely had with the huge cross. John had never really thought about tattoos on women before. He equated them with biker chicks. Maybe a part of him wished Chloe didn't have it, but then again, maybe part of him was intrigued by it because she was so different.

He recognized something within himself at that moment. For most of his life, he'd been fairly judgmental of people. He summed up their needs and problems within a few minutes of meeting them in his office. Everyone had a story, and nobody was ever wrong. It had made John carry preconceived notions about personalties. And perhaps he judged his kids by these same standards. Whatever the case, he grew reflectively quiet, thinking maybe he'd been wrong to think Zach and Kara didn't want him to be their dad.

The ways in which he'd been there for them had

been purely superficial in his role as their father. A presence, but his heart hadn't been really there. He'd been focused too long on what he'd lost, not what he had. He realized the mistake and it hit him hard.

They *needed* him as their father now more than ever.

THE LAST OF THE summer days reminded Ethel of when she'd make Wanda frozen lemonade in metal ice-cube trays. With a pull of the long tab, the cubes fell out into a bowl where Wanda gathered four or five, and put them in a plastic cup. Then she'd sit on the stoop with her cold treat. She'd smash the cubes with a fork and eat the dessert, knees bent in a pair of grass-stained pedal pushers, as she watched the neighbor kids ride bikes up and down the street.

Times like these, when Ethel grew melancholy about the past, she wondered where she'd gone wrong with her daughter. At what age had Wanda decided she didn't want any part of Boise and a so-called "normal" life? Ethel asked herself—what had she done to her child's life to cause her to go astray?

Ethel heaved a heavy sigh, forcing the thoughts away, then she continued to unpack the shipment of winter blouses that had come in. Their fabulous color, described by the manufacturer as slate-ice, gave the product a distinctly feminine quality, very different from a plain white shirt or a light print. Ethel enjoyed buying things for her shop, especially when ladies came in with their friends and bought until their arms were full.

On days like today, the sunshine streaming into her boutique despite the vague hint of crispness to it, Ethel felt a contentment in her heart. She thoroughly loved her life and the blessings given her to be able to financially support herself in a way that she called a true gift from God.

Uma, who'd come in on her off day since the shipment had been so big, set up the steamer to get the wrinkles out of the new inventory while Ethel greeted the mailman, Bernie Schmidt. He looked like a wilted head of lettuce, the day doing him in. Him being large, he was more bothered by the temperature than most. Ethel waved him into her air-conditioning.

"Come on in, Bernie. Let me get you a drink of cold water."

He nodded, his forehead red and beads of moisture forming a sheen across his face.

Grateful, he took her offering and stood a moment in her shop. He nodded his appreciation.

"Thanks, Ms. Lumm. You're a real nice lady."

Ethel beamed inside. Gracious got as gracious was. She did try and make a point of being sociable to most folks. On that note, she caught her gaze straying across the street through the glass of her front window.

Why she thought of Buzz at a time like this, she didn't care to overanalyze—other than she knew she hadn't extended herself to be nice to him.

She'd blocked him from her mind ever since she'd seen him stepping out with Lois Pearl. And thankfully, she hadn't run into Lois Pearl in the Imperial

Plaza lobby so that the woman could blab about her life in ways Ethel didn't care to hear.

Lois Pearl did like to blather on about her poodle, something that didn't bother Ethel. She liked dogs. But she surely didn't want to hear Lois Pearl blathering on about the astronaut. The very idea gave Ethel a pain in her airway.

She refused to acknowledge her feelings as anything more than indigestion. She'd overindulged on chips and salsa for lunch from the Mexican restaurant in the Grove, and the combo hadn't been settling well in her esophagus. Purely a case of heartburn.

Bernie handed over her mail, mostly catalogs and a couple utility bills. Ethel sent him on his way with a bottled water from her icebox, then she finished unpacking the blouses.

It might have been about ten minutes later when she first noticed the sirens growing louder and louder. Closer and closer.

Her ears rang from the whine of them, then the pump of the horn signaled the noise wasn't from any cops. The wail of a fire truck couldn't be confused with anything else.

Ethel's first thought was that Bernie had keeled over a few blocks away. She went to the shop door to gaze down the block in the direction the mailman had gone. But to her surprise, the fire truck barreled its heavy equipment onto their block toward her shop, its brakes jammed on directly in front of the astronaut's cigar store.

Uma stood behind Ethel, her hand on her shoulder.

"It's bad when a cigar store sets fire. It's going to stink around here."

Ethel's mind headed in that same direction, but she didn't see any evidence to that effect. No smoke curled from the building, as far as she could tell. It was hard to see because the big red-and-white truck had parked at the curb, its lights gyrating and splashing emergency colors against the brick building.

Gawkers gathered on the sidewalk, everyone nosing around to see what was going on at The Humidor.

Funny how, despite the flashing commotion, it never dawned on Ethel that this could be anything more than an ashtray fire. One would figure that sitting around in that shop all afternoon lighting stogies would be the cause of this catastrophe.

The alternative scenario didn't hit Ethel until the siren of an ambulance came screaming around the corner and stopped dead behind the fire truck.

Then her heartbeat skipped. After that, its rhythm pumped at double time. Something was very wrong.

Ethel told Uma to mind the boutique as she managed to cross the stalled traffic on the road and bound up the curb in front of Walden Griffiths's store. To her horror, she got there just in time to see him lying on a stretcher, IV lines pumping juice into his arm.

"Oh, my word!" she replied, as she felt the blood drain from her face.

Conscious, Walden's color could best be described as bleached cotton. He laid on a sheet of hospital linen, looking pale and limp.

Spotting her as the paramedics wheeled him toward

the big ambulance, he reached out and did the most unexpected thing. He clamped on to her wrist with surpris-
ing strength for a man who appeared to be on his way
to meet his maker. Walden looked her dead in the eyes,
his pupils dark pricks of black, and said in a half-
delirious voice, "Mission failure. Apollo is at home.
Can you lock the shop for me? The key is in the cash
drawer."

"I…b-but," she stammered, thinking there had to be
someone else who could do this. "Can I call someone
for you?"

On a puff of sallow breath, he whispered, "Negative.
There's nobody but you."

With that, the paramedics shoved the gurney into
the back of the ambulance and she barely managed to
ask where they were taking the poor man.

"My word," she kept saying as she dashed inside
The Humidor. *Oh, my word!*

Ethel fumbled to open the cash drawer, find the key
and then do as Walden asked. She locked the door, the
crowd fanning out to a thin trickle as everyone went
back to work or carried on with their day as if nothing
had happened.

But Ethel couldn't be so cavalier. She prayed he
wasn't having a heart attack…and would die.

For some odd reason, that just wouldn't do.

CHAPTER ELEVEN

CHLOE'S MUSCLES ached from a long day of work. She'd had two wedding-cake orders—one a traditional four-tier and the other a rose trellis pattern with extremely intricate work that took twice as long to put together—that had been assembled and delivered today.

Why did most couples pick Saturday to get married? Having to do everything last minute on that particular day exhausted Chloe mentally and physically. She took such pride in her cakes, that not only did she do many of the assemblies herself, but she also offered to help the wedding coordinators slice the cakes to keep the structural integrity sound. Quite a few of her wedding cakes relied on dowels in order for the layers to remain steady and the iced decorations to stay in place.

By the end of this particular Saturday, Chloe drove home longing for a hot bubble bath, a glass of cabernet, and wanting nothing more than to veg in front of a DVD rental while wearing her jammies.

She'd been too tired to hit the local video store and browse the shelves, so as she turned her car onto the darkened block where she lived, she mentally inventoried the movies she owned and wondered what would be a good encore viewing.

The radio played in the background, but she didn't pay much attention to the song other than being aware that its beat had kept her from falling asleep at the wheel.

Approaching her Tudor-style house, she noted the porch light had burned out. Her street was wider than most since the homes had been built in the 1930s, when land prices hadn't been at such a premium. Nowadays, developers packed as many homes as they could on postage stamp-size lots. While the homes on her street benefitted from the mature elms and sycamores shading front and side yards, the trees made for bad lighting in driveways.

Chloe began the turn into her driveway, heading toward the detached garage in back, when a flash of light caught her attention. The flashlight beam, muted and swift, came from the side yard, then evaporated into the night.

Only seconds ago she had been tired and half-asleep, but now Chloe's adrenaline amped up at an alarming degree. Her elbow hit the lock tab on her driver's door and she remained in the car, watching and listening.

From within the house, Boo's barking alerted her that her dog had run inside the doggy door that led into the yard. While Boo-Bear had a penchant for eating the mail, she was quite friendly and wouldn't attack a stranger—even if she felt threatened. The dog wouldn't harm a flea. She'd rather hide under the bed than take a bite out of someone's leg.

Chloe snapped off the car radio and now the only noise inside her small car was the *ba-bump ba-bump* of her heart as it beat against her rib cage.

The sound of an engine turning over, followed by a car accelerating, caught Chloe's attention. She hadn't paid any mind to the vehicles parked on the street. She thought she'd passed the Andersons' Ford Taurus, but she couldn't recall anything else.

"Shit on a stick," she whispered, fumbling with her purse and going for her cell phone. Whipping it out, she hit the nine, the one, then just as her thumb was on the cusp of pressing the one again, she paused and glanced at the house.

Boo had quit barking and the sounds of the night could now be heard; crickets chirped and, somewhere in the distant sky, the engines of a jet throttled back as the airplane made its descent toward the Boise Airport.

What if she were overreacting?

Calling 9-1-1, then having the cops tell her she'd been wrong about an intruder, would be awkward and embarrasing. They'd probably tell her the perps were just some neighbor kids running around on a scavenger hunt. Maybe she hadn't seen a flashlight—maybe the light had just been her imagination.

But maybe not.

She dialed Ethel.

The phone rang and rang, then Ethel's voice mail answered the call. Chloe didn't bother to leave a message.

Boo-Bear started barking again, an incessant *yap-yap* that rose the fine hairs on the back of Chloe's neck. She vacillated between calling the police, and jamming the car in Reverse and leaving.

Digging inside her purse, she felt around her wallet, lipsticks and pens for her pepper spray. Just as she made contact with the canister, she asked herself if she could really use it.

With a jerk, she dumped the contents of her purse onto the passenger seat. She sifted through the pile in the dim light. Finally finding the business card she'd been searching for, she studied the number, hesitated for all of two seconds, then dialed it.

Thank goodness a male voice answered on the other end. "This is John."

A strong hero was a lot better than a can of Mace.

"John." She breathed his name in a whooshed exhale. "It's Chloe Lawson."

His soft laugh greeted her ears. "Well, hey. You're the only Chloe I know."

Under different circumstances, she would have flirted with him. Maybe. She hadn't flirted in so long, she'd probably muck it up and say the wrong thing.

After their boat trip last weekend, she had definitely become more used to him—more comfortable with his personality and just more comfortable being around a man.

Even though he was a lawyer, John had turned out to be quite pleasant, and sometimes funny when he let his guard down. After their afternoon at the lake, she'd caught herself thinking about him. Too much for her own good. She had way too much going on in her life right now to get involved.

Why, then, had she called him to rescue her?

She put the disarming answer out of her head, as it had no business in there anyway. Not right now.

"I'm sorry to bother you." Did her voice really sound that far off in her ears? Normally she commended herself for being capable. Now she sounded like a silly female on the verge of tears. "Are you in the middle of something?"

"I'm reading some briefs for Monday. Nothing that can't—"

"Can you come over *right now?*" As she spoke, the latter part of the sentence rose an octave as she squeaked out the final words.

His voice deepened with evident concern. "Are you okay?"

Her resulting honesty surprised even her. Rather than put on a false bravado, she replied, "No, I'm not. I'm afraid to go into my house. I think somebody broke in."

"Give me your address. I'll be right there."

THE DRIVER GRIPPED the steering wheel, heartbeat pumping as the battered pickup truck swerved down the block and cut across another side street. A plastic flashlight bounced off the empty passenger's seat and rolled onto the floorboard.

That was close. Too close. Maybe it was time to just face Chloe once and for all and try to set things right between them.

A person just didn't erase Chloe from their memory and forget about her—even though there'd been those

selfish times when a sixer of beer and a night of party-
ing made a body not care about choices made in years
past.

You could only run for so long before facing facts.

Chloe was the kind of woman to be proud of, to
love. To ask for forgiveness for mistakes made a long
time ago.

If only things were that simple—to move forward
by admitting wrongdoing.

Yeah, if only.

SOMEBODY TAPPED on the car window and Chloe
started. In a flash of an instant, she focused on John's
face through the glass and relief instantly assailed her.

She opened the door, not realizing her hands shook.
She'd had plenty of time to let her fears run wild.

"Hey, come here," he said, and easily pulled her into
his strong arms. She let him lock his embrace over her
trembling shoulders while she got herself under control. The warmth of his chest soaked in next to her
cheek, where it pressed against the button-down collar
of his polo shirt. He smelled good, too. Not like shower
soap but, rather, pure testosterone. The kind of musky
scent a man carried after walking around all day just
being…well, a guy.

Chloe remembered it had been way too long since
she'd felt this protected and safe with a man around.
She liked the feeling. Too much.

Her hands slid down John's back, ready to break
free, when she felt the solid shape of a gun.

Jumping back, she gasped, "You brought a gun?"

His face, cast in shadows, seemed swarthy and determined. "I've got a permit."

"Yeah, but still." Her voice lowered to a cracked whisper. "Are you going to fire it at somebody if you see them?"

"I'm not planning on it."

"Okay, good."

"Come on. Where's your house key?"

She handed the key fob to him, her shocking pink rabbit's foot dangling alongside the gym pass tag she never used, and the video rental card for Blockbuster that she used all the time.

"Superstitious?" he asked, lifting the keys toward the light to view the pink foot.

"It can't hurt."

"Guess not, but I'd rather put my faith in a higher source." He fingered the house key.

She took a step toward him to follow, and his arm rose to keep her on the spot. "You stay here."

"But my dog's in the house. What if—"

A scowl etched into his forehead. "What if someone's waiting behind your back door with a baseball bat?"

Her pulse skipped. "You think?"

"I won't know until I go in." His determined expression said he meant business. "Don't move."

She nodded.

He disappeared behind the rosebushes and she couldn't hear a thing as he approached the house. Not even the key being inserted into the back-door lock. But Boo-Bear did. Her light barks started again. And they weren't alarming, they were the same happy barks and yaps she gave when Chloe came home.

Time seemed to tick by awfully slowly before John reappeared and waved her toward the rear yard's picket fence. "All clear."

Relief washed through her. "Could you tell if anyone had been inside?"

"I don't know how you left it."

Dawning hit Chloe like a slap. Very true. And to add insult to injury, this morning she'd run out the door leaving dirty dishes in the sink, her bed unmade, and when she'd poured dog food into Boo's bowl, the nuggets had spilled onto the hardwood floor. A nibbler when it came to dogfood, the bichon might, or might not have, eaten the overflow.

"I better go in and check." All she could think of now was her messy house. Of all the times to have him over. He'll think she's a slob.

They entered through the rear door, heading straight into the kitchen. The haphazard pile of dishes, pots and pans seemed to be mountainous. She smothered a groan. Boo had *not* eaten the food on the floor, and only half of what had landed in her bowl.

Although one wouldn't know from the appearance, Chloe did take pride in her home. She loved this house, but there were simply days where her job overwhelmed her and housework took a backseat.

John stood in her kitchen, concern marking his handsome features. He gave the room a quick perusal. "Has anything been touched?"

"No…I wish." Chloe went to the sink and began to

run the water. "I meant to get these dishes into the dishwasher but I didn't have time this morning. I'm normally really neat. I—" A dog food nugget crunched beneath her shoe as she moved to open the door of the dishwasher.

A soft smile curved John's mouth. "I have those days, too."

The man was being awfully gracious about it. He could have made a contrary comment, but he had some good points that were hard to dispute.

"Forget about this for now." After turning off the tap water, John touched her elbow and guided her to the living room, where he'd switched on a lamp. The chic micro-suede Pottery Barn sofa seemed rumpled with a chenille throw tossed over the back, its fringe brushing the floor. "Check things out in here. Everything look okay?"

"Yes."

"The pillows were like that?" he questioned.

"Yes." She'd stacked them on the floor to watch the news last night before bed. Boo had snuggled up next to her side and wanted a tummy rub.

"Okay, good."

He led her down the hallway where she'd hung family photos of her and Ethel, then passed the small bathroom and guest room. Nothing wrong in either. Lastly, her master bedroom and the disaster that waited for her inspection. Groaning inwardly, she wished she didn't have to face it with an audience.

She'd tried on a few outfits today, settling on a white muslin skirt and a pink blouse since she'd had to set up two different wedding-cake tables. Discarded clothes laid on the unmade bed: white slacks, two tops and three pairs of shoes. And, naturally, a gossamer bra that she'd decided showed too much lace-pattern through the thin fabric of her blouse, so she'd opted to wear her everyday T-shirt bra.

Seeing the disheveled area in front of her, now her bra felt as if it had tightened around her middle like a boa constrictor.

"Nobody's ransacked the bedroom?" John asked, half-seriously.

She couldn't blame him for his conclusion. Things did look a bit…untidy.

"No," she replied grudgingly. "This is how I left it. I was, uh, running late."

"I don't care if you leave it like this all the time, Chloe," John said, his eyes falling on the lacy slip of bra tossed at the foot of the bed. "It wouldn't bother me to come home to this if you came with it."

Surprise arched her brows, and she didn't comment. Just as well. John seemed abruptly uncomfortable by his admission, as if he'd spoken more than he'd intended.

"So everything's okay," he concluded, turning around and heading back into the kitchen.

Chloe trailed behind him, mindful of the gun tucked into his back jeans pocket. Not even Bobby-Tom went around armed and dangerous. There was a streak of wildness and sexiness about it that thrilled Chloe in a way she hadn't expected.

John Moretti meant business when it came to protecting a woman.

"You have a nice house," John commented casually, noting the furniture and decor.

Pride welled in Chloe. She truly did try and make her house a home. Too bad it didn't show right now. "Thanks. I've been so busy with work this week, I let a few things go. I'm not normally like this." She shrugged.

John reached out and cupped her cheek. "I think you're fine just like you are."

The words sluiced over her in a wave of heat. She felt herself blush down to her toes. Strange feelings fluttered in her stomach; it was as if she were back in high school again, thrust headlong into her first crush. How stupid was that?

While she hated that John had seen her place at its worst, she hated the thought of him leaving even more.

"What if the intruder comes back?" she blurted.

"You really think somebody was stalking the place?" His tone quietly sobered.

"I'm not sure. I really do think I saw a flashlight moving around in the backyard bushes."

"Maybe I should stay for a little while."

"Yeah, maybe you should."

Chloe went past him into the kitchen and made quick work of cleaning up the dishes. Wiping off the countertop, she asked, "Are you hungry?"

"Sort of. What do you have?"

Her mind raced through various diet entrees she had in the freezer. None sounded appealing, nor guest-worthy for a man who possessed a body made for a hefty T-bone steak. Then she recalled she did have a bag of frozen jumbo shrimp. She glanced at the lime in her fruit basket, making a mental note of the other ingredients she needed. A quick check of the cupboard revealed she had some honey. Perfect.

"Caribbean shrimp," she offered. "It'll take just a sec to make it."

"Sounds good."

"I'd offer you a beer, but I don't have any. Would you like a glass of wine?"

"That'd be great."

Chloe felt self-conscious moving around John as he stood in the middle of her kitchen, watching each movement she made with a keen eye. His unflinching dark gaze, gliding up and down over every inch of her body, disrupted her chain of thoughts, and she had difficulty opening the wine.

"Need some help?" he questioned.

"I got it," she responded too quickly, not wanting to appear like a slob *and* helpless in the same evening.

The cork popped free and she poured two glasses, sloshing wine over her rim as John fixed his attention on the column of her neck where the vee of her blouse gaped slightly. Then his gaze lowered, as if he were trying to figure out what kind of bra she was wearing.

His staring upset her balance, and a hot ache grew in her throat. The rapid thud of her pulse resounded in her ears.

Turning abruptly, she put both her hands on his upper arms and steered him to the table.

"Take a load off," she suggested, patting his broad shoulder then thrusting a wineglass filled with merlot into his hand.

Once she could focus, albeit marginally, she tunneled her thoughts on one mission. She went about getting the shrimp ready. Defrosting them was easy under warm water. After shelling and deveining the shrimp, she sprinkled them with paprika. She cooked them in some butter, deglazing the pan with chicken stock from a can, lime juice and honey.

Fixing the shrimp on a plate, she set the offering between them, taking a seat across from John.

"Would you rather have white wine?" she asked, realizing it was a faux pas to serve red with fish.

"I'm not one to stand on tradition. I drink what I like, when I like. And right now, I like this." The trouble was, the "this" in his sentence had a direct correlation to her because his eyes never left hers for a flicker of a second.

Chloe discounted his behavior as nothing more than what it was—a way to throw her off-kilter. The tactic was working beautifully, much to her annoyance.

"This smells really good." His compliment gave her pleasure. While she was great with baking, cooking was more of a challenge. She liked to use exact measurements and baking was all about that. You couldn't add a dash of this or that and have a cake turn out perfectly. Making a chicken dish or grilling a steak required a little more flexibility and skill—at least in her opinion.

As they ate, Chloe didn't say much. The stress of the day, and the relaxing power of the alcohol took their toll. She grew much more languid, her eyelids heavy.

John's voice had a low, tingling quality when he asked, "Why'd you call me?"

His question sparked a new rhythm in her heartbeat. She took a long sip of wine, then confessed, "I trust you."

"That's good. I've been trying to tell you I'm not one of the bad guys."

"I understand that. I figured out—I trust very few people. I guess I've been let down too many times."

The air grew serious. "Chloe." Her name sounded like silk when he spoke it. "I won't let you down. I promised you I'd help you and you haven't taken me seriously."

"I have so."

"Then why won't you let me get you a remuneration check?"

"Because I have three weeks' worth of signatures on my petition and I can do this myself. How many times do I have to tell you, I'm not letting Garretson win." Her relaxed mood spiked to one of agitation. Whenever she thought of the grocery giant, her blood pressure soared.

"Honey." The endearment sounded heartfelt as John laid a hand over hers. "He's already won."

CHAPTER TWELVE

JOHN WOKE AND didn't know where he was.

The television screen broadcast a late-night info-mercial and the woman's slick selling voice must have yanked him from his dream. He couldn't recall any of it, but he grew instantly aware that he wasn't alone.

And he wasn't home.

Chloe laid next to him on the sofa, neatly tucked into his side as if she'd been made to fit. After they'd eaten, they'd polished off the bottle of wine, while settling in to watch the ten o'clock news.

The last thing John remembered before drifting off was Leno.

Slowly lifting his arm over Chloe's head, John read the time on his watch dial.

2:18 a.m.

His brows rose and he gazed down at Chloe. She didn't move an inch, her body dead to the world. The steady rise and fall of her chest told him she was in a deep, deep sleep. Pure exhaustion must have taken over.

John stifled a stretch, blinked a few times, then noted the dog was curled up on the chair across from them, a light snore coming from her black nose.

Inching his way off the couch, John arranged Chloe across the cushions, but her feet slid back to the floor. A moan escaped her lips, but she didn't wake. The awkward position would give her a muscle ache in the morning.

Rather than slip into the night and go home, he walked to her bedroom. He thought of his own master bedroom, nothing ever out of place—just like he tried to live his life. But for all his best intentions, every day seemed to be messy for him.

He laid Chloe's clothes across her dresser top, picking up each piece and arranging it with care. His throat grew thick as he tried not to linger over the lacy bra. The delicate fabric was like a whisper in his hand, the feminine wisp feeling foreign to him. It had been a long time since he'd touched a woman's lingerie. His fingertips felt the lace, sliding them against the cups and imagining…

Straightening the rumpled sheets and comforter, he plumped the pillows then returned to the living room to get Chloe.

He leaned over her, quietly calling her name to rouse her.

No response.

"Chloe. You need to go to bed."

Nothing.

John softly sighed, then reached down and scooped her slack body into his arms and carried her down the hallway. Her legs dangled against his thigh as her head found a cradle next to his chest. She muttered something he couldn't comprehend.

At the bed, he lowered her onto the mattress. He could have taken her clothes off and, in her heavy sleeping state, she wouldn't have cared. But John didn't bother. She'd been sleeping just fine on the sofa wearing her skirt and blouse. When they'd turned on the TV, she'd removed her shoes.

Arranging her on the bed, he gave her cheek a light caress, then studied her face. Lashes, thick and dark, seemed exotic. The bow on her upper lip had been created perfectly, with a fullness to the lower lip he longed to kiss. The arch of her cheekbones was dusted in peach, giving her a natural look. Her blouse fit slightly snug at the waist, the top three buttons undone to give him a view of skin beneath her collarbone. The sight of it caused his body to react and heated him to the very core.

Her prettiness drew him in ways he hadn't thought possible. Being this interested gave him pause for wonder. Wanting to be with her had nothing to do with Garretson's or work, and everything to do with her being a woman and him being a man.

She had sexy feet with manicured toenails painted a silvery pink. Her calf felt smooth beneath his palm as he slid her leg under the covers.

A low moan passed over her lips as he tucked the covers up to her shoulders. Eyes still closed, she tugged at the sheets and dragged them toward her waist.

"Don't go," she murmured, her arms extending toward him as an invitation to join her.

"It's late," he said, his voice tight. Everything inside his body screamed to get on that bed next to her. Her serene expression pulled him toward her, a searing heat fusing inside his very bones.

"No," she replied, talking in her sleep. "Just another minute. Stay." Blond hair fanned out on the white pillow, her lips parting.

Her arms remained an open invitation. One he warred with. And lost.

John climbed onto the bed, fully clothed, and laid beside her. Chloe rolled onto her side, head resting on his chest, with her arm draped over his middle. A contented meow rose from her throat, and she fell back into an oblivion.

The heaviness in John's lungs threatened to suffocate him. He staved off a shiver of awareness so strong it almost sucked the breath right out of him.

He remained still, unmoving, absorbing his thoughts as he acknowledged the fact that Chloe was the first woman he'd held like this since Connie.

The sweet floral scent of her perfume drifted to him as he slowly dragged in a breath. The curves of her body and the heat that came from her warm skin heightened his awareness.

She stirred, readjusting her position and burying her face at the column of his throat. Her mouth slightly touched the stubble at his neck.

John swallowed and waited. Waited for sleep to consume his mind instead of the woman beside him.

It was a long time before he could close his eyes and surrender to the rest of the night.

T MINUS 1 minute, 30 seconds.

He had to take a leak.

T minus 1 minute, 26 seconds.

His bladder felt as if it would burst, but he couldn't move—he was strapped into the chair getting ready for lift off. He knew this would happen.

T minus 1 minute.

Dad-gum! His jaw clenched as his bladder expanded. He'd visited the john before suiting up and had taken the longest whiz known to man. He needed to get up and relieve himself, but the boosters were in full throttle and this craft was taking off.

T minus 48 seconds.

He could feel his heartbeat squeeze and constrict, then pulse and a rush of blood fill his body.

T minus 25 seconds.

Columbia's rocket booster hydraulic power units activated, ground launch sequencer online for monitoring the launch commit criteria. The noise caused a ringing in his ears, the vibrations shaking his slackened skin.

Hey, wasn't he too old to be here?

He had to pee and the *beep-beep* of the oil light or something blinking on the dash of his car momentarily distracted him. Wait, he wasn't behind the wheel. He sat in the *Columbia*. But no matter how hard he tried to give his car some gas to get it going, he could only hear the rhythmic *beep-beep, beep-beep, beep-beep*.

T minus 0. Liftoff.

And then *ka-boom*. Something rattled by and roused him from the fog inside his head, pulling him from the payload bay doors that had somehow been an airplane restroom with a lit occupied sign.

Hot and cold clashed within him. They hadn't exploded, but something had roused him to consciousness.

Slowly opening his eyes, Walden stared at ceiling-tile grids in a collage of stark white. The muted lights overhead weren't really bright, but caused him to squint just the same. He had trouble focusing clearly, and it was an effort to see through the haze.

He could feel scratchy linens against his bare legs. Sliding his hand slightly higher, he realized he didn't have any skivvies on.

Panic paralyzed him, his eyes drifting closed. He hadn't been this tanked since flight school. What had possessed him to slip up? The very notion made him feel more ill.

Where in the H-E-double-L was he?

"Thank heavens—you're back," came a familiar feminine voice.

"Hospital?" was all he managed to utter, his head unmoving but his gaze rolling toward where the voice had come from.

"Yes, Walden. St. Luke's."

The cramps in his stomach ceased as he realized he hadn't gotten drunk to feel this way. The days of suds and bars were still gone. He was in the here and now. Decades flashed forward. His beloved Fanny, gone. And his promise to the ends of eternity, thank the good Lord, still intact.

He *hadn't* been drinking. But, by God, he'd been juiced up on some kind of mind-altering poison.

A face hovering over his drew into sharper focus, like one of those fine-tuning television screens with all the knobs. The reassuring hand clamping on to his belonged to Ethel Lumm.

Then, much to his chagrin, and quite possibly to snap out of the doldrums he felt himself caught in, he confessed, "I dreamed I was lifting off on the space shuttle."

Ethel's brows lurched up. "It must be the drugs."

"What in Hades are they pumping into me?" Walden breathed, his chest tight while he stared at the IV line.

"I don't know," she said sympathetically.

His limbs could have been noodles, as if he'd had the flu for a month. "I heard this *ka-boom*. I thought—" Confusion marked his mind. "I don't know what I thought."

"The noise you heard," Ethel said, leaning forward to speak in a softer voice so nobody in the general vicinity would hear, "was a crash cart. A code blue." And in an even lower tone, she said, "In the next room." That telltale news came accompanied by a jerk of her head in the direction of the poor guy in coronary crisis.

A shiver visibly rocked Ethel's shoulders as she squared them back. "I don't like hospitals."

Walden muttered, "Me, neither."

"Well, you needed to come."

Dawning whacked him on the side of the head. He figured out that the strange feelings he'd had since waking were as clear as crystal. He'd been feeling a heaviness on one side of his body, a tingling, and in the back of his mind, he'd figured Ethel was sitting on the side of the bed making him feel unsteady. But she wasn't. She sat in a hard plastic chair. "Did…did I have a heart attack?"

"I don't know." Sliding closer to him, she said in a quiet voice, "I told a white lie and said I was your sister-in-law. Only next of kin are allowed back here. I hope you don't mind—"

Walden's eyes widened. "Was I that close to being a goner?"

Ethel flustered. "Oh, no. I don't think."

The monitor cataloging Walden's vitals obnoxiously beeped in his ears, a rhythmic sound that, for all its annoyance, encouraged him.

His geezer heart had taken a licking—but was still ticking.

He gave the room a quick glance. Typical hospital unit. On the small side, but private. He didn't share a room. Was he in the IC unit? Definitely not the emergency room.

"How long have I been in la-la land?" he asked, grazing his fingertips over the stubble on his chin.

"I don't know. They only let me see you about thirty minutes ago."

"When did I get here?"

"It's been several hours. I've been in the waiting area."

"Do you know what happened to me?" he asked, his voice dry as if he'd been out in the desert for real.

The top of his hand itched from the medical tape

sticking to it, and the line where an IV pumped fluids into him caused his fingers to be cold. His entire body felt cold. The only trickle of warmth came in the form of Ethel's hand curled around the tips of his fingers, offering marginal heat. He wondered if she consciously knew what she was doing.

Ethel's expression sobered. "I don't know for sure, but I think maybe you had a heart attack."

"Dad-gum-it."

The life-changing news put a damper on his grand day. It had started so well—the new catalog for Primo Del Rey fancy cigars had arrived in the mail, and he'd found a twenty-dollar bill in the pocket of his old lawn-mowing pants that he'd forgotten about.

"I did what you told me to," Ethel said, luring Walden out of his reflections.

He didn't recall asking Ethel to do a thing. He was having a hard enough time keeping track of what he'd said just now.

Expectancy curved his mouth. "I'm sorry...I don't..."

Shrugging off the situation and taking the vagueness on her shoulders as if the fault lay in her lap, she explained in a rush, "I don't expect you to remember. There was a lot of commotion going on."

A niggling prick of memory stayed locked in his mind. Glad for the respite, he didn't want to relive being strapped on a gurney and being shoved into an ambulance.

"I took care of your store for you," Ethel offered, grabbing hold of her handbag from the edge of the bed.

She produced a key chain and dangled it. "I brought the key with me."

An untimely thought struck Walden: Ethel's hair seemed out of place to him. As if she'd been running her fingers through it with strife and distress. Could he have affected her so? It seemed highly unlikely, and yet again, she'd been holding his hand when he'd been out to lunch.

"Back with us, are you?" The nurse in the doorway entered the tiny room, taking up half the space. The pant-and-tunic uniform she wore had tiny purple butterflies on it. So much for the days of white on white, and a dress to boot. A stethoscope circled her thick neck and her name tag dangled from her pocket. She'd braided her iron-colored hair into a sailor's rope and coiled the thick braid onto her head.

"What's wrong with me?" he questioned, worry peeling away his nerves like the shuttle losing its heat tiles on reentry. If he had a mirror to view his mug, he'd swear his face resembled the flat color of the ceiling, fear draining the blood down to his toes.

"TIA," she stated.

"TIA?" he repeated, confused.

"Transient ischemic attack."

When he still didn't register understanding, she gave him a sympathetic smile. "You had a ministroke. The doctor will talk to you about it when he comes in."

Reaching over the bed rail on his right side, she checked the monitor, her bosom close to his face. He burrowed his head deeper into the plastic-lined pillow and swallowed. Giving a nod of approval, she laid a reassuring palm on his shoulder.

The nurse attending him had hands like bananas.

When she left the sterile room, Walden stared at Ethel. A rush of embarrassment assailed him, burning his skin with shame in an unexpected manner. He hated for her to see him like this.

"Thanks for locking up," he managed to say.

"You're welcome."

A tense moment played out between them, the blips of that monitor reminding the both of them that he was prostrate on his back with medicine cocktails flowing through his arteries from IV lines.

"I'm sure you have to be someplace." He held her eyes with his own, thinking that was a good out for her. She could take her purse and go and he'd…what? He didn't know when he was going to spring this joint and get back on his feet.

Her response knocked him a little for a loop. "Wal den, would you like me to call Lois Pearl for you?"

Shock jolted him as sure as if it came from the paddles on that shock cart in the next room. "Heck no."

"I'm sure she wouldn't mind coming," Ethel said, her mouth made up with lipstick. "She might be a comfort to you."

"Why do you say that?"

"Because you're keeping company with her."

"I only took her out that one time you saw me. She needed a date for a charity mixer."

"But I thought—"

"You thought wrong. She's too much like a bird for me. Feels like a tiny bird when you dance with her— all spine-like and no meat on her bones. And she trills like a bird when she gets one too many glasses of champagne in her."

To Walden's confusion, Ethel smiled. Very satisfying. He was in no position to figure that out. He felt as if he'd been run down by a Mack truck.

The doc came in, some young guy who looked like he'd gone through medical school at age ten. Walden felt eons older than he was, his muscles and body were aching and he felt tired all over.

With Walden's permission, the doctor explained to both he and Ethel that a TIA wasn't life-threatening. Walden's CT scan had come back in good shape. But they'd have to run some more tests and he couldn't get out of here tonight.

Visiting hours had passed, but since the doc had been in the room, Ethel had stayed.

"I better get going," she said, adjusting her purse in her lap. He thought she had a pretty face, considering.

Considering she could be kind of snappish.

Considering she'd seen him at his worst moment.

Considering she had been sitting around a hospital on account of him.

Considering all that, he hated to ask her to weave herself into his life—just a little more.

"Uh, Ethel…" he said in a raspy voice as she rose to her feet. "I have to impose on you once more to help me. If you can't do it, I can call Lois Pearl." In all honesty, he knew nobody in town he could lean on, and he would call Lois Pearl if he had to, knowing full well she had a royal flush for him and would do his bidding.

He wasn't one to take advantage, but this was an emergency.

"I'll do it," Ethel prompted, snapping him to attention with her crisp response. Somehow he gathered that had he not mentioned Lois Pearl, her response would have been resistant. "Whatever it is, I'll take care of the problem."

"It's nothing I'd call a problem," he admonished. How could he explain his heartfelt love without appearing sentimental and revealing his secret soft spot?

Inexplicably, Walden found himself on the verge of tears. With great effort he worded his request, albeit with a slight detour to throw her off the scent of his emotional downfall. "I need you to get the cigar tube from my living room humidor and bring it to me. I've got an awful craving for a smoke. I could've died today and never enjoyed that fine see-gar."

"But you shouldn't—"

"I can call Lois Pearl."

"Very well."

"And while you're there…Ethel, I need you to take care of my…" He couldn't find the words to continue. Constricting, his throat tightened to a knot. Tears slipped down his cheeks and he scrubbed his face with his knuckles. Completely mortified, all he could add was, "You'll see her once you're there. The food bag is in the pantry and the rest is pretty self-explanatory."

"HOW DO YOU MAKE COFFEE?" Zach asked, shuffling through the kitchen on his bare feet. Loose-fitting Joe

Boxer shorts sagged at his hips and his black Deftones T-shirt had holes in it.

"How should I know?" Kara barked back, wearing a pair of Abercrombie sweats and a cropped, pink camisole tank. "I go to Starbucks for a mocha."

The brother and sister stood in the spacious kitchen with its expensive appliances, at odds over how to insert a coffee filter and confused over the exact amount of grounds to use. Sunrise hadn't arrived yet, and the lights shimmering outside reflected Boise and the expanse beyond.

"Why'd you wake me up?" Zach ran a hand through his hair and grumbled while sitting on a bar stool.

Kara sat next to him, her long hair falling over one shoulder. She braided the dark hair with its brown highlights, but left the end untied since she didn't have a hairband with her. "Because I was worried."

"You never worry at four-ten in the morning."

"I know, but I woke up and I had this funny feeling about the house being too empty." She took an orange from the fruit bowl, but opted not to peel it. The lining of her stomach churned, not with hunger, but with dread. "I didn't even think to check your room—I went straight to Dad's." She flicked the braid. "And that's when I figured out he wasn't home."

"So what? Maybe he had to go into the office early."

"Not at four. He's not that much of a workaholic."

"Maybe he's got a big case."

Kara shot her brother a frown. "No," she replied adamantly. "He hasn't come home. His bed is still made."

Zach tilted on the bar stool. "Did you check the answering machine? Maybe he called us and we didn't hear it."

"I checked. My cell, too. Did you look at yours?"

"The last thing I had come in on mine was a text message just after midnight from Toad."

"I'm worried." Kara bit her lip. "Should we call someone?"

"Like who?"

"I don't know. But someone."

Zach, while trying to remain unaffected about it, raised his brow in concern. "Did you try his cell again?"

"Two more times. No answer."

A look of annoyance crossed Zach's features. "Well this just bites. If this were me, I'd get holy shit for it."

"Me, too."

The pair waited, reasoning with one another for another thirty minutes before deciding they needed backup.

OPENING THE DOOR silently, John entered the house but knew full well he wouldn't be alone inside. The 1999 champagne-colored sedan parked in his driveway meant he was in for holy hell.

Summer sunshine washed the morning in brightness. He'd barely been awake when he headed home. He felt in dire need of a shower, shave and a cup of steaming-hot coffee.

As he walked through the house, Zach and Kara waited for him in the kitchen.

Kara's hand plopped on her slender hips, her long

hair swimming over her shoulders. Wearing her pajamas and fuzzy slippers, she gave him such a belligerent look it could have made an innocent man confess to something he didn't do just to get her off his back. Zach crept forward, his head shaking, and said, "It really sucks what you did."

John set his keys on the counter, running his tongue against the inside of his cheek and wondering how to get out of this. He'd never once, in his entire life, been unaccountable for his actions to his family. There had never been a single thing he'd hidden from his wife or kids.

Until now.

What happened last night, with Chloe—was personal and he wanted to keep that to himself. Even when the third party in the room came forward, her wardrobe rumpled and not a stitch of makeup on her face. Her stern voice could still set his hair on end when she got riled up.

"Giovanni Junior," Mariangela reprimanded, her finger pointing at him. "Where in God's name were you last night?"

Then for added measure, the *coup de grace* no Catholic kid wanted to face—his mother crossed herself and that meant whatever he said had better be the gospel truth.

At his age, John wouldn't be bulldozed, but coming home to find his kids *and* his mother waiting up for him packed a pretty heavy punch.

He had two choices. The truth or a lie. Seeing as he made his living off of getting to the bottom of the truth, he knew a lot about it. But on the flip side…

In the end, he went for the cross examination.

"Mom, what are you doing here?" John waited for her answer and when she remained quiet, he knew she meant business.

He gave the trio a vague response. "I got tied up and forgot to call."

Zach snorted. "This is crap. If I yanked your chain with an excuse like that, I'd get grounded for it." Then his son's face got a funny look on it as he stepped forward, snagging the car keys from the kitchen counter. "No more car for you, dude," he declared, then trudged down the hallway and downstairs to his bedroom on the lower level.

John could only give his mother and daughter a quiet stare before retreating into his study.

If this is what dating would be like, he'd have to dismiss this jury and demand a retrial.

CHAPTER THIRTEEN

AT SEVEN-THIRTY IN the morning, the bakery remained busy with customers waiting to purchase their selections. As soon as Chloe took another batch of cinnamon-and-sugar-dusted snickerdoodles out of the oven, she went to the front to help with the line.

The latest no-show clerk had been a twenty-one-year-old man she'd hired against her better judgment. She'd known he probably wouldn't work out, but he'd talked her into giving him a chance. In his short employment career, the longest time he'd spent on a job had been nine months at Journeys Shoes; previous to that, a brief two-month stint at Zumiez. But his devotion to detail had won her over—that and the fact his last boss did give him a favorable recommendation. Now he hadn't shown up for three days, and the recording on his cell said the subscriber was over his limit on minutes.

Chloe efficiently worked at the counter alongside Candace, helping customers while mentally noting the man wearing a fedora was back this time dissecting a slice of amaretto sponge cake with the back of his fork. He studied the crumbs through thick glasses, then scraped up every last one and ate them. He'd been here three times this week, and while she loved regulars, he seemed different.

Her recent scare with a possible intruder was way too fresh in her mind. While the house had been cleared of foul play by John, and he had spent the night and given her comfort, she wondered if she'd imagined the episode or if someone really had been there.

In a flash of memory, she allowed herself a few moments to relive the way John had made her feel that night. Safe, protected and cared for. Special. How long had it been since she'd slept with a man all night…not that she *slept* with him.

A long time.

Come morning, the inevitable awkwardness had strained her words and she hadn't really known what to say other than thank you. She'd talked to John every day this week since the incident at her home. He'd call to check on her, then insist she call him when she pulled into her driveway before entering the house and locking herself inside.

The whole thing had become slightly ridiculous and she began to believe that an overactive imagination had quite possibly blown the night in question out of proportion. Surely she wasn't in harm's way. If that were true, she would have continued to be pursued by some mystery person. But the calls had stopped, and there were no further late-night episodes to report.

One thing had changed in the meantime, however, and that was her impression of John. John's solicitous nature had her thinking about him in a different light.

Truth be told, she'd developed a bit of a crush on him. Silly at her age, but the feelings evoked a response in her just the same. She anticipated his calls, finding ways to keep him on the line a little longer than necessary, just to hear his voice.

After boxing a frosted white cake for a Mrs. Clark, the repeat customer remarked primly, "I hope you win against that Garretson's market. What's the latest on the petition? I've already signed it, you know."

"I'm still gathering signatures. If you know of anyone, please tell them about it."

"I already have, dear. Everyone in my complex knows and I send them your way." Her felt hat sat slightly askew on her head and her lipstick was crooked.

"Thanks, Mrs. Clark. Have a great day."

The woman tottered off, reminding Chloe somewhat of her grandmother.

Ethel had not returned her call from yesterday. In fact, ever since Saturday night, getting ahold of her grandmother proved to be a challenge. Chloe had talked with her the day after her scare at home and she'd found out Ethel had turned her phone off that night because she'd been in the hospital. Not as a patient, but as a visitor. Her grandmother stayed with the cigar-store astronaut after he'd suffered a ministroke.

The last few days, Ethel had been utterly preoccupied with Walden Griffiths. Who would have thought?

As Chloe slid the cash-register door closed, she felt as if she were being watched. The hat-wearing man's gaze trained on her every move, unblinking in its study. His presence in Not Just Cakes threw her off—which didn't make sense because seeing the same customers more than once during the week was a normal occurrence. But for some reason, he seemed out of place.

Then a notion hit her, knocking a little of the breath from her lungs. There was something familiar about him. Perhaps it was the cut of his nose or his forehead. The connection of how she knew him dangled at the fringe of her thoughts. She tried to remember the details of his features that day she'd talked with him.

Not one to overthink things when it came to business ethics, she headed in the direction of his table to introduce herself. Just then, the shop door opened and a man carrying a camera stepped inside along with a slender woman. The camera, quite expensive and probably with a card to store a million photos, caught her attention. The man had it strapped around his neck and immediately snapped a picture of her bakery.

Changing course, Chloe went straight for the couple. "Can I help you?" Her tone had a wary edge to it.

A sinking misfire of her pulse had her wondering if Garretson's had something to do with the unexpected arrival. She wouldn't put it past that snake Bob Garretson to photo the layout of her bakery just so he'd know how to demo it for his meat counter!

"Are you Chloe Lawson?" the woman asked politely.

The cameraman smiled in a friendly manner.

Ready to bite their heads off, Chloe replied, "Yes, I *am*."

Extending her card, the woman said, "I'm from *The Idaho Statesman* and we'd love to feature your bakery in our newspaper. We've heard about the petition, and while Boise *is* Garretson's territory, we like the small entrepreneur and big giant angle of it."

Relief and happiness melted together within Chloe. While Garretson's was the top dog where groceries were concerned, his "fakeries" called bakeries couldn't touch her delicious sweets.

Pride punctuated her response. "Yes, of course. That would be wonderful!"

As the reporter looked for a good place in the bakery to interview her, the fedora guy skulked behind *The Statesman* duo so fast, he bumped into the cameraman. He didn't even say excuse me as he yanked the door open, rushing out into the morning air. His abrupt exit seemed as if he'd seen Lucifer himself.

Chloe had no time to question the incident. The reporter had begun her line of questioning, and Chloe wanted to make sure she got every answer just perfect.

JOHN'S CELL PHONE rang as he rode the escalator up the Capitol Terrace.

He barely connected the talk button when a brash voice on the other end of the line barked, "Johnny-Boy, what's the latest on the case?"

It took John all of a half a second to figure out Bob Garretson waited for his response.

A couple of months had passed since their original conversation, and John had yet to specifically inform the grocery giant he wouldn't take money to get Not

Just Cakes to vacate early. John's success in convincing Chloe to change her mind remained zero. The woman was as stubborn as they came, and she was determined to fight to the end.

With an obligation born out of legal ethics rather than a desire to fill in Bob, John replied, "I don't have anything to report."

If a burst of steam could have come through the phone, John's ears would have burned from the string of barbs Bob Garretson let loose.

When he'd calmed down, he very succinctly said, "Offer her two hundred grand. You're going to make twenty percent on that, Johnny-Boy, so it's worth your while. Go the extra mile."

John's gaze narrowed as he stepped off the escalator and stood on the landing, phone cradled in his hand. Talking to him as if he needed a bribe didn't set well with John. He should tell Garretson to stand in front of a bus and wave howdy, but the partners would flay John alive if he did that.

Garretson's employed Gray, Springer, Moretti and Hayes for several of their legal needs, while also keeping good relations at other firms in town. John could have handed Bob off to Douglas or Louis—his associates—but he wouldn't do that to Chloe. Those guys, while great lawyers, wouldn't be as kind in their delivery when trying to talk her out of the lease. Best to keep things with him neutral.

"I'm good for cash, Bob," John replied in a stiff voice. "But I will take your statement under consideration. I'm working on this, but it takes time."

"Time? I'll give you time. You've got seven days to get Miss Sweetie-Cakes out of that lease early. *Or—* see if you can get her to sell off her company to me, including all her recipes."

John could have told Garretson that the latter would be a total no-go. He knew Chloe well enough to know that she'd rather torch her bakery than fork over her recipes for a price. Not even for a million bucks.

"Yeah, I'll work on it," John replied, noncommittal to either of Bob's ideas.

"See that you do or else I'm calling Lapinski and putting that pit bull on my payroll. He'll stiff me for one helluva retainer, but at least he's willing to put the screws to someone."

The call clicked to an end. John gave his cell a hostile glare before fitting it back on his belt case. But not before turning the ringer to mute first.

Clenching his teeth, John vowed to put the call behind him, as he had more important people to meet right now.

He walked along the outdoor seating area of the Piper Pub, the afternoon sun slanting in the sky.

As September wound down, the bite of a cold October to come had toyed with Boiseans each morning. Dew dotted the lawns, and the evenings got darker a little earlier each night. Frost hadn't yet made its appearance and tomatoes still bore fruit on the vines.

John had suggested his "dates" meet him for what would be the last real warm day of fall. He'd arranged an overdue lunch with his mom and sister on the second-floor patio of the pub.

Seeing them, he smiled. His sister, Francesca, looked good in a stylish dress and cardigan sweater tied loosely over her shoulders. She'd really come into her own after her marriage last year to Kyle Jagger. Kyle had arrived onto the scene after John's father had died unexpectedly and had taken over a big piece of the helm at Moretti Construction. What had begun as a curse had turned into a blessing for everyone involved.

"John, hey." Franci smiled and patted the chairback of a vacant seat next to her. "You're late."

"Got tied up at the office," he replied, sitting down.

His mom, eyes slightly narrowing in on him from across the table, still hadn't given him grace for his "stunt"—as she called his being out all night. She pursed her lips, gave him the old lift of her brows and waited. Tireless in her pursuit, she'd been waiting for an explanation from him ever since he'd come home that morning. She'd even asked him during the last Sunday supper, at the table, with all eyes on him. He hadn't responded, and instead, began to clean up the dishes—something he rarely did.

Asking in an even tone, his mom questioned, "So what's going on with you these days, *mio figlio?*"

"Same as always," he replied, examining the menu. "Been working, trying to deal with the kids—"

"Kids don't call their *nonna* in the middle of the night because their dad isn't home. If you aren't going to tell me, at least tell your children so they know what you're up to."

John perused the scene at the table—a pair of

Moretti women giving him the inquiring eye, heads tilted in the same manner, and their postures set with expectancy.

This was why he'd called the lunch date. To get things out in the open, and even go as far as asking his sister for advice.

"How've you been, Franci?" John asked, ignoring the previous comment.

"Since Sunday?" she quipped. "Still the same. Great. And how about you?"

Mariangela muttered something in Italian.

"I've been doing okay." John's gaze ran down the menu as he drew out the time in a way he felt comfortable. It wasn't a big deal to talk about a woman he had an interest in, so he'd discuss Chloe when he was ready.

After carrying on enough small talk and placing their orders, John finally leaned back into his chair, raising his sunglasses to the crown of his head.

Without an opening statement, he cut straight to the facts. "So I was with a woman that night."

"I knew it," Mariangela blustered. "I don't know whether to be relieved or smack you up the side of your head."

"I'd rather you pick choice number one, Mom."

"Who is she?" Francesca buttered a slice of bread, tearing a piece of the crust off and popping it into her mouth. "Do we know her?"

Mariangela's chin lifted as she reached over and touched John's arm. "Is she a Catholic?"

"Chloe Lawson," John said to Francesca, then to his mother, "I have no idea."

"*La madre di Dio,* my prayers have been answered, but with a sticking point. I prayed you'd move on and find yourself a nice lady to share your life with, but if she's letting you spend the night with her without marriage—and *you* taking her up on it—then she's not the right woman for you. I know of—"

"I knew you'd react this way." John's heartbeat missed a cue and snapped into an out-of-sync rhythm. "Which is precisely why I kept Chloe to myself."

"Miss Lawson—the one you said you were giving legal advice to?" Franci's smooth forehead wrinkled. "If she's who Robert says she is, that's fabulous. The baker for Pomodoro."

"Yes, that's her."

"Tell us more." Then Franci added, "Now, Mom, you listen for a minute and let him talk." His sister's voice got a delicious tone to it, all baited and ready to swallow John's story hook, line and sinker. The possibility her brother might have a girlfriend got her excited.

To John, this wasn't entirely about his relationship with Chloe, but more of an advice situation.

Marrying Connie when they were younger, and not being with another woman his entire life, John questioned himself in the dating department. He hadn't had a lot of girlfriends before his wife, and he'd had none since she'd died. Entering new territory, he wanted to ask his mother and sister for their opinions.

"She's about my age. She's going to be forty this year." Now that John thought about it, he reminded himself Chloe had said her birthday was in October. "She's divorced."

"Any children?" his mother interrupted.

"No. She can't have any."

Mariangela's features softened. "A pity. Every woman wants a baby."

"Not everyone, Mom," Franci gently pointed out. "It's okay to *not* have a baby."

"But you do, don't you?" Mariangela queried, her hand raised over her heart as if to contain it in case the answer wasn't one she wanted to hear.

"Yes, but not today."

John drank some of his cold beer, waiting for the two of them to come back to their discussion. When their attention returned, he continued. "She does really well at her bakery. It's called Not Just Cakes."

"She doesn't sell *cannoli,*" his mother declared, "but I went in there once and bought some chocolate éclairs that were to die for."

"Every dessert on Robert's menu is utterly decadent," Franci said, tucking a wisp of long black hair behind her ear. In her midthirties, she looked younger than her age. "I can see why you'd fall for her. The way to a man's heart is through his stomach."

"I can't believe you just said that." John's expression soured. "I know how to barbeque. I'm not starving."

"But you have gotten thin. You're working out too much," his mom suggested. "You need more pasta in your diet."

Franci shook her head. "No, he doesn't. The carbs are killer. And you're lucky I eat as hearty as I do on Sundays."

"Because you're deprived, *bella*. That's why diets fail."

"I'm not on a diet."

"Amen to that."

John finished the rest of his beer during their discourse, then as the waitress brought their meals, the ladies at the table gave him a soft glance of apology.

"Sorry, John," Francesca said first. "So tell us more about her and why you like her. How did you two meet? Was it fireworks?"

"No. We just met. Robert asked me to do him a favor and it was about Chloe."

"Robert never mentioned setting you up on a date," his mother remarked, taking a bite of coleslaw.

"Because he didn't." John stared across his plate of fries and a burger, his appetite waning by the minute.

"So how does Robert figure into this?" Franci kept the line of questioning in the right direction, and he was grateful for his sister.

"Chloe needed some legal counsel and it turns out that it's a lot bigger deal than she thought." While not technically working on a case for the giant grocery chain, John couldn't divulge certain information about Garretson's. "Now I'm in a situation where I'm supposed to talk Chloe into something she doesn't want to do. Even offer her some pretty big bucks to do it."

"Offer whatever it is," Franci said after taking a sip of water. "If it were me, I'd want to know everything and then decide. She may surprise you."

Judging by Chloe's resistance in the past, John already knew there wasn't a snowball's chance in hell that Chloe would take two hundred grand. But maybe his sister had a point. It wasn't his decision to make.

"Aside from business, why do you want to pursue her?" His sister stabbed a bite of salad on her fork as she waited for his reply.

The "show me the money" question.

John had thought about this, and narrowed it down to a few things. "She's attractive."

"That's a given—men are visual."

"She's motivated to do well."

Franci nodded. "A positive."

"She's fun to be around."

"So fun," his mother interrupted with a matronly tone, "she let you spend the night?"

"Mom, I told you nothing happened." John spoke with an unwelcome frankness. Sometimes his mother could beat a subject into a pulp. "She thought someone had broken into her house and she called me to check it out."

"Very chivalrous of you," Franci chimed in. "And quite appropriate for my big brother to rescue a damsel in distress."

"When do we get to meet the damsel?" Mariangela asked. "I think you should bring her over this Sunday for supper."

"I think not," John replied quickly. "We haven't even gone out on a formal date. I'm not throwing her into the fire this soon."

"Remember," Franci said with a twinkle in her eyes, "Mom invited Kyle to our house for dinner and I had no clue." To her mother, she shook her head. "I wasn't happy about that."

"But look at how well it all turned out." Mariangela straightened her shoulders and looked proud. "You've married a fine young man. Now we just need to get John and Mark settled."

Mark, John's youngest brother, had remained single his entire life, preferring to engage his sweat and strength into the family's construction business. He oversaw the physical labor side of the Grove Marketplace, and had been great with Zach, getting him on the job and mentoring him.

Gazing at the high-rise buildings panning out before him, John could see a corner of the Grove. He took great pride in his family's part in developing Boise. This town had been good to him. A real quality place to raise his kids. He didn't want to mess up.

Thoughts swimming inside his head, John spoke one of them aloud, wanting a clearer definition on the subject.

Addressing his mother and sister, he asked, "So how do I date this woman without Zach and Kara getting bent out of shape?"

His mother replied first. "Have they told you they don't want you dating?"

"No. I just assumed they'd have a problem with it."

"John, they have bigger problems." Franci's voice had a soft tone. "Maybe you should try being completely honest with them about what you're feeling, how you've taken Connie's death, how much you love them both and want what's best for them."

John had thought he'd covered all of that, especially in family counseling with the kids. But maybe the only words he'd offered hadn't been his own, but rather the psychological lingo the counselors had told him he needed to say. When had he actually had a heart-to-heart with his children?

"It would be hard," John eventually replied. "I'm not good at expressing myself like that. I don't like to talk about Connie very much."

His mother reached out to him, rubbed his shoulder. "*Mio figlio,* I pray for you every day that you don't hurt anymore. If you do the same, you'll feel better about yourself and life. You won't be alone and you can conquer anything. Francesca is right. Talk to your kids. Then see how they'd feel if you dated. I truly believe they want you to move on. You can't replace Connie, and I'm not telling you to date just to find a replacement mother for Zach and Kara, but I think you're due for some happiness."

John fought the emotional ache swelling his throat. He'd let his wife go from his soul, grieved until that process had been completed. But whenever he thought of his children not having their mother, the way they'd changed and who they were today, it choked him up. He knew if Connie came back, it would break her heart.

Putting her arm around him, Franci gave him a squeeze. "Take Chloe out on a real date and see how she feels about you. Just ask her. You might be wondering about something that isn't going to happen. But if she doesn't see what a wonderful man you are, then she's an idiot. And you can tell her I said that."

His sister's face lit up, softly illuminated with a mischievous grin that he adored. He trusted her insight.

Giving both women a loving smile of appreciation and deep-rooted affection, he said, "You're both right. It's time to let my kids into my life in every way."

CHAPTER FOURTEEN

JOHN CALLED AND invited Chloe to dinner. No strings attached. She had only taken a few seconds to reply, tamping down the unexpected thrill of hearing his voice on the phone.

Having known him for a few months now, their dealings up to this point hadn't been very personal. Except for their boat outing and the night he'd come to her rescue at her home, most of their conversations had revolved around how she would proceed against Garretson's grocery store and what she was going to do about her lease.

Friday night. The traditional "date" night. The idea of it had sent spirals of anticipation through her.

He picked her up at her house—five minutes early. She ran slightly late most times, and five minutes had meant John had to wait in the living room and play with her dog. In fast-forward speed, she applied her lipstick, put on her shoes and jewelry, then spritzed with perfume.

They ate dinner at the Red Feather Lounge on 9th, the noise level on the second-floor landing almost too much to carry on a conversation. Even so, Chloe enjoyed the evening, getting to know more about the man across from her.

The restaurant served excellent food, but mainly catered to singles on the lookout for new hookups. Couples went to feast on appetizers and enjoy award-winning martinis, and tonight's crowd felt hip and the air energized.

Chloe ordered her first ginger martini. Not one to drink hard liquor, aside from the lemonade with a buzz-in-a-bottle when she'd been a part of the car-racing group, she thought the gingery liquor tasted exotic in her mouth. Toying with the thin stem of the glass, she lingered over the cocktail, then another, throughout dinner.

John captured her attention during the leisurely two hours. The way he moved his hands when he talked, or brought a paper-thin wineglass to his perfect mouth. The time he pressed his fingertips to his temple, trying to remember part of a story he'd told her. Or a brief nod and smile of acknowledgment as she spoke. Every gesture he made enraptured her.

He had polished manners and a quality to his voice that kept her attention in a restaurant with high decibel levels. Clearly he was a gentleman through and through. His mother had raised him right.

John had insisted she select their appetizer. When the shrimp arrived, he'd served it for her on a small plate. All she could do was watch, transfixed by the play of his bicep tightening as he moved his arm.

He'd worn a short-sleeve, pullover polo shirt in white. The bleached fabric brought out the summer tan he'd maintained. Also, he told her he had a swimming pool that he sometimes sat beside, often reading the newspaper on the weekends but, by his own admission, he didn't relax much or take downtime to recharge his batteries.

John paid the check and they left the noise and crush of people to stroll Boise's streets after dark, glancing in shop windows and commenting on the merchandise.

"What guy would *really* go to a men's spa?" she questioned while peeking into the window of Napoleon's Retreat.

From behind her, the sound of John's voice caught on her neck, sending a shiver throughout her as he replied, "Guilty."

Turning toward him, the streetlight bathed them in soft hues.

Heavy embarrassment crushed any words Chloe could have added to dis the place further. Collecting herself, she formed an apology. "I didn't think you'd come here."

"Not weekly," he countered with a grin that warmed her heart and said he forgave her the blunder. "But I have come a few times."

"Good to know," she remarked lightly as they continued their slow walk to the corner. "In case I have to buy you a gift card."

"You don't have to buy me, Chloe. I'm yours for free."

His voice deepened and he took her hands, stealing her into the shadows of the storefront. Tucking the top of her head under his chin and holding her close to his chest, he stroked her back.

Chloe closed her eyes, reveling in the moment, not daring to breathe for fear this would all stop.

How had this happened? She wasn't supposed to like him so much—much less go out to dinner with him. But she'd felt herself becoming blindly infatuated by him, wanting to define their budding relationship in a more concrete manner than "just friends."

The easy lock of his arms around her offered a protective hold that only a man could give, reminding her of the night she'd slept in his embrace.

How many times had she relived that moment of waking up beside him? Too many. The long and quiet nights since had been lonely without a man to share her bed.

And she didn't mean that in a sexual way—although that, too, had crossed her mind.

Wanting to be intimate with someone hadn't pulled at her in a long while. These liquid-hot feelings that had begun to spring to life in her were a challenge to be dealt with. She wouldn't jump on the guy. She had more common sense about that. From what little she knew about him, he was a man to savor and to get to know by degrees. Not to spend one night of passion with and walk away from the next day. She didn't want to rush into anything.

The curve of her cheek resting on John's chest felt warm and comforting. The cologne he wore was subtle, and she breathed him into her lungs. Overwhelming sensations of being wanted, safe and protected, surrounded her.

She wondered what it would be like to kiss him...if

his sexy mouth would feel as soft as it looked. But she wasn't going to be the first to make the move. The idea would have to be his.

Kissing? Spending the night? Sex...

Chloe stifled an inward groan, balling her fists behind John's back, but not letting him go. Her imagination had run way too wild. The whole idea of dating a man seemed too complicated right now. And yet, here they were.

At this hour, Friday night traffic zipped by in a solid stream. The warm summer evenings, mixed with the heat of car engines, had made way for autumn temperatures. A cold snap held the night in its clutches. Chloe had had to bring out her winter coat, its wool and silk lining adding warmth where John's body heat didn't touch her. He'd slipped into a sports coat inside the restaurant and it's dark wool contrasted against the white of his shirt.

In the drowsy warmth of their nook on the sidewalk, and the relaxing aftereffects of two martinis flowing through her, she allowed the moment to carry her away.

Her hand cradled the base of his neck and stroked the warm skin there. She made a noise at the back of her throat. Most of this had been done subconsciously until she heard herself moan. Then she sobered a bit.

His smooth cheek brushed hers, his lips touching the lobe of her ear. The jolt curled her toes. Her mind took her places she'd only dreamed about, and she centered on the feeling of his mouth and the sensations he created as he kissed her cheek, then rested his forehead next to hers.

Chloe gave a slight shiver, thinking how wonderful this man felt pressed into her. She didn't want to move. To think. She just wanted to stay here forever.

"Cold?" John asked, talking into the curve of her neck at her shoulder. His moist breath created gooseflesh up and down her body.

"Mmm," she replied noncommittally.

Stroking the column of her throat with his thumb, he said, "Let's go find a place for a cup of coffee. Maybe some dessert."

They'd been so full from their dinner, they'd forgone the Red Feather's dessert menu.

The diversion gave her a moment to collect herself and her rampant thoughts, cooling her body heat.

"Sure. I know just the place," Chloe replied, taking John by the hand, then crossing the street and heading toward the Grove. She took him straight to Not Just Cakes.

"I think I've been here before," John playfully remarked.

"Have you?" The smile on her mouth gave her a good feeling in her heart. "I heard the owner is really cute."

"She's more than cute. She's beautiful."

Chloe swallowed the emotions in her throat, unlocking the door and letting them inside.

The interior remained semibright from a row of night-lights. Gleaming in the shadows, the glass case held cakes, pastries and a variety of cookies and muffins. The cooler motor hummed softly, a steady temperature to keep the items fresh.

"I'll give you a tour," she said proudly, taking his

hand once more and bringing him to the back to show him the ovens and the equipment she used to bake.

With interest, he asked questions about this and that, and she filled him in on how it all worked, telling him about baking pans and the deal she'd gotten on the freezer.

"So, name your weakness," she said at length after slipping her coat off and making herself at home. "Chocolate cake, cookies, fruit tarts? Any of those sound good?"

"Actually, you've become my weakness."

Inwardly, reservations about getting involved seemed to melt like simple syrup.

John stood across from her, handsome with his inky-black hair cut short, and his brown eyes giving her a pleased appraisal. Having him look at her so, aroused a conflict in her she'd thought dormant.

There had been a long time after her divorce when she never thought a man would look at her like this, as if she were valued and something to be cherished. Truth be told, while she'd been single for ten years, she hadn't fully recovered from the fallout of having been Mrs. Drake.

After a failed marriage, a part of the person remained with the spouse that got left behind. While not often, right at this moment it bothered her that her life resumé listed her as Chloe Ann Lawson, to be followed by Chloe Ann Drake. She'd taken her maiden name back, along with other things—personal possessions and her cookbook collection—when she'd legally gotten rid of her connection to Bobby-Tom.

In that span of time, as John looked at her as if she were somebody he could fall for, she wondered about how it would be if she'd been widowed, too. There was definitely a difference to having been madly in love and suddenly having it taken away, to being in love and having it die a slow death before mutually parting.

Chloe licked her lips, letting the thoughts go by the wayside. "Well, you have to let me know which dessert you'd like. You surely have a favorite."

With a quiet presence that seemed to swallow up the expanse of her kitchen, John replied, "Chloe, quite honestly, I don't have a sweet tooth and I'm not really partial to sugar." He leaned against the counter, folding his arms over his broad chest. "But I will say, you bake a killer blueberry muffin."

"Thanks." She smiled, but didn't give up. "I've got just the thing for someone like you. Not too sweet, airy and light."

"I like my women to have a little sugar, so don't go too light on me."

She laughed, enjoying the silly repartee they were engaged in. As she went to the front case, she grinned with happiness. For just a split second, she allowed herself an unguarded moment to just let herself smile and glow and be utterly content.

John Moretti had come to her bakery, at ten at night, and for no good reason other than to be with her.

What woman wouldn't let that feeling go to her head?

When she went back to the kitchen, she presented John with a slice of heaven on a plate. The top crust was slightly golden with a cracked crunch on top. Whipped lighter than air, the middle offered a dense-ness, yet was completely light.

Normally she would have put a spoonful of fruit or a dollop of whipping cream on the cake, but she kept the slice in its purest state for the total flavor to come out. "Angel food cake."

"Served by an angel," he said.

Chloe rolled her eyes. "Let's not go that far. We both know that I've given you my fair share of the devil's grief."

"True," he acknowledged while taking the plate. "If you'd only listen to my side of things, then you might just—"

"Take a bite," she ordered, ignoring his line of rea-soning.

He sampled the cake, thoughtfully nodding. Then he said, "Tastes a little like cardboard. Or maybe saw-dust."

"What?" she blurted, ready to yank the plate away from him.

The sound of his laughter filled the kitchen, and a roguish light caught in his eyes. "Gotcha."

"Ha-ha." A bland note marked her tone, while relief flooded her that the cake wasn't bad—but the man eating it was. "I didn't think you had it in you to be a comedian."

"I can be very funny."

Doubt punctuated her response, along with a dose of sarcasm. "I'm sure."

"I *could* make you laugh."

"Okay. Go ahead." She stood, arms on her hips. "I'm ready. Give me your best shot."

He set the plate down and came straight for her. With a squeak, she took a step back. "What are you doing?"

"I'm going to make you laugh."

"But how—"

His arms circled her and he caught her in his hold, keeping her back pressed against the big cooler door. With a swift move, he began to tickle beneath her arms.

Squirming and laughing at the same time, she wailed for him to let her go. "Stop! S-stop." She laughed, attempting to fight him off, but his strength overpowered her. "Stop-p…"

More laughter.

His voice close to her ear, he said, "I told you I was funny."

"This isn't f-funny! This is torture!"

"Oh, I have other ways to torture." His hands grabbed hold of her wrists, pinning them over her head. Heartbeats pounded in her head, her lips parted. Her breathing came in erratic pants, her hair having fallen into her face.

Motionless, she stared into his face as he studied her and the mood went from playful to serious. Mere inches from hers, his lips came closer until they covered hers and he kissed her fully on the mouth.

He slanted his mouth over hers, teasing her into submission and surrender. She didn't want to fight, not this. The need to be held by him consumed her, hot and swift.

Had her arms been free, she would have wrapped them around his neck and clung to him in bliss. Her lips melded to his, succumbing to the kiss and wanting it to deepen.

She could feel his heart thudding against her own through the layers of their clothing. She had become a willing partner and wanted to rip the shirt right from him. Feel the smoothness of his bare skin beneath her fingertips and…

John slipped his tongue into her mouth, brushing against the straight edge of her teeth and nipping at her lower lip. Sensual and slow, he feasted on her as if she were the slice of angel food cake. It made her blood heat to a fevered degree and her body ache for more than just this.

Had John not been holding her up, she would have slid to the floor in a puddle. He smelled so good…tasted even better. As he lifted his head, coming up for a breath that he jaggedly pulled into his lungs, she pressed a kiss on the slope of his shoulder.

This is lunacy.

She had to regain control, composure…whatever. If she didn't come to her senses, she'd beg him to take her right on the countertop and the consequences be damned.

"So," she said on a breathless sigh, needing to say anything that would drag her from this stupor of wanting him so badly, "what kind of obscene six figures are we talking?"

"What?" John's voice sounded garbled against the column of her neck where he gave her tiny kisses.

"The remuneration from Garretson's." She drew in a gulp of air and tried to steady herself. "What are we talking?"

"Chloe," he moaned, lowering his arms and freeing her from his hold.

Her legs felt as if they were gelatin, wobbly and unable to support her full weight. Making it to the counter opposite from were they stood, she rested against its edge, smoothing her hair with shaky hands.

"You're asking me this *now?*" John's husky tone sounded just a little irritated. "I tried to tell you about it a half-dozen times and you'd never hear me out."

"I want to hear the details." Chloe felt her heartbeat begin to slow. Slower and steadier. She felt herself returning somewhat back to normal.

As long as John didn't come close, she could get her wits and recover. She needed him to talk. He could tell her how the stock market was run and traded in long and boring detail for all she cared. She had to get her senses back.

Puzzled, John shook his head. "Maybe I should have kissed you from the very first. You might have taken the deal long ago."

"I haven't said I'd take the deal," she returned. "I'm just willing to listen to it now."

"Chloe, you are…" He let the thought trail off and she was left to wonder just exactly what he did think about her at the moment. "Okay, yeah. Sure."

John straightened, shoved his hands into the pockets of his jeans and gazed at her as if to prolong his feelings over what had just happened.

After a few heartbeats, he plunged forward and said, "Bob's willing to pay you two hundred grand to get out early."

Any smugness Chloe had been holding on to evaporated like a burst of steam.

Two hundred thousand dollars?

That was a mini-Fort Knox. Shit on a stick, she'd been saying no to that without even knowing that's what she'd been nixing. She should have her head examined.

Or go on a severe diet.

Ever since this whole thing had started with the lease, she'd been stress-eating. And sampling. The temptation of all the confections around her had been too much. Five pounds jumped right back on her frame and had made her skinny pants snug.

And now this heap of stress. She might as well dig a spoon into her sugar bowl and eat the whole thing.

Two hundred thousand dollars at her disposal if she said okay.

"That's a lot of money," Chloe finally uttered.

"Yes, it is." John's features, cleared from passion, were strong and convincing. "I told you from the beginning, you needed to take a look at this deal and consider it."

"Yes, but why?"

"Because it's to your advantage, that's why."

"And to yours?" she dared ask. She didn't know why she'd suddenly turned snippy about it. Maybe because Bob Garretson had gained some ground on her. His stupid offer piqued her interest and had her full attention. And the deliverer of the offer was the best kisser in Idaho. And how dare he be such a good kisser and put her in this pickle over how to proceed.

John admitted, "I make twenty percent on it."

"Of course."

"Let me clarify," he said matter-of-factly. "The firm makes the twenty percent, but I'm part of the firm." John took the angel food cake, ate a bite, raised his brows, but made no comment. "If you want, you can talk to Doug Gray and he can set this up for you. He's who you were supposed to originally meet with any-way."

Arms folded, a myriad of thoughts hit Chloe all at the same time. While she simmered in the middle of them, John tossed one more ingredient into the pot.

"Or, you can sell your recipes to Garretson and he takes over your place and runs it himself."

"Not a chance!" Her internal burners fired as hot as her commercial stove. "I'd torch them before I'd give over one single recipe to that man."

"Don't kill the messenger, honey," John responded. "I only work here."

John collected his jacket, looked at her and waited. Chloe didn't move.

"I'll take you home," John said after a moment.

The drive back to her house seemed interminable. Both of them had too much on their minds to talk. Neon lights and empty parking lots blurred out the car's window as Chloe tried to figure out what she should do. It had been so easy to say no. Now the tides had changed.

She had to consider the offer. Maybe.

Once in her driveway, John walked Chloe to the door, took her keys from her. "Wait here," he said, then unlocked the house.

He wouldn't let her inside until he knew it was clear.

Standing in the cold, Chloe rubbed her hands down her arms and tried to make sense of the evening. Things had started so well and she truly did like him. Very much. Too much…

John appeared in the doorway. "You're good to go."

I don't want you to go.

"John," she whispered, softly resting her hand on his broad shoulder. "Thank you. For everything."

"Sure."

"I mean it. For dinner. For telling me about Garretson's."

"I've tried all along."

"I know you have. I can be stubborn…sometimes."

"Sometimes?" His brow curved, arching high. That boyish grin returned to his mouth.

"Well…I'm sorry. I guess."

Moths bounced off the porch light, the evening chill seeping through Chloe's coat.

John's voice caught, sluicing over her like a cup of hot chocolate. "Me, too. I never finished my cake."

"I can bake you another one…maybe dinner, too?"

Putting his hand on the door frame above her head, his face loomed over hers. Handsome as he was, she could hardly think. "Is that a question or an offer?"

"Offer," she stated without falter. "Tomorrow night? Here?"

"You'd never last in a courtroom. You're way too tentative." John ran the tip of his finger along her jawline. "You tell me the facts, then I'll tell you my ruling."

"Tomorrow," she said with conviction, though the word half stuck in her throat. "My house. Seven—no make that six. Bring a bottle of wine. Red…uh, cabernet." Giving her bottom lip a soft bite, she added, "And don't be late."

"I won't."

THE OVERCAST SUNDAY sky hung around throughout the morning with no promise of sunshine. True to the season, the first day of fall had brought a noticeable drop in temperature.

Wearing a BSU sweatshirt and a backward baseball cap, John had taken the morning to winterize the pool.

As he angled the vacuum's pole across the pool bottom, back and forth, he'd taken the time to think about his life. Where he'd been and where he wanted to go. The two weren't particularly far apart.

He'd enjoyed being married. Being a husband. A father. He wanted to be that again. The whole package. Only this time he'd do things differently. He'd be different.

Change came when a heart was ready to accept it needed to be changed. He'd done that these last few months. But he hadn't told his kids he'd moved forward. He remained just the same to them.

Go to work, come home to an empty house most of the time. Not making the effort to really be here when he *was* here. Monday, he planned on telling his partners he was lightening his caseload and doing less in the office for a while. The firm had suggested this years ago when Connie died, but he'd felt that immersing himself in work was the only way to get through the pain.

He'd been very wrong.

Lunchtime loomed and both his kids were still asleep. Kara had crashed on the sofa at midnight with the television on. Waking her, he'd walked her to her bedroom. She'd flopped onto the unmade bed, dead to the world.

Retiring to his bedroom, he'd laid there until he heard Zach come in after one. Only after knowing both his children were home—safe—did John's thoughts drift to the dinner he'd had with Chloe at her house.

She'd served him meat loaf, a comfort food he hadn't eaten in forever. Their meal had been relaxing and nice, the conversation steering clear of conflict. She didn't mention Garretson's. Neither did he. She dished him a slice of the promised dessert and it tasted as good as it had the previous night. After helping her clean up the dishes, they settled onto the sofa with their wine. She suggested a DVD and he was fine with that, so she put in *Titanic*.

Halfway through the first disk, Chloe checked out.

A smile crept over John's mouth as he recalled Chloe falling asleep next to him on the sofa. He didn't blame her. He couldn't keep her hours and still be standing come Saturday night. The schedule she kept was brutal. Arrive at the bakery at 3:00 a.m., work until late afternoon, Monday through Saturday. No wonder that by the weekend, she crashed and burned.

John had tucked her into bed and come home. She'd called this morning, woken him up and apologized for last night. John had told her no problem. He'd call her later.

Taking the morning to be alone, to think, had been good for John. The swimming pool's surface rippled, reflecting the cloudy sky. He felt a sense of accomplishment, a calm peace. He'd have the pool service put the cover on tomorrow.

The chore finished, he went inside and found Kara sitting at the breakfast bar, her hair in a messy braid.

"Morning," he said, then he gave her an impulsive hug from behind. The smell of her skin filled his senses, reminding him of when she'd been a baby. Her teddy bear, blanket, pillow they all smelled like Kara.

"Hey, Dad," she murmured through a yawn. "What are you doing home?"

"It's Sunday."

"Oh, yeah." Plopping her hands in her chin, she muttered in half a yawn, "Do I have to go to Sunday dinner at Grandma's today? I have things to do."

"I'm going to skip it," John said. "I thought just the three of us could hang out."

"Is Zach home?" his daughter questioned.

"He's still sleeping." John moved to the refrigerator. "Want some eggs?"

"They're bad for you."

"Who says?"

"My health teacher. She said they're high in bad fat."

"Better the fat in an egg than the fast food you eat."

She rolled her eyes, then took a banana out of the fruit bowl. "I don't eat that stuff." Peeling the fruit, she said, "Me and Ashley have been on diets since school started. There's some really gross girls in my class."

John sat next to her. "So how's school going?"

"Okay."

"Give me the straight answer. Are you having any problems in your classes that you need help with?"

"Yeah, my math teacher is mental. Get her committed."

Kara had always been a drama queen, ever since the age of five when she'd worn her ballet outfit to bed and refused to take it off. There always seemed to be a burgeoning crisis with Kara, and nothing was ever her fault. Connie always knew how to handle it in just the right way—a way John had yet to figure out.

"I don't doubt any teacher would be disturbed having to teach you kids."

"So it's my fault?" she grumbled, breaking off a piece of the banana and popping it into her mouth.

"Not saying it is."

"You usually think I mess up."

The casual way in which she said it cut deeply for John. She actually thought he didn't think she was smart and worthy. Just because he'd given her grief a time or two—or a dozen—for her choices didn't mean he didn't love her.

"I don't think you mess up, Kara."

"Yeah, you do. You told me I was an idiot and I had to go to summer school."

Immediately clarifying his words, John corrected, "I told you flunking math was an idiotic thing to do."

"Same thing."

"Sweetheart, it's not the same thing."

Kara made no further comment. Within a few minutes, Zach came staggering up the steps, still half-asleep. He wore gym shorts and a T-shirt. Bare feet padded over the hardwood floor. "What are you guys doing?"

"Talking," John replied. "Sit down. You want some eggs?"

"Uh, yeah. Sure."

"Bad," Kara said simply.

"Yeah, I'm a badass." Zach smirked. "What's it to you?"

John disregarded their banter, got out the eggs and cracked several in a bowl. He made his son an omelet for breakfast, then punched down a slice of toast for Kara.

While his kids were eating, John studied them. Kara looked so much like her mother. The same Italian features and coloring. The same eyes. She was a proud one. A girl who knew what she wanted and usually got it— by pouting. John had given in way too much. He had taken too much for granted, had been paralyzed by his everyday thinking that time would heal all. A load of crap.

Time had only served to make things worse.

Zach looked almost exactly like John's younger

brother, Mark. He had the same hair, the same attitude. The same build. Temper, too. If Zach applied himself, he could go a long way in life. But he only put half an effort into most everything he did. And when he just didn't think—like blasting the music and the cops having to come over—he showed his ignorance. His age. Nineteen and the kid thought he had the world by the balls.

Who did that remind John of?

Within the quiet smile of his soul, John acknowledged: *Myself.*

John joined his kids at the breakfast bar, taking a seat at the end, sipping on a tepid cup of coffee.

"So how're you?" John asked Zach, sincerely wanting to know how things were going for him.

"I went to work every day last week," Zach challenged. "You can call Uncle Mark if you don't believe me."

"I believe you."

Looking through an unruly shock of black hair, Zach stared at him a long moment. "That's a first."

"That's not true, Zach. If you tell me something, I'll believe you."

His son simply snorted.

John didn't retreat, increasing his resolve. "Today just the three of us can go to dinner, then take in a movie and hang out."

"I thought you were kidding about not going to Grandma's tonight," Kara said, brushing crumbs from the counter onto her empty plate.

"I'm very serious."

"Well, I can't make it. Me and Ashley have plans. We're going to the mall."

Zach chugged back the rest of his orange juice, wiping his mouth with the back of his hand. "Me, neither. I'm meeting VeeJay and Corey at Mai Thai."

It would have been easy for John to let things go, like he always did, and give up. But he wouldn't. Not this time.

John drank his coffee, gathering his thoughts in the way he wanted them. Nothing fell into place exactly right, so he just began to talk at the starting point. A place where he felt comfortable.

"I really loved your mom," John began, causing his children to glance his way—as if questioning his motives, or worse, the sincerity of his words. "I still miss her. It's hard some days. I want her to come home. To see her face. Hear her laugh. Watch her smile. I want her to be with us again, so we can be a family again."

Kara cast her eyes down.

"But that's not going to happen," John continued softly. "We have to be thankful we had her for as long as we did. I know that I think about her a lot. But I also know that she is in my past, and the three of us have to be our future. Do you understand what I'm trying to say?"

Zach's expression grew closed. The death of his mother had been extremely hard on him. Zach had yet to open up about his true feelings, even after all this time. No therapist could crack him. He kept his emotions buried so deep, John feared they would never be dealt with.

Neither of his kids replied. John sighed. "I know it hasn't been easy for us. We're getting used to each other in a new way. I'll take my share of the blame. I've sucked at being a single dad, and I want to say I'm sorry." He kept talking, needing to say what he had to say. "I've screwed up big-time. It hasn't been fair to you, or even Grandma and the rest of the family. Robert told me something that was true about myself and I've taken it to heart. It's time for me to rebuild my life—*our* life. I'd like us to start by being totally honest from this day forward."

Zach and Kara merely looked at him, unspeaking.

John scratched his temple and stared out the windows toward the city of Boise. The many trees scattered throughout the property were stunning, their fiery majesty breathtaking. The brilliant oranges and reds, the mellowed shades of yellow, and vibrance of gold. People would kill to have this home, to have this view to look at whenever they wanted.

But for all the palatial view, nobody had been recognizing the beauty in what was right before their eyes.

The John Moretti family had each other, and memories that only they could have together. And that was a lot.

"I'm going to be different from now on," John said with a ring of clarity he didn't necessarily quite see through to the end. "It's a hard thing for me to admit, but I've really made some mistakes and I just want to start over. I'm taking a lighter caseload. And I'd like for us to keep one night a week reserved for just us three. We need to reconnect."

"Reconnect…" Zach's tone was skeptical.

Kara jabbed him with her elbow. "Shut up."

Zach frowned. "So like what night?"

"I'd like to start with tonight," John replied.

His son and daughter looked at each other, then Kara's cell phone rang from its place on the breakfast bar. Glancing at the ID she said, "It's Ashley."

The phone continued its musical ring, then Kara gave John a smile he hadn't seen since she was seven. Suddenly he was looking at his baby girl who he'd have done anything for.

Kara said, "I'll tell her I can't make it."

John nodded, swallowing the heaviness that pressed in on his chest.

Zach shrugged. "Okay. I'll go."

Not trusting himself to speak, John continued to nod; then he began cleaning the dirty dishes, desperately needing something to do or else the tears collecting in his eyes would fall.

CHAPTER FIFTEEN

AFTER THREE DIVORCES, Ethel wouldn't remotely consider adding another charm to her nuptial bracelet. She'd rather bleach her hair Marilyn Monroe platinum than get married again.

She had three rules about dating.

Never.

Ever.

Again.

This rationale kept Ethel shipshape and anchored in port on weekend nights. Wearing a blouse and lounging pants, she liked to relax on her davenport paging through fashion magazines. At times like this she would often put on a ten-minute facial mask, killing two birds with one stone. Or sometimes she enjoyed a can of beer.

Over the umpteen dozen years of being single, she'd built up a pretty nifty regime.

Count on nobody but yourself, she always said.

She hadn't counted on Walden Griffiths wanting to count on her. His request to feed his cat had really pulled a stitch out of her petticoat. She'd done as he'd asked, still disbelieving she'd actually entered his abode without him around.

With no supervision, Ethel had been let off her leash and sniffed through the joint like a bloodhound.

Walden lived in a two-year-old home. Had he not been a cigar smoker, the paint and carpet would have still smelled fresh. To give him credit, he did keep those plug-in air fresheners in all the outlets and that helped with the odor. He'd even situated the cat box in the extra bedroom and not the guest bathroom.

The one and only day she'd come to feed the cat, Apollo, Ethel had had to use the restroom, and she'd been grateful not to have to step on kitty-litter granules scattered on the bathroom floor. Quite the contrary. The lid and tank cover, and the floor rug—all in putty-colored shag—had been in fine shape. During her inspection, the countertop passed muster. Clean as a whistle. And Walden had set out pump-soap for guests to use, along with a nicely folded hand towel next to the sink.

Truth be told, she'd overstayed her welcome that day, lingering longer than she should have. Snooping. Just a little.

Walden proved no slouch in the housekeeping department, either, something that had rather surprised her. Most men were natural-born pigs. All her ex-husbands had been slobs royale, and if she'd wanted her house kept in showhome condition, she'd been the one using the elbow grease to give it some shine.

Apollo had been very friendly. Nice as could be for a cat. Ethel wasn't particularly partial to pets that did their business in the house, in a box. But Buzz did get points for solving that problem the best way he could.

After giving the cat some sympathetic loving, she'd stirred wet food into its bowl. As Apollo ate, Ethel had taken the time to give the kitchen a look-see.

Walden had a floor rug in front of the sink. A definite point-getter. Half the time, men missed the trash can under the sink. Ethel had cleaned up her fair share of olive and clam juice that had dribbled down the cabinet interior and onto the linoleum floor.

He used his dishwasher, and he stacked the dirty dishes in a very methodical way. Forks and spoons upright so the water could suds over them. Plates in a perfect row. Probably all that NASA training had rubbed off on him.

One place Ethel had not imposed on had been Walden's bedroom. She hadn't gone down the hallway or remotely near it. Even she had her limitations.

When all was said and done, the night she'd stayed with Walden in the hospital, his fib about wanting a cigar from home just to send her there to feed his cat, the notice she'd written for The Humidor's window to say it would be closed for the rest of the week, and Buzz recovering at home with nary a soul in Boise to play nursemaid to him had Ethel admitting she had become a friend to the astronaut.

When Sunday night rolled around, Ethel Lumm found herself standing on Walden Griffiths's stoop. A full shopping tote in one hand and carry-out bags from Woodchuck's in the other. Buzz had invited her over to watch *Jeopardy* reruns.

Walden, wearing a smoking jacket and slacks, let her in. She said her hellos, noting his hair stuck out on the back of his head as if he'd fallen asleep in the Bar-calounger. She also noted he could use another one of his hair color treatments.

"How are you feeling?" she asked, taking over the kitchen as if she knew her way around. Truth be told, she did. But she couldn't clue in Walden on that.

"Pretty good," he said, shuffling behind her and sniffing the aroma of food in the air. "What'd you bring?"

"Burgers and honcho fries from Woodchuck's." She took the plates down, not realizing Walden's eyes followed her every move. "And chocolate shakes."

"Deuces."

"Pardon?"

"Two." He pointed to the two tall drink cups, their exteriors sweating moisture. "You must like them, too."

"I drink my fair share." Plating the burgers and fries, Ethel then went directly to the fridge, knowing just what shelf the ketchup was on. She squirted some on each plate. "I figured they'd coat your stomach so when you take your pills, they won't give you acid reflux."

Nosing around in the other bag, she shooed Walden away from discovering the contents. She'd brought him a little something and she didn't want him making a big to-do over it.

"I don't get acid reflux," he commented. "A good see-gar after dinner cures almost anything that ails you."

"I wouldn't know about that, Walden."

"I don't suppose you would, Ethel."

Dinner ready, Ethel pulled out a chair for him. "You better sit down. You're looking pale."

"I'm always pale. I don't sit in the sun."

"Why's that?" Ethel asked, more to keep the conversation going than anything else.

"My wife had skin cancer."

Ethel paused, and suddenly refocused. She'd realized, sitting by his bedside in the hospital, he had a tender side to him, and she'd like to get to know that better.

"I'm sorry to hear that, Walden. How long ago was that?"

"She died a year ago."

Ethel didn't know why she felt a twinge against her rib cage. A widower. And his wife only gone a year. Funny he hadn't taken the rice-throwing walk again. Usually his kind, after being settled for so long, took up with another woman shortly afterward and made another jaunt down the aisle.

Sitting across from Walden at the kitchen table, Ethel opened the wrapper on his burger, then cut the sandwich down the middle with a knife.

Walden asked, "You want to eat it for me, too?"

Mortified, Ethel's hand paused, having been hovering over the salt shaker to sprinkle some over his fries. "Uh, no."

Ethel's back shot up straighter than a mannequin's, her mouth pursed, feeling every bit the mother hen.

Good Lord above. Why in the world was she fussing over the man?

"Sorry," she mumbled. "I just thought you might need some help."

"I'm a mission specialist. If I can figure out how to fly the space shuttle, I guess I'm capable of eating some chow off my plate."

"Of course." Ethel hated that he'd pointed out her fussiness. *Hovering.* Husband number two had told her she hovered just like a helicopter over a flight pad. The observation had chapped her hide in more ways than one.

They ate in relative silence after that, with only Walden doing the talking and saying how good that burger tasted and how his doc would give him heck if he knew what he was eating.

Afterward, Ethel cleaned up and they settled in on the sofa to watch the television show. She wasn't much for trivia, but she did get the answer right about the fact that Jerry Hall used to be a fashion model and had been married to Mick Jagger.

When the thirty minutes were up, and Walden had shouted out the wrong answers for half of that time, Ethel retrieved the tote she'd brought over.

An unlikely shyness crept over her as the idea of buying Buzz a few things suddenly seemed stupid. Too much, in light of the fact they were simply friends? And were they even that? More like business associates who had stores on the same street. However, only she knew that Walden had four extra toilet-paper rolls underneath the bathroom sink.

"What's in there?" he asked, his face seeming too ashen, too tired.

The Buzz she'd known and had been irritated by had a lot more piss and vinegar to him. This Buzz— well, she just wanted to wrap him in her arms and say she felt bad he wasn't up to snuff.

"I got you a few things. They're nothing, really." Ethel's attempt at brushing off her kind gesture fell short of the mark. She might as well have had a greeting card tattooed on her face that hollered *she cares*.

She rifled through the bag and handed him some tea and crackers. "I thought this might make you feel better."

"Lemon Zinger and Ritz." Walden grinned, and she wasn't quite sure if it was an impish grin or a thankful grin. "You shouldn't have."

"I know, but they were on sale. I got myself some, too," she supplied, her fingers wrapping around the neck of a bottle. "Also, some red wine. It's supposed to be good for your heart."

She'd sprung for the good stuff. The J. Lohr.

"It's not my heart that gave me a problem, it was my head."

"Well, red wine's good for you regardless." Presenting it to him with a sheepish smile, she said, "I could open it now and we could have a glass."

A distant expression caught on Walden's face, then he smiled. The smile shot straight through her heart, and packed a punch that walloped her senseless. So much so, she had to hold herself still. If ever there could have been a cupid's dart flying her way, she'd just narrowly missed this one from the look of the man's gentle smile.

"Ethel, that was very nice of you, but I can't drink it."

Flustered, she spoke in a stammer, "O-oh, well, did the doc say no booze?"

"No. Walden says no booze." Then the color of his eyes dialed in like a winter sky, vivid and sharp. She could almost see his soul, a streak of pain, in their depths. "I'm a lush. It's been a problem of mine in the past. I don't drink anymore. My wife left me once over it…you understand?"

Heartbeat pumping in her chest, Ethel nodded quietly. "I do."

And she did. The poor man…he must have put up a valiant effort to turn away from drink. A curse to be tangled up in. That was a powerful addiction, one with which she didn't have any firsthand experience.

Walden's thick fingers stirred the edge of the bag, teasing her that he'd dive in if she didn't continue. "Good thing you've got some other goodies in there that I can enjoy."

Snapping out of her thoughts, Ethel played her trump card. "I got you some birdseed and a bird feeder. You can attract birds and watch them in your yard while you're getting your sea legs back."

If ever there was a grimace, Walden gave her one.

Taken aback, Ethel asked, "Is there a problem?"

"Not really."

"Now, you needn't be polite about it," Ethel said, setting aside the bright feeder and the stupid bag of niger seeds guaranteed to attract every kind of finch within a ten-mile radius to fly in for a landing.

"But after I turned down the wine…"

"Fiddle-faddle. What gives with the birds?"

"I hate them," Walden bluntly stated. "I'm sorry, but I hate and despise birds, especially varmint cockroach pigeons." Peaked-looking and drained only a moment ago, the color seemed to return to his face in living Technicolor. "And while we're on the subject," he blathered on, "I landed a stray BB on your shop window—*by mistake*—while trying to take down a pigeon from my cigar-store awning."

Speechless, Ethel merely stared at him. For all the vim and zest he'd lost, his blood pressure had surely blown a gasket on this subject of birds.

When it kicked in, Ethel's shock came at her swift and hard. "You could have shot me."

"A BB wouldn't have taken you down."

"You could have shot me," she repeated, aghast.

"But I wasn't aiming at you."

"Where's the difference? The deadly bullet still put a pock in my window glass."

"It wasn't a bullet, and I'll replace the window."

"You're darn tooting you will!"

At that, all conversation in the room ceased as if it had been clipped off at the nub by a pair of sharp scissors.

The incessant tick of the wall clock's second hand sounded deafening. Its face showed an astronaut in full space uniform, with the lunar surface reflecting on his helmet shield.

"I'm sorry, Ethel." Walden's apology landed on her as softly as a moon landing. Through to her bones, she understood his intent and she couldn't toss it back into his face.

An accident was just that—an accident.

But still—she had long since wondered what in the world had hit her window that day. She'd concluded it had been a defect in the glass, or a rock thrown from a delivery truck.

"Forget about it," Ethel said. "No worries."

"But I will replace the window for you."

"When you get better."

"I'll be better when I see whatever's left in that bag you've got there." A spry twinkle put a brightness in his eyes.

She'd forgotten about the videos and now they seemed highly anticlimactic. So much so, she would rather have ignored them and channel surfed for something else to watch on the tube. Even though Walden was under the weather, he still had a fairly swift reaction to things and his hands were already rooting around in her tote.

When he came up with the videos, he perused the titles and got a curl on his upper lip. "*Richard Simmons Sweatin' to the Oldies.*" Then checking the second box, he read, *"Richard Simmons '60s Blast-Off."*

Wanting to sound blasé, Ethel shrugged off the truth that she had really given the videos a lot of thought and consideration before deciding to pass them along to Walden. "I don't use them anymore and I thought they might help you with your physical condition. You mentioned the doc wanted you in better shape after your attack."

Scrunching his astronaut face in a defensive glower that came across as more endearing than anything else, he countered, "Ethel, I only got hit by a foul-up in my head."

"Same thing."

"No, definitely not the same thing." He scooted closer to her on the davenport, his face looming over hers. He smelled nice, like Ivory soap from the shower. While his hair was mussed, he'd given himself a smooth shave. She could tell without even touching his cheek that he'd...

Buzz looked hard at her. "I don't have a condition in my head. But I've got one right here. On my mouth. It wants something and I guess I'm just ungentlemanly enough not to ask you, but rather, go with my intuition."

Ethel had a funny feeling she knew what he was getting at. If she were smart, she'd bolt off this couch right now, before mission control had Buzz completely locked and loaded.

"Houston," he said, leaning in closer and causing her to gasp, but hold her breath with anticipation, "we have a problem."

Then he laid a smacker on her that curled the elastic over on the waistband of her control tops.

"CRIMINY SAKES, Chloe! Slow down!"

Chloe ignored her grandmother's request and jerked a bright-colored shopping cart from the Home Depot storefront.

"I can't believe him. I just *can't* believe he had the

balls to do it!" Chloe gritted between her teeth. Anger didn't begin to describe the feeling of suffocation threatening her. Tension and fear clashed in her muscles, making her feel confused and out of control.

With its wheels rattling, she pushed the wobbly cart toward the hardware aisle.

"You aren't even sure," Ethel protested. "It could have been anyone."

"Nope. Not anyone."

"Maybe it was John."

"How could John miss me? He saw me last night and the day before that. Nope, it wasn't him."

Chloe took a sharp turn to the right, her big purse sitting on the child seat, her cell phone within easy reach of the police whistle she was going to blow into the receiver if that stinkin' prank caller she'd had in the past so much as uttered one half breath into her ear again. She almost wished the jerk would call again. His latest tactic had really unnerved her.

Under the veil of early-morning darkness, Chloe had opened her front door to shuffle out onto the driveway in her slippers, like she always did, to retrieve *The Idaho Statesman*. But she'd stopped shy of the first landing when she spotted the potted chrysanthemum plant. A note had been tucked into the bright orange flowers.

At first, Chloe had thought John had left the flowers. The thought was sentimental and nice, one to bring a sweet ache to her throat, after the evening they'd spent together, seeing a movie and then having wine at her house.

Heaven help her, they'd had a good old-fashioned make-out session on her sofa. Holding one another and kissing and kissing and kissing until she'd become totally breathless and out of her mind.

She'd hated for him to go, but he couldn't stay the night. She understood, and she wasn't even sure she wanted him to. She couldn't be trusted, not after all those kisses.

Missing him after he'd gone, she'd sat quietly on the sofa and wished he were there with her. He had nice lips and knew how to use them to his advantage. Every time he kissed her, she about melted into his shirtfront.

Then this morning, by all obvious accounts, flowers on her doorstep should have been from John. But the card had implied otherwise.

I miss you, baby doll. I'll always love you.

Definitely not John.

Definitely Bobby-Tom Drake. Dropping a flower bomb on her doorstep, then writing a sappy beer-driven note was something only he would do.

So Chloe had called Ethel and asked her to come over and help install high-tech locks on all her doors. Chloe could have called John, but she hadn't wanted to involve him in this like last time. This was her mess, she could fix it.

"I just can't see Bobby-Tom being so cowardly about the whole thing," Ethel commented as Chloe stopped next to the entry locks and dead-bolt display. "He's such a lug nut, he'd be more likely to come right over to you and start crying about how much he wants you back."

"Hah! Nothing about that man would surprise me."

"Chloe. Now, Chloe." Ethel rested a gentle hand on Chloe's shoulder, leaving it there until Chloe gave her her attention. In a wise-sounding voice, Ethel said, "But, Honey-bee, do you really think after all these years, Bobby-Tom Drake would do such a thing? It's been ten years since you divorced him. Why now?"

"I don't know." And she honestly didn't.

Well, maybe she did. Maybe she thought about him too often and gave him way too much credit for breaking her heart when she should have moved on the day the ink dried on those dumb divorce papers. Maybe the fact that he'd gotten over her faster than a lap around the track, and found a wife and created a family, bothered her more than she could ever put into words.

"I don't know," she repeated. "It doesn't make sense if you really stop and think about it, but who else would be doing this to me?"

"I think you should call the police, Chloe."

Eying the various locks and finding one that had the Defiant label written over the wrapper, Chloe chucked several packages into her cart. "I don't have any evidence to hand over. Calls with blocked caller ID, a possible intruder but nothing to prove it and now a potted plant on my front door. What are they going to do? Dust the petals for prints? Not hardly." Adding some steel plates and hardware pieces into the basket, she said, "I'd rather reinforce my house and know that I'm safe inside."

"Oh, Honey-bee, you can't live in an iron box. What about the bakery and your life? And trying to take Garretson's down a peg?"

Chloe swallowed, not wanting to go there. The truth was, she couldn't run and hide. She did have a life, a business and maybe a new man in her future. Suddenly everything felt uncertain and, in a moment of weakness, she gave a sob of frustration.

"What am I going to do?" she asked in a muffled voice.

Wrapping her arms around her, Ethel consoled Chloe's frayed nerves. "Put beefy locks on all your doors. I brought my screw gun. It'll make the job go quicker."

Choking on a laugh, Chloe kissed Ethel's cheek. "I sure love you, Mom."

After paying for the items, they went through the exit door. As soon as the fall air hit Chloe's face, every jittery nerve came back to the surface, working to undo her composure.

In a jerky motion, Chloe pulled on the cart handle and stopped cold in her tracks. Her strong heartbeat thumped like crazy in her chest.

"It's Bobby-Tom," she hissed, her pulse in knots. "At the hot-dog hut."

The aroma of garlicky dogs and grilling onions now gave her a sour stomach, when the smell usually made her hungry.

There he stood, his broad back to her. She'd know that 501 Levi butt anywhere.

He angled his face so she caught a glimpse of his profile as he took a bite out of his hot dog. Mustard smudged his upper lip and it was quickly licked off. Seeing his tongue dart out made her feel hot and itchy—and not in a good way. More like downright repulsion.

Why was it then, that she had the compulsion to hide and not let him see her?

It was Ethel who charged him with the shopping cart, like an elephant on a mission. She clipped him in the ankle with the lower, metal frame of the cart, causing him to yelp and turn their way.

"Bobby-Tom," Ethel spat, then let him have it with a string of swearwords Chloe hadn't been aware her grandmother knew. "If you so much as call Chloe one more time, I'm siccing the cops on you."

"What in the hell?" he said, eyes dark and stormy. A splatter of mustard dribbled down his shirtfront. "Chloe, is that *you?*"

It took Chloe a moment to find her voice. Funny how when faced with her ex, all those damning conversations she'd had with him in her mind vanished.

When she was able, Chloe finally asked, "Bobby-Tom, why are you following me?"

"I ain't following you," he replied in a snort of indignance. Age hadn't been kind to his face. He had crow's-feet at the corners of his eyes, his tanned skin had taken on a leathery look. "I came here to buy a safety nozzle for my air compressor."

Standing her ground, and pulling Ethel back, Chloe pointed out, "Well, you've hounded me in the past."

His face contorted as he wiped mustard from his shirt. "I ain't called you in years."

"Last month," she corrected, still hoping to trap him.

"Bull pucky," he denied. "And you could hook me up to one of them polygrams so's I could prove it."

Maybe it was his tone, or the way he smeared mustard into the knit of his T-shirt. Or the way he stood, as if he were a wrench-twist shy of doing something dangerous. Unless it was a speed race, or a football game in the front yard on Thanksgiving before carving the turkey, Bobby-Tom didn't have a real good attention span.

"I'll polygraph you, Bobby-Tom." Ethel was digging inside of Chloe's purse, then came up with the pepper spray and aimed the nozzle directly at her ex-husband's face. "Now talk."

"Ethel!" Chloe blurted. "Put that away!"

Reluctantly, her grandmother lowered her arm.

Seeing Bobby-Tom, the familiar blue of his eyes staring at her, reminded her of the past. A past where she could believe him if he said the words she wanted to hear. They might have had their bits of trouble, but there was one thing he could say and she knew for certain he meant it. She'd had to give Bobby-Tom that much. As far as she knew, he'd never deviated from the truth in his whole life.

"Bobby-Tom," Chloe said slowly. "Did you leave me a potted plant on my door this morning?"

"Why in the hell would I do that? My wife would hang me to the bedposts if I so much as thought about it." His sunglasses had slipped lower on his head. He moved them to rest behind his neck, a look he was fond of.

Some things never changed.

"So, then tell me." With her words, an understanding hung between them.

"It's the honest truth, Chloe."

Honest truth. The two words that said he was not telling a lie. At least no lies that she'd ever caught him in.

And maybe something else made her want to believe him. There was something sad in Bobby-Tom today that painted him in a sympathetic light.

Now decided, she gave him the benefit of the doubt.

"Okay then." Now feeling very self-conscious, she offered him a flat smile and added, "Nice seeing you."

She was glad neither of them commented on the other's looks, or old times or anything remotely sentimental.

"Same, I reckon." Then to Ethel, he said with a smirk, "I can't say the same to you, Ethel. Time ain't been kind to you, woman. Go out there and wrangle yourself another man to hog-tie."

CHAPTER SIXTEEN

"Hey, did you get robbed?" Zach asked Chloe, his gaze following the camera crew and reporter out the door of Not Just Cakes. Construction clothing showed the muscles he'd developed over the summer; a torn sweatshirt stretched over his chest and his jeans were dusted with drywall. A hard hat was tucked underneath his arm.

"Nope," she replied happily. "They were filming a segment on the bakery about my petition for their Monday-night community spot."

"I signed it."

"Thanks a million."

Finally relief relaxed her shoulders, and she was thankful the interview was over. While she had been very articulate about what she was doing—fighting a corporate giant—she still felt as if she'd made a few flubs here and there. Recording a news piece didn't involve do-over time. She'd have to run with what she'd given them. Too bad she couldn't edit the segment the way she'd like. But, overall, she was pleased. She'd record it with TiVo and watch at the same time.

"What can I get you today?" she asked Zach.

The lull in customers meant she was able to help Zach herself.

"No, wait—I'll pick for you." He nodded at her suggestion. "I think I have something you'll love. In fact, I'd bet money on it."

She went into the kitchen and sliced into her scarlet empress. She hadn't put it in the case yet and he'd be the first to try it. Going back into the dining area, she motioned for him to take a seat, then she sat opposite of him.

"What is it?" he queried, looking at the interesting cake.

"Scarlet empress. Raspberries and vanilla flavors."

He studied it a moment, then picked up his fork.

A scarlet empress had to rest at least eight hours, if not three days, before it could be eaten or else it wouldn't set correctly.

The outer layer was a biscuit roulade molded into a bowl to form the cake. A roulade resembled a frozen grocery-store cinnamon roll—the kind where you peeled the outer layer and cracked the cardboard tube on the side of the kitchen counter. The roulades were ten times better with their cordon rose raspberry jam spread inside before she rolled the dough. Inside the outer layer, she filled the bowl with a vanilla Bavarian cream.

Today she'd poured a homemade apricot sauce over the slice. No doubt the offering was pretty elaborate, but the tastes really were simple and pleasing to the palate.

"Well?" She watched his facial expression for a hint of Zach's thoughts. "What do you think?"

"Can you come to my house and cook for us?"

She laughed. "I don't do that. I'm not a real great

cook. I like baking better." Then on a whim, she asked, "How about your dad? How is he in the kitchen?"

"He mostly barbeques."

"Nothing wrong with that."

"And we eat a lot of pizza. *A lot* of pizza," he repeated for added emphasis.

"Maybe you should try cooking."

"Don't know how."

"Can you read?"

"Duh," he said with a cocky smile.

"Then you can read a cookbook."

Zach grinned. "You're pretty cool. I'll bet nothing gets past your kids."

The light banter faltered, and she vacillated about whether or not to tell him she didn't have any. After a few heartbeats, she said, "I'm just practical when it comes to complications that supposedly can't be overcome." Then, needing to change the subject, she said, "How is the job coming?"

"Good enough." Zach slouched in his chair, his lean and long legs stretched out before him. "It's getting cold, man. I don't know if I can last through the winter."

"Not your life's ambition, huh?"

"Not really. But I just do it. Somebody has to be stable around my house and my dad has been kind of weirded-out lately."

Chloe's brows rose. Did the man drink now, too? Or was he on drugs? "What do you mean?"

"He didn't come home one night. You shouldn't do that to a kid. And I would have gotten holy hell if I'd pulled that one."

"No doubt," she mused.

"I think he's dating some lady. He tried to tell me about it, but I was like 'whatever.' It's your life."

Chloe wondered what kind of man would put his dating life over his personal life. Probably a very selfish one.

"Maybe you can tell him you're not cool with the idea."

"I didn't say I wasn't. I guess I just think it's weird. He's my dad and I don't picture him dating anyone. Not after the way he was with my…"

The words trailed off and she was left to fill in the blank. She let him leave his sentence vague, not wanting to know intimate details of his life. Better to keep him as her customer without complications. For all she knew, his father was a real whack-job.

The young man finished his cake and nodded. "That was really good. How much do I owe you?"

"Nothing. It's on me."

"Well, hey, thanks."

"Not a problem."

He rose and went to the door. Glancing over his shoulder, he paused, then shook his head. She couldn't help asking, "What?"

Hesitation kept him still a minute. "My dad would like you."

Quickly quashing that avenue of thought, she replied, "No, thanks. I'm good."

She had all she could do to contend with her ever-growing feelings for John. Add another measure of testosterone to the mix, and she might end up with a fallen cake.

She was better when she concentrated on one recipe at a time.

"SO WHY DID YOU want to come to the zoo?" John asked, taking Chloe's slender hand as they walked through the Boise Zoo exhibits. She didn't wear gloves and her fingers were cool. Wanting to warm her, he rubbed his thumb over her knuckles.

Fall-colored leaves stirred ahead of them, dusting the pathway and dancing along the sidewalk edges. The October afternoon held a nip to the air, and both he and Chloe wore coats.

Tilting her face toward him, she replied, "I just like it. I always imagined taking my kids here." Hair swirled about her face, and she tucked an errant strand behind her ear.

A moment of regret for her welled within John, and a guilty ache that he had two kids—albeit not perfect children—but he'd been able to raise and enjoy them just the same. Chloe hadn't had that opportunity, and he could only imagine the daily emptiness she experienced.

"I'm so sorry." His sentiment seemed hollow, but it needed to be spoken just the same.

"Don't be." She gave his arm a soft hug. "How can a person feel bad missing something they never had? I don't know what it's like to have had kids around, but I've imagined it more times than I can recall."

Daringly, John said, "You could have adopted."

Her cheeks were a pink shade from the weather. "Bobby-Tom wouldn't go for that. He said if he couldn't plant the seed that gave him his baby, he wanted no part of the tree."

Rancor sharpened John's voice. "Sounds arrogant."

Chloe laughed, a bitter sound. "Yeah. Well, he's planted six kids with his new wife, so he's a happy gardener."

Now it was John's turn to laugh while giving Chloe's hand a squeeze. "You're a sweetheart," he said without reservation.

"Oh, I don't know about that," she teased as they approached the sika deer exhibit. "I can get moody once a month. I might not be fertile, but darn if I don't have a monthly reminder to prove the point."

Stopping at the lookout, John tucked Chloe into his arms, her back to his chest. He rested his chin on her head. Her blond hair whispered around her face, a soft touch against his jaw. Holding her close, he just enjoyed the moment for what it was worth.

A very simple time that he savored.

Continuing on, they visited several more exhibits. The antics of the penguins got Chloe to giggle, and John quietly watched her features, appreciating every inch of her. They viewed the "under-construction" African plains exhibit, then hit Julia Davis Park, where Chloe retrieved their picnic basket from his BMW. She'd insisted on bringing lunch, and no bachelor in his right mind would have refused.

"Chicken salad," she said, offering him a plastic

container and spoon. She kept the food coming. "Deviled eggs. Olives. Crackers and cheese. Do you like Brie? Oh, and I brought slices of pumpkin walnut cake for dessert."

"I like anything you make."

She gave him a sideways glance and a friendly frown. "No, you don't. You said yourself that you aren't partial to sweets."

"I'm partial to your sweetness." He leaned toward her, taking her chin in his hand, and bringing her mouth to his. The touch felt electric, the kiss more than sizzling. Her lips pressed against his, soft and tempting.

Her nearness kindled emotions in him he thought were dead and gone. She brought vitality into his life, the way she could make him feel literally snagged the breath out of his lungs.

In that instant, John realized that she had the potential to turn his world upside down. He hadn't experience these feelings in such a long time, that he hadn't initially recognized them.

He could fall in love with her if he let himself. Common sense warned him about the consequences of a hasty affair, yet his pulse still surged within his veins.

Hard and swift, passion overwhelmed him, kicking him soundly in the gut and making him extremely aware of every sensation in his body. He surrendered to the kiss.

Parting her lips, he cradled her next to him. Blood pounded in his brain as she curved into his body, fitting perfectly. The lunacy of it all was that he could tune out everything around him, kiss her in a park, in the middle of a Sunday afternoon, and not give a damn who saw them.

His hands rose from the back of her coat, toward her collar, then to her neck. The skin there held a fiery warmth. But as he caressed her cheeks, he found them cool.

"Too cold?" he asked against her mouth. "We could go someplace else."

"Mmm." She made a soft purring sound from her throat, and it caused his muscles to tighten and react.

"Hey," a teenage voice called, "you guys are too old to make out in public."

Breaking apart, John turned toward the group of punks walking through the park. They elbowed each other and laughed while passing by.

Chloe blushed, and John suspected the cool air had nothing to do with the deepening pink.

"Kids being dumb," he grumbled and, as he did, he wondered if his *own children* would have made the same commentary. Probably so.

His annoyance subsided. It didn't matter. He let the moment be what it was. Right now, he wanted to concentrate on getting to know everything about this wonderful woman.

Admiring the assortment of lunch offerings, he rested his plate on his lap while they sat on Chloe's picnic blanket. "There's a young man who comes into my bakery. Those boys sort of remind me of him. He seems nice, but is having a hard time at home."

"Too bad."

Chloe took a bite of her chicken-salad, then drank from her water bottle. "I wish I could help him. His father sounds like a royal jerk."

"Probably is."

"From what this boy has told me, his dad is never home. He works a lot. No time for him or anything else." A distant and wistful look caught in her eyes. "Some people who have kids take them for granted. If I had a son, I'd do everything to nurture and keep him on the straight and narrow. I know that's easier said than done, but I'd sure try my best. Even if it meant giving up hours at the bakery."

John thought about the times he'd attended Zach's Optimist football games and cheered his son on. But after Connie's death, Zach lost interest in the things that had once motivated him. If only there was something that could get Zach excited and propel him toward an achievable goal.

Working for Moretti Construction and doing a hard day's work wasn't the career choice Zach had once wanted. For a time, he'd talked about going into law. But those days had long since evaporated, the dream going south in a sky filled with gray clouds.

"Have some more crackers," Chloe coaxed, setting the plate in front of him along with the cheese. Her inviting words took him out of his thoughts, but her next ones jerked him right back in.

Holding a cracker, she asked, "So, how are your kids doing?"

Thoughtful for a few moments, John shrugged. The

truth was the truth. "Kara started her senior year and I hope she can keep up with her assignments. So far, so good. And Zach…he's going through a tough time. He's misaligned. But we're trying to rebuild our relationship. It takes time."

John gazed at the distant rows of dormant rosebushes in the tea garden. Bare stems, but the thorns still able to prick.

"Time is okay," Chloe replied, "as long as you don't waste it."

"Yeah, I know." John thought about the start he'd made with his kids last Sunday over dinner. The conversation had gone fairly well, not without a few barbed shots, but good for the most part. Then, afterward, they'd taken in a movie at the downtown Edwards theater.

Tonight they planned to eat dinner at home. He had an idea for something to do when the meal was finished. He wasn't sure how it would be received, but he'd gotten everything set up all the same.

While he'd be trying to help them heal, his own emotional wounds would be reopened. But it would be worth it if he could help the kids turn the corner and really begin to get their lives back on track.

He'd just have to pray that the outcome would be positive.

Eating an olive, John gazed at Chloe and truly regarded her as more than a beautiful woman who had intrigued him and caught his attention.

He wondered what it would be like if she joined him at home one night. If they could all sit together at his dining table. Zach, Kara, him. And Chloe. Four of them. Dinner.

How would his kids react to that? He hadn't spoken real deeply with them about dating, but he had skimmed the surface to get their take on it. Neither were opposed to the idea. But neither said, "Yeah, Dad, go for it."

Time. In all things, time healed and could help. At least that's what he hoped.

Brown squirrels ran past, carrying nuts in their mouths. The trees, most of them now nearly bare, allowed sunshine to splay across Julia Davis Park.

If the breeze had calmed, the day would have been almost warm. But a light wind came in from the west, catching and twirling the leaves on the ground, touching and kissing Chloe's hair and giving it a soft billow.

"You'd like my grandmother," Chloe said with an impish grin. "I'd love for you to meet her."

"I want to," he found himself saying. He wanted to integrate himself into her life, however that may be.

"But we'll have to catch her when she's not busy. She met this man, and while she says he's nothing, I think he's something."

"Never too old to find love," John waxed poetic, something he never did. Where that sentiment had come from, he could only speculate.

"Yeah, soon-to-be forty doesn't mean I'm on death's door." Chloe's brows arched, her violet eyes animated. It hadn't struck him that he could be referring to her. To them. But he liked the idea that she had considered it. Even vaguely.

"I'm older than you, sweetheart, and I'm not going sour on the idea. In fact, I'm all for it."

A curve lifted Chloe's supple, pink mouth. A gorgeous vision. He wanted to kiss her again. And again. The sunlight played across her delicate features, and he was struck by just how amazing she was. Not only pretty, but also talented. Smart. Funny. Any man would be crazy not to fall for her.

He wanted only what was best for Chloe, and that spilled over to all things. Happiness, fortune, well-being. Contentment was something he would like to shower on her. He knew he could give her peace of mind if she would let him.

Broaching a subject that usually caused a rift between them, he had to ask, "So, have you given any thought to the 'obscene six figures,' Chloe?"

His query was more out of personal responsibility than a sense of business. He hoped she'd take it, do well, run with a success that that kind of money could initiate.

"I'm not sure," she replied. "I'm considering it."

He nodded, not willing to push. Not today. He thought that would be the end of the subject, but she went on. "I haven't taken the time to put down on paper the pros and cons to it. I've been a little frazzled. I…well, something happened that scared me."

Every knee-jerk reaction to a statement like that soared to life in him at the same time. The chivalrous part wanted to go after the problem before even knowing what it was. "What happened?"

"Someone left flowers for me, on my porch. And I don't know who did it."

"That's scary?" He uttered the response before thinking too deeply on it.

"Yes, considering the note said they still loved me...baby doll."

John felt as if the tip of a knife blade had pierced his side. While he had no exclusive claim to Chloe, he didn't like thinking about her dating other men. She may have a dozen in contention for her love that he didn't know about. Hell, she owed him nothing.

But one of those guys might have left her flowers.

Trying to keep an unaffected exterior, he said, "Maybe it was a guy you know."

"John," she said in a pragmatic tone, "I don't know any other guys. Not like that. I don't date. Or, rather, I haven't recently. The only one I know is you."

"Well, I didn't give you the flowers. A great thought, and I'd like to send you some, but I haven't. Not yet."

He felt as if he were rambling, something he rarely, if ever, did. But the whole situation tugged at him and he had to go into protection mode.

Flowers meant something to someone.

"Got any ideas who sent them?" he asked, an air of casualness in his voice.

"I thought I did, and I confronted him."

"Him who?" John interrogated, his jaw tight.

"Bobby-Tom."

The name evoked an acidy taste in John's mouth. "Your ex-husband?"

"The one and only. Yes, I all but accosted him at the hot-dog shack at Home Depot. I asked him about it. It wasn't him. I could usually spot him in a lie if he was stupid enough to tangle himself up in one. Bobby-Tom doesn't have the smarts to concoct anything elaborate. Nope, not him."

John took a moment to process her words. So she'd run into her ex, almost literally. A stab of jealousy nicked him. He wasn't prepared for its barb.

He'd had no real experience with jealousy. He and Connie's relationship had been so solid.

Maybe that had been part of the problem at times. He vowed if he ever remarried, he'd never take his wife for granted. Not for a single second. He'd cherish every moment, every minute with her, and love her so dearly. He knew firsthand that life was damn short.

Too short.

John leaned back on his elbows. "Has anyone been nosing around your house lately?"

"I don't think so. And the phone calls have stopped." Chloe ran a hand through her hair, absently fisting a ponytail, then letting the strands loose. "I don't know what to think. My life is crazy right now." She gave a soft sigh. "What a funny time to meet you."

Her smile spoke many things, with fondness and confusion mingled together. "I'm usually more with it."

"I think you're great. Just like you are."

She rolled her eyes, the smile still bracketing her lips. "You're just a nice man with nice words."

"Ouch. I've got more than nice words."

She reached out and playfully touched his cheek. "I know. Believe me, I do."

They finished eating and put away the picnic dishes, then walked toward his car.

After settling Chloe inside the BMW, then heading in the direction of her house, John said soberly, "Chloe, you really do need to think about the Garretson offer. And soon. He may renege on it and then you'd lose a lot of money."

"I understand," she replied, lines of worry marring her forehead. "I only have four months left on my lease and then I'm out. Garretson may very well say enough is enough and let things ride. I know that. But, John—" she turned his way "—it's the principle of the matter."

"Stop. Just ignore the reason and go with it."

"I don't know. My petition's been gathering steam. *The Statesman* article increased my business, and even caused some letters directed to the editor in favor of me and nixing Garretson's."

"That's great, but it's still not enough."

Contemplation worked over her features. "Maybe…" Then her face brightened. "But the news crews from Channel Seven came by yesterday and filmed the bakery. It's going to be on Monday night. You never know. Something great could happen because of it."

John slowly shook his head, unable to give her much of a frown. "You're such an optimist, Chloe. I think that's why I like you so much."

THE TELEVISION SCREEN cast a blue hue in the sparse room, the thin curtains drawn and only one bed lamp on over the full-size bed. Fried chicken procured from the Colonel gave the small space a slightly greasy odor. The cramped studio apartment couldn't be called any kind of fancy, but it had come fully furnished and was kept relatively clean by the occupant.

Body tense with anticipation, one couldn't take much more of the suspense. The dumb channel kept airing teasers for the story before each commercial break. Upcoming. Upcoming next. Shup-coming*ing! Geez, Louise.* The story was supposed to broadcast any second.

Then—there *she* was!

Didn't she look beautiful? So pretty…so…

Baby doll.

Tears filled the viewer's eyes, the chicken dinner forgotten.

The newscaster began her introduction, with Chloe standing right beside her—looking as sweet as one of her cakes, wearing an apron and with her hair in stylish curls.

"Chloe Lawson of Not Just Cakes has built a small business into one that her faithful customers say is just what was needed in the Grove Marketplace. But is her ingenuity too much for the progress of Boise's best grocery baron, Bob Garretson?"

Only half listening to the story, tears welled and it felt as if an elephant were crushing the life breath to death.

If there was a prouder moment, it couldn't be named.

And if there was any doubt about going through with things, in that moment, seeing Chloe on the TV, it had been squashed like a June bug.

CHAPTER SEVENTEEN

JOHN BROUGHT DINNER home from Pomodoro in a thick foil pan. All he had to do was reheat it in the oven. Ziti with tender meatballs in a marinara sauce, a favorite dish of his kids. He'd bought a loaf of Italian bread, butter and a bagged salad with fresh Roma tomatoes and a cucumber. Robert had also packaged up the restaurant's house dressing, fine olive oil and vinegar seasoned with herbs. John tossed the salad with the tangy mix.

Zach was in his room, listening to music while sorting through the mile-high pile of dirty laundry he'd accumulated from the week. Both his children had learned how to operate the washer and dryer after Connie's death. John had taught them that responsibility.

Kara was late. Her cell had gone straight to voice mail when he'd tried it. It meant she was on the other line and ignoring his call. Not nice.

John set the dining table with plates and cups. He didn't want to eat at the breakfast bar where he couldn't make eye contact with the kids.

The timer went off for the ziti just as Kara came in through the garage door, cell phone to her ear, and her loud voice in what John called Valley Girl mode.

"I *know!*" she emphasized with a widening of her eyes as she walked into the room while he set the hot dinner on the side table. "Marissa's such a *be-atch.*"

John knew the slang for bitch, raised his brows at his daughter, only to have her frown at him and continue her dialogue.

Kara flopped sideways onto the leather living-room chair, her legs dangling over the chair's arm. She wore jeans and a fur-lined Abercrombie & Fitch zip-up sweatshirt. Even though it was October, she still lived in flip-flops, her toenails painted pink. "I don't know how she can even have a boyfriend. He's prob'ly cheating on her."

Motioning with his hand for his daughter to wrap things up, John went to the top of the stairs and called for his son to join them. No answer through the loud bass of blaring music. He had to walk downstairs and knock firmly on his son's door.

No reply.

John opened the door, finding the laundry still strewn all over the carpet, and Zach reclining on an unmade bed, reading a Hunter S. Thompson book.

At least he was reading.

Zach looked up.

"Dinner," John said, not commenting on the laundry. His son could do it on his own time or else wear something dirty.

"Yeah, okay."

Back in the kitchen, John brought the hot dinner to the table as Kara, who'd set her purse and cell phone on the counter, sniffed the aroma of garlic and basil.

"Yum," she said with a dreamy smile. "Uncle Robert's ziti. Just as good as Grandma's. Do you know when she's coming home?"

Mariangela Moretti had finally taken her Italy trip and had been spending time with her aunt Romilda. "I think next week."

"Can we go to Italy one day, Dad?"

"I'd like that." And John sincerely meant it. Taking his two kids to Italy would be great.

Zach joined them and John sat everyone down. They passed plates in his direction so he could serve.

John began to talk, "So how was everyone's week?"

"I hate my job, but I need the money. Want to give me some, Daddy?" Kara's voice purred. She only called him Daddy when she wanted something. The endearment flooded his memories of a cute-as-a-button, dark-haired little girl riding on her tricycle up and down the block.

"Dad gives you plenty of money," Zach said, forking a noodle. "Look at the clothes he buys you."

John broke in. "Correction. I pay for them. I don't buy them. Kara goes shopping without me." Buttering a slice of bread, he said as a reminder, "And I buy some of your clothes, too."

"Yeah, not too hard to buy some jeans and T-shirts. I'm a basic dude."

"Basic or not, they're still paid for and you're nineteen years old, buddy. When I was in high school, Grandpa Giovanni had me working all summer framing buildings for him and saving up to buy my own stuff."

"I've gotta do that, too."

"But you're older. I moved out when I was nineteen to go to college."

"I told you I didn't want to go."

"I understand. That's why you still live at home. And I'm cool with it as long as you don't get into trouble. Which, as far as I know, you haven't all week."

Zach shrugged, but added in an obligatory tone, "Thanks for everything and whatever else. And, no, I didn't get into trouble." A bite of food hovered in front of his open mouth, but he stopped to say, "Wait, does a parking ticket count?"

John stifled his groan. "That's going to cost you."

"Yeah, I know. It's my third one in the same spot. The meter runs out before I can put more quarters in it."

"Then why do you park in that spot?"

"I dunno."

"Zach, use the parking garage."

"No way. *Beaucoup dinero,* man. I'll take my chances with the meter."

While his children drank sweetened iced tea with their meal, John swallowed the last of his Chianti, needing the relaxing agent the red wine offered. Sometimes he wanted to take Zach by the shoulders and shake him.

"So, things aren't great at the mall, Kara?" John asked, desiring a conversation no matter how mundane it felt.

"I don't know. I guess it's all right. I get discounts on makeup, but still. None of my other friends have to work to buy the extra things."

"Kara, your extra things aren't necessary."

"Yeah, huh, they are."

"Like what? That purse? What'd it cost you?"

She glanced at the designer purse on the counter, stuffed to the gills with a wallet to match, cosmetics and who knew what else. "I can't remember."

"You don't remember or you won't tell me?"

She didn't reply.

John added more salad to his plate. "And if you want to buy such expensive things, you have to earn the money yourself. Otherwise, you'll never learn how to be on your own. Perhaps you need to manage your money better."

"But my friends don't have to," she whined with exasperation.

"Then they aren't being taught a good work ethic," John said. In contemplation, he continued the discussion. "How are your grades, Kara? If they're bad, then I don't want you working."

"I'm getting Bs. An A in debate and a D in math. I hate math. You know that. But the A makes the D really a B average."

"Does not," Zach said, his hair falling over his brows. "An A and a D make a C."

"You're so lame, Zach." She made a face at her brother.

While most parents would have frowned on a sibling squabble at the table, John relished every moment. The times of having both of his children home at the same time, and joining him, could be counted on one hand.

Concerned, John said, "Bring your math book home and I can check it for you. I got pretty decent grades in that subject."

"I'm good," his daughter replied, brushing off his offer. "I can ask my teacher to help me."

"But will you?"

"I said I would."

"Saying and doing are two different things, Kara."

"Dad, I said I would. Geez."

Cutting off an exasperated sigh, John changed the subject. "How're things going at the job site, Zach?"

"I dunno." Then a jocular glint filled his brown eyes. "Uncle Mark got so pissed Monday morning when the electricians bailed to go elk hunting. They never showed the rest of the week. Their floor didn't get trimmed out."

John could imagine his brother blowing a gasket about that.

Without Giovanni at the helm, Mark's duties as the project superintendent intensified, with Francesca doing double overtime as the architect and working in the trailer to hammer out detailed problems. In a way, John wished he could work with them on the Grove Marketplace, but he knew that his field was law. He'd enjoyed the challenges many of his cases presented, and he'd always been comfortable behind a desk.

Thankfully dinner fell into an easygoing span of time, one that John had dearly missed. It was the little things about their lives that he took for granted, and was glad they were able to share them, no matter how trivial.

Kara's phone burped constant text-message chimes, and when she'd moved to answer the first one, John had told her to keep her butt planted in the chair. She'd glared at him. So much for being "Daddy." When her brother laughed, Kara stuck out her tongue.

And that's when he saw *it*.

"Kara, what in the hell is that?" John blurted, shock running through him like a strong current, even making his fingernails tingle. He rarely swore, and never at the dinner table.

"Nothing," she quickly denounced, slumping in her chair.

When his gaze remained steadily affixed to her mouth, she began to squirm.

"It's not that big of a deal, Dad. Geez…"

"Let me see your tongue, Kara."

She stuck it out briefly, just long enough for him to take in the tiny ball that had pierced his little girl's tongue.

Good Lord above. John wanted to break something. "Kara, how could you do that to yourself?"

"I didn't. I had it done."

"The belly-button piercing was bad enough. And you're not eighteen so you'd need my consent on this, so how did you manage to ruin yourself without my permission?"

"I'm not ruined," she sassed, flicking her long hair over her shoulder. "And I know of a place that you don't need a consent."

"Great. Everything in there is probably germ central."

Zach, who'd been quietly chomping on a bread crust, held one corner in his hand, and talked with his mouth full. "VeeJay had his tongue pierced and it got infected. Pus city, man."

Kara shivered. "Zach, shut up. You lie half the time about everything."

"I do not."

Rising from the table, John went to pour himself another glass of wine. What had started out promising, now turned ugly. He sat down and thought about what he should do.

Looking pointedly at his daughter, he decreed, "I want you to take that thing out of your tongue before bed, and if I see it in there tomorrow, you'll be on full house arrest. No more mall employment. School and home. That's it. I'll take you myself and sit here if I have to just to make sure you're home."

He swallowed half of the Chianti in a single gulp, his insides trembling. He hated to give threats, but he meant it.

A deathly silence, much like a funeral hall, passed over the room and nobody moved or said a word. The air grew heavy. The occupants at the table hardly blinked.

John composed himself externally, but inside he fought an army of chaos. His emotions collided, his heart…broken. How had it come to this? Tattoos, body-piercings. He'd raised his kids better. Connie would turn over in her grave.

Kara broke the grey spell. "Can I be excused?"

Snapping from his thoughts, John replied, "Huh?

Um, no. I have something else. I'll clean this up later. Come into the family room."

He rose on wooden legs, trying to get stability back in them. If he hadn't been broadsided by the tongue piercing, this would have been the time where he was filled with anticipation. Instead, he began to question his choice.

But as soon as he did, he quelled the notion.

John had come to realize that during the past three years, he'd gone about things wrong. With good intentions, he'd consulted with professional people, none of whom his children had connected with and formed a trusting bond. The counselors knew nothing about turning things around with his family. He'd even had discussions—sometimes arguments—with his own parents about how to raise Zach and Kara.

Three years and nothing had worked.

Finally, John realized that he hadn't gone to the one person he could always count on. The one person who'd known his every dream and fear, who'd encouraged him and supported him. Someone his children had looked up to and loved unconditionally.

Both kids stood in the family room, neither sitting, as if they feared repercussions for even plopping on the sofas.

With one word, John told them, "Sit."

They ended up on the love seat together, and he on the large sectional sofa alone. Aiming the clicker at the flat-screen television, he punched the appropriate remote controls for the video player.

He'd planned ahead, found what he'd wanted in the tape, then set it up to begin at just the right place.

The picture came into view, the sound clear as if it had been captured yesterday.

Connie's lovely face, her infectious smile, her laughter, filled the enormous room and its vaulted ceiling. It was like an angel had arrived in the room.

His departed wife's image was on the televison. His children didn't move, fixated on the screen and watching.

There she was. At the happiest place on earth. Disneyland. Standing in front of Sleeping Beauty's castle. Connie talked about how John had been her Prince Charming. Animated in her motions with bows and curtseys, she'd embellished upon the story of how he had proposed.

Connie Moretti had been in her midthirties when the footage had been filmed on a camcorder, the summer Zach turned ten and Kara eight. They'd taken a week-long vacation to California, visiting Disneyland, Sea World and the San Diego Zoo.

The camera panned slightly right to the alcove overlooking the water under the castle drawbridge. Kara, her hair cut like a China doll's, hung her lanky arms over the side, trying to attract the ducks. To her left, Zach stood on the bench, pretending to wield an invisible sword. He'd gotten his usual summer buzz cut, the tips of his ears looking a little sunburned. In the background, the fantasy sounds of the park sang sweetly to Connie's story.

Kara said in a broken whisper, "I remember Mom's

blouse. It had Mickey Mouse on the buttons. She made it herself."

John's throat tightened, also recalling the hours his wife had put in at the sewing machine, making Kara a Minnie Mouse canvas purse, and Zach a Pirates of the Caribbean pillow to use in the car.

Stoic in expression, Zach blinked slowly. Once. Then twice. And finally rapidly. Widening his eyes, he cleared his throat.

"I remember how Mom went on Big Thunder like ten times in a row," Zach commented, his mouth curving in a vague smile.

"And I almost puked," Kara added, sniffing. "She liked roller coasters, huh, Daddy?"

"Yep," he said, tears burning the backs of his eyelids.

"And, Princess Kara," Connie cheerfully said, "is the best little girl in the entire world! She and I are going to pick out a Cinderella Barbie at the Mattel store by It's a Small World. Aren't we, honey?"

Kara's grin beamed brightly. *"Yes, Mommy. The one with the blue sparkle dress. I love you, Mommy."*

"I love you, too!" Seeing Zach, Connie moved to give his legs a hug before he jumped off his pretend horse and plopped right next to her. *"Should we get you a Pirate Ken?"* Her laughter contained a heavy dose of mischief.

Zach winkled his nose. *"I want one of those rubber snakes from Adventure Land."*

"A rubber snake. Okay. You got it, Zach-attack. Love you, son. I'm so glad you're my boy."

"I'm not a boy, Mom. I'm a pirate!" Zach gave an impression of one of the pirates from the Caribbean ride, shouting out a string of "Arghs."

"Are you going to be a pirate when you grow up, Zach?"

"Yes!"

Kara shouted out, *"And I'm going to be a princess, Mommy!"*

"And you'll be the prettiest one ever!"

The three of them, battling scarred emotions, watched Connie hamming it up for the camera at Disneyland—talking, smiling, laughing. History embedded for all time. Then at Sea World, and riding the walkway at the San Diego Zoo.

There were moments of her sitting on the beach, giving John a wink. The kids making sand castles. The video ended with a tender moment. Mother and children, hand in hand, running into the surf, the sunset ebbing into the Pacific Ocean.

When John turned the television off, both Kara and Zach were crying. He felt pretty choked up, too. Not so much for the loss of his wife, but for the innocence his children had lost because their mother had been taken away from them. His motives for putting the movie on had been to remind them that they were loved. Deeply. Unconditionally. Not only by their mother, but by their father. And it was just the three of them now.

"Zach…Kara," he said, his voice shaky, "we can make Mom proud of us. She's watching what we do, blessing us from heaven. I love you both so very, v-very…much."

His voice cracked and he could no longer keep the tears from falling. And before he consciously knew what was happening, he was flanked on either side, being hugged by children he had long since thought he'd lost.

In those heartbeats and tears, came hope.

HE NEVER SHOULD have kissed her.

Walden Griffiths paced in front of his shop-front window, the odors of fine tobacco wafting in the air. The gloomy day put a chill in his bones, the autumn skies heavy with impending rain.

With yet another glance across the street, he still hadn't made up his mind whether or not to go over to Ethel's Boutique.

It had been a week ago today that he'd made a move on Ethel and planted a kiss on her dear mouth.

Big mistake, fella, he chided.

She'd avoided him like a plate of salmonella ever since. If ever a mission had gone sour, he'd really pulled the rip cord on this one.

This morning, the commercial glass company had replaced her front window. She'd stepped onto the sidewalk, without so much as a how-do-you-do in the direction of The Humidor. Talking with the installation guy and signing the paperwork, she seemed bent on not even fluttering a lash Walden's way.

That had really chafed. Especially since the paperwork then came directly over to him and he'd written a check for the grand total. Just like he'd promised Ethel he'd do.

Perhaps he should have come clean about his foul-up sooner, but what man didn't fudge a little…or omit the truth, every now and then?

He was no dang saint.

Ruffling his hair, Walden stopped to select a cigar to smoke. Tobacco was against doctor's orders, but what was the harm in one or two? Or three puffs?

Running his gaze over his inventory, he chose a fine Brazilian cigar, darker in color, but slightly sweeter in taste. Lighting up, he relished the distinct flavors, savoring the mellow curls of smoke over his tongue.

Apollo sprawled across the cash-register counter, tail lazily switching to and fro, eyes at half-mast in drowsy contentment.

Now there was a sight. A domestic cat never had a worry. Free room and board. All the chow you could eat. Even a toilet inside the house. Never even the need to hunt down a mouse for supper when there was Friskies in the bowl.

Walden approached the window once more, and wondered, for the umpteenth time, what he should do about Ethel.

Up until this point in his life, he hadn't much considered his future as a bachelor. First there had been the move to Boise, then his energies put into getting The Humidor up and running. Beyond that, he hadn't plotted a flight chart to the moon in terms of the rest of his life.

He'd just figured he'd see where his ship took him and who'd he'd meet along the way. Never thought it would be a woman with flame-red hair and opinions as big as the lunar spaceship.

That woman had more spit in her than a desert camel. His Fanny had been a very quiet, genteel woman. Never rose her voice or had an argumentative bone in her body. He'd done most of the talking during their marriage, and all of the decision-making. That had just been how it was done.

The only time she'd had a snit was when he'd been drinking. And for that, God love her heart, he could find no blame. He'd been a horrible husband during the bottle years, and his sweetheart had obediently put up with more than she should have. Had he been her, he would have kicked himself to the curb.

Walden had come a long way, learned a lot about himself, but he'd begun to mull over the fact that maybe he didn't know squat about women. He'd only lived with one nearly his whole life, but Ethel…she was a different type of hen.

Apollo yawned, laid down and closed his eyes. Dead to the world and not a care to be reckoned with.

Now that Walden felt good enough to reopen his shop, he hadn't anticipated the restless energy that would follow. Suddenly, the days seemed too long, the nights even longer.

What had begun as an outlet to fill his time, now seemed a little on the stifling side.

He took a draw on his cigar, smoke curling in the air. Maybe his doldrums came because he wasn't supposed to sample the inventory anymore. Or maybe because he'd felt poorly for the past couple of weeks.

Or maybe because of the dang medicine he now had to take. And the barrage of tests that didn't seem to be too conclusive about anything.

From the corner of his eye, Walden caught a glimpse of a woman wearing a coat. Red alert. Ethel on the sidewalk. She was leaving the boutique, her pocketbook dangling from the crook of her arm.

Without a moment to lose, he stubbed out his cigar and boldly exited the store and made a beeline for her. Much easier to talk with her on the street, which had been his dilemma from the get-go. He could have easily stormed right into that dress gallery of hers and said a how-do-you-do. But not after that last time.

Lord knew that a man going into one of those ladies shops with unmentionables on full display shortened the hang of his apparatus. A guy just didn't need to come face-to-face with women's undergarments this way, big lacy cups and large undies and whatnot. Took the mystic out of it all.

That last time he'd nearly crossed the threshold into all that fluff, he realized he would have been a goner. Had he entered her boutique the day he'd moseyed over and introduced himself for the first time, he could have been seriously unmanned.

"Ethel!" Walden called just as she turned the corner.

The bite of the fall air cut through his sweater and the sleeved T-shirt beneath. He hadn't thought to grab a coat himself. The chill seeped into his jeans, but not into his head. His Stetson had hung on a peg beside the door, and he'd grabbed it on the run.

"Hello, Walden," she said, eyes looking more beautiful than he recalled. "How are you feeling?"

"Dandy as can be."

"That's good to hear." She lingered a moment, as if unsure what to say. Then, "Thanks for replacing my window."

"Sure. No problem. Should've done it sooner. Sorry about that."

"It's all right."

Then glancing at her shoes, she finally lifted her chin. "Well, I've got to get to the bank to make a deposit."

"Nice day for a walk," he said, just to make conversation. The truth of the matter was, the cold settled uncomfortably in his old joints.

"It's cold as all get out and I don't like it," Ethel countered, then immediately winced, as if biting her tongue. "I'm sorry. I know I should have more control over my big mouth. Husband number one always said that I—well, never mind what he said. And I'm sorry about the bird feeder and all that. And the wine."

"Ethel, dear, no problem a'tall," he immediately said, his hand touching her coat sleeve. "It's me who owes you an apology. I never should have kissed you. I should have courted you and given you your due respect. I had no right."

"I haven't known what to say to you," she confessed. "It's not that I haven't wanted to talk to you. I haven't had luck in keeping a man around and I'm gun-shy about the whole thing. I'm a sworn bachelorette—um, thrice divorced, you know."

"I don't know why you'd want to keep yourself on the shelf. You've got a nice package, Ethel."

She blushed. "I'm too set in my ways, Walden. I think I'd probably kill the life out of you."

"Seems with my head being whacked out, my life could be gone tomorrow. Why waste today?"

"Don't say such a thing!"

"But it's the truth." Walden settled his big hands on her wool-covered shoulders. Her red hair sure brightened up the day, even a cloudy one. "I'd like to get to know you better."

"I don't think you'll like the end result."

"Where's this coming from? You're a very dear woman."

For the first time since laying eyes on her, he saw a shadow of worry cross her features.

"I don't want to get married again."

"I'm not asking you."

"Not right now, but I have that effect on men. They marry me."

"I'd hope so. You seem a fine catch."

"I don't have a very good track record." Her point was uttered with half a sigh. "I was doing just fine on my own, never a thought about a man—not really, and now…" She groaned. "I can't stop thinking about you. I'm ruined. My ship has sunk. I've been…smitten by the romance bug and I…"

Walden couldn't stop grinning. She wasn't adverse to him after all, it was her own doubting mind that had kept her at bay.

He gave her no chance to say another word and

plunged right in with an offer of a date. "Say, Ethel, how about we take in the organ concert at the Egyptian this Friday night?"

"Organ concert?" She appeared as if she'd sucked on a lemon wedge. "But…aren't they rather…uh, stale?"

"I thought you might enjoy some music."

After a standoff, one in which he thought he'd lose because she was so quiet, she finally said, "I know of a piano bar and the music is divine. They do sell spirits, but quite the good cup of fine-roasted coffee. And there's dancing, too."

"Waltz or tango?"

"Both, and the fox-trot. The whole shebang," she countered.

Nodding, he gave her a bright smile. "I'll dust off my dancing shoes."

CHAPTER EIGHTEEN

THE CLOCK TICKED inexorably on for Chloe, and she knew time was against her. No matter what small scale she fought on, the grander one seemed destined to prevail. Her full-steam-ahead petition had petered to lukewarm. As many signatures as she had, they weren't enough to garner sympathy with city hall.

The feature article in the newspaper had boosted sales, and her coverage on the television brought in more customers, but the war went relatively unchanged. Sales climbed as the battle fell short of her goal.

Dismal facts had jumped out at her when she'd received her mail today and opened the official letter from the leasing company outlining the terms of her departure in February.

She was to vacate the premises by midnight on the last day of that month, taking her equipment with her. And she had to leave the rental space—albeit with her tenant improvements—just as she had found it. Nearly all signs of the lovely little bakery would be gone, as if she hadn't ever been here.

"Penny for your thoughts," Ethel said, breaking into Chloe's musings.

They were drinking creamed coffee together in Chloe's office at the bakery. Ethel had made an unexpected visit at seven in the morning. The boutique didn't open for business until ten. It had been awhile since Ethel had made an impromptu coffee stop.

Pleased, Chloe had invited her in, poured two cups and they'd secreted themselves off into Chloe's tiny office. The desk was rarely cleaned off, smudges of icing sometimes along the edges. The plant on the filing cabinet hung on by a thread, Chloe forgetting to water it more often than not.

With a sigh, Chloe said, "It's finally sinking in that I really have to move Not Just Cakes."

"But you don't have to," Ethel replied, her eyes widened. "I say fight, team, fight." She even pumped her fist.

Chloe half smiled. "I'm not a team. I'm just me."

"And a very grand 'me' if there was one."

"Thanks, Ethel."

Opening her desk drawer, Chloe produced several ads for commercial rentals. "I've been circling some alternative locations. One's in Hyde Park. It might have some potential." She showed her grandmother the building's sketch and interior layout. "With the remuneration I'd get from Garretson's, I could build a sitting area here. Not so grand as I wanted to do, but functional."

Ethel tsked. "I'm sorry you have to change your dreams for someone else's."

"I'm not changing my dream, just the road to reach it." Chloe shoved the papers aside, the smells of

Bavarian cake filling the air in a rich and delicious scent.

Inside the large kitchen, Candace and Jenny baked in the early hours.

Chloe slid the rest of the unopened mail aside. "I talked to John Moretti yesterday afternoon and I told him I'm going to take Garretson's early buyout. We're meeting on Monday to talk about the paperwork."

"Are you sure?"

"No. But the stress is packing pounds back on me. I worked so hard to lose those stinkin' eleven pounds. Now I'm nibbling on the cakes again. Five pounds have hopped a ride back on my butt."

Ethel's laughter was robust. "You aren't fat, Chloe. And your butt is very cute."

"Bah." Chloe frowned, drinking her coffee and enjoying the cream and sugar she'd stirred into it. Not wanting to think about her weight gain, Chloe gave Ethel a long stare.

With a twinkle of knowing in her eyes, she inquired after her grandmother's love life. "Tell me what's going on with you and your astronaut."

Ethel's face pinched. "He's not *my* astronaut. For heaven's sake, you'll have us bound for the altar."

"I didn't even remotely imply that. You told me you were done with weddings."

· "And I meant it."

"Well, you don't have to convince me." Chloe winked, her grin crooked. "Sounds like you have to convince yourself." Leaning into her chair, she steepled her fingers. "How's his recovery coming?"

"Dandy. He sees the doctor today."

"Nice. He tells you personal information." Chloe's teasing spirit helped alleviate the stresses she felt in her own life.

"No," Ethel admonished. "I don't know his personal dealings. I just happened to know about this because he asked me if I could mind his shop for an hour while he's up at St. Luke's."

Still smiling, Chloe asked, "You're going to sell cigars?"

"I can sell dresses," Ethel protested. "What's there to selling rolled-up tobacco leaves?"

"I think there's a small—" Chloe raised her fingers and made a visual example of them almost coming together "—difference."

"Well, most anyone who goes into Buzz's store knows what he wants anyway. All I have to do is take the money and ring up the sale."

Finishing her coffee, Chloe brushed a piece of dark lint from her white sweater. "So when are you going out on an official date?"

"Did he tell you something?" Ethel blurted. Her reaction was so quick, she sloshed some of her coffee over the cup's rim.

Taken slightly aback, Chloe shrugged. "An educated guess?"

"Don't get so smugly-wugly. It's nothing. Nothing at all. We're going to hear some music tonight."

"Music." Chloe nodded, biting on the inside of her lip to keep from driving her grandmother nuts with more inquiries. She could tell a con when she heard one.

Ethel Lumm was lovesick.

"What kind?" Chloe asked.

"Listening music."

"Where?"

"Now, Chloe, I don't have to play twenty questions with you on everything that I do." Standing, Ethel put herself together swiftly. A thrust of her arms inside her coat and a quick collection of her black leather purse. "There's nothing wrong with two friends listening to piano music."

Grinning, Chloe asked, "Piano bar, huh?"

"Never you mind."

Ethel dutifully patted Chloe's shoulder, then departed the bakery with a whoosh of cool air that she could feel all the way inside her office.

Shaking her head fondly, Chloe went to work.

The day seemed to stretch out forever, something that Chloe rarely experienced at the bakery. She usually loved the long hours, the meticulous attention to detail and the time spent building cakes.

But this evening wasn't just any Friday night, and the thought of what was to come had distracted her more than she cared to let herself admit.

John had invited her to his house for dinner. He was picking her up at six. A huge step in their relationship, as he'd mentioned his children might drop in and she could meet them. Thankfully, he hadn't set up anything formal. She didn't know if she was ready for that. Casual was better. If his son or daughter happened to be home, she'd love to say hello. But the thought of sitting down to a dinner was somewhat nerve-racking.

What if his kids didn't like her?

The possibility made her afraid. If that were the case, she'd have to tell John it was best they didn't continue to see each other. His children came first, as they should. Inside, Chloe really did want them to find favor in her. She was ready to make friends.

Then again, from the hazy picture John had painted, he had difficulties with his children these days and adding a girlfriend to the mix might prove too tricky.

Not overly pondering the scenario, Chloe had to let it be what it would be. She was excited to have John cook for her. That would be a real treat. He'd warned he wasn't polished in the kitchen, but could grill a mean steak. That worked for her.

She'd offered to bring a dessert. Marbled pumpkin cheesecake that she'd taken out of the oven after lunch today. The spicy smells had made her mouth water.

By three o'clock, when she decided she'd done what she could, and was near exhaustion, she packed it up. She had three hours to get ready. Time to walk Boo-Bear, soak in the tub, wash her hair and apply makeup.

Getting into her car, she shuddered at her appearance. The kitchen whites she'd put on fresh this morning were stained with frosting colors, and a slop of jelly from a jellyroll. Her hair, which she'd had cut recently to frame her face a little more, had been pulled into a ponytail long before noon. Since the style had more layering to it, pieces fell out of the pony, and wisps framed her cheeks.

She'd wrapped herself in her favorite coat, a forest-green car-coat she'd bought at a yard sale on her block. The garment dated back to the '60s, but it had appealed to her.

She normally didn't buy used clothes, but the coat had reminded her of one that Wanda had worn in one of the few photos Chloe kept of her mother—in a shoe box on the top shelf of her closet. Not that there was sentimental value to what her mother had attired herself in; it was just that the coat had been really cool and Chloe had liked it.

Every once in a while, Chloe would take the shoe box down and sift through the photos. She didn't have that many, so much of her childhood recollections depended on her memory versus a photo. There were moments when Chloe wished she could remember what her first or second birthday cake looked like. She'd always thought it would be fun to re-create a special "I'm 1!" cake for her shop—a whimsical reproduction of a 1960s cake that would appeal to a new audience.

But Chloe couldn't remember if the cake had been vanilla or chocolate, or had white frosting or whatever else. Ethel didn't know. At the time, Chloe and Wanda hadn't lived in Boise. From what Ethel knew about Wanda, they'd lived in a trailer park in Albany, Oregon. From there, they'd moved to Portland, then Bend, Oregon. For a time, they'd lived in Montana. Then Wyoming. Chloe had a very vague memory of sitting on a draft horse with a string-bean cowboy helping her onto the saddle. She had no clue who he was, or why she'd been there on that horse.

When Wanda left, Chloe slowly forgot about where she'd been and with whom. One good thing had been ending up in Boise as she went through puberty. If Ethel hadn't clued her in, Chloe might well have been clueless about a lot of things. But having her grandma nearby for those junior-high years had been a godsend.

With her white tennis shoes smudged, Chloe accelerated down the street and passed the Grove Marketplace. Zach stood on the corner holding the handle of a red-and-white lunch pail. He wore a quilted, blue flannel shirt, the hemline rippling in the breeze. The hard hat he always plopped down on her bakery counter was tucked under his arm.

She waved, and he waved back with a chagrined look on his face. Something in the way he motioned, told her he didn't have a ride. Again.

Keep going, Chloe, you're on a time crunch.

It must have been in the high thirties with the wind chill. The day was ugly with impending winter not too far around the corner. She'd hate to be standing outside.

Three hours to get ready. Hair, makeup…the dog.

But she found herself pulling over to the curb where Zach stood.

Chloe punched the button to lower the driver's window. "How are you?"

"Okay."

"You need a ride?" she questioned.

"I was supposed to hop a ride with a guy who works the twelfth floor, but he must have bailed on me. I dunno where he is. I've been standing out here for twenty freakin' minutes. It's cold."

A breath of frigid air had sucked the heat right out of her car's heater. She shivered.

Glancing at the clock on her car's console, she already knew that taking him home would cut forty minutes off her time to get ready. So much for a lingering bath. "Get in. I'll give you a ride."

"Hey, thanks."

She drove the same route as he'd directed her before, winding toward the foothills.

"My car's really in the shop this time," he said, slouching down on the passenger seat, his lunch bucket and hat between his long legs.

"This time?" she replied, recalling that he'd said his car was in the shop last time. The statement made her wonder if he fibbed.

"Yeah, well. I hated to say my dad copped the keys from me that day. He was pissed about something I did. I can't even recall what it was. Something stupid."

"Ah," she commented, not sure what else to say.

"Now my truck's really fried. Bad alternator. My dad couldn't get it jump-started for me this morning so we knew it was blown."

The thought of the father finally stepping up to the plate and giving his son some time encouraged Chloe. "That was nice of your dad to help you out."

"Yeah. He's trying."

"Trying is good for something."

"It's okay."

Turning into the stately entrance to Quail Ridge, she thought about the oodles of big money clustered in this one neighborhood. Palatial houses, luxury cars, foreign nannies walking babies in buggies. She'd never earn enough to live this lifestyle, not even sure she wanted to.

On an impulse, she asked, "What does everyone do for their jobs in this neighborhood?"

"Lots of corporate guys."

The thought struck her that Bob Garretson may well live right in this subdivision. She shuddered.

"Presidents of banks, prob'ly." Zach motioned for her to make the correct turn on his street. "Lawyers, I guess. That's what my dad does."

Chloe pondered that tidbit. She wondered if Zach's dad knew John Moretti.

As she angled her car into the wide and curving driveway, Zach said, "Thanks for the ride."

He got out and walked toward the massive front doors. The home was truly impressive, sprawling, rich, beyond anything she'd ever imagined herself living in.

Poor kid. All this money, and he and his father were at odds. Just like how her and Wanda had been. Money didn't change a thing. And when she'd been a little girl, she'd always thought if Wanda had a steady job, they'd be okay. But at least from the way Zach talked, his father was making a marginal effort. Better late than never, even for royal jerks.

Another notation of the time said that if she hurried, she could iron her favorite gold-toned blouse and wear that tonight. She wanted to make a good first impression, just in case his children did pop in for a quick hello and—

A sleek BMW pulled in behind her, blocking her

exit. Looking over her shoulder, she froze when she recognized the driver.

John sat behind the wheel.

"CAN I POUR YOU more wine?" John asked, gazing at her empty wineglass.

She'd already had one glass. In less than five minutes. In the time it took for her to figure out that Zach's jerk of a father was her date for this evening. She put together the pieces while looking her most hideous, convinced that this evening she would *not* be making a good impression.

Zach, already in the house when Chloe backed out, remained clueless to the scene in the driveway. Thankfully, he hadn't shown up in the living room for a "formal" introduction.

Staring into her empty glass, Chloe conceded the red wine had a calming effect that had hit her almost immediately. She'd needed it. And more.

"Please," she replied, sitting stiffly on his leather living-room sofa, praying she wouldn't get it dirty with her soiled work clothes. A glance at her stain-spotted tennis shoes and she wanted to cringe.

So this was what total humiliation felt like.

John refilled her glass, then set the bottle on the square center table. He sat opposite her on a plush chair, his forearms resting on his thighs, lean fingers loosely knit together. A white dress shirt fit him perfectly, his black trousers an expensive cut. She knew quality when she saw it.

Even from afar, she could smell his woodsy

cologne while she, on the other hand, smelled like shortening.

He came home from work looking like a male model. She left her bakery as if she'd spent ten minutes in her commercial mixer. Clothes stained, unkempt, and only wanting to get into her car and head home.

She would have done so had the BMW not boxed her in. John had quit the engine on his car, come around to hers and asked her if he'd mistaken their arrangement this evening.

She'd told him she had no way of knowing his address, and the whole reason she'd been in his driveway…an odd coincidence.

Begging off his invitation to come inside hadn't worked. He'd insisted that since she was there, she stay and tell him how she just happened to be at his residence. John had opened her car door and guided her into the grandiose home.

Now sitting in his living room, she'd yet to confess the details.

"So how'd you end up this way?" John's handsome face had a way of distracting her, of making her wonder if she'd been mistaken about Zach's disgust with his absentee father.

But one glass of wine had allowed her enough time to put two and two together. John had admitted to her that his home life had been less than stellar since his wife had passed away. He'd taken a little of the blame, but also had laid it at his son's feet. Same went to his daughter, whom Chloe hoped wouldn't make an appearance tonight.

She wondered what part of the house Zach had disappeared to. Hoping he wouldn't suddenly appear, making an awkward situation even more so.

Biting her lip, Chloe saw no way other than the truth. "I gave your son a ride home from his job site." She gave a nervous laugh. "Small world."

Hurt and betrayal washed over his features. "You've known my son all this time and you never told me?"

Countering that suggestion quickly, she replied defensively, "I had no clue. I knew one of my customers was having a tough time at home with his father, but I didn't put that together with you. You've only mentioned your children by name a handful of times, and not even that would have connected the dots for me. Zach is a fairly common name for boys. And Kara…now if I'd talked to a Kara at my bakery, for sure I'd ask if her father's name was John. But that didn't happen, so I thought Zach was someone else's Zach."

She was rambling, she knew, but with everything going on in her life, and the hundreds of customers she served, she really hadn't made the connection between Zach and John. Lots of people moaned about things in their lives to her, and she usually smiled and suggested a heavy dose of sugar to cheer them up.

"I don't know…" she said, her thoughts trailing. "Maybe you did mention enough personal information to me that I should have figured it out. But I didn't."

John remained stoic, his own agenda clearly darkening his hooded eyes. "So my son told you I was a bad dad." No question marked his words, rather, they were expressed as a blunt statement.

Chloe wanted the floor to swallow her. This conversation was proving difficult and highly uncomfortable. She'd never foreseen it in a million years.

"Not in so many words."

"But in a couple words."

"Yes, but remember, you also told me that there were some difficulties."

He inhaled, straightening and leaning into the chair's back. Deep in thought, he remained quiet. His gaze left her and focused on the large wall of windows that she just now realized overlooked all of Boise. Looking out those windows, his mind ran over the events.

She took that time to pull herself together, to reconfigure her thoughts and make sense of everything. What had she said about Zach and what hadn't she said? Her words at the zoo came back to haunt her.

"If I had a son, I'd do everything to nurture and keep him on the straight and narrow. Even if it meant giving up hours at the bakery."

She might as well have said "John—you've sucked as a parent because you work long hours and you haven't been there."

Chloe drank several slow gulps of wine, needing its warmth and comfort.

As John lost himself in thoughts, she tried to get her bearings.

The house, what little she'd seen as she'd walked in from the garage door, was massive. Grand. Impressive. Very wealthy. They had gone through the garage, into a hallway, then through a huge kitchen with a breakfast bar. Off the opening of that space, was a conversation area where they sat now.

She'd assumed John made a good living as a lawyer, but she hadn't envisioned such a fabulous home. A person could get lost around here.

"I should go," Chloe said, breaking the silence. "I—"

"No. It's okay." John's eyes leveled on her. "Stay. You're here and I'm making us dinner."

"But I haven't changed from work and I..." The sentence faded, much like the sunshine that was bathing the house in twilight and giving the promise of an impending evening.

The pain in John's brown eyes killed her.

In that moment, she understood he wasn't angry at her, but rather at himself. His intimate relationship with his son had spilled over into a stranger's life, and Zach had vented about his less-than-shining father. Any parent would find that situation disheartening. Even she could figure that one out.

Chloe set her wineglass down. "Let's make it another time."

"Let's not." John rose to his feet, coming over to sit by her.

She shied away, knowing she wore the labors of her day in a way that was less than appealing. To her horror, he sat beside her and put his arm around her shoulder.

Somberly, John said, "I'm glad he found someone he could talk to about me."

"J-John," she stammered. "It was nothing like that. Just a few casual conversations. And just today he said things were going a lot better between you."

John nodded. "Good. Glad to hear that. Maybe I should get him and he can formally meet you as my date."

"No, let's not. Let me go home and—"

"Chloe, it's all right. I'm fine with everything."

Examining his face, the slight tic at his jaw, she remarked, "You don't look fine."

Then he smiled. The familiar smile that she loved to watch capture the corners of his mouth. She'd become used to him, the sound of his voice, the safety of his embrace, and the way he kissed.

Warmth spread through her, a feeling of...she didn't even want to think it could be...love.

He extended his hand to her as he stood. "Come on. You can help me make dinner."

Letting go of an emotional sigh, she acknowledged the fact that she *wanted* to be here even though the way she'd ended up here had been less than perfect. "Okay. But can you show me where the restroom is so I can wash up?"

An hour later, the kitchen smelled wonderful from the baked potatoes and sizzling steaks sitting on a platter, ready to be served. John had told Chloe that he'd gone to his son's room on the lower level, and heard him in the shower. He'd knocked on the door and hollered he had company upstairs, and Zach had replied he'd be up when he was finished.

As Chloe put the salad on the table, Zach appeared, surprised to see her there.

"Hey," he'd said, clearly puzzled.

"Hey..." she responded, unsure of what else to add.

She recognized the heavy scent of Axe men's deodorant. His black hair had been styled into place with a light gel. The striped button-down shirt looked like it came from Banana Republic, and him wearing it seemed out of place to her, but he looked good. Dark blue denim jeans hugged his lean legs. Maybe it was her imagination, but he came across as taller. She'd never seen him dressed fresh, and now that she knew he was John's son, the resemblance hit her on the side of the head.

John stepped in. "Zach, this is Chloe."

Still confused, Zach replied, "Yeah, I know."

"She's the woman I told you and Kara about."

Shifting his stance, his jeans riding low on his hips, he scratched the back of his head. "You're dating her?"

The question was aimed smack at Chloe.

"Uh, yes." She gave a half laugh, almost apologetic in tone.

A long silence passed.

"Weird, huh. Like I already knew you but I didn't." Swiping some olives from their dinner platter, Zach said, "Toad and VeeJay are picking me up. Later."

Relieved Zach didn't make a federal case about anything, doing the typical teenager "hi and bye" thing, Chloe allowed the tension in her shoulders to slacken. A little.

"Later," John echoed, his expression unreadable.

Just as Zach turned, he looked over his shoulder. Directly at Chloe. "I told you my dad would like you."

The pair of them now alone in the kitchen, John's brows arched in Chloe's direction. "What did he mean by that?"

"Nothing…not much."

When John kept staring, she finally conceded, "Your son once implied he wanted to set us up. I turned him down flat."

"Is that so?"

"Yes. I was seeing someone." Chloe rolled her eyes. "Funny how that was *you*." And just then, she had an *ah-ha!* moment.

She remembered when Zach had complained his dad hadn't come home one night—had spent it with a woman.

That woman had been her.

Embarrassment hit her like a volcano.

"Oh, great—you don't think he'll figure out it was me you spent the night with? Nothing happened."

Resting assuring hands on her shoulders, he said, "I've told my kids that I was sitting with a friend who'd had a potential break-in at her house. It's no big deal. Come on, dinner's ready."

John and Chloe ate informally at the breakfast bar, sharing a few laughs over the turn of events. What had started as a major disaster, had been glossed over. She allowed herself the indulgence of relaxing, enjoying. Of telling herself that whatever direction things went now, they may well have gotten past a rough spot.

They smiled, brushed hands, a couple of light kisses thrown in. Chloe forgot she wasn't wearing a gold blouse and nice slacks. None of that mattered.

All that mattered was John.

And the unfolding truth…she was falling in love with him.

CHAPTER NINETEEN

GOLDY'S RESTAURANT on South Capitol, a small and average-Joe kind of place, was a Boise mainstay. Some thought it served the best breakfasts in the city. John wouldn't dispute that fact, as he'd eaten his fair share of bacon and eggs there before heading into the office.

On Monday morning, the sky still dark at 7:00 a.m., John sat in a booth with Chloe. And Kara.

Kara had missed meeting Chloe Friday night, and after some discussion about it last night during their Sunday dinner together, John suggested they invite Chloe to breakfast. Not a morning person, Kara had had a moment's reservation, but curiosity won out.

His daughter had gotten up early, applied her makeup, then dressed in jeans and a trendy sweater. She'd slipped into a pair of fur-lined UGG boots and stuffed her bucket purse to bursting with who knew what.

When he'd asked her if she needed her coat, she'd scoffed at him. At least she'd worn a long-sleeve top. She'd followed him out of Quail Ridge to the restaurant so that afterward, she could drive herself to school.

"So do you have any big graduation plans?" Chloe

asked, her hands wrapped around the cup of coffee in front of her.

John could tell she was nervous. He and Kara sat across from her, and Chloe's leg was vibrating to beat the band. Sliding his foot forward, his calf brushed, then pressed next to hers to quiet her jitters. The silent message he gave her told her to relax.

She gave him a fleeting look, placating him with a quick roll of her eyes that Kara didn't catch.

"This summer, I want to go to Los Angeles with my friend, Ashley, but Dad isn't saying yes."

John, unphased by Kara's protest, said, "I never said no, either. We'll see what your final grades look like and how well you do."

"I'm trying. I got a B minus on my chem test."

"Great."

To Chloe, Kara complained in a girlish tone, "Was your dad like this, too? Always wanting to control you?"

John knew Chloe's background and hated for her to be asked the question. He would have tried to save her, but Chloe, bless her, kept her shoulders set and smiled.

"I don't know. I never knew him."

"He died?" Kara's words warmed with sympathy, as if searching for a common bond between them.

"Actually—I really never knew him. My mom got pregnant with me and never bothered to tell my dad." Chloe gently smiled. "Or if she even knew who my dad was."

"Oh, geez," Kara remarked, the octaves in her tone rising with drama. "That sucks."

"It's fine." Chloe inhaled softly, her hair fixed neatly in a twist at the back of her head. Later today, she was going to John's office to discuss the terms of the Garretson's remuneration. Rather than wearing her bakery whites, she wore a blouse and slacks with boots. Settled at the hollow of her throat, a tiny pearl dangled from a fine gold chain. Matching earrings perched on her ears.

She looked polished, refined. Very professional.

John was proud of her. Even more so for taking the Garretson's deal and moving forward with the compensation to start over. He knew the decision had been tough, but he was glad she'd reconciled herself to it.

Chloe wiped a droplet off the edge of her water glass. "When I was little, I used to wonder what it would be like to have a father, and what he'd be like, but it was all pretend. Probably around the time I was a teenager, I stopped thinking about my father. And my mother had enough boyfriends to fill in anyway. But it was fun to pretend my father was somebody famous who had to travel a lot. I told that fib a few times in grade school before I got sent to the principal's office."

Kara smiled. "I'd probably have done the same thing."

"Well, it only worked for so long, then I had to face reality that I didn't have a dad who was famous or otherwise." Pausing in her story, Chloe thanked the waitress for her coffee refill. "And my mother…well, she more than made up for a lack of a father. We used to have parties at our house that lasted all weekend. She ran with some Bohemian friends. At the time, I didn't know what that was, but I get it now. I first learned how to put eye shadow on from her flock of biker chick friends. A woman named Free Bird shaped my eyebrows for me. She used candle wax. Geez, did that hurt. My brows are still crooked. I think she damaged the roots."

Laughing, Kara really studied Chloe. "They're okay. I like how you fix your hair for someone your age."

John snorted.

Chloe smiled, not the least bit offended. "It's fine. Hey, I'm going to be forty in four days."

That reminded John he had to finalize all the arrangements for Chloe's surprise party. He'd called Ethel at the boutique and introduced himself on the phone. He'd thrown out a few details about what he'd like to do, hoping Ethel hadn't already arranged something. She hadn't, so they agreed that throwing Chloe a birthday dinner at Epi's Basque restaurant in Meridian would be a great idea.

John watched his daughter, listening to the easy conversation she had with Chloe. He'd worried that she might be jealous over him having a woman in his life but, to the contrary, she was interested. If not very curious about the whole thing.

"So, how bad did your belly-button piercing hurt?" Chloe asked as their breakfasts arrived.

"Pretty bad," Kara confessed, giving John a sideways glance. "If Ashley hadn't have been with me and held my hand, I might not have gone through with it."

"I got my tattoo when I was fifteen. I used a fake

ID." Chloe shook some pepper on her eggs. "Of course I'd kill my daughter if she ever pulled a fake ID to do something dumb like that."

"Dad," Kara said with a huff. "You told her?"

John threw up his hands. "I didn't tell her anything about it."

The reference, of course, was about the pierced tongue and Kara having used a fake identification card to get it.

Figuring that would be the end of the touchy subject, John was surprised when Kara continued, "I got my tongue pierced with a fake ID."

"Ouch," Chloe responded. "I could never understand the appeal in that."

Kara shrugged. "I dunno. I thought it would be cool."

"Not cool—in my opinion."

"I had to take it out." Kara poured a generous amount of syrup on her pancakes. "Where's your tattoo?"

"On my ankle."

"What is it?"

"A hummingbird."

"Sweet. I didn't think women your age would ever have a tattoo."

"Well, like I said, I was fifteen when I did it."

"Would you get it again, if you could go back and have a do-over?"

Chloe pondered a long while, then finally replied, "Yes, I think I would. In fact, I probably wouldn't change much of anything in my past. I guess you live through it to make you who you are today. If I had been raised by my mother, I wouldn't have learned everything I have from my grandmother. She's the one who got me interested in baking."

"What's your favorite thing to bake?"

Not even John knew this, for he'd never asked.

A smile broke out on Chloe's mouth. "Peanut-butter cookies."

With all the elaborate things in Not Just Cakes, her answer came as a surprise to John.

"I gave up making them at home," Chloe went on, "because I was putting on some weight. It's hard enough to be around a bowl of frosting all the time—especially once a month."

Kara's laughter sounded musical, a sound John hadn't realized how much he'd missed until now. "Tell me about it. I have to have a Snickers or I'm like a loony person."

John hadn't known that. Not that he kept tabs on when she had her period…but that she confessed her feelings to Chloe brought a hint of melancholy to him. These were the things his daughter would have told Connie. But it was okay she was now talking about them with Chloe. In fact, he was happy about it.

The meal fell into a comfortable rhythm, one which John hadn't foreseen. He thought Kara would like Chloe, but he hadn't anticipated the way in which they'd clicked.

They discussed diets, hairstyles, makeup, clothing and their favorite stores at the mall. The hottest hunks in Hollywood and the actresses they admired were also discussed in great detail.

It pleased him to see the woman in his life connect with his daughter. And when they shared a spontaneous laugh, it warmed him to his very core.

SITTING IN HER OFFICE at the bakery, Chloe sifted through the rest of last Friday's mail. Because of her breakfast, she was behind. But she wouldn't change the morning for anything.

Kara had been great.

Her worries over Kara not liking her had been unfounded. It had gone better than Chloe had remotely expected. They'd hit it off and found themselves laughing about girly things and, at several points, Chloe had to remind herself that John sat at the table with them.

Contrary to the struggles John had described, Kara seemed like a normal teenager. A bit rebellious, but with a good core and heart. Kara had reminded Chloe of herself at that age. Actually, Chloe had been worse in her younger years but, by seventeen, she'd been with Ethel long enough to have begun to turn her life around.

Everyone had choices, and Chloe had made the right ones.

She suspected that Kara's choices weren't John's, and he thought his daughter could be making mistakes. Aside from bad grades and having to take summer-school classes, Chloe had not seen any red flags during their short breakfast together.

Kara didn't have a current boyfriend, but had in the past and was interested in a boy in her math class. That news had come as a surprise to John, but he hadn't countered it with a threat as if he were opposed to his daughter dating. Expecting a seventeen-year-old girl not to want to have a boyfriend would have been unrealistic.

While Chloe didn't have children, she understood that every parent wanted their children to live up to their expectations. And when they didn't, they felt disappointed, or as if the child had failed. This simply wasn't true.

Children had their own minds and creativity, and given some free rein, could express some very viable talents. Chloe was example enough of that with her culinary skills.

In any case, Chloe looked forward to getting to know Kara, and Zach, better in the coming months.

Chloe sorted the mail, tossing the junk solicitations in the trash can. She grabbed the last thing in the pile, her hand on the thick mailer.

A wry smile caught on her mouth.

The Garretson quarterly report.

Of course she received it—she had stock in the company. She hadn't opened one of the reports in forever, and now she took a moment to slide open the seal and check things out.

As she glanced at the main page, she noticed the yada-yada stuff about this and that—things the average person could care less about. She read a piece on growth, the stock situation and store summaries. Then she spotted an article on the fabulous "new mega-store" to be opening in the Grove Marketplace. That got her full attention.

She read through all the plans and hoo-rah about the whole thing. The produce department, the deli case, the butcher block. And then, of course, the fakery. That sorry excuse for a bakery that Garretson passed off as good treats. It was a joke and the whole idea that such an awful bakery would be wiping her out, brought an unexpected wave of emotion over her.

She felt like crying.

Her fingers balled into tight fists, her heartbeat snagged and she blinked hard. Then even harder so as not to let the tears fall. And then on a slow blink, she noticed something.

A photo.

Bob Garretson. A letter from the CEO on the opposite page. Thinning gray hair, blue eyes the color of winter. A bulbous nose. Chloe's pulse tripped. Swarthy.

All at once, a realization hit her so hard that it almost knocked her off the chair.

It's him!

"THE DEAL IS *OFF!*" Chloe bellowed into the telephone of Gray, Springer, Moretti and Hayes—so loud, John momentarily pulled the receiver away from his ear. "I wouldn't take a penny of that dirty, no-account, underhanded, snooping—"

"Chloe, calm down." John tried to talk over her but she continued her minitirade.

"—conniving, lying, corporate snake if you paid me to take it. Cancel our ten o'clock. I'm not coming!"

The line grew somewhat quiet. Had Chloe not been

breathing heavily into the mouthpiece, he would have assumed she'd put the phone down and quit the call.

"Chloe," he began again, only to have her, once more, talk over him as if she were a bulldozer.

"Bob Garretson has been coming into my bakery, disguised in a stupid fedora hat! He's been spying on me, trying to figure out my recipes. I want to sue him!"

"Hold up," John insisted firmly, leaning back into his oversized office chair, his feet propped on the edge of his office desk. "Chloe. Chill."

When she remained silent, he drew in a breath.

"Are you done?" he asked.

"Temporarily. But I still want to sue him. For, uh, slander. Or whatever else. You figure it out. I'm hiring you."

That gave John a slight chuckle.

"Why are you laughing at me?" she blurted. "This is not a laughing matter."

"You can't sue the man for eating your pastries."

"He was in my bakery on false pretexts."

"Nobody can prove that in a court of law. And, Chloe—it's all a moot point anyway. Will you listen to me for a sec?"

Her lack of reply told him she must have been pouting.

"Chloe?"

"Fine. Go ahead."

"I just got off the phone with Bob. He called to set up a meeting. With you. In my office. This week."

Fire shot through the phone wires. "The man's nerve sets my teeth on edge! Tell him no."

"Sweetheart." John used the endearment to try and make her stay focused on what he was saying. She'd gotten herself so worked up, she couldn't see through the smoke. "Take the meeting. You're going to want to hear this. I've never heard the guy sound remotely sincere, but when he called, there was something in his voice that actually came across as human."

"The man's not human. He's a mega-mole. A spy."

"Ah, geez, Chloe. Cut it out. He wants to make you an offer."

"I'm not taking his early payoff."

"This is something entirely different. And when you hear it, you're not going to believe it."

THE HUGE CONFERENCE ROOM into which John gently steered Chloe seemed like a cavern of doom. Waxed to a high gloss, the long table reflected the afternoon light. A line of tall windows had views to the city, but Chloe didn't pay much attention. Her focus zeroed in on the wizened man sitting at the table with a folder in front of him, hands folded on the tabletop.

"Miss Lawson," Bob Garretson greeted her formally, his angular features exactly as she recalled from his sleuthing in Not Just Cakes—minus the silly old hat.

He had the manners to rise to his feet, but her feet were planted in the doorway.

John had to nudge Chloe along, much like a puppy unwilling to walk on its leash for the first time.

For Chloe, this was new territory: Cavorting with the enemy. And it stunk.

John held out a chair for her, and she plopped into it, knitting her hands together. Unlike her nemesis, she hadn't come with any paperwork in a folder, nor a briefcase like the one heavily stuffed at his shined-to-a-high-gloss loafers.

During her short time working for Garretson's, she'd met the man himself once—at a service award banquet. But she'd neither shared his table nor gotten a good up-close look at him.

He seemed old. Tired. Almost reserved. At a near loss over what to do or how to proceed.

She almost—*almost*—felt a flicker of sympathy for him.

The emotion vanished into a vapor as she reminded herself he wanted to ruin her, to steal her very blood, sweat and tears.

His disguised presence in her bakery was more than ample proof he was a thief. No wonder he'd hightailed it out of the shop when the reporters had come. He hadn't wanted to be recognized.

For a brief moment, one evening after the flowers had been left on her door, she'd questioned if maybe the fedora man had been the one to leave them there. A stalker, of sorts.

Now she felt differently.

Examining Bob Garretson, slick and polished in a designer suit, made her aware that he was ruthless and didn't have a soft heart at all. Nary a weak bone in his body from the way his fingers gripped a fountain pen, as he tapped its capped tip on the table.

John rolled out a chair and took the head of the

table, while she and Bob sat across from each other. She staved off a snort, the tactic John had created just now dawning on her.

No table would stop her from verbally attacking the man if he so much as uttered a syllable of harassment toward her. She'd had enough of his shenanigans, and her mood was as dark as a chocolate bar.

"So, I'm not sure if you two have formally met," John said, then made the introductions.

While she knew her grandmother would take her to task for it, Chloe made no vocal response.

Bob did say, "We kind of already met."

That made Chloe pipe in. "Yes, on false pretexts. I would have thrown you out of my bakery if I'd've known who you really were in that ridiculous hat."

John's hands rose in a peaceful motion. "Chloe, cut it out."

She gave him a glower, one that said more than words could.

Are you taking his side?

"I'm here to mediate and to present an offer from Mr. Garretson to Miss Lawson. I've been hired to view the paperwork, and I've had the chance to do that. I made notations for legal changes that affect the contract, and I'm sure Miss Lawson will have her two cents—"

She opened her mouth to protest, but John's stormy warning gaze gave her pause.

"—rather, five bucks to add to the documents." John shuffled the paperwork in front of him, Bob getting out some kind of copy of his own. "But for now, it's a starting place that I'd like to open with."

Chloe had no idea what John was talking about.

Addressing Bob, John said in a business-like tone, "Since this is your project, I'm going to let you tell Miss Lawson what you told me on the phone."

For the first time since entering the room, Chloe thought she saw a flash of nervousness cross the man's features. His nose gave a twitch, as if he had an itch. His hamlike hands picked up a sheaf of paper, and he studied it—as if he'd had to write out what he wanted to say or else he wouldn't say it the way he wanted.

"Miss Lawson," he began, his voice gruff, "I've never made an emotional business decision in my life and I've been my own boss for nearly fifty years. I've listened to good and bad ideas for my stores. Even the ugly—that in-house take-home pizzeria that tanked faster than a flushing toilet—and I've given my nod to most all of it."

If he'd gotten her here to talk about toilets, Chloe was going to laugh in his face. Her expression remained neutral and she didn't move an inch, not even blinking an eyelash.

"All my decisions are pragmatic," Bob continued after clearing his throat. "They're well thought out, based on what my consultants tell me I should do and shouldn't do. They said we needed a presence in the Grove, and I didn't disagree. I thought, bully—full speed ahead and damn the torpedoes."

"But you damned me," Chloe couldn't help interrupting. "You came into my bakery, spied on me and who knows what else." The steadiness of her heartbeat kicked into a higher rhythm, even when she told herself to remain calm and unassuming in the face of the enemy.

"I only came to sample the pastries."

"Why?"

"Because I wanted to see what you were up to."

"There you go!" Chloe exclaimed, turning to John, waiting for him to throw down the gauntlet for her. "See—he admits to spying on me."

"Chloe, you're getting yourself worked up."

"I am not," she denied, but knew his words to be the truth. A prolonged buzz echoed in her ears from the agitation zapping her entire body. To Bob, she clarified, "I can understand the decision to open at the Grove. Frankly, and I don't willingly admit this, I don't blame you. It's an awesome location with a diverse group, but as a hometown boy, and Boise native, I expected a lot more from you. Going undercover…unforgivable. I want to sue you for slander or something equally as paramount, but…"

John had told her to wait and hear what Bob had to say before she started throwing stones. But John didn't have to sit here and converse with a man who'd made it his personal mission to attempt to figure out her recipes by sampling.

With a somber expression on his face, Bob said, "If you'll allow me to continue, Miss Lawson, and shut your yap for a minute, you'll see that I've had a change of plan."

Eyes widening over his insult, Chloe went to speak but John's hand came over hers, and he gave her fingers a few pats. His warm touch grounded her enough to stay quiet.

Bob said with sincerity, "The moment I tasted your recipes, they reminded me of my grandmother from Denmark. She baked with love. I had to come back to taste more and more."

Brows raising, Chloe gave him a point for the compliment, but nothing more.

"I watched you behind the counter, and would have liked to have seen you in the kitchen."

"You could have applied to be a cashier," she flippantly tossed out. "I'm always hiring, but you already have a job. Crushing little guys."

Bob Garretson guffawed, a loud and obnoxious sound that put her on alert. "You're just as stubborn as my Danish grandmother, if not more. She was one tough woman."

John moved his hand away, and Chloe realized she'd been squeezing his fingers too tightly. The blood had drained from his hand. "Sorry," she said almost mutely.

Nodding no harm, John focused in on Bob. "Just cut to the chase before she really gets mad."

"Keep your shorts on, Johnny-Boy." Then to Chloe, he said with more than an ounce of ingenuity that she found confusing, "What I'm beginning to understand is that a grocery store is more than inventory on the shelves. It becomes part of the neighborhood. We've got stores in Portland, Oregon, selling forty-dollar loaves of bread that we fly in every Thursday from Paris. It's sold out before it gets there. I think your pastries and cakes would sell for much more than you've been selling them for."

He had her attention, and she listened patiently.

"You need a mentor," Bob stressed, "and a business person to help you get rich."

He lost her just as quickly as he had her. He'd never be her mentor. No way.

"Your bakery is your heart and soul." His admission cost him from the look of jealousy on his old face. "This is what I've been lacking in my vision. So this is what I propose—Garretson's incorporates Not Just Cakes into it's mega-store at the Grove. The architect will have a hissy fit when I ask him to redraw everything, but we can make this work. I'll put the meat department elsewhere and we'll have to knock down a wall or two to expand the bakery section, with you at the helm, of course. We'll supply you with employees so no more want ads," he added dryly. "Your loyal customers will be great for my grocery store. Everyone needs a carton of milk to go with a slice of cake.

"My board members don't know anything about this, so if you nix the idea, I'd ask you one thing—keep what I just said here today in this room. But if you're okay with it, I'm the chief at my corporation, and it's time I started coming up with my own solutions and not using a hired group of bushwhackers to tell me what's best for me. The very first Garretson's grocery was slow to succeed, but it eventually grew due to my personal touch, and sales gained momentum. Over the course of fifty years, I've added stores throughout this state and others all over North America. But along the way, I lost the one-on-one touch. My aim is to get back my flagship store's feel, and your bakery in my store is vital to my vision."

Not believing what she'd just heard, she pondered the words a moment, trying to digest everything he'd said. She had to repeat it back, aloud, just to make sure she wasn't wrong.

Her breathing felt tight, and she could hardly think. "So wait a sec...do I have this right? You want my bakery—Not Just Cakes—in *your* grocery store, at my present location in the Grove."

"That's the idea. Of course there'll be a tangle of legal things we'll need to cover, but that's why we've got Johnny-Boy."

"But why...?"

"I told you why. You've got ingenuity, and I want a heap of it for my grocery store."

The generous offer began to sink in, and she gazed at John for verification.

He straightened the papers in front of him. "I've got the legal documents drawn up for you to go over. We'll take each article one by one, and you give us your thoughts."

"I'm opinionated," she replied simply.

John's laugh warmed her. "I believe I'm familiar with that side of you."

"I'll tell you exactly what I'm thinking."

Bob said, "Wouldn't have it any other way. Business people who don't cut to the chase aren't my kind of people. Miss Lawson, you lay the manure on the table and I'll bring my shovel. Let's get this deal done, and I guarantee you'll be rolling in dough. And not literally. I aim to make your bakery a household name."

With that, Chloe inhaled. "Okay. Let's see how you've spelled it all out on paper, Mr. Garretson."

CHAPTER TWENTY

"HAPPY BIRTHDAY!" the guests shouted. Chloe, visibly taken aback, leaned into John and held on to his arm. His gaze traveled over her face, her nearness kindling feelings of fire and warmth throughout him.

"What's going on?" she asked, her eyes riveting on him with mirthful accusation.

"It's your birthday party."

"I'm going to kill you," she replied. But with a good-natured scan, she took in the familiar faces at the table, clearly pleased. Recognition crossed her features, as a smile caught on her mouth. "Hi," she greeted to the family and friends waiting for her. "You guys got me. I had no idea."

John slid his hand into Chloe's, escorting her further into Epi's Basque restaurant so she could get situated for her party.

The room, intimate and cozy, held a dozen or so tables, and the owner, Chris, had a welcoming smile. Her tireless efforts to give everyone a warm embrace always made the patrons feel as if they were home. With her dark hair and infectious enthusiasm, she greeted every guest with an affectionate hug.

"Come in, beauty," Chris said to Chloe. "Happy birthday! And don't you look pretty tonight, darlin'."

Chloe had chosen an ice-blue satin blouse and winter white slacks. The cut of the blouse hugged her breasts, and she'd worn her pearl necklace and dangling earrings. She'd styled her hair in soft waves about her shoulders, and John had thought he'd never seen her look more beautiful. A glow caught on her cheekbones, and the application of gold-toned eye shadow set off her violet eyes.

She looked unconditionally happy and at peace this evening, thanks, in part, to her new business venture.

The deal with Garretson's had some minor finalizing, but the bottom line was Not Just Cakes would expand, be remodeled and incorporated into the Garretson's grocery store in the Grove. Not even John had foreseen that monumental change in plans.

Happiness didn't even begin to describe Chloe's feelings. Ecstatic was more like it. She'd taught him that keeping one's convictions all the way to the end of the line could have endless benefits. This whole thing wouldn't have happened if she'd given up on her dream at the first Garretson offer. She'd held out, and her decision had paid off in spades.

John was very proud of her.

Chloe approached the guests, her hand over her heart. She gazed at the people at the table. Ethel and Walden, Candace and Jenny, and the cashiers from Not Just Cakes. His brother Robert, and his wife, Marie. And Zach and Kara.

Over breakfast the other morning, John had mentioned the surprise party and both his kids had volunteered to come. That had pleased him, and he'd said of course they were invited. Kara must have gotten off work a little early to make it on time. She'd had to work at the mall kiosk tonight.

Chloe smiled at Zach, then waved to Kara. She nudged John with her elbow, leaning into him with pleasure. "I can't believe you did this."

"I wasn't alone. Your grandmother had her hand in it, too."

At that moment, Ethel rose from the table and came forward to give Chloe a hug. "Happy birthday, Honey-bee."

Chloe clung to her grandmother, giving her a hard, and long, hug. "Thanks, Mom," she breathed into the woman's teased hairdo. "I appreciate everything you've ever done for me."

Turning to John, Ethel gave him a bear hug. Not anticipating the friendly gesture, John stood still a few seconds, then hugged her back.

"So, I finally get to meet you," Ethel said, her eyes bright and merry. She was a rather colorful woman, completely unlike Chloe. But she had a good heart and spunky spirit that John immediately liked as soon as he'd spoken to her on the telephone.

"We've only talked on the phone to plan this," John clarified to Chloe. "This is the first time we've actually met."

Ethel studied his face, long and thoroughly. "But I can't help thinking I've met you before. Have you ever come into my boutique with your mother?"

"I haven't."

"Well, it will come to me. I'm sure we've met."

If they had, John couldn't recollect the situation.

"Never mind for now." Ethel waved her date over. A tall man stood. He had a slight paunch. He removed a felt Stetson with a link of silver conchs around the wide band, and smoothed his hair back. "Chloe, this is Walden, the man I've been telling you about."

Chloe extended her hand. "It's nice to meet you."

"Roger that," he countered, coming across as modestly shy yet with a masculine brusqueness. "Ethel's filled my ears with quite a lot of history about you two gals' lives together. She's been strung tighter than banjo strings trying to pull this one off without you sniffing out the goods. I've had your see-prize cake stowed in my fridge so I'm a guilty party to the secret, too."

"It better not be a Garretson's bakery birthday cake," Chloe teased, feigning a frown.

John had advised Chloe not to make an announcement about the merger deal until all the paperwork had been finalized. He had given her the go-ahead to tell her grandmother if she wanted, but as far as John knew, she'd kept the information under wraps.

"I baked and decorated the cake myself," Ethel said, prompted by Chloe's remark. "Your favorite. Butter cake with royal icing."

"You know what I like," Chloe replied to Ethel with perpetual merriment. Then, gazing at Walden, concern melded into her next words. "How are you feeling?"

"I'm not ready for the bone orchard yet." He puffed

out his chest and exhaled briskly. "I feel pretty good. I've got lots of time left before my final countdown."

"Let's sit down, Walden, so Chloe can get settled in," Ethel suggested, taking Walden's hand to guide him back to their spots. "We pulled it off, John. Nice going!"

With a half smile, Chloe said, "He sure snowed me. I had no idea. You two are bad news together! Ethel," she chastised, "you told me you couldn't go out tonight because you had a headache."

"I said a partial truth. I do have an ache." With flair, she laid a liver-spotted hand over her heart. "Right here in my ticker for my honey-bee. It's an ache of pride and joy!"

"Oh, Grandma. You're the best."

Ushering Chloe to a seat, John helped her with her coat and one of the wait staff took it to hang on the coatrack. Chloe sat and said a quick hello to everyone, starting from one side of the table to the other. When she got to Robert, she smiled. "So nice to see you. Thanks for coming."

Robert said, "Wouldn't miss it. Chloe, this is my wife, Marie."

"It's nice to meet you."

Marie, gracious as always, replied smoothly, "I've heard nothing but wonderful things about you. Both from my husband and brother-in-law."

"That's nice to hear." Chloe laughed, then continued her greetings, pausing at Zach. "Get the truck fixed?"

"I drove myself over in it," Zach said, nodding. He

344   ALL THAT MATTERS

toyed with the utensils in front of him, a sheepish
smile on his mouth.

"Good, then you can give *me* a ride home after dinner
because I'm going to kill your father for doing this to
me."

Zach grinned. "Yeah, man, you never know how that
guy's going to show up in your life. You better watch
out."

The jest prompted Chloe's happy laughter. "I'll be on
better guard from now on. You just can't trust this guy.
He told me we were going to an early dinner, then a
movie."

"Point proven. He lies," Zach added, with a crooked
lift to his mouth.

John shook his head, playfully going along with the
pair of them.

To Kara, Chloe said, "It's so sweet of you to come.
Thanks."

"You're welcome. I love Epi's." Her long, dark hair
fell over her left brow. Hoop earrings dangled from her
ears. "It's been forever since I've been here. We used
to come here all the time when my…"

The thought trailed, and Chloe gave her a soft smile.
"Your mom liked the restaurant?"

Kara's cheeks colored pink with embarrassment.
"Yeah, but she liked lots of other restaurants, too."

John's hand slipped over Chloe's knee, and he
whispered, "I'm sorry. I hope that didn't hurt your
feelings."

She gave her head a shake. "No," she whispered
back. "It's a small town and everyone has a favorite

restaurant. If I were to ask you to avoid every place you ever went with your wife, it would be like you asking me to avoid the places where Bobby-Tom and I went." With a mischievous wink, she added, "But I'm not picturing you at the racetrack or Mr. Q's Billiards, so I think we're pretty safe on that one."

Leaning over, John said so no one else could hear, "If you and I were alone right now, I'd have to kiss you."

Chloe replied beneath her breath, its warmth tickling the side of his neck, "Later on, I'll hold you to that."

The server came and orders were placed. A meal at Epi's was a leisurely affair with many courses: starting with plates of mushroom appetizers and their famous red bean soup, and ending with desserts and coffee.

Laughter and stories abounded at the table. Walden proved to be quite the storyteller, and Zach gave the retired astronaut more than his passing interest. He thought it beyond cool that he sat with a man who'd actually been in space.

After dinner, the cake was brought out and everyone sang "Happy Birthday" to Chloe. Her face reddened, and she seemed humbled. Gifts from the side table were brought over and she set out to opening them with many, "You shouldn't haves."

She opened John's gift last, her eyes widening in awe as she took the jewelry from the rectangular box. He'd bought her a fourteen-karat gold bracelet he'd seen featured in the American Express magazine *Departures*. The bracelet had enamel pastry charms in fun colors: yellow cupcakes, pink layer cakes, orange doughnuts and mint-green pie slices with real gem accents. A diamond for the cake's center or tiny rubies for the icing trim around the cupcakes. The whimsical piece seemed perfect for Chloe.

Giving him a big hug of thanks, she practically knocked him out of the chair. He helped her put it on, and Ethel checked the bracelet with an exclamation of wow. John had already let Kara see it before he'd wrapped the gift.

When things wound down, everyone said their congratulations and parted company in the parking lot. Ethel promised to call Chloe in the morning, and Chloe said she'd like to have Walden and Ethel over for dessert this week. All in all, John felt as if he'd pulled off a great party for his...*love*.

Somewhere between nibbles of bread, glances over the top of his wineglass, and the main course, he acknowledged to himself that he'd fallen in love with Chloe Lawson.

The tender revelation cemented itself within his heart as he'd observed the easy way Chloe conversed with his son and daughter. They fell into a casual and comfortable discussion at the table that had been neither forced nor mundane, but was rather, weighted with a burgeoning interest to learn more about each other.

John knew he was beyond lucky to have his children open up to a new woman in his life. Things could have been rocky, but maybe since Connie had been so warm, so loving, they knew that someone else could bring that same fulfillment into their lives. And possibly their home if the relationship went that far.

As the last car pulled away Chloe shivered at the night's damp chill.

"Come on," John said, putting his arm around her. "Let's get you into my car and I'll crank up the heater."

Pausing under the muted parking-lot light, Chloe lifted her wrist and studied her bracelet for the umpteeth time. "I just love this. You're so sweet."

"You're sweeter." He dropped a quick kiss on her lips.

"Are we still going to a movie?" she questioned. "Or was that a fib?"

"I was jerking you, sweetheart. I made it up."

Her brow arched. "What if I want to go to one?"

"Then I'd say it's your birthday so you get to pick."

"Well, I'd say—forget the movie." She giggled. "I want to go to my house and get my other present."

"And what would that be?"

"You promised you'd kiss me later."

"Oh, that," he said, chuckling, "would be my pleasure."

Giving him a nudge, she prodded him toward the car.

Contentment filled John. He wanted to take her home and tell her how he felt about her. This part of the surprise, he hadn't planned. His love for her had come forward, and maybe it was the good cheer and the evening, but the timing was now and he wanted her to know.

Just as John pushed the unlock feature on his car key fob, a woman approached them. In the dimly lit parking lot, John couldn't make out her features. She seemed to be of average height, and she wore a jean jacket that didn't seem to be doing a good job at keeping her warm. What struck him was the fact she carried a wrapped gift.

"Can I help you?" John asked, causing Chloe to turn in the direction of the woman.

John's arm had been around Chloe, and he felt her stiffen to the point that she began to tremble, just slightly.

"Chloe?" he whispered.

She didn't readily reply, but as the woman drew closer, the ground could have been swallowing Chloe and she wouldn't have been aware of it. Every fiber of her being focused on the woman.

Then at length, Chloe mumbled, "It's been a long time."

"Yes, it has, baby doll." The voice quivered, emotions clearly warring within her. Glancing at the gift in her hands, then at them, she said in a smoke-tinged tone, "Your momma's come to bring you a birthday present."

THERE WAS NO tear-filled reunion.

With a stiffness to her muscles that hadn't eased, Chloe sat on the edge of her sofa. Her gaze traveled across the living room to her mother occupying the Pottery Barn chair.

After a cursory inspection of the newcomer, Chloe's bichon jumped onto the sofa, and she welcomed the warmth. Petting Boo-Bear's head, as if needing the anchor of something faithful in her life, Chloe waited for the assault of questions.

They never came.

Wanda, tucking her cowboy-booted ankles together, remained quiet.

Mother and daughter were at a standstill of sorts.

After Wanda's appearance in the restaurant parking lot, John had driven Chloe home with Wanda following in a battered pickup truck.

Chloe's mind was a little confused from the evening's celebrations but she did remember John asking if she wanted him to stay, and she had said no. Perhaps she should have let him. She felt more abandoned than she had in years, Wanda's presence a reminder of those early days when she'd bailed and left Chloe behind.

Wanda had to be in her mid to late fifties. Time had not been kind, but neither had it been unforgiving. Chloe's mother had always been pretty, and remnants of that beauty still existed, but one had to look past the drugstore cosmetics and all-over blond hair dye to find it. She wore jeans with scuffed boots, and a loose-fitting sweater. Her fingernails were painted red, but had chipped leaving the manicure less than perfect.

The most noticeable things about her face were the many wrinkles at the corners of her eyes, and over her upper lip. She seemed tired, but not physically so. Rather, the kind of tired that came from a person going and going without stopping.

Wanda Lawson's wanderlust had caught up with her. She'd been rung out to dry and didn't look to be faring all that well. Still, she attempted to smile at Chloe. That kind of droopy-eyed look a puppy got when it had an accident on the carpet.

Only Chloe knew better. Wanda leaving her those many years ago hadn't been an accident.

They'd been a choice.

"You have a real nice house," Wanda said politely, dragging Chloe from her thoughts.

Staring at her mother, Chloe uttered, "It was you. You left the flowers on my porch."

Wanda blinked. "I did, baby doll."

Chloe wished she wouldn't call her that. The endearment had been given to her in her infancy and Wanda had never let up. The sound of it felt suffocating... cloying to the point where Chloe had the urge to get up and run.

A sinking notion swept through Chloe. "And it was you calling me. At home. On my cell."

Without apology, Wanda supplied, "Lonnie helped me look you up in the people finder on the Internet. Man alive, you'd be amazed at the things someone can find out about a person."

Not bothering to ask who Lonnie was, Chloe accused, "And you were snooping around outside of my house."

That comment evoked a streak of remorse on Wanda's washed-out face. She fumbled inside the depth of her silver lamé purse, as if looking for something. "I meant to knock on the door that night. I told myself I could do it, but when you came home and there you were...I got scared. I wanted to, baby doll, I truly did."

With a nervous laugh, Wanda's hand stopped moving. "I keep forgetting I quit smoking some six months ago. Still have the urge every now and then. Now being one of them. You don't have the hankering for cigarettes, do you, Chloe?"

"I've never smoked."

"Ethel told me you turned out to be a real fine woman. And I couldn't agree more. She and I talk. Did she tell you?"

"She's mentioned you'll call...*every now and then.* More then than now."

Wanda's eyes lowered. She looked like a slender twig sitting there, too thin, not fat and happy like Ethel. "I suppose you hate me. I guess you've got the right."

"I do have the right," Chloe replied without care. "I wouldn't say that I hate you, Wanda. But I'd say you sorely disappointed me in my life, but I got over it— got over *you*—a long time ago."

Chloe's anger took her by surprise, furious with herself over the vulnerability tightening her in its grips.

"I reckon that would be the truth on all accounts, and I can't say as I'd blame you."

"Does Ethel know you're back in town?" Chloe's fingers ran through Boo's soft fur.

"Nobody knows, accept for Lonnie Teluride. He got himself a cashiers job at the Flying J truck stop off the freeway, thinking we might stay in Boise. We have us a room at the motel on Chinden, but we'll see how that goes... Anyway, he's my...well, you'd not care what he is to me, but for what it's worth, he's my husband."

"Number what?" Even given the circumstances,

the barb was unjustified and left a sharp taste of guilt in Chloe's mouth.

"Six," Wanda said, appearing unaffected. But her hands kind of shook as she folded them onto her denim-clad lap. It was then that Chloe took notice of the paper-thin gold band on her mother's wedding finger.

"Sorry…" Chloe mumbled, glancing at the clock. The hour grew late and Chloe wasn't sure how to proceed. She wasn't up for an all-nighter of reminiscing, nor did she have much to say.

Times were different, they were both different people. Chloe had gone one way and her mother had gone another. Blaming and yelling wouldn't accomplish, or solve, a thing.

Let bygones be bygones.

Then, as their words had done all evening, the gist of what her mother had said caught up to Chloe in real time. "You're thinking about staying in Boise?"

"We were." As soon as she confirmed the notion, she—in true Wanda form—recanted her answer. "But Lonnie's got a job offer in Mesa and we was thinking about heading out that way to look at the prospects."

Chloe offered no reply.

Wanda toyed with the fringe of a satin pillow, glancing away, then at Chloe. "Baby doll, twenty-five years is a long time. I wish I could go back and…"

Thankfully Wanda let the thought trail off. Chloe couldn't handle a hollow apology. She'd throw it back in her mother's face and that would accomplish nothing.

Continuing, Wanda said, "It took Ethel some cooling off before she'd forward me a picture of you once in a while. I especially liked that one of you for your high-school graduation announcement. You sure looked pretty. I sent you a card."

"Ethel gave it to me."

"I'm glad she did."

Throughout the years, while Ethel had contact with Wanda, Chloe had chosen not to and it hadn't broken her heart. Well, not after a spell. Once in a while, Chloe would ask if her grandmother had heard from Wanda. She'd offer that Wanda was in Sacramento or wherever Wanda was. And that she was fine. More information than that, and it became too much for Chloe. She'd become an expert at keeping Wanda in the very furthest corner of her mind, not often bringing her up, or even wanting details.

Maybe that's how Chloe had protected herself all these years.

"Are you going to see Ethel?" Chloe asked, noting Wanda's posture as she slumped her shoulders a bit.

"I don't know. I was thinking of giving her a jingle tomorrow."

Once more, Chloe had no response. Wanda could call whomever she pleased. Or not.

And it would have pleased Chloe if she'd been one of the "or nots." Dealing face-to-face with her long-lost mother proved to be more difficult than she'd thought when she'd agreed to let Wanda come over tonight.

She'd wanted to spend the evening with John, in his

arms, a fire snapping in her fireplace and a bottle of wine. And his mouth covering hers.

The current image in her living room had been painted on a vastly different canvas.

Wanda shifted uncomfortably, as if her composure were under attack. "Is there anything you'd like to ask me about?"

"Not really." The reply came swiftly.

"I reckoned you wouldn't. You've got too much class to dig up dead pieces of history." Studying Chloe, she said with a thick throat laden with emotion, "You sure turned out well-put, Chloe. I drove by that fanciful bakery of yours, and never a prouder arrow pierced a mother's heart."

Wanda reached next to her and produced a gift, stretching her arms out to the coffee table and setting it on the center. "It was forty years ago today that I gave birth to you." Tears welled in her blue eyes. "There'd never been a happier day in my life, nor do I expect to have anything akin to those feelings from first holding you again. You have been a thought on my mind most every day. I know you don't believe me, but it's true. I don't deserve you as my daughter, so I'm not asking for a chance. Chances are for people who earn that right. I don't…but I wanted to tell you happy birthday and give you something. It's all I have to give that you actually might want from me, Chloe." Slowly, she rose to her full height. "And I reckon that's about all I have to say."

Chloe led Wanda to the front door, pausing a moment, conflict warring within her to ask her mother to stay a little longer. But the words wouldn't form and Chloe silently watched Wanda retreat over the brick steps toward her pickup.

The truck's engine fired up and Wanda pulled away from the curb. Numb, Chloe shut the door and locked it. She stared at the gift on the coffee table. After a long while, she tentatively picked it up and tore at the paper.

Sinking into the chair her mother had vacated, Chloe's fingers touched the front of a photo album, and she slowly opened its pages. Inside were photos of her at birth, as a baby, with Wanda and Ethel. Then photos of places Chloe had no recollection of, with people who had faded from her memory altogether. But it was fascinating just the same to see where she'd come from, what she'd once looked like as a child.

Ethel had a handful of photos that Wanda had mailed but, for the most part, Chloe's childhood had been undocumented. Seeing the old white-bordered pictures, some cropped black-and-whites, the images told stories that Chloe had long forgotten. She remembered the two-story farmhouse in this photo, and it brought a smile to her face. And she could place where that field was and why they'd been there. Wanda and her boyfriend had bought metal finders and were hoping to hit some kind of a jackpot. Chloe had climbed trees while they'd mined for treasures.

Then there was the picture of Chloe on her second birthday.

She brought the album closer, inspecting the tilt of the cowgirl hat on her head. Blond spiral curls framed her chubby face. Wanda must have fixed her hair. She had on a pink party dress and sat on a stool. It almost looked like a bar in the background. The cake in front of her was a single thick layer with soft pink frosting, the top bordered with colorful gumdrops. Two candles burned in the center, the firelight seemingly reflected in Chloe's eyes as she made a face ready to give a robust blow.

Wistful nostalgia softened Chloe's resolve not to be swayed by the indelible images. A lump wedged in her throat.

A couple of pages were devoted to grade-school photos. Chloe looked awkward with her gangly features and stringy hair. Those days had been painfully embarrassing, getting her first period in English class and not being prepared. Wanda had given her the entire birds-and-bees talk after school, cigarette dangling from her lips as she'd cautioned Chloe to never let a boy kiss her. It only led to one thing.

A snort found its way from Chloe's mouth.

She turned the pages, viewing her life in a way that she hadn't seen before. The photographs were both painful, and yet, comforting. There were things she saw that made her smile and recall something about Wanda that gave her a laugh. Other things…they were just notes in time, a song that had ended.

On the very last page, Wanda had pasted a letter on notebook paper, penned in her hand.

Baby doll,
I don't deserv your love and I'm OK with that. I have to be. But you never had pikters of your

life before and I thought you might like to see
what a blessing you were. I wish I could say you
had a daddy who loved you and wanted to know
you, but I cain't. Don't suffer for my mistak. I
hope you find a true love and keep him forever
in your heart.
Love, Mom

A tear splashed onto the page, smudging the ink,
and only then did Chloe realize she was crying.

CHAPTER TWENTY-ONE

JOHN'S CELL PHONE RANG less than an hour after returning home from Chloe's party. He snagged the call, sensing the person on the other end would be her. In a wavering voice, she asked if he could come over, and he'd told her he'd be right there.

After jotting a quick note to Kara and Zach, who'd gone to bed, John left the house.

Chloe opened the door for him and, without a word, closed it, then slipped into his arms. From the brief glimpse of her oval face, he could tell she'd been crying. Her upset twisted his insides, and he wished he could make her feel better. All he could do was hold her tightly, stroke her hair, whisper encouraging words to her.

She wasn't crying now, and he suspected she was spent.

"Come on, sweetheart. Sit down and tell me what happened."

Slipping onto the sofa, she patted the spot next to her. Once he was beside her, she put her hand into his. He rubbed his thumb over her knuckles.

"That bad?" he questioned.

"No. Just sad." Chloe sniffed, then scratched the

underside of her nose. "Wanda brought me a photo album."

Chloe reached for it from the coffee table and she showed him the pages, commenting on the various shots and places with her in them. Afterward, she closed the book and drew in a shaking breath.

"It's amazing I'm not messed up from my unstable childhood and my mom bailing." Chloe ran a hand into her hair, then pressed fingertips to her temple. She hadn't changed out of her blouse and slacks, but her long hair was mussed. "Unless I am a wreck and nobody's told me."

"You're not messed up, Chloe. After all you've been through, I think you're pretty incredible."

She gazed at him, her eyes red-rimmed. He'd seen her look better, but he'd never seen her soul revealed like it was now. Her eyes reflected her tumultuous adolescence, her broken heart over her abandoned mother, and ultimately, her divorce. How he knew, he couldn't pinpoint. He just did.

Loving her had broken away the layers of her armor, and he could see her so very clearly. He recognized the hurt on her face, the same forlorn expression he'd had after Connie died.

There was also a hint of defeat, as well. Almost as if she'd been trying for so long to forget her past, and now it had come back to her with such force, it shook her to her very core.

"I really thought I could care less about ever seeing my mom again," Chloe said, grabbing another tissue from the box on the coffee table. "But her being here tonight put a deeper chip on my shoulder and I don't know how to handle it." She waved her hand over the photo album. "Why did she have to go and give me that? All those images of us. It's the one damn thing she knew would get to me and it did. I'm sick at heart over being reminded about how much I've lost."

"Honey, it's still lost. You can never go back and grab on to the years you didn't have your mother."

"Thank God for Ethel." Chloe blew her nose. "I don't know if Wanda's going to see her or not. I'll have to call my grandmother in the morning and tell her my mom's in town."

"So Wanda's staying?"

Chloe made a sarcastic roll of her eyes. "Ya think? She fed me a story about trying to stay, but she'll head out. With husband number six. It's not her nature to hang around."

"Will she tell you when she's leaving?"

"Not a clue. Honestly don't care."

"Sure you care."

With a shaky reply, she countered, "I don't want to."

John handed her another tissue to wipe the tears from her cheeks.

Chloe stared off into space a moment, then in a distant voice said, "She's been calling me and hanging up—she didn't have the nerve to talk to me. And that was her in my yard that night. She also left the flowers—too much of a coward to face me."

"Some people show their feelings in different ways."

"Wanda's border on uneven."

"Not everyone's the same. It'd be a boring world if we were."

Shooting him a sideways glare, she said, "Aren't you Sigmund Freud?"

Shaking his head and cupping her cheek, he brushed her hair behind her ear. "Look at it like this—she gave you something to jog your memory with. The photo album is a part of you that you didn't have before. In Wanda's mind, she was doing good. She was giving you a piece of your childhood back. It wasn't all bad, Chloe. You're smiling in almost every picture."

"I suppose," she whispered, snuggling up against him. "I guess it's just hard."

"Nothing in life is easy." John settled his arm around her, cuddling her close. "When I lost my wife, I never thought I'd find a woman I could love as much. It was hard to go through those years of loneliness. I was in denial for most of them, losing my kids and even myself. So I understand hard."

Taking her chin with his hand, he turned her face so that her eyes met his. "Chloe, I fought change in my life. I thought my way was the right way and I was wrong. I made mistakes. But because of you, I'm turning things around. You've held me accountable to a few hard truths about myself that I hadn't been able to see. I owe you more than I can say."

She blinked, her lips parted. Compassion etched over her face. A faint smile caught on her mouth. "I wouldn't say it was all me, but I did give you an opinion. Or two."

John smiled, kissing her lightly. "If I'd have hoped

for easy, I never would have kept coming back to you with offers you had no problem refusing. In the process," he said somberly, everything in his heart warming, "something has happened to me." He ran the tip of his finger across her lower lip. "I found my happiness again. And I found myself loving you. I love you, Chloe."

A single tear rolled down Chloe's cheek. "I love you, too. It's been at the back of my mind for a while, but I didn't want to dredge it up. I was scared."

"Me, too. I don't want to rush into anything."

"Me, either."

"We have time."

"Lots."

"We can get to know all there is about each other. Take things slow. Talk slow, walk slow…kiss slow."

His mouth hovered over hers and he dipped his head for a soft kiss. A kiss that deepened and expanded, fully heightening his every sense. The depth of his love could be felt in every breath he took, in every sense that overcame him.

He captured the feelings, savored them.

Chloe's arms fit around his neck, holding him close. Then she murmured next to his mouth in a hot breath that caught on his lips, "Stay…stay the night with me, John. Can you?"

"Only if we don't sleep," he replied, lifting her onto his lap and tucking her in close. His hand fit over the curve of her bottom.

She hugged him, then lifted her head off his shoulder. "I'm not tired," she said in a whisper.

The anticipation of this moment had been coming since the day she'd walked into his office.

He kissed her softly on the lips, bringing his hand to her face, touching her cheek. Its softness fed his heart, his soul. Made him focus only on her, them. The way they were meant to be together. Like this.

Without a word, she took his hand in hers and led him to the bedroom.

Lowering herself onto the bed, he laid down beside her, tucking her close to him. They faced one another a long while, stroking and touching, measuring features with fingertips, kissing, light touches and soft sighs.

All the times he'd wanted to do this, but held back, now dissolved. This was the here and now, and he wanted to remember his every thought forever.

Chloe closed her eyes and parted her lips for him to take. He did, savoring the taste of her mouth, the touch of her teeth beneath the slow exploration of his tongue. When she took his hand and led it to her breast, his heartbeat soared and he fought to keep the groan from escaping his throat.

Knowing full well what she was doing, Chloe abandoned all her resolve. Not that she'd had much, if any. For months, John had been at the back of her mind, at the fringes of her thoughts. Sometimes she'd allowed them to take her this far, to the point where they made love. Other times, she just enjoyed the happiness he brought to her heart.

The stress of the evening seemed unimportant, and Chloe let it slip away like the flow of fabric drifting off her shoulders. John had removed her blouse, and she'd felt herself in a dreamlike state as he traced the top edge of her bra. Its lacy cups barely held her in as she laid on her side, and John's warm hand caught on the fullness of her breasts.

She could hear herself breathing. John, too. He unfastened her slacks and slid them off her hips and legs. A whimper rose on her lips as the bedroom's cool air cascaded over her near-naked flesh. She reached out to him, to undo the buttons on his shirt, to strip him of that last piece of clothing that remained between him and his chest.

When it was gone, she cuddled next to him, his body hot and aroused next to hers. Her hands wove through his hair as he pinned her onto the mattress with a gentle barrage of hot and demanding kisses. Within a heartbeat's time, they were both completely undressed.

Locking her arms around his neck, she held on to him, tears threatening. They weren't born from distress or fear or upset; rather, love. A love so powerful, it threatened to consume every sense she possessed.

He nipped his teeth against her neck, her short breath coming in choppy gasps. As his hands roamed every inch of her body, she responded to him in ways she hadn't anticipated. In the ten-year duration of her marriage, she had never once felt this loved, this cared for, or this satisfied by a man's touch.

Unable to wait any longer, she couldn't help but beg him to please…

Just please.

And then he finally came to her, joining her body and making them one. She felt his every muscle ripple and tense as she moved with him. The sensations overriding all reason, all thought, tingled in every sense of her being. She fought to catch her breath as John took her over the edge, then fell right alongside her.

In the aftermath, they lay together, bodies damp, and hearts beating in unity. He kissed the side of her neck, and she held on to him as if she never wanted to let him go.

CHLOE WAS ALONE. John had left before sunrise, wanting to return home before his children woke without him. And if they did, at least they had a note this time telling them where he was. Even so, he'd said he felt it best to be there and have breakfast going.

Sitting sideways in the living-room chair, the first glimmer of sun creeping into morning, Chloe cradled a cup of coffee in her hands, waiting until she could call Ethel. As she kept note of the time, her mind drifted to last night.

The emptiness and bereft feelings she'd had before John had come over dissipated. In his arms, her desire came alive, wanting him so much and needing him to be with her. She'd touched his very soul—she'd been able to see it in his eyes. She'd felt the same way and when his hands caressed her, the strain of the evening had melted away.

Curled into the curve of John's naked body, Chloe had fallen asleep. Some time later, they'd made love again, every sense inside Chloe awakened. When John had to get up, she'd missed him, and unable to go back to sleep, she'd put on a pot of coffee.

At seven o'clock, Chloe decided not to call Ethel. She would drive over and talk to her in person.

Parking in one of the condo's visitor slots, Chloe went into the lobby, ready to punch the button to Ethel's floor. To her surprise, a voice called her toward the parking lot.

Her grandmother waved, slow and almost sad, beckoning for Chloe to approach.

"Ethel," Chloe blurted, "are you okay?"

With a disjointed sigh, Ethel's chest sunk. "I will be in a little while."

And with those words, Chloe knew. Instinctively, her heart compressed and she smothered a cry. "My mom just came over, didn't she?"

"On her way out of town."

Chloe stoically nodded. "I figured she'd leave."

In a snappish tone, not directed at Chloe, Ethel exclaimed, "Of course she's leaving. She never stays."

Both women gazed at the parking lot, the quiet slots where cars still remained. No evidence of a wayward daughter passing through on her way out of Dodge.

"Wanda came bustling through in a beat-up truck with her husband, Lonnie." Ethel huffed. "I hate to say it, but he seemed nice enough and Wanda looked happy. Lonnie came across as polite and sweet, but kind of wore on me like a coat of molasses, though. He said he's got a job opportunity in Mesa. Said he can't take the winters here. Said he's a natural-born lizard." Ethel made a noise in the back of her throat, a mix of disgust and humor. "A man calling himself a reptile makes me wonder, but I didn't say anything about it."

"Did Wanda tell you she saw me?"

"First thing." Ethel gave Chloe a side-hug, holding tight. "I told her if she did anything to hurt my honey-bee, she'd be sorry."

"She didn't hurt me. She gave me a photo album. Some old pictures of me as a little girl…and places I didn't remember."

Ethel's brows rose. "Sounds like she made an effort, I'll give her that much."

"I guess."

Chloe and Ethel stood, embracing and still standing next to the parking lot. Finally Ethel moved. "Come on up for coffee and tell me all about it."

As they walked, Chloe took her grandmother's hand for comfort. "I always thought Wanda didn't matter to me, but she almost seemed kind of…well, caring. And remorseful."

"I got that notion, too. She said she'd call more often, even send postcards."

"Do you think she will?"

"Don't know, Honey-bee." Reaching out, Ethel pressed the elevator's button. "But what I do know is that you'll always be my girl, and that's what counts."

Chloe gave Ethel's hand a squeeze. Her grand-mother's fingers felt like dry parchment, warm beneath the thinning skin. "And you'll always be my mother, in every way that it counts."

"ETHEL, I DON'T WANT anything to do with this," Walden griped, pausing in the doorway of Ethel's Boutique.

"Oh, get over it, Walden. I need your help. Birdie's arm fell off again and, for the life of me, I can't keep it on. Bring in your tools."

When Walden agreed to do Ethel a favor, he hadn't realized it involved coming into the domain of frilly things. He'd much rather fix the usual female SOS— like unjamming a clogged garbage disposal, or pulling six feet of hair from a shower drain.

Frozen in the doorway, he tried to give himself tunnel vision before taking a step inside. He forged in, making a beeline for the window area and hopping up into it.

To his utter horror, Birdie had on a pair of lace panties and a matching lace bra the size of a '59 Buick grill. The plastic broad was as endowed as the starship *Enterprise*.

"Jeepers creepers!" he wailed. "Can't you put a frock on her, or something?"

Arms akimbo, Ethel's eyes widened. "It's not like she's a real lady."

"She looks real enough to me. So real, she's making me sweat."

Walden white-knuckled his toolbox handle and grimaced. He didn't need any help visualizing what Ethel had on underneath her blouse and slacks. A man didn't need to know the particulars in order to get fired up. Just looking at Ethel every day ignited his burner.

With an expulsion of breath, Ethel said, "For heaven's sake. I'll put a housecoat on her, but how can you fix her broken arm through the sleeve?"

"I'll figure out a way."

After Birdie was bundled up in a chenille robe, Walden set out to fix her poor mechanics. As he worked, he couldn't help thinking about the irony of being in her storefront window after popping it with a BB.

The day he'd done that seemed eons ago and his fondness for the store's owner had grown tenfold. Just the other night, he'd reveled in being included in Ethel's granddaughter's birthday party, not having seen that one coming on the horizon, but glad for it.

"So, Ethel," Walden said while picking up his screwdriver. "You never answered me about Florida. What do you say?"

He'd asked her if she could leave her shop and be a sunbird for part of November. He figured he'd hire someone to come into The Humidor to handle things for a week or two. Ethel had Uma to keep an eye on business at the dress store.

The dang Boise cold was waiting to happen, and Walden wasn't real keen on getting his butt nipped. He needed a little respite and his old stomping grounds in Florida were just the ticket.

"I'd like to," she replied while sitting on the display window's ledge. The blinding October sun slanted over her shoulders and its brilliance caught in her hair. She sure was pretty.

"Then let's set her up and go. Of course, I'll be paying for the whole kit and caboodle. And we'll get separate rooms in the hotel."

Her brows pitched upward. She had a way about her

features that set his pulse racing. "What if I don't want separate rooms?"

Stymied, he swallowed. The idea of it all coiled the heat low in his belly. Saying swell would have been easy, but Fanny raised him too well in the husband department. "Then I guess we'd have to get married first for that to happen."

"Married?" Her lipsticked-mouth fell into a thin line. "Now, Walden, I told you that I'm just no good in matrimony."

Walden dropped his screwdriver and held out his hand to her, drawing her upward so that she fit against his chest. She was warm and cushioned, sweet and nice in his arms. She blushed the shade of a garden rose.

His face lowered over hers, his heartbeat racing faster than a rabbit's. "That's because you've never been married to me." Then in a moment he'd not planned for, but felt perfectly right, he had the love in his soul to ask, "Ethel, my dear, will you co-captain with me to the moon?"

IN FEBRUARY, the new mega Garretson's opened in the Grove Marketplace with a corporate twist: The incorporation of a gourmet bakery within its walls. The concept was fresh and new, and the customers loved it.

Chloe's regulars enjoyed the convenience of grocery shopping while picking up a dozen pastries at the same time. Those who'd never been to her distinct bakery before discovered a creative selection of treats they would have missed out on.

The turn of events had brought Chloe more business than she knew what to do with. True to his word, Bob Garretson supplied her with top-notch employees, and Chloe had taken in two additional bakers to help Candace and Jenny in the kitchen.

Her best-selling cake, new to the menu, was a child's birthday cake. Two layers of butter-cake, with whipped white frosting tinted either pink or blue, decorated in rows of colorful gumdrop candies.

Wanda probably hadn't realized it when she'd given Chloe the photo album, that she had tapped into Chloe's past, and it turned out to be her best gift.

Although Wanda's correspondence was sporadic, Chloe received a postcard from her mother once in a while. The news didn't change much. Wanda talked about Lonnie this and Lonnie that. Evidenced in the prose of her writing, Wanda hung the stars on Lonnie's moon, for sure. Clearly her mom had found love. At least for the moment.

The correspondences didn't bother Chloe, and sometimes, a line Wanda wrote made her smile. She'd written back several times, telling Wanda about the bakery. She also kept Wanda up to date on Ethel. But Ethel's bigger news had been Ethel's to spill.

Ethel Lumm and Walden Griffiths had gotten married on New Year's Eve. The bride wore cheetah with black patent pumps. She swore white jinxed her so she'd decided to mix it up a little this time around. Her *last* time down the aisle.

The newlyweds honeymooned at Cocoa Beach, Florida. While they were gone, Chloe watched Walden's cat. Boo-Bear hadn't been sure if she liked Apollo or not. More often than not, the pair had a standoff in the middle of the living room.

With Valentine's Day on the horizon, Chloe had been baking heart-everything—cookies, cakes, frosted cupcakes, hearts on jelly rolls and heart decorations in the display cases. She was up to her eyeballs in hearts.

Thankfully the fourteenth dawned today, and she'd taken the afternoon off to get a manicure and pedicure. A girly luxury she enjoyed every minute of. Then she'd had her hair cut and colored. She'd bought a new outfit—an above-the-knee-length black pencil skirt and winter white satin blouse. John had set up dinner tonight downtown and wanted to celebrate with her.

Dressed and ready to go, she spritzed perfume on her neck as the doorbell rang. Boo gave several short barks, and Chloe scolded her.

Opening the door, she found John holding a bouquet of red roses. "Classic, I know," he said, stepping inside, "but they were all the grocery store had."

Chloe laughed. "You didn't get these at a grocery."

"I didn't?"

She brushed a kiss on his cheek, taking the vase laden with gorgeous deep red roses and greens. "I know you better."

"Hey, there's a card tucked inside." John followed her into the kitchen as she set the bouquet down.

"I'll open it in the car." She glanced at her watch. "Didn't you say we had reservations for seven? It's five to. We'll be late as it is."

A mask of indifference registered on John's good-looking face. "The reservations. Oh, that."

John stood there, grinning. He'd dressed in black slacks and a crisp white shirt with a black jacket. The shirt's top two buttons were undone. His hair, clipped shorter than usual with threads of silver at the temple, suited him. The warmth in his eyes caused Chloe's pulse to dance at her wrists. He could, quite simply, take her very breath away. He came across as casual yet polished, looking more handsome than any man had a right to.

Cautiously, she asked, "What do you mean by 'oh, that'?"

"Change of plans. Group dinner."

Group dinner?

Chloe didn't want to let her disappointment shine through, so she quashed it before anything could manifest. "Group dinner…with who?"

"My family."

Inwardly, Chloe kept her composure, but she may have let her true feelings show. While she had gone to many of John's Sunday suppers at his mother's house, and had enjoyed conversing with Mariangela, the table could turn boisterous and folly prevailed. Today was Valentine's, and it was special.

This evening was meant for lovers…not mothers and sisters and brothers and…others.

"Your family," she murmured. "John, I don't mean

to sound ungrateful, but well…Valentine's is like the holy grail to a baker. We spend weeks on heart cookies, heart-themed cakes, decorating with hearts. In fact, my fingers are still red from frosting dye." She held up her fingertips for his inspection, but rather than him nod his agreement and sympathy, he kissed her knuckles, lightly covering them with his mouth.

Shivers rose within and she tried to stay upset with him, but she just couldn't. Folding herself in his arms, she frowned. "You sure know how to make me forget being mad at you."

"Chloe, that hurts," he said with mock exaggeration. "I bring you roses and you're mad?"

"You know what I mean." His body heat seeped through her clothes, and she was half-tempted to take him into the bedroom and forget family dinners altogether.

Talking against his lips, she asked, "So who all is going to be there?"

"You'll have to come to find out."

Chloe backed away, straightening her blouse. "I'm sure Zach had plans with his friends." She'd met Toad and VeeJay—thought they were somewhat rough—so she was encouraging Zach to branch out and meet others. And he was. He'd started taking flight lessons at the Caldwell Airport, and had applied for a math placement test at Boise State. He'd told her Buzz's career fascinated him, and the two had met several times to talk about planes. Walden had promised Zach he'd help him get into a good military program if he wanted to pursue aviation. John had confided in Chloe that, for the first time in forever, his son had a strong sense of purpose and a drive to map out a life plan for himself.

"And I'm sure Kara's out with her boyfriend tonight," Chloe said, recalling when Kara told her about her new guy, Sean, whom she'd met at a school basketball game.

So minus two of John's kids, who else? His mother?

Well, Chloe would make the best of it. Mariangela didn't have a Valentine, so they could be it for her.

John gave a halfhearted shrug. "No, I think Zach said he'd make it. And Kara is bringing Sean."

Chloe had taken Kara to the mall last week and they'd had a fun time going shopping together. In fact, Kara had helped Chloe pick out tonight's outfit.

When Chloe thought about how fortunate she was to have her boyfriend's daughter accept her, actually like to hang out with her, she realized she had everything she could hope for.

And she and Zach continued to have daily talks in the morning when he came into the bakery on his way to the construction site.

"Oh, and Walden and Ethel will be there, as well."

"Who *didn't* you invite?" Chloe countered, rather irritated. All this effort to look fabulous—and she'd be making small talk to carry the evening. "All right then, let's go. But afterward, you're going to owe me, baby. And I don't take checks." With a threatening smile, Chloe went to grab her purse, but John stopped her.

Handing the red envelope to her, he said, "You haven't opened your Valentine's Day card."

Chloe gave him a slow gaze. "Okay, if you want me to now. I have a card and something for you, too. But part of mine," she said with a suggestive purr, "will have to wait until later."

Without Kara in tow, Chloe had bought a red lace teddy and matching thong at Victoria's Secret that would look sexy-beautiful with her red fingernail and toe polish.

Slipping open the flap of the envelope, Chloe glanced at the card's front, the pretty roses and the gold lettering. She skimmed the sentiment: *For my fiancée on Valentine's Day.* Then opening the inside, she paused, flipped the front over again, and stared at the words, then at John.

She never made it to the inside of the card.

"What…?" she asked in a quivering voice. Her legs felt like jelly, and she could hardly stand.

John, lowering onto his knee, reached inside his coat pocket.

Chloe's mind went numb and raced at the same time. Her heartbeat thumped heavily in her chest, and she couldn't seem to catch her breath.

"Chloe," John said, his eyes welled with emotion, "you know how much I love you."

She nodded, unbidden tears forming.

"You're proud, stubborn as the day is long. You can make me laugh, smile. You bake a mean blueberry muffin. You're a believer that dreams can come true as long as you try your best. I can't think of a better woman to ask to be my wife. So, Chloe…"

John lifted the dark lid of the box and took out the diamond engagement ring that sparkled in the light.

"Will you marry me?"

Falling to her knees beside him, she couldn't speak. She let the tears flow freely, wrapping her arms tightly around him, and kissing his neck, smoothly shaven cheeks, then firm mouth.

"Is that a yes?" He spoke next to her lips.

She nodded, still kissing him. Then, "Yes! Yes, of course!"

They kissed forever, a sealing of their love and devotion to one another. Chloe soaked in the sweet tenderness, in love with this man beyond measure.

When they parted, and looked into each other's eyes, they both laughed, then kissed once more as they rose to their feet.

"Let's see if that ring fits," Chloe said with the biggest smile of her life.

John slid the band on her finger, and she marveled at the cut of the clear stones, and the sparkle of the large center diamond.

With her heartbeat racing, for the longest time she couldn't stop looking at her engagement ring.

Chloe wiped the tears from her cheeks and said in a happy-shaky voice, "We'll have to tell your kids tonight."

John smoothed her hair. "They already know. I told them a couple of weeks ago."

Surprised, Chloe's lips parted. "And Kara went shopping with me, knowing what kind of outfit I was picking out…and she never said."

"That's my daughter for you."

Chloe laughed and John picked her up into his arms

and gave her a twirl around the kitchen. Boo-Bear barked and Chloe buried her face in the side of John's neck.

"We'll tell everyone else at dinner," John said against the shell of her ear. "So are you still mad I invited other people?"

She shook her head, unable to trust her voice for fear she'd break into a million shattered pieces of joy.

For Chloe, nothing could get any better.

Never mind a fancy dinner alone. Tonight she'd be with her family, those who were important to her.

Sometimes, the simplest things in life were all that mattered.

HQN™

We *are* romance™

Celebrate the holidays McKettrick style!

From *New York Times* bestselling author

LINDA LAEL MILLER

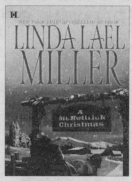

Lizzie McKettrick is homeward bound with her fiancé-to-be,
when their train is derailed by an avalanche that leaves passengers
stranded on Christmas Eve. While her fiancé is preoccupied
with his own well-being, handsome doctor Morgan Shane enlists
Lizzie's help treating injured passengers. Soon Lizzie realizes that
Christmas truly is a season of miracles…and love.

A McKettrick Christmas

Don't miss another great historical romance
by Linda Lael Miller.

In stores November 2008!

www.HQNBooks.com

PHLLM302

HQN™

We *are* romance™

Two stories that bring together the joy of Christmas and the wonder of love.

From *New York Times* bestselling author

LINDA HOWARD

STEPHANIE BOND

Don't miss your chance to share in the joys of the holiday season with this timely collection.

Under the Mistletoe

In stores November 2008!

www.HQNBooks.com

PHLHSB344

HQN™

We *are* romance™

From acclaimed authors

Liz Allison & Wendy Etherington,
Brenda Jackson,
Marisa Carroll
and Jean Brashear

Rev up your holidays with four brand-new heart-racing
NASCAR-licensed romances, sure to send you
into overdrive this winter!

A NASCAR Holiday 3

Don't miss this exciting collection, available in November!

www.HQNBooks.com

PHNH337

REQUEST YOUR FREE BOOKS!

2 FREE NOVELS
FROM THE ROMANCE/SUSPENSE
COLLECTION PLUS 2 FREE GIFTS!

YES! Please send me 2 FREE novels from the Romance/Suspense Collection and my 2 FREE gifts (gifts are worth about $10). After receiving them, if I don't wish to receive any more books, I can return the shipping statement marked "cancel." If I don't cancel, I will receive 4 brand-new novels every month and be billed just $5.49 per book in the U.S. or $5.99 per book in Canada, plus 25¢ shipping and handling per book plus applicable taxes, if any*. That's a savings of at least 20% off the cover price! I understand that accepting the 2 free books and gifts places me under no obligation to buy anything. I can always return a shipment and cancel at any time. Even if I never buy another book from the Reader Service, the two free books and gifts are mine to keep forever.

185 MDN EF5Y 385 MDN EF6C

Name _____ (PLEASE PRINT) _____

Address _____ Apt. # _____

City _____ State/Prov. _____ Zip/Postal Code _____

Signature (if under 18, a parent or guardian must sign)

Mail to **The Reader Service:**
IN U.S.A.: P.O. Box 1867, Buffalo, NY 14240-1867
IN CANADA: P.O. Box 609, Fort Erie, Ontario L2A 5X3

Not valid to current subscribers to the Romance Collection,
the Suspense Collection or the Romance/Suspense Collection.

Want to try two free books from another line?
Call 1-800-873-8635 or visit www.morefreebooks.com.

* Terms and prices subject to change without notice. N.Y. residents add applicable sales tax. Canadian residents will be charged applicable provincial taxes and GST. Offer not valid in Quebec. This offer is limited to one order per household. All orders subject to approval. Credit or debit balances in a customer's account(s) may be offset by any other outstanding balance owed by or to the customer. Please allow 4 to 6 weeks for delivery. Offer available while quantities last.

Your Privacy: Harlequin is committed to protecting your privacy. Our Privacy Policy is available online at www.eHarlequin.com or upon request from the Reader Service. From time to time we make our lists of customers available to reputable third parties who may have a product or service of interest to you. If you would prefer we not share your name and address, please check here. ☐

BOB08R

This Christmas, "holiday getaway"
has an entirely new meaning....

From popular authors
ANNE STUART
TINA LEONARD
MARION LENNOX

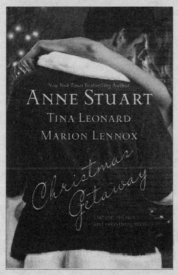

Three women, connected by friendship and fate,
are taking cover...with men sexy enough to unwrap!

Christmas Getaway

Catch this holiday anthology in stores November 2008!

www.eHarlequin.com   PHANTH729

#1 *New York Times* bestselling author

NORA ROBERTS

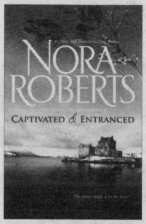

Fascinating and irresistible, the mysterious
Donovan cousins share a secret that's been
handed down through generations—a secret that
sets them apart from ordinary beings.

CAPTIVATED & ENTRANCED

**Indulge in two classic
Donovan clan tales.**

Available November 2008 wherever trade paperbacks are sold!

Where love comes alive™

Visit Silhouette Books at www.eHarlequin.com   PSNR572